love me

JENN PLUMMER

Love Me

Aspen Ridge, Book 3

Published by Wild Lupine Books LLC

Editing by Katie Ducharme - Between The Covers Editorial

Cover Design by Melissa Doughty - Mel D. Designs

Photographer - Cadwallader Photography

Model - Storm Wilson

Formatting by Destiny Blake LLC

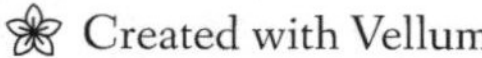

Join Jenn Plummer's Readers' Group

Stay up to date with Jenn Plummer by joining her Facebook readers' group, Jenn's Harlots. Ask questions, get first looks at new books/series, and have fun with other book lovers!

https://www.facebook.com/groups/jennsharlots/

A Note From the Author

Dear Readers,

Welcome to Aspen Ridge. Love Me is book three in a five book, interconnected standalone series. You do not have to read them in order but for the best experience, I recommend that you do.

Themes in Love Me include parental abandonment, explicit language, and sexual situations.

Please read responsibly. If you have any questions about this list, please don't hesitate to reach out to me directly.

Sending all of you love.

Playlist

Good as Hell - Lizzo
All On Me - Devin Dawson
Chillin' It - Cole Swindell
Rumor - Lee Brice
Stargazing - Myles Smith
Don't It - Billy Currington
Perfect - Ed Sheeran
You Belong With Me - Taylor Swift
Paper Rings - Taylor Swift
Walking on a Dream - Empire of the Sun
All Over You - The Spill Canvas
Swing Life Away - Rise Against
Love Lies - Khalid & Normani
Dance Inside - All American Rejects
Lucky - Colbie Caillat and Jason Mraz
The Bones - Maren Morris

For all my single mommas out there in the trenches being dicked around by little boys who think they're men . . . they aren't. Until you find your real one, Liam is for you.

For all the amazing men who embrace the role of daddy to the children you didn't create, but love just as fiercely and want just as much.

For Michael, you know why. We love you.

Four Years Ago

Liam

Running my hands nervously through my hair, I sit in my truck, trying to convince myself to not be such a pussy and tell her how I feel. That I'm obsessively, hopelessly, in love with her. Fuck, why is this so hard? It's not like I haven't talked to girls before, I'm twenty-two for fuck's sake. But this is Hannah we're talking about. My best friend since we were in preschool.

We were too little to remember the facts, but according to my parents, I was playing with a stuffed bear that she wanted, and we fought over it until the teacher told her that I had it first and gave it back to me, causing her to cry. I immediately gave it to her to get her to stop. I made sure she had that stuffed bear every single day so that I never had to see her cry again. *A stuffed bear.* That's what brought us together. She refused to give it up, and luckily, the teacher was sweet and understanding. She still has the old thing somewhere in her room at her parents' house.

The following year, once we got to kindergarten, we were assigned to different classrooms, and I terrorized everyone around me. I became defiant and uncooperative, screaming like a banshee until the school was forced to keep the two of us together. I behaved once I was able to be with her, and we've been inseparable ever since. I didn't realize the depth of my feelings until Hannah dropped out of college and I had to continue there without her. It was our first time apart, and it was that persistent ache that caused me to drive three hours each way every weekend just to see her. That was my first sign she's it for me.

I'm staring blankly at my dashboard when a flash of pink catches my eye as Hannah jogs down the steps of her parents' house. She's wearing black leggings, a large *Scream* T-shirt that hides her body, a pair of black Chuck Taylors, and the tips of her blonde hair are dyed the color of bubblegum. She's so damn edgy, in a cute, punk kind of way that is totally unique to her. She's missing that stereotypical emo personality that you'd typically find in girls who dress like she does. But Hannah is a ray of sunshine, constantly smiling and happy, full of life. She's the sweetest damn girl I've ever met. I'm a man obsessed.

Fuck, I need to get this over with and tell her, fear of ruining our friendship has kept this a secret for far too long. I also didn't want to drop this bomb on her until after I graduated. The time apart was hard enough, and if she felt the same, there was no way I'd have been able to walk away from her. I want this girl to be wholly mine, and she needs to know how I truly feel.

Hannah opens the passenger side door, reaching up to use the grab handle before pulling herself into my large truck. She's a short thing at roughly five foot five, and I find her always having to haul her ass into the passenger seat comical.

"Hey, beauty," I say as I take stock of her now that she's sitting next to me on the bench seat. Her typical glowing face is withdrawn, her eyes slightly red and bloodshot. She works too damn much, and I wish she would pull back her hours at her family's coffee shop.

"We need to talk—"

"—I've got something that I need to tell you," we say at the same time, my eyebrows arching in question.

"You go first," I tell her.

"I'm pregnant."

Two words. Time comes to a standstill as I sit frozen to my spot trying to make sense of what I just heard. She couldn't have said what I think she did. The air in the truck evaporates, replaced with a tension thick and heavy. My eyes blur with the confusion swirling in my head. There's no way I heard her correctly.

"Hannah, *you're what?*"

"I'm pregnant, bear."

And just like that, the life I dreamed of having with her goes out the window. She's creating a family with someone who isn't me, who will never be me. The pain in my chest comes on strong and I rub my knuckles against the spot to alleviate the pressure that won't subside. Nausea rolls around in the pit of my stomach, a hard knot in my throat. Fuck, it's hot in here. Why is it so hot all of a sudden?

"Who's the father?" I choke out the words, clearing my throat.

"Promise me you won't be mad."

"If you say Levi Jenkins, Han . . ."

"Bear . . . *please.* I need you through this. I haven't told anyone yet. Not even Levi. I can't do this without you."

I look at the girl next to me, her fingers playing with the cotton-candy tips of her hair, her eyes darting back and forth between mine. She looks so vulnerable right now—lost and confused. Something Hannah typically isn't. She's always been confident, edgy, unafraid to go against the grain. Seeing her uncertain—almost fearful—I know I'll do anything to help her, and another man's baby or not, I'll be damned if I abandon her when she needs me the most.

"Alright, beauty. Looks like you're having a baby. I got you. Anything for you," I tell her, resigned and heartbroken.

"You're the best, I don't know what I'd do without you."

"Remember that when I curb stomp Levi if he ever hurts you."

She chuckles nervously at that, but her posture is more relaxed, a smile playing on her pretty face.

"What did you want to tell me?" she asks.

That I'm in love with you. That I've always been in love with you. That I want to start a life with you.

"Oh, uhm, they're doing a double feature of *Halloween* and *Friday the 13th* at the drive-in this weekend, wanted to convince you to go."

"Duh. Like I need to be convinced. Scary movies in the summer are always a yes."

"Attagirl. You okay?"

"Better now. You and me?"

"You and me."

Chapter One
Liam

Present Day

The floodlights blur past me before they disappear altogether in my rearview mirror as I drive out of the distillery property and pull onto the open country road. I grip the steering wheel of my Ford F-250 and focus on the empty road in front of me, the familiar flutter of anticipation stirring in my chest just as it has every Thursday for the last five years. It's the one day a week that is guaranteed to be spent with my best friend, just the two of us, no interruptions.

My headlights barely cut through the pitch black of the night, the only light the glow from the moon above me, casting shadows from the tall Sitka spruce trees that line the long, winding road. I live for the quiet stillness of nights like these, when the sky is so dark it looks endless, when the world is asleep and there is only you and your thoughts. I was born and raised in Aspen Ridge, Washington and I would probably suffocate to death in a city.

Some people grow up in small country towns and count down the days until they jet off to bigger, brighter, and better, but not me. Aspen Ridge buried itself deep within my bones and is just as much a part of me as I am it.

I love our small community, but mostly, I love the location. Nestled on the coast of Washington State, it's a secluded gem hidden under the watchful protection of the Olympic Mountains, with the Pacific Ocean at our back. There's a sense of peace here that's not found in the concrete jungle, as if everything moves slower, suspended in time while the rest of the world continues on at a rapid pace.

Snow falls lightly from the sky, hitting my windshield and immediately melting away as I take each bend in the road, just like I've done thousands of times. As I near the edge of Downtown Aspen Ridge, the tiny gold twinkling Christmas lights that stay wrapped around light poles year-round come into view, like a beacon leading me in.

Snow crunches under my tires as I slow my speed, taking the turn down an alley just big enough for one vehicle, barely wide enough for my big-ass truck. Parking behind the brick building, I eagerly climb out, grabbing the cold beer from the passenger seat that I know she's looking forward to drinking with me. Pizza, beer, horror movies, no phones, no cancellations. It's been our rule, and we've stuck with it, prioritizing detoxing together and not feeling the pressure of any of the responsibilities weighing on either of us.

Walking into Hannah's after the long week I had, I'm ready for our weekly movie night. The door was left unlocked like usual, so after taking off my snow-caked boots, I step out of the cold Washington winter air and into the warmth of the little loft apartment, eyeing the pizza on the kitchen counter waiting for me. Her apartment sits above her family's coffee shop and bakery—Bean Haven. It's small and cozy, and just like Hannah has done with everything else she touches, she's made it a vibrant and happy home for her and her three-year-old daughter, Charlotte.

"Hey, beauty. You ready to argue over which horror movie we're watching tonight?" I shout out, dropping the beer next to the pizza. When I don't hear her reply, I leave the kitchen to find her, kicking myself in the ass because she's probably putting Charlie to bed. As I round the corner, the door to her room is slightly ajar and I push it open a bit more, peering in at the little girl's sleeping form. She's cozied up in a bed I built her that looks like a little house. After watching her back rise and fall for a moment, I close the door, moving through the apartment to continue my search for Hannah.

Soft whimpers hit my ears before my eyes are on her, my heart squeezing painfully in my chest. There's something about seeing Hannah cry that triggers me, like I'm fucking helpless, and it makes me feral. There's not much I hate more than seeing her sad, but I'm willing to do anything to take her pain away.

Pushing through the bedroom door, I finally see her, rolled up into a ball on her bed, squeezing a pillow to drown out her cries. My heart constricts, that well-known ache in my chest a vise grip as my knees sink into the mattress, body on autopilot. I settle in behind her, pulling her by the hip until her back connects with my chest, cocooning her body with mine in comfort.

"I'm here, beauty. What happened?" I whisper, my lips against the back of her head as I do my best to console her.

She turns in my arms, burying her face into my chest and gripping my T-shirt with her fists. Ever since we were little kids, nothing could get me pissed off faster than seeing Hannah Haven cry. There's nothing that can bring me to my knees faster than seeing her upset. I would gladly light the match that sets the world up in flames if it meant she never had to feel an ounce of pain again.

"I hate him," she whimpers, her tone thick with anger.

"What did he do this time?" It's difficult to hold back the animosity I hold for her boyfriend, Charlotte's deadbeat sperm donor. Hannah and Levi had a string of one-night stands four years ago that resulted in the creation of Charlie, who's now almost four. He never wanted anything serious and has made that clear since the beginning. For some reason, Hannah has it in her pretty little head that since she shares a child with the douche-canoe-shit-bag, she's stuck with him. He works in Seattle as a commercial fisherman and has used that as his excuse to never be around. I know she doesn't love him, but she feels stuck with him, even though she owes him no loyalty.

"I'm tired of him making plans and never following through. He never calls Charlotte when he's scheduled to, and I know she's not even four yet, but she has no idea who he is. He promises to come into town when he's not on the boat, but he never does. I thought we would make this work, be a family. That was the plan. My parents are expecting us to get married."

"What?" I breathe the words incredulously. To say this comes as a complete shock would be an understatement.

She huffs a deep breath. "I'm sorry I didn't tell you until now. I'm just so lost. My mom doesn't want to go back and forth anymore between California and Washington. She refuses to spend winters in AR as it is, they're moving there permanently." She sighs, her breath warm against my chest, my shirt wet with tears. "With my grandma getting older, and Harlow and Hailey doing mother knows what, they gave me an ultimatum—settle down with Levi here and prove to them that I've got my shit together, or they'll sell Bean Haven, and I can move to California with them so they can help me with Charlie. They don't think I'll be able to handle it all long-term in Aspen Ridge unless I'm in a stable position, because apparently single moms can't run a business and be a parent simultaneously. It's bullshit. And outdated. And patriarchal. I've been working at and running this place since I was a teenager."

I do my best to remain calm, knowing she doesn't need me to come out swinging, raging like an out-of-control, hot-headed caveman like my two older brothers would. But I'm about to lose my shit, and it's taking every ounce of self-control that I have not to blow. Like fuck is Hannah leaving me. Over my dead body will the two of them move to California because her parents can't get their heads out of their asses and see that their daughter is already settled and stable. She's doing the damn thing all on her own.

"Fuck," I huff, flicking off my hat and running my hands through my hair. "I'm so sorry. They seriously put that on you? That's such bullshit, Han, and you don't deserve that. They're not taking Bean Haven from you, and you're definitely not moving to California, like hell will that be happening. Do they not see how happy you are here? You're doing amazing things all on your own. We'll figure this out." *Because we have to.*

Hannah's parents can be great, but they still look at her as that lost teenager who never quite fit in with anyone around her, who always pushed the boundaries and went through life to her own beat. She dropped out of college because she knew she wanted to run Bean Haven. That, plus the unplanned pregnancy, and they've never quite looked at her like she had the ability to be successful or stand on her own, even though that's exactly what she's doing.

It's fucking bullshit and has put a strain on my relationship with her parents, who've known me my entire life. This just makes it all that much worse. Hannah is the strongest, hardest worker I've ever met. Not to mention the best mom, she gives her all to Charlotte. Hell, she gives her all to everything she does, and she does it with a smile on her face. Because that's just who Hannah is. But, at some point, if someone gets knocked down enough, they start to expect it and just stay down. I'll be damned if I let that happen to her.

"They feel so strongly about it, bear. Like, how could I possibly be a single mom, run a bakery, and survive in the world on my own? They'll never believe in me. It's fucked. I'm fucked. Apparently, I've been sucked through a time portal where I need to leave my father's home and go directly to my husband's, and if there is no husband, then I need to go back to my father's." Her voice cracks on the last word as the tears flow freely, not ashamed or worried about how she looks right now, or how vulnerable she is. I love that she is always one hundred percent herself with me—unashamed, honest, and raw. I wouldn't have it any other way.

"Han, it's their issue, because you're not fucking leaving. We just need to figure out how you can keep the bakery, and it won't be an issue. You and I both know you're kicking ass in every area of your life. Your parents, Levi, anyone who doesn't support you, is missing out on seeing you grow. I'm damn fucking proud of you."

"I love you for saying that. The shit with Levi though, bear." She continues to vent, and I listen to every word. "I really had it in my head that we would get married and be a family because we shared a baby and cared about each other. But I'm stupid and delusional, it's been years. I actually hate him. Why the hell would I want to marry him? All I wanted was to give Charlotte a family, and I can't even do that. Why aren't we enough?"

"Hannah, you *are* enough. You're more than enough. Levi is just a selfish bastard who can't see past his own shit. Don't you dare think you and that little girl aren't enough. You two are everything, do you hear me?"

Hannah cries herself to sleep in my arms as I lightly rub her back, my fingers trailing up the length of her spine and back down again. She gives off this tough girl, can't-penetrate-her-defenses exterior, but those lucky enough to know her like I do get glimpses of her soft side too. She has never cared what anyone thinks and has always worn the confidence of a warrior, but when it comes to providing a life for her family, she is much more delicate.

I gently push her beautiful, lavender-colored hair out of her face and take a moment to watch her sleep. She's going to survive this, and I'm going to make damn sure of it. There are moments when life shifts whether you're ready for it or not. This is one of mine. I won't let her parents take her from everything she loves. And I sure as shit won't let Levi be what breaks her. He needs to get his goddamn priorities straight. This ends now. One way or another.

My fist connects with the solid wood door in three rapid knocks, purposefully louder than they should be. The night is chilly, but I don't register the cold, anger and adrenaline pumping through my veins making my body feel hot. I pace for a moment on the stoop of the apartment in Downtown Seattle, removing my hat and running my hands through my hair as frustration courses through me. Putting my hat on backwards, I lift my fist to knock again just as it swings open. Levi stands in front of me, bleary-eyed from the sleep I just pulled him from, slightly shorter than

I am, and much thinner. He's a lanky motherfucker and with his shaved head, he looks more like a propaganda poster for the U.S. Air Force than he does a Seattle fisherman.

"What the fuck do you want?"

Ahh. Good morning motherfucker, my old nemesis. Rise and fucking shine, asshole. You get to deal with me today.

"For you to stop fuckin' around in Seattle and get your ass back to AR to take care of your family. Enough is enough, Levi," I grind out.

"How about you mind your own goddamn business for a change, huh, Liam? Always gotta come to her rescue. She really that pathetic she's gotta sic her bulldog on me? Get back in your fuckin' truck and don't come back here."

"Levi? What's going on, I can hear you yelling from the bedroom."

Levi stiffens as a little blonde waltzes up behind him and tucks herself into his side. I've never thought Levi was faithful to Hannah, but it's the swollen, pregnant belly that I can't take my eyes off of and stuns me silent. Slowly, I turn my attention back on Levi, and I see the moment he registers how fucked he is, my face surely giving him the vibes that back that up. My hands ball into fists at my sides, and the petite female bristles, taking a step back to retreat farther into the apartment. Smart girl. She wouldn't want to watch her man get pummeled to death in his doorway.

"It's time for you to go," the piece of shit says to me.

I lean forward into his space and whisper, "You ever show your fucking face back in AR, I'll fucking kill you myself."

"If I wanted to be there, I'd be there. But I'm here. Tell her to take a hint."

My arm cocks back in an automatic response to punch this motherfucker right in the teeth—like I've done before—but I stop myself. He's a sleazy asshole and it'll only make things worse for Hannah. Turning on my heels and jogging down the steps, I pull myself into my truck and spin out—snow, dirt, and salt picked up and spraying—eager to get the fuck home to figure out how to deal with this disaster.

The drive back to Aspen Ridge is more than three hours, and given the time now, I'll be lucky to get home in time to take a nap before showing up for work. Which means I've got the next few hours to figure out how the fuck I'm going to tell my best friend that her "boyfriend" and father of her daughter is a lying, two-timing, low-life piece of dogshit that shouldn't have been allowed to breathe the same air as her from the beginning, let alone be inside her.

To add the cherry on her shit sundae, the ultimatum she received from her parents is contingent on her marrying that asshole. Her life is about to be blown to bits, and it fucking figures that I have to be the one who pulls the clip.

Hannah and I have known each other our entire lives, and in that time, I've never left her side. Through the fun elementary years, the awkwardness of middle school, to high school, when we both started to morph into mini adults, all the way to planning to go to college together. I was there through her unexpected pregnancy with Charlotte, and even caught that little girl as she rushed to enter the world on Hannah's kitchen floor, and now I have to be the one to set off a massive fucking bomb in the center of her world. Being away from Hannah while I was in college was torture, now that Charlotte is in the mix? Fuck that. I will do anything to help Hannah keep Bean Haven, and her parents will have to pry both of them from my cold dead hands before they move to California. She has all the support she needs here. The two of them leaving Aspen Ridge isn't even an option.

My palm connects with the steering wheel as I hit it repeatedly, pissed that anyone in this world could willingly hurt the two most perfect people in it. Hannah and Charlie are everything that is good, and they deserve someone who will put them first and show up for them. Levi has always been a deadbeat dad and an even worse boyfriend. He was all too satisfied to fuck Hannah, but the moment she got pregnant, he suddenly had better shit to do. He's been dicking her around for years, and I'll be damned if it continues after this.

Instead of going home, I turn onto the long dirt road that leads to the distillery and drive my truck around to the back parking lot. It's about five in the morning, too late (or early) to have a drink, so I throw myself into the work that brings me peace. I head to the vats to try to focus on my new project but after a few hours, I can't shake the anger that threatens to consume me. Picking up my phone, I call my brother, Dallas, only for it to go to voicemail after several rings. I'm one of five siblings, and most of the time it's a madhouse of uncontrolled chaos, heavy banter, and fistfights with a whole lot of love and loyalty. But Dallas is the glue, and if I have a problem, he's who I want to talk to.

"Marcus!" I snap at our intern as he pulls into his parking spot near where I'm pacing outside, the freezing winter air biting at my skin and keeping me awake.

"Yes, sir? What can I do for you?"

I sling my arm around his shoulders and pull him close. He tries to slink away, clearly intimidated by me. Good. He needs to listen and get my dumbass brother.

"This is what's going to happen. You're going to go into the office building and park your ass right outside Dallas' door and you aren't going to move until he gets there."

"Of course. Consider it done," he says as he starts to pull away.

"Oh, no. That's not all. When you see him, I want you to tell him, verbatim, 'get your ass to the fucking fermenting vats.'

Can you do that, Marcus?" I say as I squeeze his shoulder firmly.

"Yep. You got it. On my way . . . right . . . now," he replies as he finally dislodges from my hold. I turn quickly and head back inside, irritated as fuck that the one time I actually need something important, the brother I want to talk to is busy doing God knows what.

My oldest brother, Sawyer, is without a doubt busy with his new wife, Ivy. Dallas is Sawyer's twin and typically readily available to all of us. Carter is the youngest male and is always busy with either work, marketing, or his playboy lifestyle. Then there's our little sister, Kinsey. She graduated from college a year early and started her first year teaching at Aspen Ridge Elementary School last September.

Unable to sit still, my footsteps echo through the room as I pace back and forth, running my hands, almost obsessively, through my thick hair, wondering when the hell Dallas will show up, when the door finally opens.

"Hey, man, you summoned me?"

"Yeah, I'm losing my shit and I need you to talk me off the ledge. You weren't answering your damn phone."

His face falls momentarily. God knows what the fuck he was doing.

"What's going on? Tell me what you need."

"It's fuckin' Hannah. I'm so goddamn tired of Levi jerking her around. I'm so sick of seeing her treated like shit over and over and over again. You know where I was last night? Fuckin' holding her while she cried because she's running on fumes."

Dallas looks at me like he already knows that my night didn't end holding Hannah through her meltdown.

"What'd you do, Liam?"

"I drove to Seattle to find the asshole and tell him to get his ass back in Aspen Ridge and take care of his family. And you know what I found?"

"Shit, man. Does Hannah know?"

"Know that her lying, piece of shit baby daddy that she thinks she's still involved with has a girlfriend he's living with? That she's fucking pregnant!"

"Oh, fuck."

Rage hits me like a tidal wave all over again. I need to fucking hit something.

"You didn't beat the shit out of him, did you? That's the last thing Hannah needs to deal with."

"I saw it, right in front of me at his door, and I turned and left. Dal, it was the hardest fucking thing I've ever done, and the longer I stay here and keep it from her . . . fuck. I want to fucking kill him. How could he do that to them?"

"We'll all get her through it, they're going to be okay."

"You don't get it. Her parents want to cut her off, Dallas. With Ms. Nettie getting older, unless Hannah gets married and settles down, they're selling Bean Haven. Her mom is sick of going back and forth every winter and they want to move to San Diego permanently."

And bring Hannah and Charlie with them. Not that I'm going to let that fucking happen.

"What kind of fucked-up ultimatum is that?"

You're telling me. Hannah is such a free spirit and will never complain. She takes everything she's given as a gift and is the happiest person I've ever met. Even when she's dealt shitty blows by the people she loves, she just takes it, adapts, and moves on. Not this time. This time, the weight of it all is crushing her. I'm not about to sit back and let it.

"I don't know how to tell her about Levi. I want to go put him six feet under. That's what he fuckin' deserves."

"I agree with you, brother, but that's not how this can be

handled. Levi's a fucking weasel and he'll make Hannah's life hell because of it."

"What do I do?"

Because right now, outside of committing murder, I don't know what to do anymore. The idea of causing her pain is killing me.

"Just sleep on it. You know her better than anyone else. But you get your shit straight and then talk to her. You'll know what to do."

How the fuck do I fix this for her?

Chapter Two
Hannah

My EarPods blast Florence and the Machine as I flow through the same early morning routine I've had since I was a teenager. My family owns Bean Haven, the only coffee shop in our small town of Aspen Ridge, Washington. The storefront sits on Main Street, a gorgeous, weathered brick building nestled up between Book Bound, an indie bookstore, and Rosemary and Runes Apothecary, with alleyways just wide enough for a vehicle separating them. My grandparents opened it a few decades ago and it's been a town staple ever since. I'm biased but I think we have the best spot on Main Street.

The dough deflates slowly under the weight of my hands, and I lose myself to a steady rhythm. I knead what will turn into my cinnamon rolls, working it by hand the way my grandmother taught me. I was barely old enough to see over the counter when she first let me help her in the bakery's kitchen. The fact that both of my sisters were either too young, or too busy to be bothered with learning her craft—one filled with love and passion—made it even more personal for me. It was something just she and I shared, and that same love and passion fuels me to this day.

The air was thick with the scent of butter, sugar, and cinnamon, just as it always is, and I remember how she pulled over a stool and dropped the first heap of dough onto the floured surface of the butcher block table with a loud thwack. She dug her palms into the squishy mass, pressing and moving with this steady, hypnotic rhythm, working the dough until she was satisfied, like it was as natural as breathing.

My grandmother is known for being loud, brash, and unfiltered—notoriously so—but when she baked, she created a silent magic that I was captured by. She gave me patience, something that was rare for me to feel. The lines around her eyes softened, and her smile was delicate and encouraging as she showed me how to fold the dough, how to knead it just right, how to feel the texture, to know when it was done, sharing her secret that it was all in your hands and intuition. She taught me everything I know, and baking is just as much a part of who I am as it is her.

Ever since that first day with my grandmother, I found any excuse to be in the kitchen with her, where she taught me how to bake her recipes. As I got older, it became therapeutic for me, a way to channel all of my teenage angst and hormonal rage that had nowhere to go, and it has never felt like work—despite what my family believes. Running this place fills me with purpose and joy, and I couldn't imagine doing anything else.

Over the last few years, I've taken over running Bean Haven, revamping the interior decor to something livelier and more enticing for customers. My best friend Liam repainted the walls to a creamy off-white, leaving the fourth in its natural brick red. *Bean Haven* is painted in a gorgeous loopy font above the counter in a deep green. Live plants hang from the ceiling in some of the corners, while others are in huge wicker baskets that I've placed strategically throughout the room. It's got a lively bohemian vibe that I live for and matches my personality, while also making my grandmother proud.

Last night I exhausted myself once again, stressing about my current situation. I can't even call Levi my boyfriend anymore because he's never around. I feel this inherent need to keep fighting for him to be in our lives because he's my daughter's father. But as I've had to learn—unfortunately the hard way—we can't force anyone to be in our lives. Plans change. Just like people, hopes, and dreams. If Charlie and I were important, Levi would be here. Full stop. He would be with us every moment he wasn't out at sea. He would be calling, he'd be aching to be home with us—a place that I've only ever shared with my daughter.

After I got pregnant with her, my grandmother offered to turn the loft above Bean Haven into an apartment for me to start a life, and I assumed Levi would join me. But not long after we remodeled the place, Levi was hired on a commercial fishing vessel out of Seattle, and he never moved in. I was left alone the majority of the time.

I've always been quite the loner, always keeping people at arm's length but never letting them get closer. My sisters, Harlow and Hailey, would visit fairly regularly, but having their own lives, they just wanted a place to hide out from our parents and their strict rules. My best friend, Liam, is over all the time since we're still as inseparable as we were twenty years ago. He's what's kept me sane all these years. My rock.

I am not my parents' favorite person. I know they love me and love Charlie, but I'm their college dropout, pregnant out of wedlock, misbehaving, rebellious child, even though I have grown up so much over the last four years. I feel the weight of their disappointment like a heavy cloud, blanketing me anytime I give it thought.

Transferring the dough to a bowl to proof, I dump a fully-proofed ball onto my floured surface, rolling it out until it's flat and glossy, brushing butter across its surface. I follow up with a heavy dusting of cinnamon, sugar, and a special ingredient, before rolling it together and cutting it into round pieces. Between prepping the ingredients and baking all of the pastries for the day, I wake up at three in the morning to get down here.

We open at 5 a.m. and it's always a hustle of listening to the bell chime announcing a customer, and baking in the back. Luckily, we close at three during the week, which allows me to pick up my munchkin from preschool and spend the afternoons and evenings with her, doubling roles as mom and dad.

My grandmother joins me around seven a few days a week, keeping me company throughout the day as I juggle baking and coffee orders, and making sure our town is happy and fueled. There's something so inherently calming about the process of baking—the smells it creates, the ingredients that come together to make something taste so good and comforting. I live for it. I know my grandma does, too, and that even though she misses my grandpa daily, being here, a place that they built together from the ground up, brings her joy and peace . . . most of the time.

After pulling out the first few batches of my top sellers—apple cinnamon muffins, cinnamon rolls, chocolate croissants, and banana bread—I wash my hands and walk to the front of the building to unlock the door. Hands slightly shaky, I return to the back to eat something quickly before the morning rush starts. Liam will kick my ass if I faint again because I let my blood sugar get too low.

I manage to scarf down my oatmeal and fruit just as the bell chimes from the front door. Popping some gum in my mouth, I return to the counter to greet them. The next two hours are a constant rotation of customers coming in and out to get their caffeine fix and baked goods, while I check my baby monitor every few minutes to keep an eye on my sleeping daughter upstairs. My grandmother comes in and takes a seat at the small table by the bay window, with her little dog, Winnie, on her lap.

The bell chimes again just as I'm setting it down from staring at her perfect, relaxed little face on the screen.

"Well, look who it is. Don't you normally get your fix down the street at The Night Owl?" I tease Liam's brother, Carter, as he walks up to the counter.

"Han, don't you know alcohol is frowned upon this early in the morning? C'mon."

"But is it the alcohol you go there for?"

"Hey, now. That's not fair. The ladies come to me, I'm just an innocent bystander trying to get a drink at the local bar after a hard day's work. I can't help their desires, sis."

A laugh bursts from my lips. Carter is fifteen months younger than Liam. His poor mom had them all back-to-back, minus Kinsey who came a little later. He's their wild child, and the rumors about him being a lady killer run strong in town. There's an aura around him that demands attention, and women are throwing their panties at him left and right. The man has never been in a relationship, and I've known him his entire life.

"You need a chastity belt, sir. Or someone to lock you down for good. So, what can I get you?"

"Actually, not here for coffee, Liam sent me over to see if you needed any help with Charlie since he got caught up at work."

My head jerks back in slight shock. It's not abnormal for Liam's family to jump in and help me with Charlotte. All of his siblings are surrogate uncles and aunts, and his parents are especially involved. But Carter?

"And he sent you? You hate kids."

"I don't hate kids," he admonishes. "I'm not a monster, Han. I just don't want any of my own. I'm a fun uncle though," he says, flashing what he thinks is his million-dollar smile. I just find his arrogance annoying, and I roll my eyes. His charm has never had an effect on me, and it certainly won't now. "For real. I'm here to take her to school. Liam even made me take his monster truck for the kid harness thing."

A smile tugs at my lips at the memory of Liam purchasing a car seat.

"Let me get the car seat from my car, that way your gigantic body doesn't have to be squished behind the wheel of it again," I say as I hand my daughter to Liam. He scoops her into his arms where her hands immediately find his cheeks. She loves to touch the cheeks of the people she loves. It's such a comfort for her.

"No need, beauty. Ones already in there."

"In your truck? When did you move it?" I ask, confused when he had the time to do that.

"I didn't. After it took fifteen minutes last time to switch it out, I took a photo of the one you have and bought a second one so that it's easier."

"Wait, what?" I can't hide the shock his revelation brings out in me. My tone lifting higher on the last word.

"I can't talk any slower than that, Han." He bounces my almost two-year-old in his arms, making her giggle. "Your momma is crazy, munchkin."

"Bear, you bought a car seat to go in your truck?"

"Yes."

"And it's the exact same one I have in my car?"

"I know how long you did research on that thing so she could stay rear-facing, I'm not stupid enough to mess with you and the safety of Charlie. It's the exact same make and model."

I blink at him slowly and my eyes start to water with tears. When I had Charlotte, I didn't think I would be doing this without her father. Blinded by hormones. The red flags were always there, I just chose to ignore them. Liam hasn't left my side since the moment I told him I was expecting her. This shouldn't surprise me. But the extra mile he continues to go doesn't go unnoticed or unappreciated. I'd be lost without my best friend.

"Fuck, beauty. Don't cry."

"Language, bear, please!"

"I can't help it, when you cry it kills me. Don't cry. It's just a car seat. This will make things easier on us."

Us.

Christ. What am I going to do once he finds a woman to settle down with? Explain to her that I need him, too? I need to get my shit together. Time for another heart-to-heart with Charlie's father, Levi.

"Yeah. This will make things easier. You're amazing. You know that, right?"

"You're not wrong. I'm pretty cool." He turns his attention back on my little girl. "Aren't I? I'm your favorite, huh? Not momma, me."

"Charlotte Sidney. Who's your favorite?" I ask her, rubbing my nose against hers.

"Bear."

Of course he is.

"You really don't mind taking her? Liam usually scoots out of work, is everything okay?"

He rubs the back of his neck while looking over the menu behind me.

"Yeah, everything's cool. He and Graham are just working

on a wood supply issue from the cooperage. Her school is right up town, I'll go the speed limit the entire way."

I squint my eyes at him for a long moment before the bell chimes again and I'm forced to make a decision.

"Please, Ms. Nettie, get this thing off of me. Why? Why do we have to go through this every single time?" The eldest Hayes sibling says as my grandmother's dog, Winnie, loses her ever loving mind, jumping at Sawyer's ankles and barking as if she's the most vicious little thing in the world.

"What are you doing here?" Sawyer asks Carter as he joins his brother at my counter.

"Being the fun uncle and taking Charlie to school."

"What the fuck? Why do you get to take her to school?"

"Because Liam asked me to, shithead. Why is that surprising?"

"Because you hate kids."

"Why the fuck does everyone keep saying that? I don't hate kids. Just because I don't want any doesn't mean I hate them. Get off my case, shitstain. Hey, maybe we should update your nickname from shithead to shitstain. Gonna need to run that by Dallas." Carter pulls out his phone and starts to text. These boys are all at or over six feet tall, athletically built, successful businessmen, and they behave like prepubescent children.

"Han, you really gonna let this fool take Charlie to school?"

"You all are insane. We just need Dallas to walk in and it'll be a party. Liam is the only sane one out of you boys. Poor Kinsey. No wonder she's out trying to do her own thing."

"That didn't answer my question," Sawyer deadpans.

"Mother give me strength," I mumble under my breath as I look up at the ceiling to compose myself. "Yes. I'm going to let him take her to school. He has Liam's truck."

Sawyer looks at me like I've grown three heads before he

nearly whines. "But I need the practice. Ivy and I are going to have a hockey team someday."

"I don't think driving Charlotte to school is going to give you the practice that you're looking for. Read a baby book. Carter, you can go on upstairs and wake her up. She'll be excited to see you. After she's ready, bring her through here so I can say bye to her, will you?

"You got it, boss."

Turning back to Sawyer, he looks genuinely offended, and I can't help but laugh at him. He's a large fucker at six feet tall and built like a damn brick house with how often he works out. Still, he's smaller in stature than Liam, but there was definitely something in the water when these boys were procreated.

"You'll be fine. Buck up. Here for muffins?"

"Fine. Yeah, she's craving them. You got a dozen?"

"Dude, where does Ivy put them? How are you going through so many?"

He shrugs and takes a seat at a table to wait for me to pack up his order.

The rest of the morning goes by in a blur and like every other day, I'm racing to close up and get Charlie from school. I'm exhausted, but I've got this. I live for this little shop and my daughter. Nothing is going to take either one of them away from me.

Chapter Three

Liam

Sundays are spent at my parents' house for mandatory family dinners. We've been doing it since we were kids, and as we all trickled out of the house to live on our own, my mom made it a very strict rule that every Sunday is the day dedicated to each other. She may be a sweet little thing, but she's fierce, and none of us want to cross her. My mood only got worse as the week went on. Sitting on this information and keeping it from Hannah is eating me alive. But I can't bring myself to tell her yet. Every time I think the time is right, I fucking panic. I don't know how to help her through this mess, and it's eating me alive.

My tires crunch over the packed snow as I pull around the back of Bean Haven to pick Hannah and Charlie up for dinner. She's so in tune that I know she feels my anxiety, but no matter how hard she pushes, I'm just not ready to talk and blow her life to pieces, at least not until I can find a way to help her first.

Before I even put my truck in park, my phone starts to vibrate from the console next to me, going off with rapid-fire text messages that can be from none other than my sibling group chat. Groaning, I pick up the phone and unlock it, and sure as shit, the assholes are rambling.

CARTER:

Who's going to dinner?

KINS:

Uh? All of us?

DALLAS:

Wait, since when do we have a choice?

SAWYER:

You don't, dickhead.

DALLAS:

Sounds like we do...

CARTER:

Wait, is dinner mandatory?

KINS:

Oh for fuck's sake

SAWYER:

You've been in this family your entire life, wtf do you mean is it mandatory?

DALLAS:

Someone smack this idiot

ME:

What do you think you've been doing all these years?

CARTER:

Have you fuckers been tasting Mom's food? I wouldn't miss that shit. I go for her food. I thought you all were doing the same

KINS:

Holy shit

SAWYER:

Are you fucking with us right now?

CARTER:

Yup. Sad how stupid you assholes think I am. Who is everyone bringing?

SAWYER:

Holy fuck. Lose my number will you, lover boy?

ME:

I don't think I'm actually related to any of you

KINS:

Hey! Rude!

DALLAS:

You're not. Didn't Mom tell you? Why do you think we're so close in age?

We're all so close in age because my damn father couldn't keep his filthy paws off of our perfect saint of a mother. Poor thing spent nine months pregnant with spawn one and two, then immediately got pregnant with me, and then Carter not long after I was born. She's had her hands full, and hell, the four of us boys didn't make it easy on her. We still don't. Kinsey was a complete surprise and has been an angel since the day she was born.

ME:

Done with this conversation, I slam the door of my truck, leaving it running to keep it warm, and jog up the stairs to the second-story door that leads to Hannah's apartment, knocking twice before opening it. Not wanting to take off my boots, I lean into the doorway before shouting.

"Han! I'm here. Ready when you two are!"

The pitter-patter of little feet hits my ears before I see her. Barreling around the corner dressed in fleece leggings with a long sleeve dress, comes Charlie, flying at me with a hairbrush in her hand.

"Munchkin!" I yell as she launches herself into my waiting arms. I scoop her up, standing to my full height and bringing her outside with me, my nerves and anger settling instantly.

"Mumma was right. It's freezing today!" she squeals and shivers in my arms.

"It's a cold one. But we love the cold, don't we?"

"Yes! Will you do my hair? I want braids but Mumma said we don't have time."

"We always have time for braids."

Kicking off my boots, I step into the kitchen and set Charlie's feet back on the tiled floor.

I sit on the ground and take the hairbrush from her hands as she settles in front of me.

"One braid or two?"

"TWO! It's Sunday, so it's safe to wear two. Pigtail braids are my favorite," she says, her little three-year-old voice laced with a bit of sadness instead of her usual excitement.

"Is it not safe to wear pigtail braids on other days?"

"Julian said my braids are stupid."

Oh hell no. Just like that, I've got beef with a four-year-old. Julian is stupid. Her braids are perfect. Julian is a little jerk face, and I hope I run into his dad one of these days. I finish up one braid before turning her around to face me.

"Charlotte Sidney. Repeat after me. I am strong."

"I am strong."

"I am smart."

"I am smart."

"I am brave."

"I am brave."

"I am beautiful."

"I am beautiful."

"My braids are not stupid."

"But Julian said . . ."

"It doesn't matter what Julian said. It matters what *you* think. Do you like your braids?"

"I love my braids."

"Then say it. My braids are not stupid."

"My braids are not stupid."

"Good. Now let's get this one done so we can hit the road. Where's your momma?"

I turn her back around and get started brushing through her thick, dark-blonde hair and separating it into three pieces, the natural highlights popping as I cross over the strands.

"She's getting dressed. She had chocolate all over her. I think she got messy downstairs, 'cause she had it allllllllll over her."

I laugh while finishing up the last wrap of elastic on the end of Charlie's hair.

"Okay, munchkin, grab your shoes, put them on please, and I'll be right back so we can hit the road."

"Tell her to hurry! I want to see Pappy!"

Leaving Charlie in the kitchen, I walk through the little apartment until I reach Hannah's room. The door is open, so I creep up to it, my socks on the floor quieting each of my steps. Hannah and I have been jump-scaring each other our entire lives, and neither of us gets sick of seeing the other rattled.

As I move into the doorway, I stop in my tracks. Mission aborted. Hannah is standing in front of her full-length mirror in nothing but a strappy thong and matching bra. The breath leaves my lungs as my eyes take in her flawless body. I reach up and brace my hands against the top of the door frame, my nails digging into the wood to hold myself back from crawling across the damn floor with my tongue lolling out of my mouth and begging at her feet to worship her body like she deserves.

My eyes roam up her toned legs and stop at the swell of her perfect ass. I stand there shocked as hell, staring straight at her curves like a man seeing water after wandering a barren desert. I bite my bottom lip to hold back the groan that wants to break free. Fuck if I don't want to squeeze that ass between my palms, feel her smooth skin under my rough, calloused hands. I'm desperate to bend her over the bed and bury my face between her legs, devouring her pussy from behind. God, she's so damn sexy. My cock rapidly hardens behind my jeans, throbbing against the zipper, reminding me how desperate I am to feel her sheathed tightly around me.

My eyes trail over her body, taking in the floral tattoo that hugs her right hip, dipping into her trim waist and rising higher before disappearing under her breast. My eyes glance in the mirror, finding hers already on mine, a shit-eating grin plastered to her pretty face.

"Take a picture, it'll last longer," she teases, having no idea the effect she just had on me.

"Don't tempt me, beauty. You are fine as hell."

"Shut up, bear. Now quit staring at my ass and let me get dressed. Seriously, you know it's time for you to go out and get laid if you're ogling me of all people."

If she only fucking knew. Her half naked body just went into my permanent spank bank to imagine while I beat off later. No one has ever, nor could they ever, compare to her.

Walking into my parents' house, I'm tense, and although my irritation has simmered, I know that spending a meal with my siblings is not what I need right now when I should be taking Hannah back home and explaining everything that I learned. I wasn't about to tell her before we left and no doubt ruin the night. Even if I know it's all bullshit and that I'm finding every excuse I can to not break her heart.

Hannah and I haven't kept things from each other before, so keeping this is causing me a foreign type of pain in my chest that makes me constantly uncomfortable. I'm irritable, grouchy, and two seconds away from losing my shit. Maybe I should have taken out my anger on Levi's face.

"Hello, my darlings!" my mom yells from the kitchen as the three of us arrive, the house quieter than normal given all the cars in the driveway.

"Hey, Mom," I say as I lean in and kiss her head before moving to the fridge to pull out a cold beer.

"Hi, Momma Amy. You need anything?"

"Hi, Mimi! Can I go find Pappy?"

"Hi, my sweet Miss Charlotte. Yes, he's in the living room watching the hockey game."

"The Kraken are playing?"

"Yes! Go give them good luck!"

"I'm going to go join them. Let's see if we keep up this winning streak."

Hannah follows Charlie to go see my dad, and I head downstairs to find my siblings. The boys and I work together at our family-owned-and-operated distillery. I love them all, but we spend way too much damn time together, and there are no boundaries in our lives. We've all got unfiltered access to each other, and a group chat that's constantly going off—basically, we're all nosey as shit.

"Hey, fuckers."

"What up little brother?"

"Fuck off, Sawyer," I say as I flip him off, putting my hand directly into his face. He smacks it out of the way, and I keep walking, taking long pulls from my beer and heading toward my sister.

"Hey, sweet sister. How are you?"

"Hey, big brother. I'm freaking amazing. You doing okay?"

"Just fuckin' dandy," I say, a hint patronizingly. Life fucking sucks right now.

"How about some ping pong?" Carter suggests.

Little competition sounds like a good enough stress reliever.

"Let's make it beer pong, make it interesting."

"Fine, but you're cleaning up the mess, 'cause last time Mom was pissed."

"Dude, she wasn't pissed about the beer pong, she was pissed you puked all over her braided rug," I remind him.

My brothers and I work together to set up the solo cups, filling them with beer, and splitting into teams. Dallas and I on one side, Carter and Sawyer on the other, and the game begins.

The balls get lobbed into cups, and after a few rounds, I realize that Dallas is throwing the game, distracted as all fuck, and Sawyer and Carter aren't missing a damn toss, causing me to have to drink. So much for being a stress reliever. My asshole brothers are just pissing me off more.

I try to let my shit mood go and enjoy myself, but it's difficult. I feel the moment Hannah walks downstairs, joining Kinsey, Ivy, and Blaire behind us, and my irritation over the situation increases tenfold. Fuck all of this shit happening to her.

"Drink up, motherfucker!" Carter yells as his ball slams into another cup.

I flip them all off, knowing they were all teaming up on me and purposefully doing some shady shit.

"Fuck off! You're a bunch of goddamn cheaters!" I yell over my shoulder, walking away from the assholes.

"How can you cheat at fuckin' beer pong, lint licker?" Dallas yells back.

I try to tamp my frustration with my dickhead brother and join Hannah, Ivy, and Blaire off to the side. Ivy just married my older brother, Sawyer. They were childhood sweethearts until Ivy up and ran away, staying hidden for ten years. She only just returned last September, and they haven't been apart since. He knocked her up and married her so fast our heads spun. They're definitely making up for lost time. Something I wish I could do with Hannah.

"They're cheats, huh?" Ivy asks.

"They're assholes. All of them."

"But, lint licker?" Blaire, our newest Aspen Ridge Distillery employee, asks. She works as our new event coordinator. She's pretty damn smart-mouthed and makes us all laugh. Drives our brother Dallas insane, which cements her as irreplaceable at work, in my opinion.

Ivy covers her mouth and laughs as Sawyer walks up to her. He grabs her wrist and pulls it away from her face while saying something to her that I don't catch. The two of them live in their own little world now, and that's fine. We're all happy to have Ivy back in our lives and our brother finally happy again.

"That's Liam's nickname. You haven't heard it yet?" Sawyer answers the question I was dodging. I fucking hate this nickname. My brothers are such assholes and I'm not in the mood for this shit right now.

"Apparently not, how did he get such an awful one? No offense to you and the other two, but Liam's the most level-headed one out of all of you, so how does he end up with the worst nickname?"

"Cause they're all assholes and they don't like that I'm bigger than them," I tell Blaire, interjecting the question she posed to Sawyer. Fuck if I'm going to stand here and let him drag me through some more shit.

"Size doesn't mean shit. How many times have I taken you? I'm happy to do it again right here."

Finally, something tangible that I can take my frustration out on. My brothers and I have been boxing together since I was a preteen. We've always been extremely physical when it comes to dealing with issues, and after one good fight between my older brothers, our dad put us all in weekly boxing lessons at Knockout, run by a former professional Russian boxing champion. Sawyer practices all sorts of other shit too—Krav Maga, and MMA—and I swear he would have tried to go pro if the distillery hadn't called us all to run the family business. I box with them since it's all I know, but I prefer to weightlift, which puts me at an advantage when fighting these dicks.

I step into Sawyer's space, we're about the same height, so we're looking eye to eye. I've got him in weight and muscle, but I know he's ruthless in the ring and not to be underestimated. Good thing we're in our parents' basement and the rules don't apply here.

Out of my peripheral, I see all the women take large steps back, my brother Dallas stepping to stand between them and whatever's about to go down between me and shithead here.

"What the fuck is your problem lately? You got some shit you need to work out, then you let us know, but we're not here to be treated like shit by you, so what's it goin' to fuckin' be?" Sawyer raises his voice directly in my face, which pisses me off more. Rage bubbles to the surface, not allowing me to back down.

Fuck this shit.

I jerk forward with my fist posed to clock him in the jaw, but I hold it back, just wanting to challenge him. Sawyer takes the bait, tackling me, bending down like a fucking linebacker, his arms wrapping around my waist and moving me back a few steps. The momentum causes my body to lean forward over his shoulder, but I use it to my advantage, throwing a punch into the soft part of his side, under his ribs.

"Get it out of your system, little brother," Sawyer grunts out as I connect two more punches to his stomach.

"Fuck you!" I yell.

We grapple with each other until we end up on the hard floor. Sawyer doesn't throw any punches, just holds me in close and braces for each of my hits. It pisses me off even more.

"Fight back, shithead! We all know you love a good fight!"

"Not when you're clearly working through something. So hit me if you have to, but get it the fuck out so you're dealing with it with a level head!"

"Fuck," I jerk out of his hold around my neck, shoving him hard.

"You gonna talk or continue to take it out on me? Do what you gotta do."

Straightening, I pick up my hat from where it fell on the floor and run my hand through my hair, pacing in front of Sawyer. I look behind me up the stairs where the women retreated while we fought, to make sure no one is nearby who could potentially hear me before talking, but decide I don't want to do this shit here.

"I'm done. I don't want to talk about it." I shoot Dallas a

hard glare when he goes to open his big mouth. This isn't the time nor the place, and I don't want to spread Hannah's business before she even knows about it.

"Let's just get through dinner so I can get home. I'll deal with my shit."

"You know we're here for you, right?" Sawyer reminds me.

"Yeah, I know. Just, some things need to be handled alone."

I'm not going to be able to lean on my family to help with this one.

Chapter Four
Hannah

Monday evenings suck.

It's Levi's day to call, and it's the same excuses every week. Sometimes I don't even get the courtesy of an excuse, so I guess those are better than being ghosted. It always puts such a damper on the start of the week, especially after spending the previous day with my favorite people. I've been going to the majority of the Hayes family dinners for as long as I can remember. They're my second family, and I'd be lost without that crazy bunch.

Living in a small town, everyone pretty much knows everyone. But I didn't really know Levi until later in high school. We were both seniors, and I had spent the majority of the year working at Bean Haven, studying, and spending my weekends at the drive-in theater with Liam. Levi pursued me, and what started as casual fun nights of hooking up, got shitty real fast when I found out he was cheating on me with some chick from a school in the next town over. We weren't in a monogamous relationship, and that was later thrown in my face when I confronted him about it.

We didn't speak again for a few years. I went away with Liam to college in Oregon and hated every moment of it. Our junior year I dropped out and moved back to Aspen Ridge to work at my grandmother's coffee shop and bakery full-time. A year later, after one drunken night at The Night Owl, I found myself pants down in the back of Levi's car. What started as a one-night stand continued.

I was easily wrapped up in the heat of all of it. My parents were at me constantly about going back to school, when all I wanted to do was bake in our small town. I love Aspen Ridge, and I feel happiest when my hands are covered with flour in my grandmother's bakery. Why can't that be enough?

I was at a low point, desperate, feeling bad about myself, and I easily got wrapped up in the feeling of being desired. Or what I thought at the time was desire. I used what little time Levi gave me as an escape. It wasn't ever love, or passion. It was two young adults being idiots fucking in the back of a car. I found out I was pregnant with my daughter the same month I would have graduated from college. When Levi found out, he lost his shit, and I have never been more thankful for my sisters, Liam, and the entire Hayes family for getting me through the last few years. Levi certainly hasn't been around to do it.

When he got the contract aboard a commercial fishing vessel out of Seattle, it was honestly a relief. It was never a question of whether I would go with him or not. I didn't feel the urge to ask, and he didn't offer. I assumed we would do the long-distance thing and work on building our lives as a family, even if that meant living apart for a while.

I moved into my apartment above Bean Haven, Levi moved to Seattle, and I've been trying to force this thing for the last several years, for the sake of my daughter. I should have expected to be out of sight out of mind, but because I can't fathom not seeing my daughter every day, I assumed he would feel the same. I guess some people just don't get the paternal/maternal genes and some do.

An hour after he was due to call, I drop down onto my bed and pick up my phone, my fingers hovering over the call button. I'm so tired. Tired of fighting. Tired of the missed opportunities and the disappointment. Tired of feeling like I'm attached to another person who doesn't seem to want anything to do with us.

Becoming a mom as young as I did and doing it without the support of my partner and parents has been more than difficult. I lost the opportunity to take time for myself, to experience life and figure out what I like and what I don't. I've been too busy working my ass off to ensure that my daughter doesn't feel the loss of not having two parents, or grandparents that are present and active in her life. I deserve more than my situation. My daughter deserves more.

Resigned to get this over with, I connect the call and wait. Just as I'm about to hang up, Levi answers.

"Hey." His voice is monotone, withdrawn, almost annoyed.

"Hey? You were supposed to call an hour ago," I bark, my tone clipped and short.

"Oh, shit. Yeah, is it Monday already?"

"Yeah, Levi. It's Monday. We were going to plan our daughter's fourth birthday party. You remember her, Charlotte?"

"Of course, I remember her, Hannah, you remind me she exists every chance you get."

"I wouldn't have to if you put in some goddamn effort to be her father."

"Here comes the fucking nagging. I don't need to listen to this shit. I've got my own shit going on here."

The goddamn audacity. It's not supposed to be this way. How can he not want to be with her as often as possible? We made the most beautiful tiny human, and he doesn't want to be a part of our family.

"Wow. I'm sorry we're such an inconvenience for you, Levi. You think you're the only one who has stuff going on? I'm running Bean Haven and raising our daughter alone. While you're what? On a damn boat? What are you even doing right now, Levi? What's stopping you from driving the few hours here to see us? To see Charlie. To be with us."

"Will you shut up with this shit already, Hannah? Poor you, life's so hard," he mocks. "You asked for this. You decided to keep her. Not me. You made your bed, Hannah, now you get to lay in it alone. If I wanted you, I'd be there. Hope you're happy 'cause no one else is gonna fuckin' want you now."

"Wow. Fuck yourself, Levi."

"Yep, because I sure as hell won't fuck you again."

I jam my finger into the end button, hanging up on the bastard, adrenaline making me feel nauseous. I wipe at my face furiously, refusing to shed any more tears over him and my failed relationship. I'm just sad for my daughter. How can someone create something so perfectly beautiful and not feel any desire at all to take care of her? To have a relationship with her at a minimum. My heart breaks for that precious girl who only knows good. She doesn't deserve to be tainted by such vile selfishness.

My rage simmers, leaving nothing but hate for a man who gave me the greatest gift in the world. My stomach flips over again, nausea rising further. It's hard to fathom I ever saw anything in him to begin with. Liam warned me about Levi multiple times, had a deeply rooted hate for him that I still don't understand outside of how Levi treats me and Charlie. But I was so desperate for attention that I fell back into a pattern with a man who had already hurt me once before. They don't change, and it's a lesson I learned too late. At least I got Charlie out of it.

The only reason I hang on to him anymore is for her. But what good is it doing? My parents may not be winning any parenting awards, but at the end of the day, I know they love me and my sisters. They always want the best for us, even if what we want isn't what their idea of success is. Not a day went by that my dad didn't rush right home to my mom, or to spend time with us girls. They may be holding Bean Haven over my head, but at least the offer to move to California with them is there, not that I would ever take it.

Levi is deeply flawed if he doesn't want a relationship with Charlie. I will just have to work overtime to make sure she feels all the love and protect her from all the future disappointment that is bound to come from her piece of shit sperm donor. Because that's all he is at this point. I don't know how to go on from this, from failing at something so basic as starting and keeping a family.

I'm at a point where I just need something. An epiphany? A fairy godmother? A sign from some higher being? Maybe a yellow brick road will magically appear and show me the way. How the hell do I figure out where to go from here? I'm going to lose everything I've worked hard for because I wasn't enough to keep the man I share a child with. He's right, who the hell is going to want me now? A single mother, workaholic.

After pulling myself together and letting my rage drop to a rolling simmer, I go find my daughter, who's playing with dolls in her room.

"Hey, baby cakes. Want to help your mama make dinner?"

"Yes! What are we having?" she squeals.

"We're having your FAVORITE!" I yell the last word, amplifying my excitement for her.

"FRENCH TOAST?"

"FRENCH TOAST!" I echo back, matching her enthusiasm.

"Can bear come? He loves French toast, too!"

"He does love French toast, but he can't come over until late tonight 'cause he's working on something new and exciting. You'll be asleep. But guess who's taking you to school tomorrow?"

"Bear is? Cause Uncle Carter didn't do the dance."

I gasp in horror, and her light little laugh—that is music to my ears—floats through the air.

"We're gonna have to talk to Uncle Carter because he needs to learn the dance if he's going to drop you off again."

Charlie and I work in the kitchen together with our '90s music playlist blaring in the background. Nights like this with just me and my girl make me feel better. She's happy and has no idea what she's missing. It's just that lingering fear that I'm not giving her everything she could have that makes me feel like such a failure. I so badly want to give her a stable home with two parents who love each other and love her just as much.

After dinner, we move through her bedtime routine—taking a bath and getting into her favorite PJs. Pulling out her favorite book, *When the World Is Ready for Bed*, we take turns reading. Well, me saying a line and pausing, and her saying the next. We've read this one no less than a few times a night for the last year, and she has the entire book memorized.

Kissing my baby goodnight, I leave her in her big girl bed to go about the rest of my evening alone.

Needing to decompress, I strip out of my clothes and get into the shower, not bothering to wait for the water to heat up. I've always been good at deflecting what anyone has to say or think of me. I have a tough exterior, and I've never fallen prey to people's harsh words or opinions.

But Levi's struck a chord. Am I going to be alone forever? Charlie's part of this package, and I wouldn't want to be with anyone who didn't love her just as much. I wouldn't trade her for anything, but I can't help but wonder if I didn't inadvertently sign myself up for a lifetime of loneliness.

The early morning hustle and bustle has gradually faded, allowing me a few moments of peace and quiet before it picks back up again around lunchtime. My phone rings from the kitchen, the erratic alarm blaring as a warning of the caller. Dropping my head back and groaning to the ceiling, I snatch it off of the counter and click "accept".

"Hello, life giver, to what do I owe this pleasure?"

"Hello, Hannah, nice to hear you're your usual snarky self. Very cute. How's our granddaughter?"

"Thank you, warden, I do try my hardest for you. Charlie is doing amazing, loving preschool, learning so much, and making friends. Complete opposite of her mother."

"That's great, that's what we love to hear. And how is Levi?"

My teeth gnash at the inside of my cheek to keep from losing my mind. She asks this every week when she calls, and my answer is always the same.

"I wouldn't know. Levi doesn't come around often, and he hardly calls anymore."

"Well, you know, if you didn't work so hard, and focused on raising Charlotte, things would be easier. No one wants to have a long-distance relationship, Hannah. If you just put in some effort with him, maybe he would come home."

Always the same conversation. Over and over and over again.

"It was Levi's choice to leave, our lives are here."

"Yes, but to provide for his family, Hannah."

"No, mom. It wasn't. It was a selfish decision that I wasn't even a part of when he made it. Charlie and I are doing just fine by ourselves. More than fine."

She sighs into the phone, no doubt to make sure I hear her disappointment through the speaker. I feel like a robot on repeat, going nowhere fast.

"You can't continue to run yourself into the ground, Hannah. This nonsense has gone on for far too long, and you can't do it all on your own. Not to mention what a travesty it would be for Charlotte to be raised without a father. Either you get it together and make things work with Levi, or you are coming to California with us. End of conversation."

God, does she even hear herself? I am surviving just fine on my own, raising Charlie and running Bean Haven. Why the hell can't anyone see that? She's always been like this, refuses to see that pushing me toward *her* version of happiness and success isn't what works for me. I'm living my happy life, with a joyful, healthy daughter. But I don't want to lose Bean Haven if that's what she is truly threatening. This place is deeply rooted in the marrow of my bones, and if they take it from me because I don't meet their outdated expectations of what my life should look like, I don't know what I would do.

I don't even want to think about having that conversation with my grandmother. Just the thought of her no longer being with us and her bakery being sold is enough to steal the air from my lungs, the pain squeezing tightly. I would do anything to keep Bean Haven.

I haven't even given a single thought to moving to California, because it's not an option. I wouldn't—I couldn't—leave Aspen Ridge, even if they take Bean Haven from me.

"No, mom," I object, my voice monotone and withdrawn. "Charlie and I are happy in Aspen Ridge, our lives are here. Please trust me. We are thriving, and I am figuring things out." Quickly changing the topic, I add in over her audible huffs of disappointment, "Will you be coming back to Aspen Ridge for Charlie's birthday party?"

She sighs again before answering, and I have to pull the phone away from my face so that I don't freak out on her. Bringing it back up to my ear just in time to catch her reply, I roll my eyes and let my shoulders sag in relief.

"We wish we could, but we just can't make it work to hop up there for just a weekend. We will be back for the summer in the last week of May, and we'll take her out to celebrate and spoil her. I'll call her on her birthday, okay?"

"Sounds great, Mom. We'll talk soon then, k? Thank you for calling, it's always such a good start to my week."

The moment I click "end" on my phone, I drop it on the counter, let out a frustrated wail, and stomp my feet.

"Whoa! Everything okay?"

A startled, high-pitched scream bursts from my lungs as I turn and come face-to-face with the gigantic, tattooed, muscled mass of a man in a leather jacket. His long hair is combed back and pulled into a ponytail, a few stray strands falling around his face, his beard thick and scruffy. To a stranger, they'd assume this big bad wolf would be here to eat them alive and use their bones as toothpicks, but his soft emerald-green eyes give away that he's really just a bunch of gooey melted chocolate on the inside.

"Dammit, Reid! I think I just peed my freaking pants! For fuck's sake!"

"I thought you heard the bell. I didn't mean to scare you.

Then you screamed and I thought you were hurt so I came running back here."

"Not hurt. Not physically at least," I sputter, rolling my eyes and walking into the café area. "Parental bullshit. They want me to marry Levi so that Charlotte is being raised the 'proper way,' with both mommy and daddy in the same house," I confess, my tone dripping with condescension. "Oh! And they're holding Bean Haven over my head to get me to comply."

Reid rubs the back of his neck as he walks to the front of the counter so I can take his order and get it started. He's been best friends with Liam's older brother, Sawyer, since Sawyer was in college. A few years ago, he opened up a tattoo shop a couple blocks up the street from me called Rogue, and pops in a few times a week to satiate his sweet tooth and get a coffee fix.

"I know something about difficult parents, pretty sure I'm the poster child for doing the opposite of what they envisioned for me."

"What, lawyer daddy not proud of his tattoo artist, motorcycle-riding, tattooed-from-neck-to-toe son?"

"Somethin' like that," he says, fairly sheepishly. "We just need to live the life we want. We've only got one of them and it's a privilege to wake up every day."

"So wise, big guy. But I'm in the mood to burn shit down. I'm so over being fucked with. Anyway, your usual?"

"Please. We starting any new projects this year?"

Over the last two years, Reid has completed my floral sleeve and a large piece that curves from the very top of my thigh, flows around my hip, and comes up my side to cup under my breast. He's so talented, and I wear them with pride. Even if my mother died when she saw my sleeve for the first time. It was worth it. It's not like being covered in tattoos is out of character for me. My hair has been vibrant colors for years.

"Possibly! It's always tempting and such a stress reliever."

"You're an enigma, not many people get tattooed and enjoy the pain part."

"It's not that I enjoy it." I pause to think for a second. "Well, maybe I do, but it's more like an endorphin release. Maybe I should look into acupuncture."

I hand Reid his drink and he looks at me with soulful, sincere eyes. Not with pity, but concern for a friend.

"If you ever need to talk, I'm just up the road. And if you need an excuse to vent, just book an appointment and we'll think of something."

"You're a gem, Reid. Now, get outta my shop and get back to work!"

He laughs as he walks out of the door and more customers squeeze in. I glance at the clock and count down the hours until I can go pick up my little girl and spend the afternoon with her. As much as I love being at Bean Haven, I'm craving being surrounded by her little ray of sunshine.

Chapter Five

Liam

Unlucky for me, our annual Hayes brothers snowboarding trip to Mount Baker was this week. There was no way I was going to tell Hannah the shit news and leave her to pick up the pieces by herself. I couldn't come up with a decent enough excuse to skip the trip, so I set myself a deadline to tell her the day we came back.

Lucky for me, Sawyer couldn't stand to be away from Ivy for longer than forty-eight hours, so we got back to Aspen Ridge much quicker than our typical three full days. Dallas was also itching to get back here, but I've had too much on my mind to get to the bottom of *that*. Too bad for him, it all came crashing down on us not long after we got to work after driving straight through from Mount Baker. *Literally*.

Turns out brother dearest is sleeping with the event coordinator of our distillery, whom he "hates." Blaire was hired last fall and has brought so much visibility to us that we're feeling the pressure to keep up with our rapid growth on the property, even through the harsh winter months. After the mess my brothers and I just walked into, and seeing how pissed Sawyer is about it, I feel the need to check on his ass. He'd do the same for any of us—after rubbing our faces in it a bit.

Finding Dallas in the hallway coming from Sawyer's office, which I'm sure was a fun time considering the bomb he just set off, Dallas nods his head at me to follow him into his down the hall.

"She alright?" I ask as I shut the door behind me to give us some privacy, worried about how our newest employee is feeling now that we've discovered their relationship.

"Mortified, but she's the strongest woman I've ever met," he says, seemingly okay despite the circumstances. But that's just Dallas. He owns his shit and moves on.

"Well, shit, that's sayin' something considering the last six months."

Life has been fucking nuts around here. What the fuck could be next?

"How's Han, everything okay?"

Running my hand nervously through my hair, I start to pace the length of his office. I came here to check in on him, and typical Dallas, he wants to make sure that I'm doing okay.

"Still trying to process how I'm going to break it to her that her boyfriend-slash-ex-boyfriend-slash-baby daddy is a cheating piece of shit with a live-in girlfriend and another baby on the way. Oh, and he's most definitely not going to marry you, so plan on losing your family's business that you love so much."

"Shit. Yeah. So, advice?"

"Please."

"I wouldn't say it like that."

"Well, no shit, Sherlock. Thanks for helping."

Dickhead.

"Like I said before, you know Hannah better than anyone in the world, and you literally were the first person to see

Charlie when she delivered her on the kitchen floor. No one knows how better to help them through this than you do."

"Shit sucks, man," I admit, feeling helpless as fuck. I just want to fix this. I would do anything to make life easier for her.

"Trust me, I get it. Just be there. It's all you can do. Give her a safe space and shoulder to lean on, something you've been doing for twenty years already."

His words trigger something inside me. That isn't all I can do, is it? I *can* fix it. It may be a hard sell but if her parents want her settled and married, I can get her to marry *me*. Her parents have wanted this since we were little, and they would definitely get off of her case about settling down. Plus, with me behind her, Levi wouldn't fuck with her anymore. And this would keep her and Charlotte here, because I'm not letting them go. Yeah. This could work.

"Thanks, brother. I got shit to do but I'll see you Sunday."

"Sounds good."

Decision made, I leave Dallas' office on a mission to make Hannah mine. Levi's loss is my gain. She's always been mine anyway, Levi was just a heartache that she needed to endure to bring Charlotte into the world. And I am more than okay with that. I wouldn't trade that girl for anything, no matter who created her. And Hannah's parents? Fuck them. That girl has been running Bean Haven by herself for years, and if Ms. Nettie has faith in her, then her parents can fuck themselves.

Swinging into Carter's office before I head out, I find him tapping away at his computer.

"Hey, Casanova, I got some shit to take care of, I'm out of here."

"Everything good?"

"Yeah, it's all good."

"Thank fuck," he sighs as he leans back in his chair. "Between all that shit with Ivy, and now Dallas fucking Blaire,

I can't take another damn thing in this family. You all are working overtime to make *me* look good."

I inwardly cringe, knowing that I'm about to drop a bomb of my own when I get Hannah to agree to be mine. Carter is about to look like the golden child. Even if he's slept his way through our town and the next three. We're surprised a baby or two haven't resulted from his extracurricular activities.

"Don't worry, I'm sure you'll find a way to top us all," I say with a wink before heading out. I want to be ready for tonight. And the sure way to Hannah's heart is pizza and old slasher movies. Both of which just happen to be my favorite, too.

Unsure when the last time I was this worked up over something, I step through Hannah's apartment feeling anxious as fuck. I know that this Band-Aid needs to be pulled off, but being the one to cause her pain makes me feel like dog shit. But I already have a plan to pick up the pieces, she just needs to trust me. I won't abandon her now, not ever.

"Yo! Why do you look so pale? Are you getting sick?" Hannah says as I walk into the living room, finding her curled up on her side of the couch flipping through old slasher movies on Netflix. Great minds think alike. She's wearing a thin tank top and loose pajama pants with Freddy Krueger masks all over them that I bought her for Christmas.

"I wish. That'd be easier than this is gonna be. Look, we need to talk, Han."

She sits up straighter, pulling her legs under her, and faces me as I drop the pizza onto her coffee table. Fuck, this sucks. I have no idea how she's going to take the news. I pace in front of her, taking off my backwards hat and running my hands through my thick hair.

"Oh for fuck's sake, bear, sit down and spit it out. I'm not made of glass."

"Fuck, I know that, Hannah. Just . . . okay, wait, first we're going to need alcohol."

Walking to Hannah's kitchen, I grab a bottle of tequila from the cabinet above the stove and return to the living room. I plop down in the middle of the couch, my big body taking up the entire cushion and part of the one she's on. Opening the cap, I take a swig before passing it to her.

"I'm a big girl. Let's hear it."

"Take a swig then, *big girl.*"

With a dramatic eye roll, she puts the bottle to her plump lips and takes a hefty pull of tequila without a wince. It's been our alcohol of choice since we were dumbass teenagers, stealing it from my parent's liquor cabinet and refilling the bottles with water. Kind of ironic considering my family owns a successful whiskey distillery and that I'm now a master distiller, maybe that's why we always went for the tequila. Maybe we figured they weren't reaching for that one as much.

"After I walked in on that meltdown from Levi and all the shit with your parents, I'd reached my end of the bullshit—and before you get pissed, I didn't touch him. I wouldn't do anything to make things harder on you, you damn well know that," I declare, pointing my finger at her before her crazy comes out.

"So you drove all the way to Seattle? And then what? Drove back home and worked all day?"

"Yeah," I say sheepishly, scratching the back of my neck.

"Well, seeing as he's not here, I guess whatever you said didn't work. Plus, I've since gotten into it with him. *Again.*"

"Han, it's not about anything either of us said. It's what I found."

Her eyes squint into slits, her head cocking to the side a bit as she waits patiently, something that's not usually her strong suit.

"I love you, beauty. Remember that, okay?"

"Unless you want me to knock your teeth out, bear, talk."

"Levi's got a pregnant girlfriend living with him."

Her face pales, her mouth dropping open a bit and forming an "O" before closing and opening again like a fish. My lungs seize up, and my palms get sweaty as I watch her take it all in, bracing myself for her reaction when it hits.

"HOLY SHIT! That lying motherfucker! Holy fucking shit! Whelp, our last conversation makes so much more fucking sense. That cheating asshole! Holy fuck!" Hannah stands abruptly, pacing back and forth in front of me. Her hair is dancing around her face, the violet color reflecting the light and making it almost shimmer. "You know, I can't even say that I don't believe it because it makes so much fucking sense. Ugh! I goddamn hate him, bear!" She stomps around for a moment before the information seems to settle in before the crash.

"This ends it completely between us. What about Charlotte? Bean Haven? Oh my god, I don't know what I'm going to do." Aaaand there it is. Panic. Fuck. Hard part over. Now the final blow.

"I do. But you need to sit back down first." I pass the tequila bottle back to her. "And drink more."

She looks at me, her eyebrows arching in confusion. Mixed with the anger, it would be pretty cute if her world wasn't crashing down around her. She takes a seat across from me, pulling her knees up to her chest and grabbing the bottle roughly from my hand.

"You're going to marry me."

"Ha. You're smoking crack," she says, brushing me off as she takes another long pull and wipes her mouth with the back of her hand.

"Beauty, listen to me. You're out of options, and that fucker will never be an option again. We're going to start dating, right now," I tell her firmly, pointing to the ground. "We'll make it a whirlwind romance and then we'll get married. Everyone in this town thought we would end up together anyway, so that's just making it that much more believable. This is how you get your parents off your back so you can keep Bean Haven. You never loved him, Hannah."

"Holy shit balls, you're actually serious right now. We can't do this. We're best friends, you idiot, what about Charlie?"

"Even better, because it'll make it easier for everyone to fall for it. The three of us are together all the time, we just need to date a bit first. Beauty, if you think about it, it's not that farfetched." I try to keep the desperation from leaking through my words. Am I doing this for Hannah or because I'm so desperate for this woman to be mine that I'm willing to do anything to make that happen? Probably equal parts of both.

"Bear . . . this is a bad idea."

"Is it? You get to keep Bean Haven, your parents will fuck off with their bullshit, and Levi will finally realize that you're off the market to be continuously fucked with. It'll allow you to really stick it to all of them. And nothing has to even change much."

"What do you get out of this, freak? You trying to get in my pants after all these years?"

If she only fucking knew. God, the things I would do to her if I could.

"I'm not going to say no if it's in my face, Hannah, have you seen yourself?"

As if I was only attracted to her sexy, tattooed body. It's that personality of hers that brings me to my knees.

"Listen to me, I fucking hate that they're hurting you. That Levi continues to fuck with you. You deserve so much more than that piece of shit. So does Charlie. I'm pissed at your parents for their archaic beliefs and that they can't see what a hard worker you are and how deserving you are of running Bean Haven. You can handle anything on your own. But if it makes things easier for me to be behind you while you give everyone the finger, then that's what I'm going to do."

Her face softens as she listens to my words, and my heart melts right there.

"I love you. You're an idiot, though. This will blow up in our faces." Her rage has melted away, and I'm not sure if it's the tequila she continues to sip or if she is actually leaning into this idea.

"I'll make sure it doesn't. Trust me, beauty?"

She really looks at me now, her eyes filled with uncertainty before resignation slowly sets in, and a bolt shoots through my entire body. Holy shit, she's going to do this. My heart nearly beats out of my chest. Dropping down to my knees in front of her, I take her left hand in mine. Her head drops back as she nervously laughs, the soft sound floating through the air and easing some of the tension I'm carrying. I try to swallow hard, my mouth suddenly devoid of any moisture, and work to steady my voice when I speak.

"Hannah Jade Haven, I promise that someday you will get the proposal of your dreams, but for right now, will you fake marry me?"

Because I will make all your dreams come true.

Because I'll show you what it means to really be loved.

Because I'm so in love with you that I can't bear another moment that you aren't mine.

"You're absolutely crazy. I can't believe I'm agreeing to this. Yes, bear, I'll marry you."

Chapter Six

Hannah

Three little words ring through my head, and I have to close my eyes briefly to center myself.

I'll marry you.

Lucid dreams are a thing, right? I think I remember reading about them at one point. This seems like a textbook case because there's no way I just agreed to marry my best friend. This is Liam for fuck's sake. There is zero mystery between us, except for the obvious.

As my eyes flutter open, Liam is still on his knees in front of me, my hand in his. I watch as he brings it slowly to his mouth, his eyes never leaving mine as he kisses the spot where a ring would sit. It's something so simple, but he makes it so intimate. A shockwave flows through me, and as though my heart has never beaten for another person before, it finds a rhythm that makes it sing—beating rapidly, my chest rising and falling harder.

What the hell is happening right now? These feelings are coming out of nowhere and I seriously need to get my shit together if this is going to work. What the fuck even was that? I hold out the bottle in front of me and look at it. Goddamn tequila. Why do we always have to go straight for the tequila?

"We're really doing this?" I ask, breaking the tension suspended between us.

"Yeah, we're really doing this. You ready to date the shit out of me, beauty? Cause this is gonna go fast. We're gonna give everyone something to talk about."

I laugh because what else am I supposed to do? This is sure to get me what I want, my parents will probably die of happiness when they find out, the patriarchal assholes.

"So, how is this supposed to work?"

He moves off the ground to sit next to me on the couch, not bothering to put space between us. Something I wouldn't have even noticed before, but now . . .

"We're going to date. And in a few months, we're going to run off and get married."

I swallow another swig of tequila, feeling the warmth of the alcohol flowing through my veins. Tomorrow morning is going to be a bitch.

"You think it's that easy?"

"Han, be real. You don't live under a rock. You run Bean Haven for fuck's sake, which is like town central. You know there's rumors about us. There's always been rumors."

He's not wrong, as much as I've done my best to ignore them. I can't stand that people think that a man and woman can't be close friends without having a sexual relationship or one of them hiding their secret love for the other person. Bear and I have been best friends our entire lives and the rumors have followed us for just as long. Even our parents made jokes when we were younger about an arranged marriage. Which is honestly pretty funny given the current situation.

"Okay. So, as much as I hate to breathe life into them, I hear what you're saying. People will believe it and I don't think much even needs to change. What about the logistics? I don't want to confuse Charlie."

"Nothing changes in front of her. I don't want to do anything that would confuse or potentially hurt her. I'd die first, Han."

My heart warms at his statement because I know it's the truth. He has loved her just as much as I do since the moment she was born.

"Alright. That's easy enough then. I mean, you're practically here all the time anyway, and you already help so much with her."

"Exactly. Now ask me what you really want to ask, beauty. I see it turning over in that pretty little mind of yours."

My cheeks flame with heat but I meet his eyes straight on, not backing away from this.

"What about the physical stuff? We need rules in place."

"People aren't going to believe it if we aren't physical at all, Han. You're a smart girl, you know that."

Shit. I know he's right, but I also know myself, and that will turn my brain into a hormonal, confused, tangled mess. It doesn't matter how desperate I am to be touched, that can't come from my best friend—that will muddle everything.

"So, we definitely need rules then."

"What rules would make you feel better?"

How is he so calm? He seems almost . . . excited. I look at the bottle of tequila again and try to remember how much was in it before we started because it's the only explanation for everything happening right now. I say the first thing that comes to my head.

"Only touching in public when we need to. Simple touches, holding hands . . . that kinda thing. And no touching . . . you know . . . *intimately*."

"Intimately? What are you a sixth-grade sex ed teacher? Do you mean no sex, Hannah?"

My face pales because of his words and the thought of sex, period. Something I haven't had in quite some time. And the last time was devastating to my ego and emotional state.

"I'm hurt, Han. You don't want me? I'm your fiancé!"

I smack him in his big stupid chest for making fun of me. Levi and I were hot and heavy before I got pregnant with Charlotte, but since he moved to Seattle, it's been strained. While he never made me feel desired or wanted, it was better than nothing that he wanted me enough to use me to get off, even if he didn't care about my pleasure. I was just desperate for affection and took whatever I could get. But nothing has happened since the last time he was here. I couldn't put myself back in one of those situations again. The last time crushed me.

I know that I'm touch starved, using my vibrator only takes the edge off, and that's after I've held off so long, I feel like I'm going to erupt. What I really want is to feel someone wanting me in a way that I'm now wondering if I've ever even felt before. Something all-consuming, life-shattering.

The last time Levi and I had sex was after a huge fight. I used it to try to smooth things over, to try to reconnect with him and show him that I wanted him to come around more, that we could be a family. After he fucked me, using me as a vessel for a quick lay, he abruptly stood up, looked down at me, and told me I was pathetic. I haven't tried since.

"You're an ass. That would be a terrible mistake and you know it. Sex is off the table. No touching. That's our rule."

"Fine. No touching, except light touches when needed in public. What about kissing?"

My head jerks back and I look at him like he's crazy. "What about it?" I ask with a little more shock and attitude than probably necessary.

"I may have to kiss you, Hannah. You are my fiancée, after all." His voice drops, no longer filled with teasing, his eyes flicking to my lips. My tongue darts out and swipes across them in response, and for the first time in my life, the thought of kissing Liam crosses my mind.

And it doesn't sound bad at all.

Shit. I really am touch starved.

He moves closer, his eyes heavily lidded and pupils dilated as his palm rises to my face, pushing my hair out of the way and tucking it behind my ear, barely a whisper of a touch. My breath hitches as he lays his warm hand against my cheek, and I jerk back at the contact.

"Bear, knock it off. We said no touching."

"Han, with the way you just flinched away from me, it's clear you need to get used to me touching you the way a husband touches his wife."

My mouth falls open because I never thought I would hear those words come from his mouth. Shock hits me first, but then a surprising part of me, a part that I don't want to dissect right now, wants to know exactly what it would feel like to be touched the way a *husband* touches what's his. He reaches his hand back up to repeat the action and I slap his hand away.

Shit. He's good. This must be how the women fall at his feet. Warmth pools at my center, my body prickling with anticipation. He's nailed his moves. Liam exudes confidence, sexual prowess that I've never been on the receiving end of before. That explains it.

And the tequila.

"I know how to act, bear, trust me. Don't forget I've been with Levi for the last five years. I'm the best actress that ever lived. I can act with you, too."

Liam's eyes squint as he leans into my space, his lips next to my ear, his breath tickling me as he speaks. "Beauty, if you were with me, there would be no need to fake a goddamn thing."

My skin breaks out in goosebumps as he pulls back, flipping open the lid to the pizza box and pulling out a slice like he didn't just successfully leave me hot and bothered.

And confused as fuck.

I wake up with a jolt, the alarm of my phone blaring obnoxiously next to my face, where it fell out of my hand as my body finally gave in to sleep not long ago. I sit up slowly, bracing for a wave of nausea, the room swaying for a second before steadying. My head is pounding thanks to last night's tequila marathon, and my dry, gritty eyes protest as I force them open in my dark room. Last night was near sleepless, my mind racing, spinning on its own axis and out of control. None of it truly seems real, just a drunken hazy memory of something that couldn't possibly have happened to begin with.

Forcing myself out of bed and into a hot shower, I wash, albeit sluggishly, and then step out to dry off and blow dry my hair. After getting through my morning routine and pulling on a pair of jeans and a Bean Haven T-shirt, I check on my sleeping baby girl before starting my long day.

I feel the tension in the pit of my stomach that never seems to leave anymore as I pull myself together to sneak downstairs through the interior door that leads directly to the bakery, body operating on autopilot. Pulling out all of my ingredients, I get started on the goods that keep driving everyone into my little shop day after day, slowly waking up in the process. I lose track of time as I let myself go to the same routine I follow every morning—mixing ingredients, rolling out dough, scooping batter, in the oven and out, rinse and repeat, all while watching my daughter sleep right above me on the baby monitor, the soft tunes of Third Eye Blind coming from my headphones.

The revelation of Levi's secret life in Seattle shouldn't have come as a surprise to me, but the weight of it sits like a bomb in the pit of my stomach. What is wrong with me and Charlie that kept him away from us? That made him not want to be a family? My emotions warred with each other all night as my body fought off the effects of the tequila, and this morning isn't any better. While I realized I wasn't in love with Levi a long time ago, I've been living in this never-ending cycle, trying to force a square into a round hole. We share a child, why wouldn't we share a life? And if Levi doesn't want me, then what now?

His new life cements a new fear. He and I won't ever be anything, so where does that leave my daughter? Just the thought of her traveling back and forth to live with him and his new girlfriend and child—a child that is technically her sibling—makes me anxious, and I don't know if my heart could take it. It would be an entirely different feeling if he played an active role in her life and we simply didn't work. But Charlie doesn't know him. He's never made it a priority to create a relationship with her. Would I be expected to share custody with him? Would he even want that? He doesn't care about her now, so why should I even worry about that?

The back of my mind is also acutely aware of the icing on my shitty life cake, that my parents have threatened to sell Bean Haven if I don't settle down and get my shit together. Even if Liam thinks he's found the cure to all of my problems, all I can see right now is that my life is literally crashing and burning around me in a rapid blaze and no matter what I do, how hard I work, or how much effort I put in, it will never be enough for anyone. The saddest part of it all? I don't even feel the heat of the flames anymore.

My alarm goes off, reminding me to open Bean Haven, so I wash my hands of the sticky dough and pull out my headphones. Flour coats my apron and while I would normally take it off and hang it up to make myself more presentable for customers, this morning, I just don't have it in me to care.

When I get to the glass door, I'm not surprised to see people waiting, even though it's five in the morning. The sun is peeking through the thick cloud cover today and I have to squint as it reflects off the snow-covered sidewalk. Doing my best to stifle a yawn, I unlock the door and hold it open for Wes and his wife Lily to walk in, followed by Liam's good friend, Officer Owen Hopkins, who must be coming off of his night shift.

"Hey, you two!" I greet Wes and Lily. Their relationship is still a little shocking to everyone, considering Wes is her ex-boyfriend's dad and all. But honestly, I called it way before it happened. The way that man looked at her was anything but innocent.

"Hi, Hannah. Are you still selling pumpkin spice lattes by any chance?" Wes asks.

"I'm sorry, I'm out for the season. I promise they will be back in September. Is there anything else I can get you?"

"Black coffee for me, and a caramel latte for Lilith."

"You got it."

While I make their coffees, I can't help but admire the way Wes holds onto Lily. His arm is wrapped around her waist, keeping her close to him, like her touch gives him everything he needs. She is so clearly smitten with him that she just exudes happiness. I guess when you're loved the way you need to be loved, why wouldn't that show outwardly?

After handing them their drinks, they head out as Liam is

walking in. Butterflies take flight in my stomach because it's the first time I've seen him since our agreement last night. I need to speak with him alone to see if it was all a fever dream or if it really happened.

He's wearing denim jeans with his tan boots and a jacket, a backwards Aspen Ridge Distillery hat, and looking effortlessly put together like we hadn't polished off a bottle of hard alcohol last night, the big jerk.

"What up, Owen?" Liam says to Officer Hopkins, giving him a fist bump. The two of them have been friends for years, and when Owen decided to be a police officer, it was an ongoing joke that he'd no doubt have to arrest his friend at some point, with all the crazy shit the Hayes siblings get themselves into. *Especially as of late.*

Liam walks around the counter and my breath seizes in my lungs as I watch him take purposeful strides in my direction. What the hell is he doing? He's a man on a mission, and he slides his big hand around my waist, confidently pressing my body flush with his. I inhale deeply, breathing in the intoxicating scent of burnt sugar and oak.

His lips press against my temple and my eyes close briefly, enjoying such an intimate hug, my brain signaling the rapid sendoff of happy hormones. Fingers deftly toy with the tiny space where my shirt ends and my jeans begin, lightly touching the bare skin with skillful fingertips. My breathing is shallow and ragged, but I feel a calmness wash over me that is associated with and so specific to him. All my worry and anxiety, all of it washes out into the abyss as he holds me close and forces my senses to hyperfocus on him—his delicious woodsy, sweet smell, the feel of his fingers, the warmth of his big body, the sound of his steady heartbeat. *Peace.*

Owen coughing loudly into his fist snaps me out of this spell and my spine straightens. Liam pulls back just enough to look at me, but my eyes are stuck on Owen, trying to gauge his reaction. Liam's fingers make contact with my chin, gently tilting my head back to him and I go willingly. Mother above, what is happening?

"Eyes on me, beauty. How was your morning?"

I can't help but smile brightly at him, although I'm confused as fuck. My body and brain are not on the same page. Abort! I need to put space between us, stat. This is Liam for fuck's sake. I can't be so desperate for physical affection that the first time I receive any, I'm a lost puppy begging for more. Am I truly that starved for attention? I inwardly cringe and squirm, suddenly not feeling confident in my own skin as I can't imagine what a desperate mess I must look like to him. Taking a deep breath, I answer his question with a well-practiced smile.

"I'm exhausted but it's been a good morning. How are you?"

"Better now." He smirks. "Charlie still sleeping?"

"Yes," I reply, slightly breathy.

"Either of you assholes going to tell me what the fuck is going on right now or are you going to continue to pretend I'm not here?" Owen says and we both snap our attention back to him. Slapping Liam's chest hard, I try to push him away, but he doesn't budge. Instead, he holds his grip around my hip steady and jerks me back into his big-ass body.

"Good morning, Owen. I'm sure you're tired. Your usual?" I ask, hoping like hell he isn't going to ask questions.

"Yup. But you're not going to get out of telling me what's happening right now. It's freaking me the fuck out."

"Hannah and I are dating—"

"—It's nothing," Liam and I say in unison.

"It's not nothing. She's just worried about what people are going to think. Isn't that right, beauty?"

Liam continues to move his fingers back and forth on the

tiny strip of bare skin at my lower back and it's distracting as hell, the bastard. He's playing dirty and successfully screwing with my already-fucked-with head.

"Hmm?" I ask, not hearing what was just said past the sound of my blood rushing in my ears unable to focus on anything other than that slow glide of his fingers, back and forth, back and forth.

"You're shittin' me right now. You two finally got together? Well, shit. Who knows?"

"Honestly, man, we've been keeping it to ourselves for a while now. We haven't wanted to make an announcement of it. You know how people are," Liam says resolutely, like this is the easiest thing he's ever had to do.

"You idiot, you need to tell people, you know how many people all have bets on this?"

I nearly choke on my saliva, now firmly back in reality. I've heard the rumors, but bets? I internally die over the fact that I'm proving their point that a male and female can't be as close as Liam and I are without having some type of feelings. Ugh. Kill me now, please.

"Can you keep it PG in public though, don't want Hannah to be arrested for her second offense."

I shoot Owen an evil glare, narrowing my eyes at him.

"Try to keep it to yourself for a bit, huh? We still need to tell our families. It'll spread like wildfire as soon as Han tells Ms. Nettie," Liam states.

"Fucking right it will. Everyone three towns over will know."

I roll my eyes and move away from these idiots to pour him his coffee, Liam's hands falling from my waist, the cool air replacing his warm touch. Handing the to-go mug to Owen, I don't release it after he reaches for it.

"It's on the house, but some discretion for more than five minutes, please?"

"Only cause I'm happy for you two. Keep her, Liam, it's about time you got your girl," Owen says as he turns and walks away. His statement makes me freeze in my spot. About time? When I turn around, Liam has moved to the open doorway that separates the bakery kitchen from the actual shop and is bracing himself on the door frame, hands above his head, stretching out his body slightly. His brown Carhartt jacket is unzipped and hanging open, and a formfitting white pocket tee lifts up, exposing the area right above his jeans, a barely noticeable happy trail disappearing below his belt.

Shit.

I may need to find a one-night stand because there is no way that I'm being turned on by the same man who has held my hair back while I puked into bushes after a drunken night, whose truck seats I stained when I bled through my tampon, who has seen me give birth and cleaned up all the lovely birthing juices from my kitchen floor. For fuck's sake, with those thoughts, it's a wonder he wants to marry me at all. At least I don't have to worry about him wanting me in a sexual way, with all the bodily fluids he's seen come out of me, I'm sure I've scarred him for life.

"Like what you see, beauty?"

"Oh, shut up, bear. What was that?" I chastise him.

"Me being your boyfriend. Don't act like you weren't into it."

"I wasn't. It's acting, you dink hole. Remember? We're playing pretend."

I'm starting to wonder if this is a good idea at all. This is going to no doubt crash and burn with the rest of my dumpster fire life and then I'll truly be alone.

"This is stupid, right? We were drunk last night?"

He lets go of the frame and walks right up to me, combing his fingers through my hair and holding my face to look up at him. My heart does that weird thing in my chest again like I'm about to have a heart attack, but more fluttery?

"Listen to me, I'm not about to stand by and do nothing while you lose everything that you have worked hard for. If you need me to stand behind you, I will be whatever you need me to be so that you can prove you've got this." He pulls gently on my hair to make sure I'm listening before continuing, "So, get out of that pretty little head of yours. Let's make this work so you can give a huge fuck you to Levi and your parents."

"Okay," I agree. How could I say no when he puts it like that?

Chapter Seven

Liam

The end of the week came hard and fast, and I was feeling worked up enough that I either needed a hard workout that included pummeling one of my dipshit brothers in the ring, or a stiff drink. Choosing the latter, I roll my truck up to the only bar in Aspen Ridge—The Night Owl—and order a beer to unwind for a beat.

The Night Owl has a rustic vibe while also being surprisingly edgy. The ceiling is supported by thick wooden beams and open pipework, giving the space that industrial yet modern vibe. It's the bar itself that steals the show, though. Crafted from live-edge black walnut, a silky black epoxy river run detail flows through the center. Each of the tables around the open dance floor match. Leather barstools are scattered about, and the craftsman in me appreciates the aesthetic of the place. It fits in seamlessly with the town.

Taking a deep pull of my beer, which always gets me funny looks since I'm one of the lead master distillers at work, I do my best to chill out. I haven't been able to shake thoughts of Hannah out of my head, the events of the week on a steady replay the entire day as I tried to focus on my tasks at the distillery. Being a master distiller takes focus and clarity, neither of which I have at the moment. I had to pass tasks to Graham on more than one occasion, and I'm grateful for my right-hand man. Technically we share the same title, and while he'd never say differently, I look up to him since he and my grandfather taught me everything I know.

Graham has been working for the distillery since I was in grade school, and even though he's fifteen years older than me, we've got a great relationship. He's a single dad and while I'm not one, I've leaned on him more than once as I was there to help support Hannah with a baby neither of us knew how to take care of. It helped that he's known Hannah most of her life since he's best friends with her dad.

Her words echo again and again, making my heart rate pick up, the beer doing nothing to settle my thoughts and nerves. *"Yes, bear, I'll marry you."* Fuck if I don't want to hear those words from her lips with deep meaning behind them. The other morning, I thought for sure she was going to go back on it all, but what I didn't expect was for her to be so compliant. Melting right in front of me. She's not as unaffected by me as I thought she was. I just need to show her that I'm more than her best friend, that I can be everything she wants and needs. Because, let's face it, come hell or high water, once I make Hannah mine, fake arrangement or not, I'm not giving her up.

I pull out my phone to text my brother, in need of some backup to get some time in with Hannah outside of Bean Haven and her apartment. I know only one brother who can handle it right now, and my sister would see right through the bullshit and call me out.

ME:

Grandpa caught me drinking his whiskey again.

CARTER:

Fuck asshole. You couldn't send it to the group chat? Where are you?

Me:

The Night Owl

CARTER:

Okay. I get why you texted me. Our brothers aren't any fun anymore

Well, shit. I'm about to piss on his good day.

ME:

You gonna come or what?

CARTER:

Yeah, be there in 5, I'm close

Pocketing my phone, I order Carter a drink and sit at the bar to wait for him. I'm torn between telling him the truth or just going for it and keeping everyone in the dark. I know Dallas will put it together since he knows the pressure Hannah's parents are putting on her, but I can't take the chance of word getting out. Carter is a gamble. Dallas is a sure thing.

By the time he walks in, I've got my game face on. Really not hard to do when I've wanted Hannah for as long as I have and had to keep it to myself. There won't be anything fake about this arrangement.

"Hey, man, where's the fire?" Carter greets me as he loosens the tie around his neck.

"Take a seat, little brother."

He picks up the whiskey on the rocks I ordered him and does a scan of the room. My hand comes quick and hard to the backside of his head, causing his teeth to clang against the glass and slosh alcohol across the bar top.

"Eyes over here, fucker. We're not here to pick up pussy."

"Asshole. That's what you think. Get on with it, what's the emergency?"

"I'm in love with Hannah."

He finishes dabbing up the spilled alcohol and takes another sip, his expression unchanged before facing me, the picture of composure. What the fuck?

"Okay? You think everyone in AR hasn't known that? Surprised Han doesn't know that. And don't abuse the code phrase, asshole. What if I was doing something important?"

"Were you?"

He shoves his middle finger in my face like a prepubescent boy, and I smack it away.

"We're dating. And I want to take her out this weekend, just the two of us, but we don't have a sitter."

Hannah's sisters, Harlow and Hailey, would be a sure thing to help out but they won't be back in Aspen Ridge this weekend.

"You're shitting me right now. No. Ask Mom."

"I'm not ready to tell Mom we're dating. We've been keeping it to ourselves for as long as possible," I lie. "I just want to take her to the drive-in. Charlie will be sleeping for like ninety percent of the time we're gone."

"Who the fuck wants to go to the drive-in in the middle of winter? What about Ivy?"

"Dude. No. You. I used the code phrase. It's important."

He drops his head back and groans up at the ceiling, and I know I've got him.

"You'll owe me."

"Big time. Cash in whenever you want."

As I leave my brother to corrupt whatever innocent women

may be left in Aspen Ridge, I pull out my phone to text Hannah.

ME:

I'm on my way over.

The walk up Main Street is a cold one. It's been a harsh winter this year, and my breath turns to mist as I exhale into my fists to warm them up. Snow crunches under my boots in a thick layer that has built up over the last few weeks; people are getting lazier and lazier about shoveling as the season wanes.

The town is already still as I continue up the cobblestone sidewalk toward Bean Haven, the kind of stillness that only a small mountain town can bring. The smell of fresh pine mixed with the smokiness from woodstoves burning is strong as I take a deep breath, the air sharp as it fills my lungs. I love this town. The seasons. The elements. The people. I especially love the distillery and being able to create a product that people can enjoy. The only thing I'm missing in life is a family of my own. A family with Hannah and Charlie.

I make the trek up the back stairs of Hannah's apartment, stomping my boots until the snow shakes free. Opening her door, I toe them off and drop the boots outside before walking into the warmth of the little place, excitement over seeing her heating up my veins faster than the house can.

I find Hannah lying on her side on the couch, stretched out like a cat sunbathing in a window. Her tiny sleep shorts leave little covered, the thin, delicate vines of her floral tattoo peeking out the bottom of the hem as I take a moment to peruse her fine body. A crop top reveals a strip of bare skin on her midriff, and knee-high chunky wool socks cover toes that she keeps painted black. Her eyes are closed, and she looks so goddamn peaceful like this.

Gently picking up her legs, I take a seat at the end of the

couch, resting them back on my lap and rubbing her feet to rouse her. She comes to slowly, her eyes heavily lidded and slightly groggy as if she's been sleeping for a while.

"Hi, beauty."

"Hi. What are you doing here?"

"Wanted to hang with my favorite girls. You two aren't up for partying?"

She playfully snaps her leg out to smack me in the chest, my instincts kicking in and grabbing her foot in my hand.

"The other night nearly killed me, you jackass. I'm not young anymore."

I gently press my thumb into the center of her sock-covered foot and slide it up and down, earning me the sweetest sigh from her in response. Fuck, I love touching her.

See me, baby. See me as more than just your best friend.

"Got us a sitter for next Friday night. You up for going to the drive-in with me?"

"Depends. What's playing?"

"Does it matter? It's a date, Hannah. It could be *Mrs. Doubtfire* and you'd go because that's the rules."

I continue to rub her foot, squeezing and making circles in the center, watching the expression on her face as she fights with the blissed-out feeling I'm pulling from her.

"You're such an idiot," she laughs. "For real. What's playing? Or I'm just gonna look it up on my phone."

"Holy shit, God forbid you're surprised," I jest as I give her foot a hard squeeze, switching to the other one, wishing like hell we were skin-to-skin instead. "A double feature, obviously. *The Nun* and *Annabelle: Creation.*"

She jumps in excitement, nearly heel-striking me in the balls. "Fuck, Han! Watch it!"

"Oh, don't be such a baby, your package isn't that big, I barely grazed it!"

"Fuck, that sass," I grind out with my teeth clenched. "One of these days I'm gonna spank it outta you."

I can't help but smile as she rolls her eyes in a dramatic display, forcing herself to shiver like she could ever truly be scared of me.

"Yes, obviously we're going to the drive-in. I love that they'll still play them through the winter. I'm so glad they're showing those movies in order. How people don't realize they should be watched in chronological order instead of by release date is so annoying!"

Here we go . . .

Hannah spends the next ten minutes venting about the whole picture people are missing when they watch franchises in order of release date instead of chronologically. She's passionate about four things: her daughter, baking, hockey, and horror movies.

After she's settled down, I decide I need to hit her with the heavy questions, needing to check in on her headspace and where she's at after the atomic-sized bomb I dropped on her.

"How are you handling everything? Have you had time to digest it all?"

She answers right away, which doesn't surprise me. Hannah typically says exactly what she's thinking or feeling. You get what you see with her, something I love. I hate having to fucking guess how someone is feeling or what they're thinking.

"I haven't had time to digest it, no. I battled a hangover—thanks for that by the way—and then went into mama-mode, and café owner. He really has a pregnant girlfriend?"

"Yeah, beauty. She's far enough along for me to notice right away, too."

"What a piece of shit. Actually, no, he's less than a piece of shit. Ugh. I hate him, bear. How did you not knock his teeth out?"

I laugh because I don't know how I didn't.

"Your guess is as good as mine. Fuck, I wanted to. I saw red, but also, I saw you and Charlie. I just went into protection mode. If I curb-stomped his ass, it would have made things a whole helluva lot worse."

She shakes her head in agreement, seemingly lost in thought as she takes it in.

"Why have you always hated him?"

Shit.

Owen and I finish lacing up our skates, ready to hit the ice, feeling good about tonight's game against Forks. Playing hockey feels good, and since I'm the only one of my siblings who took it up, it gives me some much-needed separation from being lumped in as one of them. Especially when our dad already makes us box together at the gym.

"Hell yeah, I hit that. Not that great of a lay, but she's hot enough, I'd fuck her again."

"Who'd you hit, Jenkins? Your hand again? You're gonna burn a hole through that damn thing if you're not careful," my friend Owen says to the arrogant asshole who just entered the locker room with his posse of braindead fuckwits.

"Fuck you, Hopkins. Don't be jealous," Levi spits in our direction. He's such a sleazeball and has always annoyed the shit out of me with how he conducts himself on and off the ice.

"He hooked up with Hannah Haven last night. Took her virginity in the back of his car."

My blood boils as my posture goes rigid, balling my hands into fists, unable to control my reaction.

"That true?" I grind out, standing up to my full height. My teeth clenched so hard I'm surprised I'm not breaking them.

"What, Hayes? You pissed I got to her first? Surprised you didn't get to pop her little cherry? She bled all over my dick so good."

My body reacts before my brain consciously catches up with what's happening. My fist connects with Levi's nose, a deafening crack as it breaks, blood immediately pooling. I don't stop my swings as he stumbles back. I guess those years of training in boxing paid off. Feels good to actually pummel something not in a ring or wearing a helmet on the ice.

Levi is slow to respond, his right arm swinging out to take a shot at my face but I easily dodge the hit, connecting another one to his ribs. Yelling ensues behind us.

"Don't fucking talk about her like that! I don't want to hear her name outta your fuckin' mouth you piece of shit!"

His reply comes out nasally and diluted but his words are like ice over my body.

"I'll fuck her until I'm done with her, maybe I'll even pass her around to my boys."

I get one last hit to the side of his face before he stumbles back into our teammates, eyes rolling to the back of his head.

"Fuck you, Jenkins!" I spit, as Owen and one of our coaches stop me from going after him again.

"We've just got some shitty-ass history, Han."

Her face falls as she looks at me, and I know she's not going to let this go until I come clean.

"It has to do with me, doesn't it?"

"You don't wanna do this. You've got enough on your plate."

"For fuck's sake, bear, when did you start treating me like I'm made of glass?"

"He was bragging about taking your virginity in the back of his car before one of our hockey games senior year. I lost it."

"Holy shit, that's how his face got so busted up?" she says with a laugh, which surprises the hell out of me.

"It's not funny. I got a five-game suspension for that, Hannah. My senior year of hockey."

"Yeah, but I know you and it was worth it, wasn't it?"

I smile wildly at her because she's right.

"Disappointed I didn't get to break more than just his nose."

"Yeah, but that fucker is still crooked, so he's got to live with that forever, thanks to you."

I join her in a laugh this time.

"Thanks for always having my back, bear. Even now, you're coming in like a knight on his white horse."

"I think there's a good chance I'm over the weight limit for a horse, but the idea is cute. I've always got you. You and me."

"You and me."

Chapter Eight
Hannah

My alarm goes off before I've even had a chance to fall asleep. I spent the entire night staring at the ceiling thinking about the state of my life and knowing I need to make some decisions to move forward on the path that's right for me and my daughter. Levi and my parents be damned.

Tying my hair up into a messy bun, I take a quick shower, knowing I need to get my ass moving. Throwing on a pair of ripped denim jeans, a Goo Goo Dolls concert T-shirt, brown ankle booties, and my pleather jacket, I walk into the living room to find Liam sleeping sprawled out on my couch.

His large body is way too big for the tiny space, and without thought, I take out my phone and snap a quick picture. His face is calm and relaxed, his breathing extremely shallow. Actually, it's hard to tell that he is breathing at all. Suddenly, nerves skate down my spine, I move to the side of the couch and watch his chest and the lack of normal rising and falling. What the fuck? His arm falls off the edge, dangling lifelessly, body way too relaxed.

Standing to face him, panic starts to take over. Leaning over his body, I rest my hand on his chest, my face less than a foot away from his. I hold my breath, focusing on feeling his pulse. After thirty seconds or so, I feel his strong, steady heart beating beneath my hands, and his chest starts to rise slightly.

"For fuck's sake," I huff.

Just as I start to pull my hand away, his snaps out, coiling around my wrist and holding it there. The quick reaction scares the fuck out of me, my scream echoing through the small room in an ear-piercing startle.

"Morning, beauty. Coping a feel? All you had to do is ask. I am yours now," he says with a wink, his voice steady and wide awake.

"You asshole, you were already awake!"

"Got ya."

"Ugh! You're so annoying! Payback is gonna be a bitch, big boy. Sleep with one eye open," I reply, trying to pull my wrist free and stand up straight. Instead, he pulls me harder, causing my body weight to slam down on top of his.

My eyes go wide as his squint heavily, both of our breaths coming in quick pants now.

"Wh-what are you doing?"

"Saying good morning to my fiancée, what's it look like?"

"Bear, don't call me that."

"Why's that, beauty? That's what you are." His voice is a breathy whisper as he leans forward, dragging his nose along my jaw, causing goosebumps to break out over my skin. My eyes flutter closed as I suck in a quick breath.

For fuck's sake why does that feel so good? His free hand moves to my waist, barely touching my body, but enough that an electric zap shoots through me. My body jerks slightly at the sensation, and what I feel next has me jumping off of him and pulling away. Standing up straight, I brush my hair out of my face, trying to compose myself.

"Put that," I whisper yell while pointing at the steel rod that's in his pants, "away. Right now. What the fuck is in there? A tree trunk?"

"Why don't you come find out for yourself?"

"Ha! You're such a dink." I pick up one of the throw pillows and drop it over his lap with a little force, causing him to wince and grab his junk with both hands. Shit, you'd need both hands to handle that thing.

"Quit messing with me, or next time I'll be sure to make it hurt," I threaten. "Now, Charlie already knows you're going to take her to school today but I'm going to close Bean Haven and take care of some things."

Liam sits up on the couch, his forehead creased in confusion, and looking at me like I've grown horns.

"What?" I spit. "What's the problem?"

"I don't think you've ever closed Bean Haven before."

"Yeah, well, I also have never had my boyfriend-slash-baby daddy have a secret life in another city before, or fake date my best friend either, so, looks like I'm just all about new things now!"

"Han, don't say it like that."

"It's the truth. And I need to see it for myself. Glutton for punishment and all that. So if there is any way you could please get her from school today, there will be no chance I will be able to drive back before two to do it myself."

"Let me call Dallas or Sawyer, or hell, even Carter, I'm going with you." Liam stands, tossing the blanket off to the side and pulling on his jeans that were thrown haphazardly on the chair next to us. I watch his strong, muscular legs disappear into them as he pulls the denim over his hips and zips up. My hair bounces around my face as I shake my head clear of the thoughts. I need to get my shit together.

"Love you for it, but that's gonna be a hard no. I've got to do this myself."

He looks at me, stoney and resolute, but he knows I won't back down from this.

"You're right. You've got this. Call me if you get arrested again. Don't need your dad pissed off when I have to tell him I'm marrying you."

"For fuck's sake! Why can't everyone let that go? It was one time! Who doesn't want to steal a street sign that says Booty Street when you're sixteen? It's funny!"

"Hey," he says, his voice taking on a more serious tone, "you've got this. You're strong as fuck and he never deserved you. Hand him his balls, baby."

My head bounces back slightly because he's never called me that before. He drops a quick kiss to the top of my head before walking past me to the kitchen without saying another word, leaving me flustered once again.

By the time I get to Seattle, any trace of sadness I felt over this situation has completely dissipated. All that remains is a scorned woman who wanted nothing more than to protect her child. If Levi wants to be Father of the Year to his new child, so be it. But he needs to make a decision about his role in Charlotte's life and stick to it. A nagging feeling in the back of my head tells me that there's going to be a long fight ahead of me either way. Bring it, asshole.

Parking across the street from his apartment, I take a moment to think through how I want to play this. A huge part of me wants to go in guns blazing and set him and his house on fire but the other part wants to see what he'll do if I act like I don't know a damn thing. But he has to know Liam wouldn't keep a bomb like this from me.

Fuck it. Let's light this shit up.

I slam my Jeep door and march up the stairs to pound my fist against the big, ugly green entrance, waiting for Levi—or whoever the hell could also be living here—to answer it. Just as I'm about to knock again, the door opens, Levi's dumbass self looking back at me in surprise.

"What are you doing here, Hannah?"

"Hi to you, too," I say as I duck beneath his arm that he's braced against the doorframe and walk into his apartment. "Why, yes, I would love to come in, thanks for inviting me."

The entryway leads to a small open-concept living space, a sleek kitchen off of that, and a set of stairs leading to the second story off the main room. It's decorated with a large black leather couch and matching industrial looking coffee and end tables. There's zero art on the white walls, but the fireplace is a nice touch. It's all very modern and . . . *sterile.* I would be so unhappy here. It's clear he never learned to clean up after himself because soda bottles, wrappers, and used plates litter the coffee table, complete with an Xbox remote lying on one of the cushions as if I interrupted his game. I do a quick spin, taking it all in with a disgusted look gracing my face.

"Mommy and Daddy helping you pay for this place or is the fishing paying you that well?"

"Always with the bitchiness, you wonder why I stopped fucking you."

"Oh, no biggie, I'm being thoroughly well fucked," I lie. "You could at least hire a maid if you're pulling in the dough," I mock as I knock a sock off the back of the couch.

Levi hasn't left his spot at the front door, his arms crossed tightly over his chest as he watches me walk through his space for the first time, his stare angry and pinched. I've always been so busy with Bean Haven and raising Charlie that we relied on Levi to come home to visit us. I guess now I know why he never invited us up here. The second family and all.

I take in the man I've been tied to for the last eight years, and it dawns on me that I don't know him at all anymore, if I ever did. We started seeing each other off-and-on our senior of high school, then took a break when I went to college with Liam, and since he was home when I dropped out, we just fell back into the same pattern. We were never in love with each other. The room never lit up when he walked into it. I've never had butterflies when he looked at me or even touched me.

He'd been my first real relationship—if you can even call it that—and while he holds so many of my firsts, looking at him right now, I feel nothing but disdain and disappointment. Was there a time I wished he would race home at the end of the day to be with me and Charlotte? Of course. Do I lay in bed at night and wish someone held me tightly wrapped up in their arms? More times than I'd like to admit. Do I use my vibrator a few times a week and pretend someone else is ravishing my body? Making me feel desired, worshiped, just fucking *wanted*?

The more I think about it, the more it hits me that it was never *him* that I wished for. It was just the absolute loneliness of my circumstance that made me find myself desperately wanting those things. But not with Levi.

"So, who is she?"

He doesn't even flinch, expression blank and fucking dead. Was he always such a pathetic piece of shit and I was just too blind to it?

"Figured your little dog would run and tell you, always such a loyal fuck."

"Oh, he's a good fuck alright," I quip without missing a beat.

His eyes flash to mine, finally an expression. I don't even feel the slightest bit ashamed that I'm letting him think such a thing. That's right, asshole. Fuck with me.

"Finally got to fuck you, huh? He's only been trying for a lifetime. Too bad you're washed up now. He knock you up, too? Only reason he'd continue to fuck your sorry ass, Hannah, don't be an idiot."

"I'm not a fucking idiot, Levi! You're the daft piece of shit with a second life over here in Seattle. You think I'd never find out, you pig? Liam says she's pretty far along. Must be close to her due date. Hmm." I tap my finger on my chin patronizingly, pretending to think hard. "That means she must be at least what? Seven? Eight months along? At least, right? Wait, didn't you just fuck me a few months ago?"

"Shut the fuck up, Hannah!" He steps forward and I slip my hand into my jacket pocket, firmly grasping the mace Liam gave me to carry for whenever I leave the safety of Aspen Ridge.

"What's your plan then, huh, you fucking tool? We share a child! Does she even know about me? About Charlotte?"

His eyes squint, and I release a maniacal laugh.

"Wow. Just fucking wow. So, what? Just going to ignore your responsibilities like you have been? Charlie doesn't even know who you are!"

"Because of YOU!"

I take a step back like he slapped me.

"Wh-what do you mean because of me?"

"I stay away because I don't want to deal with you. All you do is nag and bitch and complain. You used to be fun, a decent enough lay when I was bored. Then you got pregnant with her and turned into an uptight bitch who stopped putting out. The last time I fucked you, I meant what I said. You're pathetic, Hannah. You've always been pathetic." I'm stunned silent as he takes steps in my direction. "I'm not like the other girls," he mimics the voice of a teenage girl, "I'm different. Edgy. I love spooky shit and baking all goddamn day." He stands directly in front of me now, picking up a lock of my violet-colored hair and looking at it with disgust before dropping it like it burned him. "Enjoy Liam while you got 'em, 'cause once he's gotten his fill of your used-up pussy, he's gonna run for the hills just like I did."

I blink away the tears threatening to spill over at his words. Fuck him. Fuck this. His opinion of me doesn't mean shit. Whatever.

"Fuck you, Levi, you lying, cheating, piece of shit. And don't you ever touch me again or I swear to God it'll be the last goddamn thing you ever do. You have a week to tell her about Charlotte or I will hunt her down and tell her myself. Especially the part where you stuck your shriveled up dick inside me while she was here carrying your child. Figure out how you want to proceed with Charlotte, or I will happily take your ass to court."

I push past him and storm out of his stupid-ass apartment, stomping all the way across the stupid-ass street to my Jeep. I drive the three and a half hours straight through, and it's not until I'm safely in my bedroom that I let myself cry.

I snuggle into my body pillow and allow the waves of sadness and fear to crash over me. Levi managed to hit me where it hurts, filling my head with already-present insecurities and pulling them to the surface. How did I end up here? These are supposed to be the best years of my life and I'm living them like a zombie, barely functioning through the days, working long hours, focusing on raising my daughter as a single mom, and holding onto a relationship that has been nonexistent for a very long time. I was just too stupid to see it.

I held on to Levi because it's what I already thought I had. I settled. Desperate to create a family for my daughter when that's all I wanted for both of us. Maybe my parents are right, I'm burning out and there's no way I can sustain this way of living. I just wanted to have a little family for my daughter and didn't want to be alone.

But here I am, feeling more alone than ever.

Chapter Nine

Liam

Friday night finally rolls around and I'm eager as fuck to get Hannah out and alone. We spent last weekend together taking Charlotte ice skating and had two movie nights over the week. But it's not enough. People are starting to whisper, but we haven't outright come out and confirmed anything except to Owen. Besides not living together and the physical displays of affection, Hannah and I have been operating like a married couple since Charlie was born. I take her to school most days of the week, leaving work to help get her ready for the day while Hannah juggles Bean Haven, and whenever Hannah is running late, I pick her up. Our lives are already deeply embedded with each other, it's been tricky to change anything up and expect people to notice. But that all changes tonight.

Carter and I meet up behind Bean Haven so that I can talk to him in person before heading up to Hannah's.

"What up, Casanova? You ready for your fun Friday night?"

"Fuckin' babysitting. I'm the goddamn king of this little

town, could spend it with whoever I want, and you got me chillin' with Little Miss Sass."

"Hey, I'd say that's the best Friday night if you ask me."

"Didn't though, did I, lint licker?"

"For fuck's sake you all gotta find a better nickname," I blurt, rolling my eyes. "Hannah is probably already putting Charlie to sleep, but she may get out of bed a few hundred times before she finally stays put and crashes. Just keep taking her back there and she'll eventually give in."

"Sounds easy enough. I'm the cool uncle anyway, she's gonna wanna hang. She can't stay up?"

"No, idiot. She's three. She needs to stick to her routine, she'll be crabby as shit tomorrow if you keep her up."

"Well what the fuck am I supposed to do while she sleeps?"

"What are you, twelve? Watch a damn movie or start a new show for all I care. Stay out of Hannah's bedroom or I'll fuckin' strangle you slowly, bring you right to the brink of death, let you think you're gonna survive, and then do it again and again before finally watching your life slip from your eyes. Got it?"

He bristles. "Fuck, you're scary when you wanna be."

I poke him hard in the chest. "Yep. So remember that. C'mon, let's get upstairs so Han and I can hit the road."

I take confident strides across the small parking lot and up the stairs to the apartment, nothing but excitement fueling each step. All bets are off starting tonight. It's time I show Hannah that I can be so much more. She may be fake dating me to change her circumstances, but there isn't anything fake about any of this for me.

I knock twice on the door before opening it slowly since Carter is with me. I'm not about to allow him to see Hannah less than fully dressed. She's probably one of the only girls he hasn't messed around with.

"Han? I'm here, and I brought the dipshit with me. You ready?"

Hannah pops around the corner, her violet hair left down, falling around her shoulders in big waves. She's done her makeup in a way that makes her pretty light brown eyes pop, and is wearing a pair of denim jeans that look like they were painted on, a pair of boots that come up slightly past her ankle with big buckles, a large T-shirt with Valek on the front, and her leather jacket. She's so fucking cute.

"Casanova! You'll be flying pretty solo tonight. She is wiped out and it's only seven. I'd be surprised if she got up, but you never know," Hannah tells Carter.

"Lame. We'll be fine, I brought my laptop to get some work done anyway."

"Working on anything fun?"

Carter scoffs. "Nah, big fucking headache lately. A huge Pacific Northwest magazine wants to feature the distillery but narrowing down the details has proven to be ridiculous. They could make or break us, and I want everything to be perfect. It's almost like they want to find a story and not just celebrate and promote the distillery and everything we're doing over in our tiny-ass part of the world."

"I'm sure you'll figure it out and they'll all love you."

"Psh," I add. "Just as long as it's a female. Maybe he can fuck his way into a good feature."

"Shut up, lint licker. Don't you guys have a movie to get to?"

"Yep. On that note, you ready, Han?"

"Been ready! Mama needs a night off. Let's go eat our weight in junk food and get jump scared!"

Hannah pushes past us, doing a little shimmy as she does, looking cute as hell as I watch her walk out of the apartment.

"Damn, you're not even holding it back anymore."

"The fuck are you talking about now?" I ask my brother.

"The way you just watched her leave. You're a goner."

He's not wrong.

Hannah and I drive up the road a few blocks to Barrel House. Normally we would walk, but it's too damn cold for that shit, plus we need to grab our food and get over to the drive-in. After pulling into a spot, I jump out of my truck before rounding the hood and opening up her door, grabbing her little waist and easing her out. When she's planted firmly on the ground, I crowd her space, caging her in with my hands on either side of her head against the side of the truck.

"Remember, this isn't two friends grabbing a bite, we're dating, time to act like it. Can you do that for me?"

Her eyes blink rapidly like she's attempting to clear her thoughts.

"Yeah, yeah. I know how to act, bear. I got this."

I feel like testing the waters, and maybe I'm playing with fire here, but damn, if she was mine, this is exactly how I'd behave anyway. It's time she sees that. Lifting my hand from the truck, I rub the back of my knuckles down the side of her face, temple to jaw in a slow motion. She doesn't jerk away but fuck if she doesn't hiss in a quick breath of air and hold it, her eyes glassing over slightly, the pulse point in her neck throbbing rapidly.

"That's my girl. God, you're pretty."

Her eyes light up in surprise, like she didn't know I thought that, and I make a mental note to tell her more often.

"You ready?"

"Ye—" She clears her throat before trying again, leaving me grinning like a fucking idiot. "Yes. I'm good, I'm ready."

Clasping her hand in my own, we walk around the corner

and down the steps to Barrel House to pick up the to-go order I had placed earlier. Sawyer's wife, Ivy, is the head chef here and the food is beyond good. She's extremely talented and all of us frequent the place for lunch and dinner. Holding the heavy steel door open for Hannah, I place my palm on the small of her back and guide her inside before taking her hand in mine again, keeping her body close.

The hostess greets us with a huge smile, eyes flashing down to Hannah's and my clasped hands before going wide, nearly bugging out of her head. They're fairly sizable to begin with, and enlarged, they remind me of one of Charlie's toys that you squeeze and the eyes pop out of the sockets. It's actually a little concerning, and I cock my head at her.

"Liam Hayes, what do you have here?"

"Hey, Luna. Picking up a to-go order for Hannah and me."

"Eeek!" she squeals and we both flinch, Hannah's back pressing to my front. Whelp, I don't mind this position at all. I release her hand and settle mine on her hip, right under her leather jacket. Luna goes to the back with a skip in her step, clapping her hands together the entire way.

"I wanted to get our first date in and be seen a little before we come clean to your grandmother tomorrow. So, let's give 'em something to talk about."

"Pretty presumptuous of you that we're going to tell her tomorrow, bear, Jesus."

"We are. Didn't expect Luna to be this happy."

"Yeah, me either. Did you tell your brothers? Cause here comes Ivy."

I look up to find my sister-in-law in all her pregnant glory heading right for us, Luna behind her carrying our to-go boxes.

"Is it true?"

"That Hannah and I are together?"

"Holy hell, finally!"

Hannah throws her hands in the air. "Why does everyone keep saying that?"

I lean my mouth to her ear, rubbing my thumb against her skin softly, and whisper just for her to hear, "Because it's the truth."

"Took me long enough, but I got her locked down," I tell Ivy.

"Who knows?"

"You two, Carter, and Owen," I reply confidently. "Been together a bit now, just over keeping it a secret."

"Holy shit. How did I miss this? Well, don't I feel special to know before Sawyer. Is it still a secret? I can't keep anything from him, he'll know something is up right away. He reads me like a damn book."

"Nah, Iv, it's not a secret. Wouldn't ask you to keep anything from the shithead. But I'll tell Dallas. He's been a little preoccupied."

"Ya think? Preoccupied would be an understatement," she says with concern in her eyes.

Hannah and I accept our food from Luna and say goodbye to Ivy before packing back up in my truck and heading to the drive-in, a place where Hannah and I have been going since we were teenagers. They're notorious for showing classic thriller and horror movies and that's where we fell in love with the genre. It's been our thing for years, and I knew it would be the perfect place for our first real date.

"Do you want to get stabbed? Quit eating my nonpareils! Mother above, bear, I swear. You've eaten half the box!"

"Are you kidding me right now, Hannah? You picked out all of the red and green Skittles from my bag, ate more than half of my popcorn—that you said you didn't want, by the way—and

I'm scared to pick up my box of Hot Tamales 'cause you're not as sneaky as you think you are. And I can't have some of your precious nonpareils?"

"They're only sold here, and you know I save them to bring home!"

"You're being a baby. Quit yapping and watch the movie. This is my favorite part."

"You hate this part, you big liar!"

"Shh! No talking at movies!" I push her farther away from me in the bed of my truck to annoy her. Her feet come fast and hard as she retaliates by kicking me in the thigh and ribs. Thank God she took her shoes off and is only wearing socks or that would have hurt like a sonofabitch. I grab her ankle and yank her closer so I can pin her legs under mine to keep her still when her quick little hand comes out of nowhere and slaps me in the chest.

"That's it."

Popcorn flies as I sit upright and yank Hannah into my lap, grabbing her wrists and wrapping her arms like a straitjacket, holding her back to my chest, my legs wrapped around hers, holding her still. The little monster keeps trying to fight me, even though I'm at least triple her size, her battle cries loud enough for everyone parked nearby to hear.

"Quit." I jerk her closer, trying my hardest not to hurt her but not letting go as she wrestles me in the back of my truck. Her head falls back onto my shoulder, and I should have expected what she was about to do but goddamn she's fucking quick. Her wet tongue licks up the side of my face as she struggles to breathe through her laughs. I release her arms and legs pushing her back so that she flops off of me, using the back of my sweatshirt to wipe her saliva from my face.

"For fuck's sake, Hannah! Gross!"

"Gotcha to let me go. It always works."

"You're pure evil. Payback is always a bitch, watch your back, beauty. I'm comin' for ya."

She throws a handful of popcorn in my face, and the two of us drown out the noise of the movie with our fit of laughter. It's always been like this between us. Easy, fun. I never wished my best friend was a guy because I've had my three brothers and that comes with enough competition and masculine pressure to keep up with them. With Hannah, I just get to be me. No judgment. No pressure to be anything or do things a certain way. I've never had to think. She just lets me be me.

After the double feature, Hannah and I pack up the bed of my truck and clean up our mess before driving back to her parents' house.

"Hey, only ten minutes after curfew. Not too bad. Should only be questioned by the parental units for an hour."

"Stay strong. Text me if you need anything." Opening up the middle console of my truck, I pull out the box of nonpareils and toss them in her lap.

"Holy shit! When did you get these?"

"When you went to the bathroom—before you started bitching that I ate half of the ones you bought, by the way. Wanted you to have extra until we made it back up here to get more.

"What would I do without you? You're too good to me."

"You'd probably have just the half-eaten box of your favorites, so you should probably keep me around." I shrug, not understanding what the big deal is. She loves them, I ate them and knew she would want some later. Seemed like an easy thing to do to make her happy.

I drive into The Moonlit Theater and pay our fee to the attendant, pulling into a slot at the very back so that everyone is in front of us. May not be the best spot in the lot, but I didn't want eyes on us all night.

"It's freezing, you want me to run in and get snacks or do you want to come with me?"

"And trust that you're going to get exactly what I want? Not a chance. I'm coming!" she says as she unbuckles her seat-belt and reaches for the door.

"Two boxes of nonpareils, one Snickers bar, popcorn with extra butter, and a vanilla cream Dr Pepper."

Hannah's head whips in my direction, the skin around her eyes crinkling as a huge smile fills the face I'm obsessed with.

"Plus, you'll eat my Hot Tamales, only the green and red Skittles out of my bag, and my salted popcorn when you pretend you hate the salt on top."

She shrugs. "Lucky guess."

"Not luck, or a guess. I know everything about you, Han."

She squints as she bites her bottom lip in a devilish little look. "Not *everything*."

"Fair. But I plan to change that."

Leaving her stunned, mouth falling open, I jump out of the truck and head around the hood in her direction when I see a group of people from town that we went to high school with. They nod their heads at me in a hello and I wave back. When I get to Hannah's side of the truck, she's already got the damn door open and is bracing herself to climb out when I slide my hands up her thighs and settle them around her trim waist.

"I've got it, bear, I've jumped out of this beast a million times."

"Yeah, but that was before you agreed you were *mine*."

I easily lift her out of the truck, setting her down on her feet in front of me, crowding her space with my body just as I did in front of Barrel House. My hand threads through the pretty muted locks of her violet hair that I love so much, tilting her head back to look at me. The little intake of air she pulls in through her teeth every time I'm this close is so fucking cute. And goes directly to my dick.

Leaning into her, her eyes flick to my mouth, her tongue peeking out and slowly swiping across her soft pink lips before disappearing. Shit, she thinks I'm going to kiss her and seems more than okay with it. My eyes shutter closed for a brief minute while I reel the control I'm losing back firmly into place. I wasn't planning on that happening tonight.

Instead of kissing her, I lean my head down, running my nose up her jaw from chin to the bottom of her ear, inhaling as I go. "Mmm." She smells like vanilla, chocolate, and something that is just so inherently *her,* and it wakes my dick right up. Hannah stands stock-still, frozen, probably in shock at how the close proximity is making her feel, fighting it.

"People are watching, *fiancé*. Thought you could act better than this."

Her hand shoots out, clasping the back of my neck, nudging me closer to her. "Why didn't you say so? You want me to act, I can fucking act."

Her hips gyrate against mine ever so slightly, and I nearly groan out loud at the feel of her pelvis against mine. My dick is rapidly hardening now, and I wouldn't be able to hide from her if she keeps this up.

She must see someone behind us because her spine straightens for a split second and before I can process what's happening, Hannah's hands grab the sides of my face, pulling me down, her lips crashing hard against mine. I stumble for a second before my brain catches the fuck up.

Hannah is fucking kissing me. Tightening my hold around her waist, my other hand still holding the back of her head, I press my lips more forcefully against hers. There's no tongue, nothing about it is romantic or how I envisioned what kissing

Hannah would be like. The entire thing is over quicker than it started, and I'm left stunned that she did it at all. When I pull back, she's looking up at me with a smug-as-shit look plastered to her face, while I'm left dazed and confused.

Goddamn, Hannah just kissed me.

"Gotcha. Told ya I could act."

"You're gonna pay for that one."

"Payback. Payback. Always with the threats. Our food is getting cold, let's go get our snacks so we can eat!"

Hannah pushes against my chest, effectively bringing me back to Earth, grabbing my hand and pulling me behind her into the theater's concession stand. We order our food and drinks and then pile back into my truck, Hannah kicking off her shoes and getting comfortable before the first movie starts.

I can't take my eyes off her as we eat and relax into the comfortable silence between two people who have known each other, and been close, their entire lives. I just hope that I can change the future for us, because I want to keep my girls forever, I just need to get her on board.

Chapter Ten
Hannah

I can't believe I kissed Liam. I've never thought about what type of kisser he would be, even if I've seen him kissing other girls before. He seemed decent enough, and the man is too good-looking for his own good. He's bigger than all three of his brothers, which is saying something because they're all massive genetic freaks. I don't know what the Hayes were drinking when they procreated, but they made some gorgeous humans. Liam has broad shoulders that I've caught myself looking at more often than not over the last two weeks, hair that is such a light brown it could pass for dirty blond, dark chocolate eyes, a strong jaw, chiseled abs from working out at the gym every day, and thick, strong legs. He's a goddamn beautiful man. I'm not blind for fuck's sake.

But I wasn't prepared for how good it would feel to have his lips on mine. The kiss was PG at best. Just a firm press of lips on lips. But dammit to mother above, every single cell in my body woke up from hibernation. Add to that the way he held me close, turning my blood to molten lava from his body heat alone. Just that small peck overwhelmed my senses. The thought of kissing Liam for real? It would be devastating. All-consuming. The kind of kiss that you can't come back from. Best friend or not.

I focus on eating my garlic pommes frites, savoring every single bite, and dip into the garlic aioli before picking up my falafel banh mi, trying not to think too much into the fact that he ordered my favorite two things off of the menu. But, that kiss. The way he felt against me consumes my thoughts.

I really am desperate for physical touch. But, even on the rare occasion Levi was in town and I gave him my body, it never filled my cup, never left me satisfied. In fact, I often felt worse than I did before. It's completely different from this feeling ignited by Liam, and I'm struggling to understand it.

"You're quiet, beauty. What's goin' on in that head of yours?"

Liam's already done eating, having smashed his gourmet bacon cheeseburger and fries in just a few bites. I peek up from over my sandwich, purposefully having taken a huge bite so I'm not forced to talk. He's looking at me intently, body illuminated only by the light from the large movie screen in front of us, the dim glow casting shadows across the strong features of his face. He looks almost ethereal—gorgeous, and untouchable. Fuck, what is happening to me right now?

"Spill it."

I swallow my food down hard and set the sandwich back in the container that's balancing precariously in my lap. Twisting my lips side to side, I quickly contemplate whether or not to be open. We've never kept secrets from each other before, so I'm not going to start now. That's where relationships go to die, and I wouldn't survive losing Liam.

"I think I'm touch starved."

Liam's face falls flat. Whelp. Not exactly what I had in mind with how to start, but my brain and mouth failed me.

Could have started with, hey, this situation is super weird and messing with my hormones, making me feel all sorts of things that I didn't think were possible. But, no, let's just drop that bomb on the man who is literally doing everything in his power to keep you on a life raft right now.

"Han . . ."

"Nope. Don't do that. Do not pity me. I am not—"

"Made of glass. I know. I guess I just assumed you were, you know."

"Sleeping with Levi?"

I don't miss the tick in his jaw or how his hands fist in his lap.

"Yeah."

"It's been months. And even longer before that. The last time I was using it as a way to get closer to him, to try to convince him to stay, he, well you know, and as soon as he finished, he couldn't get off me fast enough, got dressed and told me I was pathetic." Rage simmers strong behind Liam's eyes, and I watch as he works hard to tamp it down. I know how much he hates Levi, and I'm sure that sharing that little bit of info could have just signed Levi's death warrant.

"I get affection from Charlie, but my parents are away, my sisters are never home, and I'm too busy for the friends I used to have. I don't get physical touch. Certainly not romantic or passionate touch. I don't even know if I ever have . . ." I return to look down at my food, not wanting to make eye contact, even though Liam is the furthest thing from judgmental. I let out a long deep exhale. "I don't know if I've ever felt really desired. And whatever this is between us right now"—I wave my hand haphazardly through the empty space separating us—"is really messing with my head and my hormones."

I expect him to speak, to say something in an attempt to cheer me up, instead, my body melts as his large palm slides across my face, gently pulling my head in his direction. I let my eyes flutter open, finding his stormy gaze trained right on me. His expression is a mix of empathy, love, protection, and something that looks a hell of a lot like longing.

"I'm sorry. I know you don't want to hear it but I'm saying it anyway. I'm sorry. You deserve to be with someone who can't stand to be away from you for even a minute, who makes sure you know you're the first thing on his mind the moment he wakes up and the last thing before he goes to sleep. That's after he's made you feel it with his body. The right man will make sure you never doubt his love for you, beauty. You should never want for touch because you would feel it constantly." His fingertips gently caress my scalp behind my ear, and I lean into the feeling of his touch, his words hitting their mark hard. It's so challenging to believe his pretty words when the actions of that kind of man seem like a fairytale. "Things are going to change, just trust me, okay?" He drops his hand, and I miss the touch immediately.

"I trust you, bear. But I think I may need to find a one-night stand or something to take the edge off or I may end up ruining our relationship by jumping you."

Liam's head snaps in my direction so violently, I'm surprised he didn't pull a muscle. His spine straightens, his hands curling into tight fists. Everything about him right now screams *seriously pissed off alpha*, a complete contrast to the sweet, tender side I just had.

"The fuck you will, Hannah!"

His reaction surprises me. He's never told me what I could or couldn't do and has only ever encouraged me to do what I want.

"Excuse me? You did not just tell me that I can't sleep with someone if I want to."

"I sure as fuck did and I mean every word. Want me to say it again?"

"You can't be freaking serious right now!"

"You're my fiancée, Hannah."

"Fake. Fake fiancée. And I just got done telling you how starved for affection I am. I thought you would understand."

"And you're telling me that some random dink you pick up at a bar is going to make you feel better? Did you not hear what I said? About what you deserve?"

He can't be serious right now.

"Oh, I heard you, bear. Pretty little words wrapped in a bright bow. Those are fantasies. It's not real life."

The rage seems to vacate his body, leaving him dejected and morose.

"I've known you forever, which means I know everything about you, and I'm telling you right now, a one-night stand is going to make you feel worse. If you need something, I'll give it to you."

"Wow," I say, shaking my head and laughing under my breath. "So, what? You want to pity fuck me, bear? How is that going to make me feel any better than a one-night stand would."

He moves as fast as lightning and I'm reminded that Liam holds his control at bay, his normal loose, laid-back personality, is just one part of him. He can be just as ruthless and over-bearing as his brothers. He grips my chin between two fingers, his other hand curling behind my neck, pulling me toward the center of the truck.

"Listen to me, Han, if you give yourself to me, there won't be anything about it that's out of pity. It'll be because we want each other so fucking bad we can't go another second without me deep inside you."

My breath hitches, my heart like a tumbleweed in the

wind. My eyes bounce back and forth between his, trying to find meaning behind what he just said.

"I've got you and I'm going to teach you how to take what you want, even your pleasure, Hannah. You'll never want for touch with me, and you're going to take what you want when you want it. Now, let's enjoy these movies. This is the best part, and I don't want you to miss it. You love this scene with all the nuns praying."

I swallow hard as he releases me, and for the millionth time tonight, I find myself wishing he wouldn't. Instead of over-thinking things, I study my best friend's face for a moment longer, his strong features, the coarse stubble of his cheeks and jaw. I do trust him, and even though everything he just said confuses the living hell out of me, I pack up the rest of my dinner, setting it behind me in the to-go bag, pull out the blanket, and scoot across the bench seat. Liam lifts his arm automatically, tucking me into his side, and my brain settles almost instantaneously.

I've always found peace and comfort with Liam. He's seen me through my hardest days, held me through ups and downs, and I know that this is just one more thing he'll see me through. Liam is my rock, at the end of the day, it's me and him, always has been, always will be.

Sitting in the nurse's office of my high school sucking on a honey stick is not how I wanted to spend the afternoon when I should be getting ready for Liam's hockey game. I've missed so many of them this season because of work at Bean Haven after school. But here I am, headache, still shaking like a leaf, nauseous, and holding an ice pack to my head from where I hit the lockers as I passed out and crumbled to the ground. I don't even care about the looks, or how everyone freaked out. I'm grateful no one called an ambulance. I was only out for a moment and Ms. Gagnon knows I don't take care of myself like I should.

She pulled my blood sugar monitor from my bag, set it up, and checked my levels before giving me a honey stick. She has glucose tabs and gel on hand, but I hate them. Living with reactive hypoglycemia is so fun when you're too busy to eat, or eat and drink all the wrong things. It's living in a constant state of having to think about food and I rebel against it. And more days than not, I end up feeling like shit. I've only passed out a few times, today being an unfortunate addition, but the symptoms suck when the crash happens.

Ms. Gagnon leaves me to rest and finish my snack when the door opens again, the curtain to my hidey hole ripped open, causing me to jump, followed by a wince as I jerk my head. Liam stands in front of me, red-faced and sweaty, like he ran all the way here. His top half is in his hockey pads and jersey. He moves quickly, sitting next to me on the bed, surveying the damage under the ice pack.

"Where are you hurt? What happened?"

"It's just my hairline, right here. I hit my head on a locker."

"Han, you passed out? What have you eaten today?"

I roll my eyes at his overprotectiveness. It knows no bounds.

"Two coffees."

"And? With what?" He gives me a look that says, you can't seriously be that dumb. *But apparently, I'm proving that I can. Hold my beer.*

"Sugar and milk?"

"For the love of God, Hannah, tell me you've eaten."

I hold up the empty plastic that held the honey stick and shrug my shoulders innocently. My attempt at a sweet whoopsie, silly me *fails miserably. If possible, Liam's face turns an even darker shade of red, near crimson, as his eyes squint at me. My eyes widen as I scoot back farther on the bed, nudging his side with my bare foot, trying to put some needed space between us. Liam is so levelheaded, chill, just go with the flow, until he's mad. Then he's basically The Hulk.*

"Can you walk?"

"Uh, yes?"

"Then put your shoes on and let's go."

"What do you mean, 'let's go?'" I mock his deep voice, and he shoots me a glare. "You have a hockey game to get ready for. Shouldn't you already be on the ice for a skate?"

"I'm not going. You need to eat a meal. Can you move your ass, please?"

I stare blankly at my best friend. He can't be serious right now.

"Bear, I'm fine. I'll call my parents, in fact, Ms. Gagnon probably already has. You can't miss your game."

"I can, and I will. I have stuff to change into in my dad's truck, let's get going."

Liam picks up my backpack as I shift off the bed, slipping into my Converse. He grabs my arm like I'm an invalid, refusing to let me walk on my own in case I suddenly pass out again on him. Once we're settled into the truck, he drives us to the grocery store where he tells me to stay put and jogs in, returning a few minutes later with deli subs and a bag of BBQ chips. He puts everything in my lap and drives to the outskirts of town, taking a familiar dirt road that leads to Grace Beach.

Liam parks with the bed of the truck facing the ocean and pulls a big blanket from the backseat, opening his door and climbing out.

"Move your ass, Han, get the food and get over here."

Doing as he says, I set the food down and Liam hauls me into the bed of his huge truck, tossing my sandwich into my lap and snapping, "Eat."

Opening the white wrapper, I check the contents of my sub

and do my best not to give him the satisfaction of my smile. It's packed with a rainbow of veggies, with a thick layer of spicy, chipotle hummus. Any time I have a hypoglycemic episode, my parents try to force meat down my throat. I've been a pescatarian since freshman year of high school. I hate how most meat makes my body feel. I'll eat fish in small doses but for some reason, land animals make my body feel sluggish and just downright awful.

"Don't be too excited, there's some tuna at the bottom."

"I'm okay with that. Thank you, bear."

We eat in silence, sitting in the bed of his truck with nothing but the ocean in front and the tall Sitka spruce trees and salty air surrounding us.

"Don't need to thank me, Han, it's you and me."

"You and me."

Chapter Eleven

Liam

The next morning, I'm at Bean Haven right before opening. Knowing Hannah has her headphones on, I use my key to sneak in, hoping like hell she's blaring that music like she typically does so that I can scare the piss out of her. I told her payback was coming and scaring each other is something we've done for as long as I can remember. Careful not to let the door connect with the bell, I squeeze my big-ass body through the space and with all the care I can muster, shut the door behind me. Sneaking through the shop, I stand still next to the open doorway that leads to the bakery kitchen and listen for her footsteps, hearing nothing but her clanking around and humming. The moment I hear the loud noise of her industrial mixer, I know she's facing away from me, and the noise will work to my advantage. I slip the Ghostface mask down over my head and take a peek around the doorframe. Hannah sways her hips side to side while she adds pre-measured ingredients to the mixing bowl. I hesitate for a brief moment, lost to the shake of her plump ass in a pair of tight black leggings as she dances to music that only she can hear.

Fuck it. It's now or never. Squatting down to my haunches, I shuffle around the corner, letting the butcher block counter in the center of the room block her view of me if she were to turn around. Once she's in view, I sneak right up behind her. Standing to my full height—six foot two inches, to Hannah's five foot five—I'm several inches taller, and nearly double her width. She continues to sway, completely out of touch with her surroundings.

Shooting my arms out, I quickly snake one around her waist, the other clasping my hand over her mouth. She lets out a muffled scream as I pull her back into me. Just as quickly as I've captured her does her non-restricted elbow connect with my rib cage. Hard. I immediately release her as she turns, ready to fight.

I put my hands up in defense and as she takes in the Ghost-face mask, she doesn't react how I thought she would. Her hand is placed over her heart, chest rapidly rising and falling. Her cheeks are pink, but her eyes? They're heavily lidded and glassy as she sways slightly on her feet.

Hannah loves being scared, and *Scream* has always been her favorite movie franchise. She even gave Charlotte the middle name Sidney. But this reaction is more than someone being scared. I watch as she squirms on her feet, her face flushed from a mix of fear and what I'm guessing is arousal. Holy fuck, did this turn her on?

Leaving the mask on, I prowl toward her, backing her against the stainless-steel counter between the mixer and sink. Hannah braces her hands on the edge, leaning back away from me. I squat down slightly, coming face-to-face with her and cocking my head to the side, as she struggles to maintain regular breathing. Yeah, she's turned on. I don't hesitate to run my hands slowly up the length of her arms and over her shoulders and neck until I'm clasping her face in my hands, goosebumps scattering behind my touch.

"This tracks, you know," I whisper through my mask, enjoying seeing her like this.

"Probably not a normal reaction to an intruder."

"Nah. But, I can't say that I don't like it."

Her pretty eyes close as I move her head backward so that her neck is stretched and bared to me. She's so goddamn pliable like this. So sexy. Goddamn, I want this woman. *My* woman. Her confession last night nearly broke me, but it cemented my need to give her everything she's been missing, show her what this could be like.

"Han . . ." I breathe out on a rough exhale, my control rapidly slipping. My dick is rock hard behind my jeans, my breathing coming heavier now. I want to rip her pants off, lay her back on the table, and eat her pussy until she screams. Make her feel better than she ever has before. Fuck, I want to taste her so badly that my mouth is salivating at just the thought. This woman has me in a goddamn chokehold. She always has.

Just as my fingers touch the plastic of my mask to remove it, ready for my lips to kiss along the length of her neck, the baby monitor goes off with Charlotte's little voice, breaking the spell between us.

Hannah's hands move to my shoulders, pushing me back from her. I go willingly, removing the mask and setting it on the counter. Hannah looks at the monitor and sees that Charlie has in fact woken up for the day, earlier than she typically does. Disappointment doesn't hit me as I look over her shoulder at Charlie sitting up in her bed.

"You finish up down here, beauty. I'll go get the munchkin. She's fun in the mornings."

She turns to face me, a sweet look plastered on her face that is starkly different from moments ago when she was hot and bothered.

"Thank you, bear. She's much nicer to you in the morning than she is to me."

"Isn't that par for the course though? Daughters driving their mothers mad?"

I drop a kiss to the top of her head and walk farther into the back to the interior stairs that lead to the apartment.

"Bear!" Charlie squeals as she sees me enter her room.

"Munchkin monster!"

"Mumma's downstairs?"

"Yep. And she's in the best mood and said you can have whatever you want for breakfast today!"

"Even pickles?!" she squeals, clasping her hands together in excitement. I can't do anything other than laugh.

After helping Charlotte get ready for the day and feeding her a breakfast of pickles and—after some serious begging—a waffle with peanut butter and banana on top, we braid her hair and grab her backpack to head downstairs so Hannah can say goodbye before school. I love the flexibility my job at the distillery gives me, and being able to help Hannah most mornings with Charlie is the best way to start my day. She is so full of life and always so excited to go to school to learn. Granted, school right now is full-day preschool, but she's still learning and eager. I don't ever want that light for learning to dim.

"Hey, my baby girl. Did you have a good breakfast?"

"Yep! I had pickles!"

Hannah's eyes widen and she whips her head in my direction, brows arching in question.

"She also had a yummy peanut butter waffle with half a banana."

"Okay, that I'm happy with. Good choices. I hope you have the best day learning."

"I will. Best friends forever?" Charlie asks Hannah.

"Best friends forever and always."

I smile like a fool watching the two of them, pride and love filling my chest. Fuck, I want to permanently make the two of them mine. Levi may have helped make this family, but there is no doubt that they are mine.

Once I find a parking spot at the elementary school, Charlie unbuckles her seatbelt, and I pick her up to climb safely out of my truck. Hannah about kicked my ass a few months ago when Charlotte decided to full-on launch herself out of the side of it, skydiving style. She landed pretty gracefully, the little daredevil. But Hannah threatened to cut my balls off with a butter knife if I let it happen again.

"Dance time!"

I face Charlie in the parking lot, ignoring everyone around us and only focusing on the sweet girl in front of me. Going to Pre-K was a huge adjustment for her, and when it wasn't getting any easier, I got her to make up a silly dance with me to help pump her up for the day ahead. So far so good, and it's working.

"You ready, munchkin?"

"Ready!"

We sing our bravery song, stomp our feet and clap our hands, do a shake in a circle and then hip bump—thank Christ I have no problem squatting, but this shit will hurt if we're still doing it at graduation—all to the tune of *Twinkle Twinkle Little Star*. Charlotte skips off to her teacher and I watch until she disappears inside, already missing her, remembering the day she was born and realizing it's already been almost four years.

"Oh my god!"

"Shit, Hannah, did you just piss on me?"

I jump up off the couch where we're sitting watching The Cabin in the Woods. My entire thigh is wet with warm fluid.

"Oh my god, bear. I think my water broke."

"Wait, seriously?" My concern over my jeans being covered in her urine suddenly evaporates.

She stands from the couch, waddling like a penguin to the bathroom. Grabbing some towels from the closet, I try to soak up whatever fluid is on the couch.

"Bear! It did! My water broke! Oh, fucking shitballs asshole motherfucker!"

I laugh at her array of curse words as I walk over to the bathroom door.

"Han, you okay? Once you get changed, we'll head to the hospital."

She opens the door wearing a large Hellraiser T-shirt, holding a folded-up towel between her thighs.

"You going like that?"

"Yep. This isn't a fashion show, a small human is about to exit my body through a tiny hole between my legs. Bring me my phone so I can let Levi know to meet us there."

I turn and roll my eyes. This'll be a good ol' time. Despite Hannah's pregnancy news, Levi hasn't stepped up. Surprise fucking surprise.

Handing the phone over to her, she calls the dipshit. He picks up on the third attempt and each time she has to call him, my anger increases. He fucking knows how far along she is, knows that this baby could come at any moment. Knowing his ass isn't on a ship right now and that he is choosing not to be here, I want to knock his teeth to the back of his throat and watch him slowly choke to death on them.

"Labor takes a while, Levi. If you leave now, you can make it."

"I don't care how late it is. You're going to willingly miss the birth of your child?"

"Wow. Okay. Fine. I'll update you tomorrow."

She hangs up and throws the phone to the couch as a contraction hits her hard.

"Fucking shitballs. These hurt like a mofo," she says through clenched teeth once the contraction passes. I hate seeing her in pain and don't know what to do to fix it for her. I've never felt so goddamn useless before.

"You good, beauty?"

Seems like a fucked-up thing to ask considering she's obviously in physical pain and Levi just massively let her down. She straightens her spine as best she can with the weight of her pregnant belly in front of her.

"Nothing I can't handle. He's an asshole. He doesn't feel like driving. Told me to update him in the morning. So, fuck him."

Things turn from anticipation to concern really quick as the contractions increase in severity. Hannah doubles over in pain, breathing hard through each one as they come rapidly back-to-back. She's unable to take more than a few steps at a time, and with my help, we stop in the kitchen. On her next contraction, I dial 9-1-1. Based on all the pregnancy books I read so that I could support her, I don't think getting her in my truck and driving to the hospital is a safe bet.

"I can't do this. We need to get to a hospital. Please, bear. Please, get me to a hospital."

I move directly in front of her, grabbing her face between my hands, forcing her to focus on me and me alone. When I speak, my words are firm, honest, and leave no room for discussion.

"Hannah. Listen to me. This baby is coming. The paramedics are on their way. You can do this. I won't let anything happen to you."

"I'm so scared."

"You don't need to be. You've got me, and we're about to meet this baby. Girl or boy?"

She laughs for a moment before another contraction hits her hard. She leans over the edge of the kitchen counter, one hand bracing herself, the other hand on her lower back. Moving up behind her, I put my palms there, massaging the tight muscles, trying my best to give her some relief.

"Boy. I think it's a boy," she says on a rushed exhale.

"Nah. Totally a girl. Only a girl would be giving their momma this hard of a time."

"Fuck, bear. It hurts so much. There's so much pressure."

Fuck.

"Han, I need you to lay down. Paramedics might not make it in time."

"WHAT?" Her scream could wake the goddamn dead, and her eyes are wide and terrified.

"Okay, psycho, no need to scream. But you need to lay down." She levels me with a stare that could bring down an entire kingdom, but relents, thank fucking god.

I quickly snatch up the towels that were pulled out when her water broke and lay them down on the floor with a pillow. Grabbing Hannah by the hands, I guide her on top of them and force her to lay on her back. I don't know what the fuck I'm doing but I've seen enough movies that hopefully I can catch a slippery-ass baby as it leaves her body. I just hope to fuck there's no complications. I'm not a religious person, but right now, I'm sending up prayers to every god that could possibly exist to see my girl through this.

"Do you know what you're doing?" she bellows, panic, pain, and fear laced in her tone.

"Remember that scene from Alien?"

"Fuck! That comes out of her stomach, you fucker!"

"Same, same!"

"Oh, fuck. Bear, I don't want you to see me down there!"

"I think we're past that, I was laying in your fluid, Hannah! And for fuck's sake, I've seen you pee a thousand times!"

"This is different, you buffoon, and you can't see anything when I pee! Oh, fuck my life, why does the universe hate me?"

She grips her pillow hard, biting her bottom lip until blood pools as she braces through another contraction.

"Han, you need to breathe for me, okay? This is nothing. We've been through so much, what's a little childbirth on the kitchen floor?"

"Fuck, it burns!!! Fuck! Fuck! FUUUCK!"

I lift the T-shirt over her bent knees and close my eyes, taking a deep breath. I can't believe this is fucking happening. When I'm alone and dreaming about being between Hannah's legs, it definitely doesn't include childbirth. I need to get it together, and now. She needs you, motherfucker. Man up and look. She fucking needs you.

Opening my eyes, I let myself look between her legs. Hannah is being stretched to the max, a head of wet hair clearly visible. I steady my breathing, doing everything I can to stay calm.

"Alright, Han. Baby is coming. I hear the sirens but I'm gonna need you to push, okay? I can see the head."

"Oh, fuck. Fuck. Fuck. Fuck. FUCK!"

Hannah grabs her knees and lifts herself into a curling position, pushing until she's bright red in the face. The head slips right out. Holy fuck, that's a head coming out of my best friend.

"Breathe, Han. Push again."

She pushes once more, and I reach out with a towel in my hand as the baby twists a bit, shoulders popping free. I steady the body as Hannah pushes again, the baby slipping free of her body and into my waiting hands. I pull away just enough, seeing the cord fucking hanging out of Hannah, and wrap the baby in the towel just as the paramedics rush through the door and take over.

Everything else happens in a blur. I hold Hannah's head in my palms, praising her as the paramedics deliver her placenta, Hannah screaming at everyone to put the fucking sea creature on ice so she can do fuck knows with it later, and check the vitals on the baby. When the baby is finally wrapped up tight and put in Hannah's arms, my heart nearly explodes out of my chest.

"Boy or girl, bear?"

"You've got a daughter, beauty. I hope you're ready."

Her eyes fill with tears as she kisses the head of the baby girl in her arms.

"Alright, we need to get you moved onto the stretcher, ma'am. You'll be able to hold your baby on the way to the hospital."

"Please hold her, bear."

No hesitations, I eagerly scoop up the tiny bundle into my arms and look down into her bright watery eyes. And just like that, I've fallen in love with two girls.

"Beauty, what's her name?"

"Charlotte. We're going to call her Charlie."

My heart stops beating and my eyes flash back to meet Hannah's.

"After the goddamn bear we fought over? Hannah, think about this. It's your daughter."

"And you brought her to me, just like the bear brought you. That's her name. Now I'll have my Charlie bear forever."

"Well, fuckin' finally! Thought I was gonna join your grandpa in that jar at your dad's house before you two got your heads outta your asses."

I sit across from Ms. Nettie, Hannah's grandmother, after we just dropped what Hannah thought was going to be a bomb on her. Apparently, her reaction is the same as everyone else's.

"Grandma!" Hannah covers her mouth, shock written all over her face. "Mother above give me strength." Ms. Nettie is a loud-mouthed, crass elderly woman, so this doesn't come as a surprise to me at all. But clearly Hannah has chosen to completely ignore the rumors and whispers that have been going around our town for years about us.

I squeeze her hand lightly once before bringing it up to my mouth and placing a kiss on the back of it. Her eyes flick to me, nerves and shock settling down and leaving her more composed. Seeing how I affect her makes me feel so good, there's a deep connection between us that's always lain dormant, but now that I'm pulling that up, neither of us can deny it. She just needs to give in to it.

"Grandma, you're good with this?"

"Yep! 'Bout time you dropped that little weasel, what was his name? Leon? Lance? Labia?"

"Levi, Grandma. Charlotte's father."

I bristle at her words, and I know she felt it based on how she looks at me out of the corner of her eye. The fuck he is. Deadbeat piece of shit is not that girl's father.

"What a stupid name. That's a brand. I like Labia better."

"Holy shit, Grandma, what meds did you take today?"

"The good ones, my girl, always the good ones."

"For fuck's sake," I whisper under my breath, leaning back in the chair. Time to get this train back on the tracks.

"Ms. Nettie, things are moving quickly, and I just want you

to know how serious I am about Hannah. I'm crazy about her and I feel like we have a lot of time to make up for."

"You're a good egg, Liam Hayes. All you boys are. Not the eldest one though, something fishy about him. Winnie doesn't like 'em much, which is a sign if you ask me."

Sawyer and Ms. Nettie have been clashing since the beginning of time, and for some reason, the calm pup sitting in her lap loses her shit every time he comes into Bean Haven.

"Grandma, you've known these boys their entire lives. There's nothing fishy about Sawyer."

"Agree to disagree! You two have fun. Put a baby in her, Liam, I want more grandkids, and lord knows Harlow and Hailey aren't gonna give me any before I croak. And keep Labia away from her."

"Shit, Grandma, are you sure you're okay?"

"Feeling great, quit askin' me. Now, go. Let me watch Graham Colson cross the street. That man is a silver fox if I've ever seen one. Fine piece of ass that one."

"Holy shit, I've had enough."

Hannah scoots out of her chair and walks to the back of the bakery while I drop my head back in a deep laugh that I can't contain. Once I've pulled myself together, I lean back until I can make sure that Hannah isn't within earshot.

"Ms. Nettie, I know I've known Hannah forever and things have always been platonic, but I've been in love with her for a damn long time. She's it for me. I'm gonna marry her. Soon."

Her hand reaches out and pats the top of mine in a loving, grandmotherly way, and I settle into my seat.

"I know, my boy. She'll figure it out. That other one left his mark on her, but you can heal her, help put her back together again. Soulmates are real and you're hers. You remind me of my James. This kinda love only comes once, so when you get it, don't let her go."

Pride and happiness swell in my chest as her words settle in my heart. Some conversations will stick with you for a lifetime, and this is one for me. It was important to me that she knew where I stood before her time on Earth ended.

"Thank you, Ms. Nettie. I'll take care of them."

She suddenly gasps, her hand flying to her heart in shock, causing mine to stop. What the fuck?

"No! I will not run away with you, Liam Hayes! You're not my type!" she yells, and I sit fucking stunned as shit. She knows no bounds. Fuck, to be old and give zero shits will be such a gift.

"Grandma!" Hannah snaps from the bakery counter. "Leave him alone!"

Later that afternoon, I drove to the other side of town to pick up Charlie from school. The pickup line traffic is a goddamn madhouse and too many parents parking their cars to chitchat like it's fucking happy hour caused an even worse traffic jam. By the time we got back into town, there was zero parking within three blocks of Bean Haven, forcing us to park down the street and walk.

Carrying Charlie's backpack, her little hand in mine so she doesn't slip on any ice, we walk down Main Street, chatting the entire way about school and friends, all the while I'm trying to hurry her along so that we aren't late for dance. Typically Hannah is able to close Bean Haven on time to do afternoon pickup but on the rare occasion she can't, I get to jump in and help out.

"Shh. Stop. You hear dat?" Charlie asks me, pulling my hand back to get me to stop.

I crouch down to her level and listen, giving her patience even though I know we're behind schedule.

"Munchkin, I don't hear anything."

"No! Shh! Don't talk. Listen."

She puts her little hand up to her ear, cupping it around and leaning forward. She can be extremely bossy when her mind is set on something. It's difficult not to encourage her to use her voice because I don't ever want her to feel like her's isn't important or valued. But right now? In an alley in the freezing cold when we're running late? I need to pick my battles, and unfortunately, this is one of them.

Releasing my hand, she starts to walk away. Trailing close behind her, I start to hear the faint whimpers and scratches of a small animal. Moving on instinct, I scoop Charlie up with one arm around her waist, holding her sideways like a sack of flour. She immediately starts to flail.

"Charlie, it's a rat, and they carry diseases. Let's get going."

"No, listen! It's crying. Rats don't cry! Ms. Katie said so!"

"Your teacher told you that rats don't cry?"

"Yep!" she pops the "p" for good measure, the little fibber. Deciding to indulge her, thinking back to the last time she had all her immunizations and wondering if any of them cover feral animals, I put her back on her feet and follow her into the alley. A little bark echoes through the dank space and Charlie looks back at me with an iconic "told ya so" face that she could have only gotten from her mother.

"Okay, okay. Let's investigate."

"What's investigrate?" she whispers, butchering the pronunciation.

"It's when you check something out closer."

Grabbing the hood of her raincoat, I pull her behind me while I move some boxes away from the dumpster. Sitting in the corner, shivering, is a tiny, dirty dog that looks more like a large rat than anything else.

"A puppy!" Charlie squeals as she barrels out from behind me, reaching for it.

"Hey, hey! Freeze, little miss! Did Ms. Katie teach you about rabies? Cause that thing could definitely have it."

"It doesn't have the raybeez." And I can't help the laugh that comes out of me at her pronunciation. "It's sooooooo cute!" she squeals as she balls her little hands into fists and shakes her head violently, eyes large and wide.

I squat down and hold out my hand for the little rat-dog. The dirt and grime matted to his short fur is so thick it's hard to tell what the natural color is but I'm assuming it's a mixed breed. Knowing I can't leave it out here to starve, the moment that tail starts wagging wildly and its nose bumps my fingers—clear signs it's not going to try to bite me—I scoop it up into my arms.

Still on my haunches, I turn so Charlie can see it better. She jumps from foot to foot, clapping her hands and squealing.

"Calm, Charlie, calm. We don't want to scare"—I lift it really quick and check the undercarriage—"him."

"'Kay. Whisper voices."

"That's right."

"Hi, Garbage. We're taking you home now."

The chuckle that I release is far from quiet and booms through the alley as I study her. Dark brown eyes, the color of rich molasses, blink back tears as she oohs and aahs over the ball of matted fur in the crook of my arm.

"Garbage?"

"Yep! That's where we found him."

I laugh again.

"That doesn't mean we need to name him Garbage, munchkin. You were born on a kitchen floor, but your momma didn't name you Kitchen."

"I like Garbage. His name is Garbage."

"We're going to have to talk about this."

Standing to my full height, I pull the dog close and grab Charlie's hand, walking the rest of the way up Main Street. We take a short path between two buildings and climb the stairs to the second-floor door so we aren't waltzing through Bean Haven with the dang thing. Hannah is going to kick my ass.

Instead of getting Charlie ready for dance class, we stop by the grocery store and purchase dog food, ten bottles of dog shampoo, tick and flea treatment, and head back home. We spend the rest of the afternoon bathing our new little friend five times before it resembles an actual dog, and one more time for good measure. I think, and I use that term loosely because I don't actually have any fucking idea, that he may be crossed with a Cairn Terrier, but what the fuck do I know? I'm relying on Google here. He has an appointment with the town vet tomorrow, so we'll have a better idea. Hopefully we can find its owners.

My phone vibrates in my pocket, and I know who it is before taking it out.

SAWYER:

The fuck am I finding out about you and Han from my wife?

KINS:

And Ms. Nettie

CARTER:

I'd just like to state for the record that I knew before anyone and successfully kept a secret

ME:

Piss off Casanova, no one asked you

SAWYER:

Talk or I'm coming over

ME:

We're dating, it's serious

KINS:

Eek! About time!

My phone buzzes again and I realize the chat name isn't "Nosey Assholes" but just all of our names, Dallas conveniently missing from the chat.

SAWYER:

You need to tell him

I contemplate what he's saying, and I know I do. It's eating me alive to not talk to my brother, the one who always has our backs. But he's got shit on his plate right now he needs to focus on. Plus, he's the only one who knows the truth and could potentially blow this whole thing up in our faces.

ME:

I will, when I'm ready. He needs to focus on his own stuff right now.

SAWYER:

I won't hold him back when he comes for you if he finds out from someone else

ME:

I can handle Dallas, shithead

SAWYER:

🖕

I'm happy for you, brother

CARTER:

So exciting! Yay! Another brother off the market turning lame as fuck. I'm jumping for joy for you assholes.

KINS:

Uhm, I'm not taken? Am I not cool?

SAWYER:

You don't count because you're an angel and you'll never do anything terrible like dating or getting married

CARTER:

Our sweet little sister forever

ME:

Perfect Kinsey! No men for you!

SAWYER:

We would literally hunt them down and murder them while they're awake so they knew exactly who was taking their life

ME:

Slowly

CARTER:

Painfully

KINS:

The fuck is wrong with you three? Can't believe I actually miss Dallas being on here

SAWYER:

Dallas is more protective than we are…

KINS:

I beg to differ, psycho. Pretty sure you almost murdered your own best friend for looking at Ivy

SAWYER:

He shouldn't have looked at her

ME:

I don't see the problem here

CARTER:

I do.

SAWYER:

???

CARTER:

He's still breathing

KINS:

Bye. Happy for you, Liam

I drop my phone on the coffee table, glad that's over with, but slightly nervous about how to handle Dallas finding out the news. I still need to tell my parents, but now just isn't the time with everything they're focusing on with Dallas and Blaire.

Charlie is on the floor rolling around with the dog when the front door opens and closes, Hannah's graceful footfall leading her closer and closer to us. I brace myself for what I know is going to be the loss of my life.

Hannah rounds the corner leaving the kitchen and comes into my line of sight, freezing and staring at the scene in front of her.

"Hi, beauty. Welcome home."

"Bear . . . What is that and why is it in my house?"

"Hi, Mumma, that's Garbage, my puppyyyyyy!"

I use my hand to cover my smile and choke down my laugh, coughing on my own saliva.

"But we don't have a puppy."

"Technically, it's a dog. We don't know if it's a puppy or not. And his name is not Garbage," I inform Hannah, loving watching her face morph from shock to confusion, and then settling on mama bear rage.

"Oh no. Absolutely not. We don't have a puppy, or a dog, or a cat, or a hamster, or a pet wasp . . ." She gives Charlotte a pointed look because, unfortunately, she caught a wasp under a cup last summer, named it Platypus, and tried to keep it.

"But, Mumma, it's sooo cuuuute! It loves me and I love him! Bear said I could keep it."

My eyebrows shoot to my forehead, and I look at the little traitor before me as Hannah turns her back to Charlie and stares me down in a way that could only be described as Carrie right before prom burns to the ground. I bristle as Charlie puts her hands together in a clasped prayer, pops out her lip, and blinks her eyes rapidly at me from behind Hannah. Damnit.

"That true?"

My eyes drift slowly back to Hannah's. Her hip is popped out, arms akimbo, and she's death-glaring me, daring me not to have her back on this. She's so sexy when she's riled up, but I don't let myself go there.

"I may have said something along those lines."

"Oh, really? Okay. Well. He can't stay here, so hopefully you're excited about your new little companion."

Fuck.

The next day, I'm a zombie on my drive to work. My new little buddy cried and whined the entire night. He finally settled when I put him at my feet on the couch, burying himself into my body heat and crashing hard. Unfortunately, I had to wake up and get to work two hours later.

The crunching of my large truck tires over the snow-covered gravel startles him from where he sits in the passenger seat of my truck as I drive through the familiar barren roads on my way into the distillery. It's one of those gray Washington mornings, the kind that makes you feel like the sun is hiding just beyond reach, trying to make up its indecisive fucking mind. The sky's overcast, a dull blanket that stretches out for miles, promising rain, or maybe even very late-season snow. I wouldn't complain about either. I pet the little guy around his face and neck to calm his nerves. For a dog who's been surviving on his own out in these elements, he sure does get scared easily.

Once settled at the distillery, my buddy sitting to the side of my desk, I throw myself into work, preparing for a finance meeting with our CFO, Lorelei, checking on the production and maturation process of more than a few single barrel recipes we've got going, and making sure everything is running smoothly. Carter walks into my office for our meeting, and I don't bother looking up from my laptop, not really feeling like talking marketing plans today.

"What the fuck is that thing? Is that a rat?"

"It's a dog, Casanova," I deadpan.

"Are we sure? How the fuck did you end up with a dog?"

"Charlotte. We found it yesterday next to a dumpster on Main and Hannah won't let her keep it in the apartment."

Carter bellows a laugh, but I ignore him, trying to keep my focus on new sourcing options for wood for the barrels. I pride myself on using locally sourced ingredients, everything from the corn, barley, and wheat, down to the white oak used to make our barrels. We toast or char them depending on what we're putting in it, but we do it all here. We're one of the few distilleries in America that do this in-house instead of sourcing made barrels from a cooperage.

"That little girl has you wound so tight around her fingers, bro. So now you're the proud new papa of a dog that looks a whole helluva lot like a rat. What's its name?"

"Charlie named it Garbage. But we gotta think of something else, 'cause no man needs to be called Garbage for their short little life."

"What about Winchester?"

"What are you, the Queen of England? No."

"Magpie?"

"No."

"Kanye Westie? Pup tart? Dogzilla? Jimmy Chew? Oh! I got it!" He snaps his fingers. "Chew-barka!"

I look up at him from my desk, dumbfounded. "What the fuck is wrong with you?"

He shrugs his shoulders before taking a seat in one of the chairs placed haphazardly around the empty space. I'm hardly in my office, spending the majority of my days working with my hands or in meetings.

"How's things with Dallas and Blaire?"

"They're hanging in there. Stopped by yesterday. If you ever checked your phone, you'd be getting more updates. What are you working on?"

"What am I not working on right now? I need to spend more time on this recipe and getting it going. Everything needs to be perfect."

"You're putting way too much pressure on yourself. Anything new you've added has been incredible, why are you so worked up over this one?"

I lean back in my chair, pulling my hat off and running my hand through my shaggy hair while thinking about his question. I've been working on perfecting the recipe for the straight bourbon whiskey for a while now. There's a shit ton of rules, which I'm used to, and confident that we can meet the standards, but I want this to blow everyone away. I want to crack that baby open in a few years and have it be a game changer on the market.

"Legacy? I guess. Yeah, I've adjusted some of the recipes,

but this would be mine. Something we haven't done yet. Long after I'm gone, whoever inherits Aspen Ridge Distillery will still have my make. I want to leave my mark, not just as one of the founder's grandsons, but as someone who's earned his title and place here."

"Alright, shit. Yeah, I can relate to that."

"It's hard to bitch when we've all been lucky to find our places here, but I don't want it to be just because we're all family and keeping it in the family."

"I get that, and I hear you. But we've worked our asses off. Dad and Grandpa didn't give us shit." I give him a look, arching my eyebrows. "Alright, fair," he concurs. "Dad may have created my position, but I've got two degrees in marketing and business. You know we needed someone to come in and focus on what I do. I'm busy non-fucking-stop. You know why I sleep around? 'Cause it takes the edge and the pressure off. I don't have to think, there's no pressure, and I'm damn good at it."

"So, we're all a little fucked-up then."

He chuckles. "Yeah, I guess so. Except for maybe Kins. She seems to have her shit together."

"Little angel. She'll never do anything wrong."

"Never."

"Not having Sunday dinner sucks. Never thought I'd say it. Hopefully we'll all be able to get back to our normal routine as soon as things settle down with Blaire."

"Agree. You tell Mom and Dad about you and Hannah yet?"

"I'm sure everyone has started to hear the rumors. It's moving quick though, so I should probably get on that."

"I don't know if she has. She hasn't left them. Sawyer's been stepping up and taking care of everything."

Shit. I feel like an asshole for not being there for my brother, even though he's asked everyone for space. But Dallas is a straight shooter, while he's the most loyal and dedicated to his family, he will still be the first to call any of us out. But if we're already married when he finds out . . .

"Alright, I'll talk to Han and figure out a plan."

"Good. Now, let's talk about this bullshit coming up."

Carter and I jump into our meeting, but my mind is on Hannah, wondering what's the best way to play this and how to address the elephant in the room. We need to tell her parents, and we need to get married.

Soon.

Chapter Twelve

Hannah

The next few weeks fly by. Liam and I fall back into our normal routine, the same one we've had for years. People in town smile when they see us together, some making comments that it's about time we got together. I'm realizing that I did a really great job at living in my little bubble, ignoring the whispers and rumors that surrounded Liam and I through every stage of our lives.

He's continued to stay close to me, being affectionate but not sexual, and has stayed within our rules. I find myself looking forward to him wrapping his huge arms around me every morning when he gets to Bean Haven, and when he pulls me in close to him on the nights he comes over for our weekly movie and pizza night, even though no one is around to see it. He feels like comfort and safety. Liam feels like *home*.

My phone chimes on the counter with my sister's notification. Wiping my flour-covered hands on my apron, I grab my phone to check the message.

HAILEY:

Yo, I'm bored. Need any help at the bakery?

ME:

I always need help at the bakery

HARLOW:

Put her to work, she can't get lazy. Make her find a real job

I outwardly roll my eyes. Like me hiring Hailey wouldn't be a real job. Annoying.

ME:

Get over here, you can run the counter while I get caught up on backorders.

HAILEY:

Putting myself together and then I'll be over

The three of us couldn't be more different. I completely missed the stereotypical firstborn genes. I rebelled from an early age, forcing Harlow to step into that type A always-have-her-shit-together role. Harlow may be the middle child, but she acts more like the eldest. She's uppity, opinionated, brash, and can come off as a fairly uptight bitch if I'm being honest. Hailey is the complete opposite of both of us. She's kind, soft-spoken, and a genuinely good person to be around. While she's the baby of the family, she's the sweetest girl you'll ever meet and really just trying to find her way in life. I don't think she's ever done anything wrong and if my parents had a favorite, it would be her.

Harlow is in grad school and never home unless it's a holiday or special occasion, but Hailey just finished getting her degree at the University of Washington after changing her major five times. They're my parents' pride and joy. I'm the outsider, the one they're stuck with but are thoroughly disappointed in.

The bell chimes out over the shop and Graham walks in with his daughter, Mila. She's the cutest thing, and while Graham has had his fair share of troubles raising her as a single dad, he's so attentive. He may work at the distillery hand in hand with Liam, but he's also my dad's best friend.

"Hey, you two. No school today, Mila?"

"I had a doctor's appointment," she replies while looking through my bakery case.

"It's too late in the day to take her back to school so I'm bribing her with sweets before taking her back to work with me."

My heart drops for him. Being a single parent is not for the weak. It's a constant game of adaptation and hustling. He's been single for as long as we've known him, just him and his little girl for the last ten years.

"I bet spending your afternoons at the distillery is fun, Mila." But even as I say the words I realize that the distillery really isn't a place for anyone under eighteen, and I wonder if anyone other than Liam even knows. The bell chimes again, in walks Hailey, and a lightbulb goes off in my head.

"Hey, Mr. Colson, Miss Mila! Stocking up on the good stuff?" Hailey chirps.

"Hi, Hailey. Welcome back home," Graham greets her, and I quickly debate if I should talk to Hailey privately or just go for it.

Mila waves and continues to browse, even though she always gets the same thing, same as her dad.

"So, Hailey is home for good now, and she was just saying how she's looking for a job."

Hailey's eyes snap up to mine, eyebrows raising in confusion, trying to figure out what I'm playing at.

"That so? I'll keep my eye out if any places are hiring."

"Well, you know, she majored in early education and there aren't any teaching positions open right now in Aspen Ridge where she wants to stay, buuut she'd make one hell of a nanny."

Graham finally looks up from the bakery case and faces me, then Hailey, my not-so-subtle idea planted.

"Is that something you'd be interested in doing, Hailey?" he rushes out eagerly. Poor guy. We grew up around him, he was always invited to family functions and holiday dinners since he never had a family of his own.

"Nannying? I've never really given it thought." Her eyes flit to Mila, and I can see her wheels turning. Mila is ten and a very mature ten at that. This would be perfect for Hailey, and honestly, Mila, too.

"I mean, are you looking for full-time help?"

"Here, why don't I take your order and you guys can talk and figure it out? Honestly, Graham, you'd be doing me a favor by keeping the girl out from under my feet," I jest while giving him a wink.

That settled, I return to my work, juggling the hustle and bustle of my little coffee shop alone. I can't imagine not working and running this place. The fact that my parents would honestly give me the ultimatum to settle down or they would sell Bean Haven, strains our relationship even further. I wish they could see how happy it makes me, how good I am at it, and how hard I work.

But all they'll ever see is that I never met their unrealistic expectations of what success should look like. It's not like I was a teen mom, either. A point I've tried making dozens of times. Was I living at their house when I got pregnant? Yes. But was I still working full-time at Bean Haven, taking over for my grandmother at that point and running it by myself? A thousand times, yes. I've never shied away from a challenge, and I've always met my goals. It may take me a little longer because I have Charlotte, but I'm still reaching them.

I've been putting off telling them about Liam and me because I know I'll just be giving into their demands. But I know I need to bite the bullet and get it over with, especially because they're the reason we're together anyway. The sooner, the better. I had to practically beg my sisters not to say anything, and I had to actually bribe Harlow, the bitch.

Later that night, after I've tucked Charlie into bed, I decide to make some tough phone calls. Starting with Levi. When he surprisingly answers, I stutter for a moment because of how unexpected the action is.

"Hi. It's Hannah."

"I know, what's up?" His tone is clipped and short, making sure I know how irritated he is with my interruption of his life.

"Do you have plans to have anything to do with Charlotte's birthday?"

"When is that again?"

"You're telling me you don't even know when her birthday is, Levi? Are you stupid?"

"If you're just going to be a bitch, Hannah, I'm hanging up."

"It's this weekend, Saturday at three. We're having a party for her."

"Pretty late notice."

"I've been trying to talk to you about it since late February. You've ignored my attempts. You also haven't called her in even longer than that. Are you coming or not?"

"Where's it at?"

"Liam's. My apartment isn't big enough."

"Pass. Look, I gotta go, tell her happy birthday for me."

"Wow. Told your new girl about her yet? I told you a week and it's been a helluva lot longer than that."

"'Cause you're weak and I knew you were all talk. It's none of your damn business. So fuck off, Hannah."

The line goes dead before I can tell him to go fuck himself. What the hell have I done? How did I create something so good and wonderful with such an absolute piece of shit? Before calling my mom, I take a moment to Google custody laws in Washington State and lawyers in our area. I need to do something and putting it off is only going to prolong the inevitable. I need to protect my baby and having a legal plan in place is what's going to benefit her. After sending a few emails requesting consultations, I steady my breathing and hover my finger over the call button to get the conversation with my parents over with. But I just can't bring myself to do it.

Instead, I call the one person I can't stop thinking about. The one person I can count on. He picks up on the first ring, making me smile and changing my entire mood.

"Hi, beauty, everything okay?"

"Yes and no. Are you busy?" I ask nervously, not wanting to be needy.

"For you? Never. Want me to come over?"

"Please."

"Pizza or ice cream?"

"Ice cream."

"Anything for you. See you in fifteen."

"K. Bye."

For the first time in the twenty-something years we've been friends, I jump up and run to my bathroom, brushing my teeth and finger combing my wavy hair. I slip into a pair of PJ shorts and a spaghetti strap tank top, pulling up my wool socks, hoping that I look semi-cute and not like an exhausted sewer rat.

I get comfortable on my couch, flipping through Shudder and then Netflix to find a horror movie so that it's queued up for us to watch. Liam is walking through my kitchen door less than ten minutes later, his heavy steps leading him directly to me. His steps falter as he walks into my small living room, his eyes roaming over my bare legs that are stretched out in front of me, crossed at my ankles, heels resting on the coffee table. He tracks the length of them as my breathing picks up, over my belly, eyes squinting over my breasts—my nipples pebbled from the heat of his stare, poking through the thin fabric of my tank top—before finally meeting my eyes. I bite my bottom lip to stifle the smile that threatens to consume my face, the bastard.

"Hi, beauty."

"Hi. Want to watch a movie?"

"Like it's even a question. What are my choices tonight?"

He sets the paper bag down on the coffee table and drops himself next to me, legs brushing mine, his arm stretching behind my head and tucking me into his side. I inhale a deep breath of his woodsy, sweet smell. He's always smelled like charred sugar and oak from the distillery and rickhouses, and I've always taken that smell for granted until now. Now, I crave it.

"Thought we could binge *Fear Street*?"

"*Fear Street* it is."

After devouring some ice cream and starting the second movie, my eyes get heavy as I play with Liam's fingers currently resting on my leg. I don't know how much time passes but I'm jostled awake as Liam picks me up off the couch, holding me bridal style and carrying me into my bedroom. He pulls my quilt back before setting me down, brushing the hair from my face. I tuck my feet under the blanket, as he pulls it up over my waist, leaning down to kiss my head. My heart flips over in my chest, and instead of fighting what I really want, I ask for it.

"Will you stay?"

"It's late, beauty, you know I'm not driving home. I'll be on the couch."

"No, will you stay with me? I just . . ."

The faint light shining through my window illuminates the slight smirk rising on his handsome face.

"You don't need to explain, I know. Let me shut everything off and lock the door. I'll be right back."

I release the breath I was holding. Even though he's slept in here with me before, something about this is different. It's more than wanting physical touch, I just want to be close to him. The boy who has loved me through everything.

I lay down on my pillow, getting comfortable on my side just as Liam slips back into the room, leaving the door open halfway because he knows I don't want to be separated from Charlotte in case she needs me in the middle of the night. I hear the rustle of his clothes being removed and then feel the dip of the bed as he lays down. My heartbeat settles as Liam's strong arm wraps around my waist, dragging me to the middle of the bed, cocooning my back flush against his hard, naked chest.

"You doin' okay?" he asks after a few moments of silence.

"I think so. Getting everyone to believe we're dating was a joke. We didn't even need to change anything."

"I know."

"So, let's just get married."

His body stills, not even a breath against my neck or the rise and fall of his chest against my back.

"Bear? Isn't that the plan? If you've changed your mind . . ."

"Yeah, that's the plan. We're getting married. Do you want to tell your parents? Need any help planning it?"

"I don't want a wedding. I've never wanted a wedding. Let's elope. We'll tell everyone after."

"Han, are you serious?"

"Please. This is the plan anyway, no sense wasting a ton of money. Courthouse next week work for you?"

He's silent for a long moment and I wonder if he's fallen asleep. The truth is, while I don't actually want a big wedding, the idea of experiencing that and having it fail or end, would be painful. It's better to keep this what it is. Liam's reaction seems almost disappointed as the silence stretches on. Just as I'm about to doze off myself, he speaks up.

"I would marry you any time, any place. If you want to get married at the courthouse, then that's what we'll do. But then you'll be my wife, Hannah, and everything that comes with it."

He says the last sentence in a whisper, but there is no denying the powerful and matter-of-fact way he says it. As if there is no going back. Next week I'll be Liam Hayes' wife.

The thought is on repeat as I fall asleep with him wrapped around me, my heart pounding in my chest, my head full of what-ifs, the one thing that I'm not feeling though?

Hesitation.

Chapter Thirteen

Liam

The week drags on as Graham and I focus on perfecting the mash bill for our straight bourbon whiskey. I pulled him to help give some advice to get it right. My new little buddy, who has still yet to be named anything other than Garbage, hasn't left my side a month later. After taking him to the vet, getting him shots, scheduling his neuter, and finding out that he isn't microchipped, I'm now the proud owner of a little mixed mutt. Charlie is beside herself with happiness, Hannah still hasn't come around.

I haven't stayed over at Hannah's since the night she asked me to sleep in the bed with her. I knew she was going through something, and my guess was that she talked to Levi.

For some reason, he has a hold on her that I don't know how to sever. She feels loyalty to him just because they share Charlie, even though time and time again, he has shown that he couldn't care less about either one of them. Hannah is the happiest person you'll ever meet, until she's fucked with by that piece of shit, then she gets quiet and dejected, all of her fire doused.

I know he gets sick satisfaction from the little control he has over her, which is why he continues to fuck with her. What he doesn't know is, that as soon as she's my wife, that shit ends. He'll go through me from now on. I'll be damned if he causes either one of them harm again.

Hannah is so pure and full of life, I refuse to see her defeated and solemn. She's going to find her strength when it comes to him and her parents, and I'm going to show her that she's had the power all along.

It's way past when I should have left for the day but when I'm on a roll, I tend to lose track of time. Good thing I can get ready fast. Every year the distillery is invited to a masquerade ball held by the sitting governor in Olympia, and this year Carter and I are the only two forced to go. Our other two asshole brothers are usually in attendance, but Sawyer won't leave Ivy since she's struggling with her pregnancy, and Dallas wouldn't leave Blaire for anything right now—which I respect.

While I usually attend alone, asking Hannah to be my date was a much better option. I adjust my tie before opening the front door, walking into the little apartment she's made a home. Hailey is sitting lazily on the couch, Charlie in her lap watching Moana for the millionth time.

"Hi, munchkin!"

"Bear!" she squeals as she jumps off her Aunt Hailey and runs into my arms. I snuggle my face into her damp hair, smelling her perfectly sweet green apple scent.

"How's my favorite girl?"

"Great, thanks for asking. So excited to move home for good. Yippie," Hailey drones on.

"You're not his favorite girl. I'm his favorite girl," Charlie tells her with all the sass she can muster. Hailey and I both laugh at her little 'tude.

"That's right, munchkin, tell her. You gonna be good for your Aunt Hailey?"

"Yep! Mumma said I could have French toast for breakfast and then cotton candy for dessert if I'm good!"

"That's my girl! Alright, I'm gonna go find your momma now, go lay down with Aunt Hailey and get nice and sleepy, okay?"

Charlotte gets back on the couch, snuggling into her aunt as I walk away to find my other girl. Hannah is sitting on the edge of her bed, messing with the clasp of a high heel as all the air whooshes from my lungs. She's wearing an all-black, floor-length dress with no straps, the top making a tiny v between her breasts that are looking a helluva lot more voluptuous than normal. Her floral black and gray tattoos travel and twist up her entire arm, an accessory all on their own. Her shoes are gold and pointy and clearly frustrating the shit out of her.

"Fuck, Hannah, you look beautiful."

Her eyes finally meet mine before roaming slowly over every inch of my body.

"Don't think I've ever seen you clean up so well, Mr. Hayes. Borrow a suit from one of your brothers?"

"Like any of theirs would fit me. You do know I go to this event every year, right?"

"Yes, dork. But you literally wear jeans, boots, a baseball cap, and a T-shirt every day. I never see you like this. You look good."

"Thanks for the compliment, Han," I joke with her. "I actually don't think I've ever seen you dress up either. I'm kinda at a loss for words here."

"Yeah? Rendered your ass speechless? Wait until you see the back."

My knees nearly give out on me as Hannah slowly spins in a circle, hands in the air like she's fully showing off, swaying her hips side to side as she turns for me. Holy fucking shit. The back scoops all the fucking way down, exposing *everything*, stopping right under the dip of her lower back before her ass.

"Fuck, Hannah. You're *so* fucking sexy." The words are out of my mouth before I could even process the severity of them. But right now, it doesn't even matter. She's so fucking gorgeous it's almost painful. "How is that even staying up?" I ask, because like hell will I be taking her out in that dress if there's a chance she could slip a peek to every greedy-ass motherfucker that will be checking her out tonight.

"Tape," she lilts, like that's the most obvious answer.

"Of course. Tape. Duh." I smack myself in the forehead with my palm to feign my ignorance.

She sits back down on the bed and starts to mess with her shoe again and I don't think, I just react. Stepping into her space, I slowly kneel before her, grabbing her dainty ankle and stretching her leg out in front of me. Resting her heel on my knee, I buckle the little strap and because I can't help myself, I lift her foot, placing a chaste kiss to the inside of her ankle with my eyes closed.

Not wanting her to get weird and pull away before I have the opportunity to get closer to her tonight, I act like nothing happened. Placing her foot on the ground, she accepts my outstretched hand and stands, getting familiar with walking in heels.

"Are you about ready? Have you eaten?"

"Yep, and yes, Dad, I ate. Also have a honey stick in my purse. I plan to watch the shit out of people, drink far too much free champagne, and go to the hotel room to watch *Scream* until I pass out."

"Sounds like a plan, let's hit the road."

We say our goodbyes to Hailey and Charlie before getting on the road to Olympia. After a five-fucking-minute walk down half of the stairs because of her shoes, I bend over and scoop her into my arms, her squeal echoing through the backyard.

"Put me down!"

"Not a chance, beauty. I'd like to get there before tomorrow, and at the rate you're walking, Charlie will have graduated from college by the time we get to the bottom. Stop squirming."

She settles in my arms and there's a chance I walk slightly slower than normal to prolong the feeling of her pressed against me. Once at my truck, she reaches over to open the passenger door, and I easily set her ass down on the bench seat. Reaching to pull the seatbelt down, I start to cross it over her chest when her eyes meet mine. I'm witness to the quick emotions that flash through her, first shock, then arousal, finally settling on denial.

"Give me that! Don't baby me, bear, I'm a big girl."

She's gonna keep fighting this even though I know damn well she feels this heat between us. Chemistry like this doesn't just happen. We're made for each other, she just needs to wake up and see it. I release the seat belt once she has it firmly in her grasp, and watch as she pulls it across her body, hearing the click of it locking into place.

"Hey, look at me," I say gently.

"I'm not babying you. You are more than capable of handling everything the world throws at you by yourself. But there is nothing wrong with leaning on me to handle shit with you. You're the strongest woman I've ever met, I'm not doing it because I don't think you can do it on your own, I'm doing it because I *want* to. Because it makes me feel good to take care of you."

She blinks at me a few times before nodding, her voice coming out slightly choked with emotion. "Okay."

It's a little more than an hour's drive into Olympia, and we spend the time talking about the new movies releasing this year, summer plans, Charlie's birthday party tomorrow, and then she shocks me by bringing up her parents.

"I told them about us."

I nearly swerve off the road, snapping my attention back in front of me and putting both of my hands on the wheel. I thought we were waiting until after we got married.

"You what?"

"I told them that we are dating and things were getting serious quickly. I know I said I was going to wait, but Hailey told me to just rip the Band-Aid off."

"Shit, Han, how did they react?"

She snaps her head in my direction, giving me a "really?" look.

"That well, huh?"

"Pretty sure I need hearing aids because of the way my mother screamed in joy. Nearly blew my fucking eardrum," Hannah deadpans, her voice monotone and slightly annoyed.

I bark out a laugh.

"Sounds about right. Pretty sure both of our parents have been wanting this since we were kids and refused to be away from each other."

"Yeah. Whatever."

"Hey." I reach over with my right hand, resting it on her thigh and shaking her slightly to get her attention. "You and me. Screw everyone else. We know what you're capable of. You don't need me or anyone else's opinion or approval. This is just making things easier on your parents so they give you what you ultimately earned yourself and deserve. Bean Haven is going to be yours, beauty."

"It's just shitty. All this talk, for years, about how I need to settle down with Levi because he's Charlie's dad, and the moment I tell her that I've moved on and we're dating, she's overjoyed. Bear, my mom is happy with me because of the man

I'm with. As if I have no worth at all besides that. It's not the fucking 1800s."

"Your parents are old school and out of touch, Han. They love you in their own way, but yeah, they're assholes. Little do they know, I'm not doing jack shit. Sure, I help with Charlie here and there, but this is all you, beauty. How many people our age are running a full-time business on their own while also being a single parent? Fuck them."

She smiles and nods her head in agreement before looking out the window. The rest of the trip is spent in silence, nothing but the highway in front of us, my mind reeling with how I can get this night back on track.

Once we arrive at the hotel where the event is being held, I say a quick thanks to the sky for not being it's typical moody, temperamental self this time of year. No rain, no extremely late-season snow, just overcast skies and a decent temperature tonight. I pull up to the valet, grab our masks, and leave my truck, rounding the hood to get Hannah. This time, she waited for me to open her door and help her out. Before we enter, I pull her to the side and secure her mask over her eyes, tying the lace behind her head. Luckily, I went with all black for both of us, so it matches her dress perfectly. Hannah's is adorned with tiny crystals around the edges and a bit of lace in a dainty pattern through the center. She's gorgeous, and I have to mentally prepare for everyone to be eyeing her all night.

After tying mine, I hold out my arm like a gentleman and guide us inside. We step through the grand doors of the ballroom, and it's like we've walked into another world outside of our tiny town. The air smells rich and stuffy—nothing like the fresh air, aged whiskey, charred sugar, and oak that I'm used to. Strong perfume lingers in the air and assaults my nose, but Hannah seems either unbothered or unaffected.

The room is bathed in a warm golden light that makes

everything glow softly, crystal chandeliers hanging above making it truly feel like we've stepped into a time machine. The whole space sparkles and shines, and a rush goes through me that I get to give Hannah this extravagant experience.

The event is already in full swing, hundreds of attendees dressed to the nines, wearing sleek tuxedos and flowing gowns, some variation of masks hiding parts of their faces. Hannah squeezes my arm, pulling me closer to her. I lean in, dropping a quick kiss to the top of her head and squeezing her back in comfort.

I lead us to the bar, knowing a drink will help calm her nerves and take the edge off for both of us. While tonight is about representing my family and the distillery, it's also about connecting and being alone with her, and I want to make the best of it.

"Champagne, and a whiskey on the rocks," I tell the bartender as he greets us.

"Aspen Ridge?"

I smile at the bartender, having forgotten that our whiskey and bourbon were being served as the featured brand tonight. "Only the best," I answer him and find Hannah smiling up at me, her focus homed in on my face.

"What?" I ask her, leaning down to whisper in her ear so she can hear me over the classical music floating through the air from the string quartet playing.

"In all the years we've known each other, this is the first time I've seen your whiskey served in a place that wasn't in Aspen Ridge."

"His?" the bartender interrupts.

Hannah turns to face him, and I don't miss the way his eyes drop to her cleavage. Hannah must hear the growl that works its way up my throat, because she drops her hand to my chest and leans into me, pressing her little body flush against my side. It makes me feel like the most important man here.

"Yes, his. He made it. This is Aspen Ridge's master distiller, my fiancé, Liam."

If I died right now, hearing Hannah say those words would be enough to let me go in peace.

"Well, shit! It's nice to meet you, Mr. Hayes." He reaches out to shake my hand and I reluctantly accept it, squeezing much harder than I normally would.

"Mr. Hayes is my father, Liam is good. Thanks for the drinks." I turn to face Hannah, giving her my full attention and brushing off the bartender who had the audacity to check her out when she's clearly with me. "Are you ready to find our table, baby?"

She looks up at me like I hung the fucking moon, a smile spreading across her entire face as she agrees. Hand in hand, we walk through the throngs of people, greeting the few that I know from networking, and find our table near the front, closest to the stage, Carter already sitting with a drink in his hand.

"Hey, hey, Casanova!" Hannah greets him.

"Hey, you two. Looking fine as hell! Damn, Han! Shit, mama! You sure you want this Hayes brother?"

I smack the shit out of the back of his head, not giving a single fuck if we're at a classy event. Fucking idiot.

"Down, boy. I'm a taken woman," Hannah purrs, snuggling back into my chest. I don't know what switch went off when we walked in here, but it's fucking with my head. Is she acting or is she finally seeing me?

We sit with Carter at the table, drinking and catching up on everything going on with our family. Sunday dinners are still on perma-hold while my mom helps take care of the personal things our brother Dallas is currently going through with Blaire. Even though we are all in fairly constant contact with each other, it's still a shake-up to our normal weekly schedule, and dinners on Sundays have been a mandatory part of that for as long as I can remember. Even Charlotte has been asking when we're going over again.

When the governor takes the stage to thank everyone for coming and singles out the large businesses that continually give back to Washington and our community—Aspen Ridge Distillery being one—Carter and I stand to accept the applause. Before I sit back down, I don't miss the look of pride that gleams on Hannah's face. I know she's proud of the hard work I've put in, but it feels good to see it. From a very young age, I knew I wanted to be a master distiller like my grandfather, and I worked hard to get to this point. Being trusted to be one of the lead developers of our distillery is monumental. The weight is a heavy one, but the reward is so worth it.

When Sawyer took over the CEO position from our father after his stroke, I was worried he would change things up, keep me as an apprentice under Graham, but he and Dallas have been nothing but supportive.

The party starts to pick up now that the formalities of the evening have passed, and people take to the dance floor. Wanting nothing more than to hold Hannah in my arms, I stand, buttoning my jacket and holding out my hand in front of her.

"Dance with me, beauty?"

Taking my hand, she follows me to the dance floor, her heels clinking on the glossy surface, her long dress flowing down her frame in a gorgeous wave. Spinning her delicately to face me, I pull her in close, my hand finding its home at the base of her exposed spine, holding her little hand at my chest with my other one. After her confession about being touch starved, I've been trying to give her everything she needs. It hasn't been difficult to reach for her, to hug her, and hold her close to me, when that's all I want as well—her touch.

"Are you having fun?" I whisper in her ear.

"I really am. I've never dressed up like this before. It's like you're giving me my prom."

"Still pissed that you missed that."

"It is what it is. Focusing on the future. Thank you for bringing me here, bear."

Bear.

My heart deflates. Fuck, what I'd give to just be Liam in her eyes.

"You're the most beautiful woman here."

"Thank you for saying that, but you're so full of shit," she laughs.

"I haven't noticed another female since we arrived, you're all I see, and I've caught more than half the men here staring at you tonight. Trust me, I've thought of a million different ways to gouge out their eyes."

"I didn't expect you to be so territorial. I can see it with Sawyer, even Dallas, but you're so chill. Are you like this with all the ladies?"

Everyone knows me as the easygoing Hayes brother, the one who doesn't lose his cool often. Levelheaded Liam. Never makes any mistakes, always keeps his nose clean and works hard. But fuck if I'm not sick of playing by the rules.

"There aren't any other ladies, Han."

She smothers her laugh by burying her face in my chest.

"You forget that we're best friends, bear. I know that you date."

"Yeah? Who was the last one?"

She thinks hard for a moment, eyes starting to go wide as panic sets in.

"Yeah, that's what I thought," I tell her, rolling my eyes, because there hasn't been anyone in a very long time.

"Okay, so it's been a minute."

"It's been longer than a minute, Hannah, give me a break."

"So what do you do then to, you know, take the edge off?"

"Change the topic, Han."

She laughs and lays her cheek against my chest, her little fingers moving slightly against the breast of my jacket where her hand lays under mine. Fuck, it feels so good to have her close to me. The song changes again as the string quartet plays classical tunes, and Hannah and I continue to dance, not altering our rhythm, even as the songs do. Eventually, the music dies out altogether.

"They stopped playing," she whispers, her head still resting on my chest, right above my heart.

"Yeah . . ."

But neither of us makes the move to break apart. I feel the eyes from onlookers focused on us as I keep my arm wrapped around her waist, my thumb rubbing back and forth on the exposed skin at the small of her back. Just that small touch is lighting up every fuse in my body, making rational thought completely dissipate. She's all I want. With the dance floor empty, I keep Hannah tucked into me, swaying slightly back and forth, our bodies completely flush against one another.

Moving back just enough for my hand to gently nudge her chin up to look at me, I'm completely lost to her in this moment. Wisps of her pretty hair have fallen loose from the chignon she had twisted it into. Her face is slightly flushed, the apples of her cheeks rosy, eyes holding so much depth you could get lost looking into them.

"You are so fucking beautiful, Hannah."

"Bear . . ."

"It's true."

Hannah slowly closes her eyes, and when she opens them, I see nothing but desire reflected back at me. She meets my eyes then glances at my lips and slowly swipes her own with her tongue in a teasing, seductive movement that I couldn't have looked away from if I wanted to.

Sliding my hand to frame her jaw against her soft face, I angle her head back so that she's forced to look up at me, giving me complete access to what I want more than anything. I haven't been able to think about anything else since our kiss at the theater, how badly I want a redo, how badly I want to kiss her for real.

Her breath hitches, and fuck do I love her response. In a painfully slow motion, I bend and lower my head to hers so our foreheads are pressed together, sharing air, so close that our lips brush against each other when I speak.

"Hannah . . . I desperately want to kiss you right now."

"People are watching."

"Let 'em."

I erase the space between us, my lips settling on hers. Her body immediately softens against me, her hand gripping the lapel of my tux and pulling me closer as our lips move in unison. A sweet little moan escapes her as she opens for me, not needing much more than a slight coax from my tongue at her soft lips. She meets me in the middle, caressing and tangling, our tongues moving together in a gentle caress.

I leave my eyes open and watch as hers close, wanting to burn her facial expression as she finally surrenders into my memory. I throw every bit of feeling I can into this kiss, giving it my all to show her how I feel about her, how I've always felt about her.

My hand flexes on her lower back, closing that tiny gap between us, my hand edging down slightly, right to the top of her ass. When she responds by moving closer to me, her breath hitching the moment she feels just how she's affecting me pressing hard on her stomach, I keep going. To hell with what people think.

I thread my free hand into her hair, more strands falling loose from the bun, tilting her back, deepening the kiss, drinking up every one of her soft mewls. I could stand here and kiss her like this forever. The world around us could burn down and I would stand right here with my woman in my arms, kissing the shit out of her while the flames lick at our feet.

It's not until I feel Hannah's pelvis grind against me that the rational part of my brain clicks on and reminds me that we're at an event and I'm here representing my family's company, and as much as I want to let her dry hump my leg until she comes, that would probably reflect poorly on all of us, not to mention, embarrass the hell out of Hannah.

Pulling back slowly, I drop several small pecks to her lips before separating us completely. Her eyes are slow to flutter open, searching mine for answers as to how she felt the way she just did. The best part of being in love with your best friend is that you know absolutely everything. I know every single expression, every quirk, the smallest, most mundane actions and twitches—I have them memorized. There's nothing this girl could hide from me. I know exactly how I just affected her. My chest fills with so much hope.

Instead of letting her freak out, I grasp the back of her head, pulling her to rest on my chest for a moment to compose herself before clasping her hand in mine and leading her back to our table where Carter is sitting with a shit-eating grin.

"Some kiss."

"Who knew you were a voyeur, creep," I snap at him as he dodges my slap to the back of his head.

"That was hot, I'd definitely watch if I could somehow block your ugly mug out of it."

"Anyone need a drink? I think it's time for a drink." Hannah excuses herself, rising, and walking quickly to the bar. I watch her until she's out of eyesight, disappearing into the crowd of other business owners, investors, and philanthropists. I let out a sigh as I turn back to the table, loosening my tie slightly for some extra breathing space. Fuck, I hope she isn't freaking out right now.

"Surprised you're still here. Aren't you usually in a broom closet with some rich, old asshole's daughter or a waitress or something?"

"Already done it, brother."

"Fuck, do you have any decorum? Humility?"

"I like to fuck, sue me. You should try it sometime, you uptight celibate fucker."

"I'm not celibate."

"You sure as hell aren't fucking Hannah, based on that kiss."

I point my finger at him harshly, giving him a look that says not to fucking talk about her like that. Carter puts his hands up in the air defensively. Looking at my watch and seeing it's after midnight already, I decide to find Hannah and just bounce instead of murdering my brother right here for the governor and his guests to witness. After saying a few necessary good-byes, Hannah and I take the elevator to our hotel room, where our bags have already been delivered.

I got us a suite, not wanting to assume Hannah would want me in bed with her, even if I'm desperate for it. It has a separate bedroom, a small living room, and an en suite bathroom, plenty of space if that's what she needs. Hannah takes her bag to the bedroom, silence permeating the air. I know she's processing how she feels after that kiss, and I'll give her a moment, but fuck if I'm going to let her retreat.

After the bathroom door unlocks, Hannah comes out in

nothing but a big T-shirt, makeup removed from her face, hair down and bouncing around her shoulders. She's so goddamn pretty.

"You take the bed, I'll crash on the couch, not quite ready to fall asleep yet," I tell her after I've brushed my teeth and taken my suit off, just wearing a pair of loose gym shorts. Hannah's sitting on one side of the bed, her back resting against the headboard, looking so sleepy and cute. I don't miss the way her eyes trace over my chest, down my abs to the V at my pelvis.

Walking over to her, I lean down and kiss her forehead goodnight. "Get some sleep, beauty. We'll be heading home early."

"I had a great night. Thank you for bringing me," she whispers as I leave the room, closing the door behind me. I get settled on the couch, not far from where she's sleeping, just a damn door separating me from who I want to be with. I want a repeat of that damn kiss downstairs, I want her molded to me the way she was when I claimed her mouth, hear her soft little moans, like when she finally let herself go and just feel. She was fucking perfect. That was how I imagined what kissing Hannah would be like. I know it left her stunned, and the look she gave me after told me everything I needed to know. She may be confused right now, but there is no denying that she wanted me, badly. Her brain will catch up, but her body is so in tune with mine, eager to accept whatever I'm willing to give.

After an hour of mindless scrolling on my phone, soft whimpers and the low unmistakable hum of vibrating wakes my dick up, thickening and lengthening to a heavy, thick pipe in my thin shorts. I rub my palm hard against my length to alleviate the ache. There's no way she's doing what I think she is. No way she brought a fucking vibrator with her.

Not about to sit out here while she makes herself come, I get up, adjusting my raging hard-on and heading for the only damn thing I want. Pushing the door open as quietly as possible, I get my first glimpse of her. The room is dark, but I can see the outline of where Hannah lays on her back, her knees bent and spread open as she slowly runs a vibrator along her center. It's too dark to make out the details from where I'm standing, but it's enough to make me lose my mind.

Goddamn, it's the sexiest vision I've ever seen. My mouth waters at the sight in front of me and hell if I don't want to taste her, bring her to orgasm on my tongue, feel her shake beneath me, and fuck, if she screamed out my name, I'd die right on the spot. I step into the room, refusing to slink around. I want her to know I'm here, I want to see her reaction to being caught.

"Shit, bear!" Hannah snaps her legs shut and jerks up the blanket to cover herself. I don't bother hiding my disappointment at the loss.

"Don't stop on my account, beauty."

Her face pales but her eyes are so glassy, heavily lidded, and full of desire. She's desperate for relief. Her chest rises and falls rapidly but she's so damn unsure. I need to fix that. I need her to get used to me, to thinking of me this way. I can be so much more than just her best friend.

"You heard me. Please, don't stop."

"I-I can't."

"I can help you out, it's not like it would be a hardship for me." I do my best to mask the nerves in my voice because all I want to do right now is make her feel good.

"Yeah right. That's not funny."

"I mean it, beauty. Let me take care of you. You're worked up, I'm right here. I already told you, if you needed something, I would take care of you. Let me."

"Kissing was the line, we can't cross that."

"It doesn't have to be. You're mine now. I will always take care of what's mine. Let me make you feel good."

Walking up to the side of the bed, I pick up the vibrator that's lying next to her and press the button to turn it back on, bringing it to life, buzzing in my hand. Without taking my eyes off of her, I slowly pull the blankets down, letting my fingers trail back up her shin until I reach her knee, pushing it outward to spread her open for me. It's taking every bit of restraint not to look at her laid bare for me, but I keep my focus on her eyes, waiting for permission. She's breathing harder than I've ever seen her, practically panting as she watches me with rapt attention.

"Let me make you feel good. I want to, so fucking bad."

"We can't do this."

Fuck, if she says no and I'm forced to walk away now, I may die.

"I won't touch you. It's not crossing any lines if I don't touch you. Let me take care of you, *please*."

She holds my stare for a beat longer before relaxing into the bed and letting her knees fall open, giving me permission.

"Fuck, yes, Hannah, that's it, baby." My eyes trail down her body until they reach the apex between her thighs, where I get my first real look at her. There's a thin landing strip of short curly hair from the top of her pubic area leading straight down to her glistening pussy.

"Fuck, you're perfect. Such a pretty pussy." The words come out before I realize I've said them, my voice thick with desire and need. I hear Hannah's quick intake of air, and I know my words are washing over her, settling and hitting exactly where I want them to.

Keeping my promise not to touch her, I drag the vibrator slowly down the inside of one thigh before repeating the motion on the other side, her legs trembling softly as I go. My eyes track the path as I tease her, running the tip over her hips and over her pelvis. Neither of us says a word as I explore her as close as I can without touching her skin with my own. Not able to wait any longer, I slide the vibrator through her slick center, her hand reaching out and circling my wrist, little puffs of air coming from her lips as she gasps.

"Feels good, doesn't it?"

"Oh god. Yeah. It feels good."

I change the angle of my hand as I move the vibrator down, finding her dripping entrance and circling around it before pressing in just an inch, pulling back out, and repeating the process, teasing her more with it, getting the device nice and wet. Her hips move, and I love that she's chasing the feeling it's giving her. Fuck, I just wish it was me.

My fingers, my tongue, my cock.

Pushing it in deeper, I start to slowly fuck her with it, moans slipping free from those perfect, lush lips that she can't hold back. I've never been happier than at this moment. This right here, making her feel good after all this time. Fuck. She looks so good like this, spread out in front of me, her pussy dripping the arousal I'm coaxing out of her little body, responding so damn well to me.

Pulling the vibrator out, I drag it up to her clit, her moisture easing the way, pressing down and seeing how she likes it, figuring out exactly what will make her see stars.

"Oh! God! Fuck! Yes! Liam!"

Liam.

Not bear.

Liam.

It takes everything in me not to stop, lay down on top of her, and fuck her with my cock. To claim her once and for all and make her mine in every way possible.

"You like that, baby?"

"Yes! Please don't stop. It feels . . . Aah, fuck! It feels sooo good."

"Fuck, you're so wet. Look at you, Hannah. You're making a mess all over the bed. Fuck, you look so good right now. You're killing me. You gonna come for me?" My chest is heaving now, so caught up with making her feel good, my hips slowly thrusting the air, wanting friction, wanting *her*.

"Yes! Make me come, Liam," she whines.

I move the vibrator back to her center, filling her with it, the filthy squelching sounds of how slick she is turning me on further. I want to prolong this, I don't want her to come too soon and break this heated, electrically charged moment between us. I want to suspend us right here together for as long as possible.

I repeat the process two more times, letting the vibrations and pressure hit her clit, bringing her close to the edge before dipping back down and fucking her with it.

"You look so good, baby. Fuck, I want you." Her hips move with me, chasing her orgasm, and it's so fucking hot to see. Her cheeks are flushed, hand digging into my wrist, chest rising and falling rapidly. She doesn't take her eyes off of us, and knowing that she wants to watch this as much as I do is such a huge turn-on. My damn dick throbs painfully against the fabric of my briefs, and I'm desperate to stroke it but I don't want to ruin this perfect moment.

"Oh god, please! I can't take it anymore. Make me come, Liam. I need you."

Fuck it.

"Anything for you, Hannah."

I waste no time pulling the toy from her pussy and moving it back to her clit, loving how it looks sliding between her little lips, her glistening clit swollen and aching. The self-restraint it's taking not to devour her with my mouth is monumental. I should earn a fucking award for being able to hold myself back.

"Come for me, baby. If I don't get to touch you, if I don't get to taste you, at least let me see you fall apart. Let me hear you scream."

She shatters, and I get to watch all of it. The hand around my wrist squeezes painfully and I relish in the sting of her nails biting into my flesh. Her other hand grips the sheets tightly, her head thrashing side to side, legs shaking. Fuck if it isn't the most beautiful goddamn sight in the world. The only thing that could make it better was if my cock was buried deep inside her perfect pussy. What I wouldn't give to feel her walls clenching around my dick.

As her orgasm ebbs, I turn the vibrator off with my thumb, moving the toy down and dragging languidly through her drenched core. Bringing the vibrator to my mouth, I know I'll regret what I'm about to do, because I'll never stop craving it, never stop desiring it, never stop wanting more.

Hannah watches me through hooded eyes as I put the vibrator into my mouth, licking and sucking all of her cum off, loving the taste of her essence for the first time. She's so sweet, so perfect as it coats my tongue and slides down my throat. I don't stop until it's clean. I already want more.

Once I'm finished, I lean down and press a chaste kiss onto her lips before meeting her eyes, her face a sexy mix of shock and post-orgasm bliss.

"Feel better?"

Her cheeks heat, flushing across her high cheekbones as she flops her arm over her eyes.

"Yes. Thank you."

"Don't ever thank me for giving you something you deserve. I wanted that just as bad as you did."

"Bea—"

"Let me clean you up," I interrupt, not wanting to hear her retreat backward and place me in the friend zone. I walk to the bathroom and quickly wash her toy, setting it on the counter for her to pack in the morning and wetting a washcloth with warm water. When I return to the room, she's still dazed, sleep heavy in her eyes.

"I'm not going to touch you with my hands, but I am going to clean you up," I whisper softly. Being as gentle as I can, I use the washcloth to wipe her down before tossing it to the side. I pull off my bottoms, my dick still painfully erect behind my briefs, and crawl into bed next to her. I help her slip under the blankets, and as she turns to her side, I don't hesitate to pull her to the center of the bed and slide my palm under her T-shirt, settling it flat right across her navel. She sighs softly, contentedly, but we don't share another word.

There should be no doubt in her head just how badly I want her now. I'm going to break down these walls, she's going to fall in love with me. Hannah doesn't know it yet, but now that I have her, I'm not stopping until she loves me back.

Chapter Fourteen
Hannah

Morning comes faster than I'd hoped, but after sleeping more soundly than I have in months, even though I only got a few hours, I feel rested. Probably because I fell fast asleep after the most intense orgasm of my life was given to me by my lifelong best friend, and then I was held the entire night with his warm body wrapped around me.

Bringing my vibrator was a last-minute decision. I've been so worked up lately and thought that the mix of alcohol with having an outlet that wasn't my fingers—something I haven't been able to get good at getting myself off with—was a safer bet than jumping my best friend's body and climbing him like a freaking tree.

The way he licked the vibrator clean was the dirtiest, sexiest, most erotic thing I've ever seen, and when I replay the moment, it almost feels unreal. I've only been with three people, and none of them had ever been so . . . feral. Only one had gone down on me, a guy named Colin who I met in college, and it only lasted for a few moments before he was over his sad attempt at getting me to come before he gave up. Liam seems like the type of man that wouldn't come up for air.

I've never experienced something so intense—and he didn't even touch me. More shocking than *Liam* giving me the orgasm was how badly I *wanted* him to touch me. The thought alone was driving me crazy. The wonder, the heady anticipation, the deep desire of wanting to feel his skin on mine—his thick, calloused fingers, his mouth . . . I nearly groan out loud and rub my thighs together to ease the ache that's already returned between my legs.

Everything is changing between us. The scariest part is that I've never seen Liam so confident, so sure of anything. And he doesn't seem like he's faking. This seems very, very real to him. Last night he was just as present as I was. I don't know what's scarier.

Dragging myself out of bed, I straighten out my tank top, slip on a pair of PJ shorts, and leave the safety of the bedroom to find Liam and get cleaned up. As I step into the living space of the hotel suite, I hear the running water from the shower and see that the door was left cracked open.

Curiosity getting the best of me, I walk to the door, and instead of sneaking around, I push it wide open and step inside. The glass enclosure is foggy, distorting my view of his naked body. But . . . the outline. Mother above, Liam is a work of art. His body is thick, muscular, and tight everywhere. He has the sculpted silhouette of someone who works out regularly, with the soft facial features of someone who can be so tender and sweet.

His ass is perky and firm, and my eyes roam upward to the large expanse of his back, strong and fit, straining as he washes his body. As he turns, I know he registers me watching him, but he doesn't shy away.

"Need something, beauty?"

"A shower," I reply, my voice shaking slightly with nerves. What the fuck am I doing right now? This is Liam.

He pushes open the glass door, giving me a full-frontal view of his entire naked body if I wanted to check him out. I do my best to keep my eyes locked on his, as tempting as it is to look lower, I just can't bring myself to do it. His face is a mix of desire and heat as he waits for me to make a decision. There's no denying anymore that he wants me, and I don't know what to do with that.

"You can look, beauty. I'm yours."

"You can't keep saying things like that. It's making things confusing."

"Get in the shower, Hannah."

"I shouldn't . . ."

"*Please.*"

"Bea—"

His reflexes are so goddamn quick, his arm snapping out and grabbing my wrist, pulling me quickly into the shower with my clothes on. I squeal as he turns me to face him, water cascading down his naked body. The hot water hits my tank top, soaking through the material as my nipples harden from the change in temperature. His eyes don't leave my face though, searching mine for any clue that this is okay.

"Baby. You're so pretty in the morning. I'm gonna kiss you now."

"We can't do this. This is such a bad, bad idea. Last night was a slip of judgement."

He shakes his head and laughs quietly under his breath. I cross my arms over my breasts, grateful for at least the barrier of my clothes—even though they're soaked through—clinging to my body. Liam's hand grazes my hip, gently pushing me backward until I'm flush against the tile wall.

My breath hitches as I watch him, his stormy eyes peering down at me with all the confidence in the world. It's the confidence of a man who knows what he wants and isn't afraid to take it. But am I really what Liam wants?

He keeps just enough space between us that our bodies aren't touching, but with the power of his stare, it feels like every inch of him is against me, filling me, consuming me.

His hand stays on my hip, a barely there touch that I feel as if he was a hot iron branding me with his initials. His head dips slowly, eyes never breaking contact as his lips connect with mine. Our eyes stay locked as his lips move, and when his tongue slides across my seam and I open for him, my eyes flutter closed, the weight of the moment too much. I don't need to see Liam to understand. I can feel everything through his kiss. Unspoken words of longing, promises, and desire.

His tongue meets mine in the middle, and everything in my head disappears. My hand reaches out, running up his taut waist and over his chest, running my fingers through the light dusting of hair there, loving how it feels threaded through my fingers.

"Fuck, Hannah, you taste so goddamn good," he rasps, his voice a deep growl as he kisses down my jaw before dragging his tongue down my neck and up again, sucking my earlobe into his mouth.

"Aah."

"Mmm. Let me watch you come again. I won't touch you. Please, just give me that, beauty."

Without thinking, I push down my drenched pj shorts, letting them flop heavily to the shower floor. His gaze tracks down my chest until he stops between my legs, but I don't dare take my eyes off his face.

"Will you spread your legs for me?" I do as he says, placing my foot on the shower bench, the position spreading me wide and opening me up. Liam drops to his knees and my breathing picks up, nearly hyperventilating at his point. Mother above, I want this man so bad my legs are shaking, and I haven't done anything yet.

"Use your fingers, baby. Touch yourself. Show me how wet you are."

Dragging my fingers up my thigh, I brush across my sensitive center the way I would if I were alone, teasing myself slightly before dipping my finger inside. I pump a few times before adding in a second, then inching them upward to my clit, rubbing small circles around it with the moisture I collected. It feels so good, my body tight and vibrating with need. Knowing Liam is kneeling in front of me, watching from mere inches away makes the entire thing unlike anything I've ever experienced before.

I have no idea what I want, what I like, having to grow up way before I was ready to when I became a mom, I didn't have time to experiment. And when I was with Levi, I couldn't count on him to get me off at all. But this? This is doing it for me.

"Just like that, beauty. You like how that feels? Fuck, you have no idea how good you look right now."

My reply is just a garbled moan and shaking my head in agreement. Liam's shoulder starts to move just out of my line of sight and without looking, I know what he's doing. I suck in a quick breath, moaning as I breathe out my next words, wanting to hear the confirmation of what I already know.

"Are you?"

"Jerking off? Yeah, baby. You're gonna make me come just from watching you, I'm so damn hard, Hannah. It's killing me not touching you."

"Oh, fuck."

"You want that, Hannah? You want me to come without even touching you? Just from watching your fingers play with your little wet pussy?"

"Shit, Liam. Ohmygod," my words rush out of me, Liam's dirty mouth heightening the feeling currently coursing through my body like a tidal wave. Barely able to keep my legs spread open because they're shaking so badly, my breathing becomes erratic as the sensations build and build, every cell in my body extra sensitive and ready to fire.

"Come for me, beauty. Let me watch you come undone."

"Ohhhh! Yessss!" My body arches, my head falling back against the tile as I orgasm, pleasure vibrating through every nerve.

"That's my girl, ride it out, baby."

"Fuuuuuuck, Liam!"

My eyes fall closed as I fall rapidly through the pleasure. A smack next to my head has me snapping my eyes back open, finding Liam standing, hovering over me, his hand braced in front of me as he strokes himself off with the other. He moans, and it's such a sexy damn noise that I nearly spiral into another orgasm.

"Fuck, Han, I'm gonna come," his words are followed by a deep, long moan, my name on repeat as he comes and comes. I watch his face the entire time as he keeps his eyes on me, witnessing the pleasure as it hits him, peaks, and then crashes. It's so hot that I'm stunned silent, frozen in place as his hand finally rings the last drop of cum from his body and he slumps forward, still keeping our bodies separated, his forehead falling to mine.

"You're gonna be the death of me, beauty."

"I was thinking the same thing."

"I'll give you some space. Let's try to get on the road soon so we can get things ready for Charlotte's party."

My mouth drops open as he kisses my forehead and leaves the shower. If the orgasms don't kill me, his selfless love for my daughter and her well-being will.

We get back to Aspen Ridge around eight, and I'm anxious to see my baby girl, having never left her overnight before. The ride home was more relaxed than I would have expected for two people who've been best friends for their entire lives watching each other orgasm just minutes prior. Neither of us breaches the topic, and it's probably better that we don't discuss it. We slipped up, caught up in heated moments between two people who are clearly desperate for physical intimacy. There's no way it will happen again, and it's not like we touched each other.

Even if I wanted him to.

I expect Liam to drop me off at Bean Haven, but he parks around back and gets out of the truck with me, following me silently up the stairs to my apartment, the smell of bacon already permeating the air, making me want to gag.

"I'm sorry, Han," he sighs, looking at me with sympathy.

"It's fine. It's party day, it's just a smell. It's not like I don't cook with meat on the daily for Charlie."

"Yeah, but not bacon. You can't stand that smell."

"I'll survive. Nothing is going to ruin this day."

We walk into my house and find my sisters, Harlow and Hailey, sitting at my little table with Charlotte eating homemade breakfast sandwiches. Charlie jumps up from where she's sitting, running in my direction with her arms in the air like she hasn't seen me in a month.

"Mumma!" she squeals as I kneel down and wrap her in my arms. I breathe her in deeply, filling my lungs with her green apple shampoo.

"I missed you, my bestie. Did you have fun with your aunt? I see the grumpy one got here."

"Real nice, Han. Good to see you too," Harlow chastises.

"We had fun. I got to stay up late, and we had popcorn with M&M'S!" After she's done hugging me, she moves to Liam, who scoops her into his arms. She's far too big to be held like a baby at this point, but I wonder if he'll ever stop.

"You're back, bear! What did you do?"

"I danced all night with your momma. She's a terrible dancer though, stepped on my toes a lot." Charlie explodes into a fit of laughter at my expense and I can't help but join in.

"Where's Garbage? I miss him and I know he misses me and it's not fair. I want to see him. He's so sad. Mumma, Garbage is so sad! I can hear him crying."

"We can't keep calling him Garbage, Charlie, remember? Do you want us to call you Kitchen?"

"No. 'Cause I already have a name and it's Charlotte Sidney Haven. Garbage didn't have a name. Ms. Katie said everyone needs a name. He can't not have a name. Duhhhh."

Liam and I look at each other before losing it completely. He sets Charlie down on the ground, bent over laughing at her absurdity.

"Well, aren't you three just the cutest family? One of you gonna spill how this finally happened? Cause I'm callin' horseshit now that I've seen it." Harlow's voice breaks our fit of laughter. My eyes go wide at my sister, who's now standing with her arms crossed, leaning against the wall of the kitchen watching us.

"Charlie, why don't you and Hailey go pick out the best outfit to wear today for your party. You can wear anything you want as long as you feel good in it. I'll be right there."

Charlie skips off to her bedroom and I arch a brow at my asshole, skeptical sister.

"Start over," I tell her with an attitude.

"This"—she waves her hand between Liam and I—"whatever it is between you two, didn't just happen overnight. So, what gives?"

"You're right, Lo, it's been twenty years in the making. You got a problem with it? Or are you still butthurt Dallas is off the market now and you can't possibly be happy for me?"

"That man is fine as hell, but there is no way I wanted anything more than one night with him. We're not talking about me though, we're talking about you, jumping from one relationship to the next, with no time in between to figure your own shit out. You have a daughter to think about."

I feel Liam stiffen next to me, Hulk hovering right under the surface. I drop my head back and let a deep laugh escape me as his hand rubs my back, letting me know that he's right there for support.

"Wow. You are so much like Mom it's like looking directly at her. First off, you have no damn right to come into my home and give me your unsolicited opinion about my life. I juggle every single day by myself with the help of friends. Grandma is too old to be anything but a sounding board for me at this point. I bust my ass to run Bean Haven—by myself, I might add—and raise my daughter without the help of her father or any family around. I've been a single mom since the day I got pregnant with her. And as far as jumping from relationship to relationship—Lo, what relationship did I have with Levi? The one where he showed up randomly every few months to get his dick wet and then bounce? No, you don't get to judge me. You have no damn idea what's between me and Liam, and it's none of your business. So either get out or get on board because I don't need anyone's blessing in order to be with him. He's not going anywhere."

Liam's arm wraps around my waist and tugs me into his side, holding me close to him as I work to steady my breathing and not launch myself across the kitchen at the Wicked Witch of the West and claw out her eyes.

"You're right. I'm sorry. I was just trying to look out for you, but I can see how that isn't what you need or what is helpful. I love you, Han, and I'm sorry."

I let out a rough exhale, letting the situation defuse and my emotions calm down.

"Thanks for saying that. Just don't come at me, Lo, it's not needed. I'm a big girl. Let's just move on and celebrate Charlie today. She needs a happy mom, I'm playing the role of two parents here, it's hard enough as it is. Let's just get through the day and focus on making her feel special."

With that, I grab Liam's hand and pull him behind me to my bedroom to decompress for a moment before going downstairs to put the finishing touches on the cupcakes and all the other party prep that needs to be done.

Liam shuts the door behind us and grabs me by the shoulders, pulling me into a tight hug, his huge arms wrapping around me. I relax my head on his chest, hugging him back around his firm waist, filling my lungs with his clean, woodsy smell.

"Are you okay?"

"I'm fine."

"You don't have to lie to me, you know. I can see right through you. Perks of knowing you our entire lives."

"She's such a bitch sometimes. A mini-Cynthia but with

claws. I want to smack the shit out of her smug-ass face sometimes. Ugh!"

"I get it. Why do you think my dad forced the four of us boys to take boxing lessons from a young age? He wanted us to have an outlet to channel all that rage."

"And now look at you four, still pummeling the shit out of each other on the regular."

"Yeah, but the love between us is damn strong. I would die for any one of my siblings. Even if I do need to throttle them every once in a while."

I step back from his hold, sitting on the edge of my bed, lost in my own thoughts, when he drops down in front of me.

"Hey, everything's going to be okay. I've got you. You can handle anything because you're a badass. So take a minute, but then pull yourself together and let's get shit done. Today's not about us, we'll focus on all the other crap tomorrow."

I reach out, running my fingers through his messy locks before settling my fingers along the scruff of his jaw. Without thinking, I lean in, pecking him on the corner of his mouth. When I pull back, his lips have turned up into a smile that reaches his eyes, crinkling them slightly.

"What was that for?"

"For always having my back. You and me?"

"You and me."

After several hours of party prep and two trips back and forth from Bean Haven to Liam's house right outside the distillery property, it's party time for my sweet Charlotte. My parents called not long ago to video chat with her, which I appreciated, and so did Charlie. Even if our relationship may be strained, they are good grandparents, and I know they love their granddaughter. How could you not? Unless you're Levi.

Liam had completely transformed his garage into a magical *Moana-themed* party, complete with large character cut-outs of Moana, Maui, HeiHei, and Pua for the kids to take photos with. Luckily for everyone here, the rain has held back, and we've been gifted a rare sunny day. The rays beat down on our little part of the world, melting away what little is left of the snow, and bringing some much-needed warmth and sunshine into my little girl's life.

There are two types of people who live in Aspen Ridge. Ones who thrive under the near-constant cloud cover, and those who leave the first opportunity they can for warmer, sunnier weather. I hope to mother above that my daughter is like me and is the first. But if her life calls her away, I'll be cheering her on always.

The majority of Liam's family is here, along with both of my sisters, our friends Reid and Owen, and what seems like Charlotte's entire Pre-K classroom and their parents. It's such a good turnout.

Sawyer, Ivy, and Reid find me at the craft table after helping the kids get set up with their little sensory bottle projects. Ivy's belly has completely popped out at this point, but she looks so full of life, happy, and glowing. The complete opposite of me when I was pregnant with Charlie.

"Look at you, I don't think I've ever seen a more beautiful expectant mother."

"Mother. Jesus. It sounds so surreal," she replies.

"Better get used to it, butterfly, I plan to have you pregnant for the next few years."

I give Ivy a sympathetic look, but she waves me off. "I'm ready for it. We want five."

"At least," Sawyer adds.

"For fuck's sake, more power to you. My hands are full with just the one right now. I couldn't even imagine multiple of them. How are you, Reid? I feel like I haven't seen you in weeks!"

He shrugs his big shoulders. "Life's been busy, Han, but I'm decent enough. No complaints."

"Drogo will never complain," Ivy adds, rolling her eyes at him.

"Hey, baby cakes. Having fun?" I ask Kinsey as she joins our little circle.

"Yes. Didn't you know I love working five days a week and then spending my Saturdays with the children who I'm supposed to be getting a break from?" she jokes, and we all laugh.

"I know, I know! I'm sorry. But I'm grateful you're here. Anything new going on with you?"

"Nothing. Work. Looking for a new place to live, actually, but it is ridiculous in this town. Someone either needs to move out of AR or die. And if someone could please do that, I would love to get out of my parents' house STAT."

Sawyer laughs, and Ivy and I both narrow our eyes at him. These boys are so ridiculous with how they treat their poor sister. They think by putting her on a pedestal, that they're keeping her safe and loved, when all they're doing is smothering her and keeping her from living her life.

"I'll keep my ears open in case something comes up, and I'll let you know," Reid chimes in.

"Thanks, Reid," Kinsey says fairly sheepishly before continuing. "Actually, I was hoping to talk to you about something."

"What's up?"

"I want to get a tattoo."

"Ha! Fuck no," Sawyer snaps.

"Sorry, sweetheart. Not a chance. You tryin' to get me killed?"

"That's fine, I expected that. I'll find someone else."

"The fuck you will, Kinsey," Sawyer demands. I link my arm through hers and drag her away from the group of them, sticking my tongue out and leaving them for Ivy to deal with. She can control Sawyer and pull him off the ledge, and the two of them are both best friends with Reid. They'll sort out their shit.

"So, a tattoo, huh?"

"I want one, I want to experience it. Something small and hidden. My brothers are fucking ridiculous. Who did yours?"

I squirm, my face bunching up as I wince.

"Fuck, really? Reid?"

"Yeah, babe. He's a master at fine line and his florals are to die for. I wouldn't go to anyone else."

"Shit. Whelp. That's out."

"Don't stress about it, we'll figure something out. I'll help you."

"Thanks, love you, Han. By the way, I can't tell you how happy I am for you and Liam. First Ivy coming back and now you. It really feels like our family is coming together the way it was always meant to."

And with that statement, part of my heart shatters. The weight of what Liam and I are doing, and all of the people it will impact and affect once this ends will be devastating. Kinsey walks away as I stand slightly stunned next to the outdoor tables set up between the house and the garage.

"Hannah, you're looking a little flushed, sweetie. Are you feeling okay?" Liam's mom, Amy, says to me, her words sounding a little too far away.

My cheeks flame as I put both of my shaky hands on the

table to stop the swaying, the feeling of standing on a boat out at sea washing over me. My head starts to pound, and I squint my eyes against the onslaught of the ice pick assaulting my brain. Shit. It hits me just as the world starts to fade to black.

Two lattes.

No food.

Chapter Fifteen

Liam

Sawyer yells my name over the commotion of the kids playing at the craft table set up for the party inside my garage. When I turn to face him, his expression makes my heart drop into the pit of my stomach.

"What's wrong?"

"Hannah passed out. I carried her inside, Mom's with her."

"Fuck." My brother stays put to assist with watching the small group of four-year-olds as I jog across my driveway to my house, wracking my brain for the last time I saw her eat today and cursing myself for not making sure she had. Tearing through my front door, I pull open the drawer where I keep Hannah's spare blood sugar monitor and then jog into the living room. She's relaxed on the couch, her face pale and flushed all at the same time. I don't see or hear anything but her as I kneel down at her side, running my hand over her forehead and cheek.

"Baby, I'm so sorry. I should have taken you out for breakfast or made sure you had a snack throughout the day. I was so focused on getting us home to get ready for the party."

She looks at me with her eyes squinted into slits, a "you're an idiot" look plastered to her face. But this is a fight I will gladly take on. I don't ever want to see her hurt or feeling like shit. I unzip her pack and pull out the monitor with the other supplies, sliding a testing strip into the monitor and pressing the lancet into the device to prick her finger.

"I'm a grown-ass woman, bear, I know I need to eat and watch what I eat. It was stupid. Haven't passed out in a bit. Grateful Sawyer was next to me, or it could have been worse. No one wants brain matter all over the place at a birthday party."

My hand reaches out to pinch the bottom of her chin, turning her head to face me so that there is no doubt of the severity of my next words.

"Hey, that's not funny. You have to take care of yourself, or I'll do it for you. You want to be a big girl? Don't want to be babied? Then don't let this happen again. What if you were by yourself? Or alone with Charlie? Promise me, Han, promise me you'll do better?"

She bites her bottom lip, and I use my thumb to pry it free. "Words, baby, use them. Please."

"I promise."

Not thinking, I lean forward and let my lips touch hers for a small kiss, just enough pressure to feel the warmth of them against me, needing to feel her breath.

"When did this happen?" my mother's voice breaks the silence, thick with emotion and cracking on the last word. I back away slowly from Hannah to catch her eyebrows rising, her pupils blown as we both realize who's in the room with us.

"Hey, Mom. Didn't see you there," I say innocently as I turn to face her where she sits in the chair across from us. How long has she been there? "You mean Hannah passing out or us being together?"

"I'm aware she passed out, Liam, I was there. When did you two finally figure things out?"

I look back at Hannah in a groggy state, and I know she's feeling like shit. I grab her hand to distract myself, wiping an alcohol swab over the side of her little pointer finger, before letting the lancet device disengage to prick it.

"A while ago, we've been keeping it low-key since people in town like to talk so much."

"You two are actually together?" she asks, like her whole heart is on the line and she's just as invested in this as I am.

My parents' house was the hub for all of us kids plus our friends. More nights of the week than not, the dinner table was overflowing with kids, Hannah being one of them. We've always been inseparable, and while my mom and dad have never outright called me out on my feelings, they are extremely inquisitive and it's a solid assumption that they've clued into how I feel about this girl. That I'm head over heels in love with her.

"We're really together. We haven't sat Charlie down and told her, so we're still keeping it a bit of a secret, but it's the real deal," I tell my mom matter-of-factly, refusing to look at Hannah's face and see the trepidation etched into her features. "I'm surprised you haven't heard on your own, Ms. Nettie has been yapping about it to everyone who will listen."

"Oh, I've heard the gossip mill, but I just assumed it was talk because it's always been there following the two of you. This is really happening? Your siblings all know?"

"Everyone except the one you've got at your place. I'll tell him on my own though."

"Fair enough. I've been a little preoccupied, so I forgive you all for not telling me. But I'm beyond happy for you both. Hannah, my sweet girl, I have loved you since you were three, this news couldn't make me happier. You've always been family, and this changes nothing." My mom nearly squeals in joy and claps her hands together before rising and kissing Hannah on the head. It fills my heart with so much fucking love. She's so accepted by my family, always has been, and this will only cement her place within it.

My mom leaves Hannah and I to ourselves, and with last night and this morning still on repeat in my mind, I just want to lay down next to her and kiss her for the rest of the night. If it's up to me, we'll be repeating that as soon as possible.

"What can I get you to eat besides a honey stick?"

"Bear, we're going to hurt everyone we love when this crashes. What the hell are we thinking?"

I sigh and look away.

"Just trust me, beauty. This isn't going to crash and burn. I won't let it."

After getting Hannah food, and she starts to regulate a little more, we return to the party where Charlie is happily playing games with her friends, Kinsey saving the day with her mad kindergarten teacher skills. Carter is holding my little fluff ball in his arms, and I cock my head at him. The little guy won me over and I am not about to have him stolen by my idiot brother.

"Who's ready for cake and presents?" I yell over the little voices and laughter ringing out through the open garage. They cheer loudly, Charlie runs over to me, and I scoop her up.

"Happy birthday, munchkin!"

"It's just my party, bear!" she squeals. "My birthday is in three days!"

"Oh, I know! I delivered you, remember?"

"You were the first one to hold me."

"I sure was. You were slippery and covered in goo!" I tickle her and she flails around in my arms, forcing me to put her back down on her feet.

Hannah brings in Charlotte's birthday cake, which she spent hours working on. The cake is made to look like Te Fiti from the *Moana* movie and is surrounded by cupcakes decorated to be the green heart of Te Fiti. She outdid herself, and the look of pure happiness and excitement on Charlie's face is priceless.

Charlotte is surrounded at the table by her friends, my entire family minus a few, Hannah's sisters, and all of our friends. While we all sing Happy Birthday, I slip my hand behind Hannah's waist, giving her a gentle tug into my side, and she drops her head onto my bicep. I take a second to appreciate the moment. Hannah on my arm, Charlotte happy as can be, surrounded by my family, in a place that I love.

This. This is what life is all about.

After the party, my family stays back to help clean everything up and put my garage back together. Once everyone heads home, I walk inside to find Hannah and Charlotte lounging together on my large couch. It's a massive L-shaped, plush sofa with huge pillows.

When I started house hunting two years ago, this house had just gone on the market, and I didn't hesitate to put in an offer. I wanted to live on the side of town where the distillery is located, attracted by how much farther from downtown it sits, giving me ultimate privacy. The house sits on three acres, but it's a wooded paradise for someone like me.

It's a beautiful log cabin with tall, vaulted ceilings held up by thick, exposed beams, an open-concept living area, with floor-to-ceiling windows expanding the length of the back of the house, and an upgraded kitchen. It has three bedrooms, two on the second floor, and the large master suite on the bottom with its own master en suite. The master bathroom was nothing to write home about until I updated it. It was the first place I gutted and renovated. A part of me always hoped that one day the stars would align, and Hannah would move in here with me, help make this big house a home with me. She complains at least once a month about how much she misses taking baths since her little apartment only has a small stand-up shower. I chuckle when I remember her reaction.

Pulling up in front of my new house, Hannah jumps out to get a head start to scope out the place and the new updates I've made to it. She jogs up the stairs, opening the front door and stepping in with me right behind her, Charlie in my arms, watching her reaction as she takes in the new furniture, the wall I took out to make it more of an open concept, and the new paint.

"Holy shit, you ass! I'm obsessed! It looks totally different already! You've really put the work in. Ugh, I love it so much, I don't want to leave," she nearly whines. I knew she would love it, and part of me feels guilty for being able to purchase such a lavish place while she and Charlie are stuck in the small apartment above Bean Haven.

"C'mon, go check out the bathroom."

She gives me a look that says "no, you fucking didn't" and I just smile at her. I follow behind as she skips through the living space into the master bedroom, floating through the room until she gets to the en suite. Her chin drops, mouth falling open as she stares at the large, vintage, enameled cast-iron clawfoot tub. There's a massive four-person shower across from it, tiled in gorgeous stone, with multiple spray heads and attachments. I even hung eucalyptus from them because I knew she would like it. On the other side of the room sits a large counter with two porcelain sinks, individual round mirrors above, and some plants that I have no fucking idea how to keep alive. Several more hang in the corner, placed strategically in front of the large window that faces my sizable, private, and wooded backyard. Which also happens to be the wall that the tub sits on.

"Holy. Fucking. Shit."

"You like it? It really needed a fuckin' upgrade. Whatever old bitty decided to put carpet in a bathroom is hopefully long gone. There are some things you just can't come back from."

"Bear, this is literally what dreams are made of! You outdid yourself."

She continues to stand in the entryway of the bathroom, just looking at it, and after a moment I start to laugh at her.

"You ready to go?"

"What? NO! Do you have Charlie for a bit?"

My eyebrows rise as I look at her in confusion.

"Yeah . . . but—"

"Good, bye! Get out! Get out!"

"What? Why?" I yell at her as she shoves me to push me out of the bathroom.

"Momma needs a bath. Desperately. So, bye!"

"You don't have clean clothes, nutjob! What are you doing?" I start to really laugh now, not expecting her to want to take a soak in the tub this very moment, even if I did secretly buy the damn thing with her in mind.

"I'll wear yours! I don't care, this tub is screaming at me to christen it! Please, Liam."

She crosses her arms and lifts her shirt up and over her head, leaving her standing in front of me in just her denim jeans and bra, the thin material leaving nothing to the imagination, including the barbells pierced through each of her nipples, which I didn't know she had. Fuck, that's the hottest thing I've ever seen.

"Mother above, bear, if you don't leave now, I swear I will

strip down right in front of you. Are you going to leave, you perv?"

"Wouldn't you like that, beauty? Nah, Charlie and I will go hang and we'll order some pizzas. You relax. Towels are in the closet right there," I say as I point to the area behind the bathroom door. "We'll be hanging in the living room. Clean clothes are in my drawers in the walk-in closet." As much as I want to watch you slowly strip naked in front of me.

She squeals loudly, screaming a thank you as I turn on my heels to go do exactly what I said I would to keep myself distracted from thinking about Hannah naked in my tub and the things I want to do to her in it.

The memory stirs an idea as I plop down between the two of them on the big couch, making Charlotte squeal and bounce slightly, the pup barking, ready to play. We just need to get Charlotte settled and to sleep before I can execute it.

"Either of you hungry? Or still stuffed from all the pizza and cake?" I ask my girls.

"I couldn't eat anything else today if I wanted to," Hannah replies, looking over at Charlie to see how she's feeling.

"I'm soooo full. Are we staying here with you and Garbage?"

My eyes meet Hannah in question but she's already nodding her head yes before answering out loud.

"Yes, baby girl, it's getting late. You want to stay in the cool kids' room tonight?"

"Can Garbage sleep in there with me?"

This time it's me who answers, "Yes, but he needs lots of cuddles or he cries. He'll sleep right at the end of the bed at your feet. I hope they aren't too stinky!"

Charlotte giggles as she stands up on the couch, bracing her hands on the back of it and sticking up one of her feet and pressing it into my face. I fall into Hannah in a dramatic display and feign passing out.

"They don't stink! They smell like roses, bear! Momma, tell him they smell like roses!"

"Jeez, bear! Don't you know girls' feet only smell like flowers? Get with the program!"

"Roses, huh?" I laugh as I sit back up and lightly toss Charlie onto her back, tickling her until her laughs leave her gasping for air. The three of us settle in together on the couch until Charlotte starts to doze off, the long, exciting day finally catching up with her. I nudge Hannah as I sit up and scoop Charlie into my arms, carrying her into the bedroom that I keep made up just for her and Hannah when they crash at my house.

Hannah pulls down the blankets as I set Charlotte into the center of the queen-sized bed, my little dog jumping up and settling at her feet under a throw blanket that lays at the end. Hannah and I take turns kissing her head and saying good night as she falls asleep right in front of our eyes. We close the door behind us, and excitement fills me at what comes next.

Time to get my girl nice and relaxed.

Chapter Sixteen

Hannah

Liam gives me a look that is heated and foreboding, his eyes darkening right before me, eyelids heavy, his bottom lip pulled between his teeth in a sexy move that has my panties dampening with arousal. He grabs my wrist without saying a word, gently pulling me behind him through his house and into the master bedroom. After the events of last night and this morning—for fuck's sake was it only just this morning I was getting myself off as he watched while in the shower together—being in his bedroom feels a whole helluva lot different. But my heart is the same, flipping over in my chest, butterflies taking flight in my stomach.

He doesn't stop though, pulling me into his dream of an en suite. His hand releases mine, moving to my lower back as he leads me inside the massive, serene space that is every bit my perfect sanctuary before spinning me to face him again.

"Strip for me, beauty." His voice is a warm caress over my entire body, just four little words striking the match that will ignite the inferno that I've felt every other time I've been on the receiving end of his desire.

Liam walks over to the clawfoot tub and turns on the hot water, letting it heat up before adjusting it with a tiny bit of cold and putting the stopper in the drain. I watch as he meticulously dries his hands off with a towel and then pulls out a fancy glass jar with green soaking salts. I immediately know what they are, and my heart does that damn flip and flutter behind my ribcage. After unscrewing the top, he shakes out a hearty amount into the bathwater, the smell of eucalyptus, lavender, and dried rose petals slowly engulfing the room.

My chest starts to rise and fall rapidly as he finally turns to look at me, his head cocking to the side, eyes squinted into slits.

"You're still dressed," he tsks.

It's now that I realize what a grave mistake I made by not heading in his direction the first time. Liam prowls over to me, his eyes roaming all over my face as his hands reach out to grasp the hem of my T-shirt, slowly lifting it over my head. I feel every centimeter of his knuckles brushing up against the skin of my sides as he does it. Once the shirt has been discarded onto the heated floor, he kneels in front of me, his deft fingers expertly flicking open the button of my jeans, slowly sliding down the zipper. His fingers hook into the side of the waistband, and at a torturously slow pace, start to drag them down my hips and legs. I keep my eyes focused on him the entire time, still struggling to believe that this is Liam with me right now.

"We shouldn't do this . . ." I whisper, my words coming out on a shaky exhale. He looks up at me from under his eyelashes, his heated expression causing my breathing to hitch and a flood of arousal at my aching core.

"Then tell me to stop."

Goosebumps scatter across my hypersensitive skin as he works the material down my body. After my pants are removed, he takes his time repeating the motion, sliding my panties down until they're added to the heap of clothes. I'm suddenly extremely aware that my thin baby pink satin panties will give away just how turned on I am by this man right now.

But Liam doesn't comment, instead, he bunches them in his hand and brings the damp material to his nose, breathing in heavily, eyes shuttering closed as he inhales my scent. Holy fucking shit. I thought I knew everything there was about this man, but any assumptions I may have made about what this side of him was like were nothing close to the real thing. Liam is an unhinged, primal alpha male right now and my brain isn't catching up to my body—which is screaming at me to climb him like a fucking tree and bury him deep inside me. My stubborn-ass brain, however, is flashing a neon sign that says "warning!"

Rising to his full height, he takes a single step into my space, our bodies nearly flush with each other but not touching. If my breaths come any harder, my nipples will graze his lower chest . . . something I find myself wanting to happen.

Instead, his hands reach behind me, head tilting to the side as he watches my expression. An expression that I'm sure is conveying what a desperate hussy I am. I'm scared to move an inch, I'll be rubbing myself all over him like a cat in heat if I do.

Within a split second, I feel the release of my bra, my breasts suddenly hanging much heavier, fuller at my chest. And as Liam pulls the bra off of my arms, the air brushes against me, my nipples pebbling, reaching out, begging for touch.

"God, Hannah, you're so sexy, I wish you could see yourself right now."

His words finally break the silence between us, caressing over my body and finding their home at my aching, desperate pussy. Hell, what would it be like to be filled by him?

Liam steps back and I sway slightly on my feet, lust-drunk

without even being touched. Instead of feeling self-conscious, instead of covering myself up, I watch him as he runs his hand through his shaggy dirty blond hair, and then drags it over the coarse stubble at his jaw. For the second time in the last twenty-four hours, I find myself naked in front of him while he's clothed, as his eyes bathe me in a thick coat of desire.

I don't dare ask him what he's thinking right now, I just let him eat his fill, his gaze lingering on my breasts, his tongue slipping out and sliding through the seam of his lips before pulling the bottom one between his teeth again. It's such a sexy move that I nearly moan just from watching him look at me.

After a moment, he leans down and turns the water off, holding out his hand for me to take.

"You know, when I bought this thing, I definitely thought it would get more use."

Accepting his hand, he helps me step into the large tub where I sink into the deep water, resting back and laying my head on the folded towel he set there for me. I close my eyes and settle into the warmth and the aromatherapy of the bath salts.

"You're telling me you bought this gorgeous tub and you don't use it regularly? I'm so disappointed in you. I would use this every single day."

Liam is silent for so long that I'm forced to open my eyes, finding him sitting next to me, his arm resting on the rim of the bathtub, looking at my face and lost in his thoughts.

"So, why don't you then?"

"Mmm. I wish," I dream as I close my eyes and sink into the hot water, loving being submerged and relaxed like this. I love baths. There's something so simple about relaxing in a body of hot water that has the ability to melt away every ounce of tension or ache your body is holding on to.

"You and Charlie should move in here with me, Han."

My eyes fly open, all that tension quickly finding its way right back into my body.

"Liam . . . this will end, and it will only confuse Charlie if we do that."

He nods in agreement.

"Right." He says the words, but I know this man better than to think this is the end of the conversation. "But we'll be married, and we need your parents to not have any reason to think that this could be anything less than real. Plus, beauty, we're not going to be able to suddenly walk away from this as soon as your parents agree to leave you Bean Haven. You're stuck with me for a bit, we need to sell it."

"I just don't want to do anything to confuse her."

"How do you feel about telling her a little fib then?"

"Terrible."

"Han, just last week you told her that if she didn't drink her milk her bones would turn to jelly. We just tell her that you guys have to stay with me for a while because the dog needs her to take care of him. Something little, skirting the truth."

I think about his words, and while Liam lives on the other side of town and it would give me a little commute, it would also make this look more legit to my parents, which is the whole point of this arrangement anyway. To have the added perk of using this gift of a bathtub every night isn't a bad sell.

"Alright, maybe you're right. But ask me again when I'm not being manipulated by you and your elite bathroom."

"That's fair. But I'm not letting this go. Especially if you're my wife."

My breath catches in my throat, my eyelids fluttering closed from the rush of emotions flowing through my veins. My heart begins to race, quick and erratic, as I work to steady my reaction to his words. Liam's hand reaches out, brushing his fingertips over my forehead, my temple, and settling with his open palm cradling my face. I tilt my head slightly, savoring the feeling of his touch. But, in typical Liam fashion, he doesn't miss a thing when it comes to me.

"You like that. Don't you? It turns you on."

"What does?"

"When I call you *my wife*."

The little gasp that leaves my lips is uncontrolled and gives me away. Why the hell does that sound so good? *"It's clear you need to get used to me touching you the way a husband touches his wife."* I'm fucked. Because right now, everything else be damned.

"Yeah, you like it, beauty. No use in trying to hide it from me because I notice everything when it comes to you."

Feeling confident and irresponsible, I lift my hand above the water, sweeping my fingers across my collarbone before dragging them between my breasts, pausing there to grab both in each of my palms, squeezing and massaging before gently tugging at the piercings through each of my nipples. The little sting of pain goes straight to my clit.

"Hannah . . ." The way my name sounds rolling off of his tongue should be a sin. His voice has dropped to that husky, rich tone that holds so much depth.

I flatten my palms and slide them farther down until I reach my hips, letting my eyes fall closed as I let go. My fingers brush through the trimmed landing strip of hair at my center, anticipation and the strong craving to feel good overcoming me.

A deep masculine groan rumbles from his chest through his throat as my fingers spread open my pussy lips, my other hand slipping between and finding my clit.

"That's my girl. Play with that pretty pussy. Tell me how it feels."

Mother above and all things good, I had no idea Liam

would have such a dirty mouth and that it would do such filthy things to me.

"It feels so good."

"Good, baby. Shit, you don't know how badly I want to touch you. Feel how silky your skin is, how wet your pussy is. Spread your legs farther for me, Hannah. Let me watch."

I do as he says, opening my legs as wide as the tub allows. I hear him shuffling around, and when I open my eyes, he's changed his seating, now positioned closer to where my legs are currently spread wide enough to give him another full view between them.

"That's my good girl. Dip your fingers inside, fuck yourself with them."

Following his directions, I slide my fingers down, pressing my middle finger inside, pumping twice before adding a second, rubbing my palm along my clit as I do.

"Just like that. Fuck, you look so good spread out like this for me. Bring those fingers back up to your clit." I eagerly pull out, dragging them to circle around my throbbing clit, chasing my orgasm that seems just out of reach. "Yeah, baby. Make yourself come for me."

"Oh, yessss."

"I love watching you come, Hannah. So fucking pretty."

"Aah. Liam. I need . . . Fuck."

"Anything, baby. Tell me what you need." Fuck, his voice sounds so desperate, like he's on the cusp of snapping, the restraint too taut to be stretched any farther. But we can't cross that line. No matter how badly I want to right now. Fuck.

"I don't know," I tell him, my voice needy and nearly a whine.

"Fuck, Hannah. If I could touch you right now, I'd sit your ass on the edge, spread your legs, and lick your pussy."

"Oh, fuck, yes, Liam."

"I'd take my time, letting my tongue trail over every inch of you, fucking you with it before sucking on your little swollen clit."

"Don't stop, please, Liam, yes." I had no idea I would have a voice kink, but here we are. Liam talking to me with his dirty mouth is edging me closer and closer to orgasm.

"Fuck, baby. I'd make you come with my mouth, and as soon as you came down from it, I'd start all over again. I'd spend all night feasting on this pretty pussy, letting you come all over my tongue, swallowing you down over and over again."

"Holy. Shit. Liam! I'm gonna come. Fuck. Fuck!"

"That's my girl, come for me. Let me see you fall apart. Picture my face buried in your pussy, my tongue flicking your sensitive little clit, baby. Fuck, Hannah. Come, right now."

It starts deep in my belly, a fire rising like an inferno before it combusts, spreading rapidly through my entire body. My legs shake, and just as I'm about to scream, my moans are muffled by Liam's mouth on mine. Wave after wave of pleasure burns through me as he fucks my mouth with his tongue. I moan into him, his lips moving against mine as our tongues tangle and caress, licking into each other in a desperate attempt to be closer. It prolongs my orgasm, the waves of pleasure continuing to pulse through me until it becomes too much.

He breaks the kiss, eyes heavily lidded, and rests his forehead against mine as I struggle to pull air into my lungs. So much longing is etched into the strong features of his face, but it's the dark mischievous challenge that has me sobering, anticipating what he's thinking.

"Again, beauty. Give me another one."

My internal clock never letting me down, I wake up before the sun, knowing that I need to get moving so that I can get started at Bean Haven. But, instead of jumping out of bed, eager to get to the bakery, I'm enveloped in a heavy warmth that I don't want to leave the safety and comfort of.

The first thing I register is the heat emanating from his large body, his front flush against my back, the slow rise and fall of his chest a soothing rhythm. His heavy arm wraps across my middle, palm splayed over my belly in a way that is both cherishing and possessive. His scent is all around me, clean linen, but also his signature woodsy oak and sweet sugar. He cocoons me like there's no place in the world he'd rather be, and at this moment, I agree. Right now, the world outside doesn't exist—our problems out of sight and mind, the weight of our decisions lifted—right now, nothing else matters except the feeling of being tucked up into him. I want to stay hidden away from all the demands of everything but this.

For a brief moment, I let my brain rest and enjoy what my heart wants. The world outside might be calling, but in this moment, I don't care. His fingers tighten around me, pulling me in just a little closer, my heart flipping over again my chest. His thick thigh is threaded through mine, lifted high so that I'm practically sitting on it. The warm pressure at my core feels so damn good. My mind drifts to last night, as Liam coached me through multiple orgasms until my body was mush. His restraint didn't snap, but it was close. He was unhinged for me, and somehow, without even touching me, Liam has managed to erase every experience that came before him.

I've never felt so desired, so desperately wanted, and it's a feeling that all of me wants to continue to chase. Liam nuzzles his face into the back of my neck, his breath warm and sending goosebumps across my body. I know I'll have to get up and face the day, but for now, I rock back slightly on his thigh, just to scoot as close as I possibly can when I feel the unmistaken hard rod against my ass. Fuck, that definitely feels good.

I allow myself to tentatively move backward again, rubbing against the stiff cock wedged against me, when he doesn't seem to stir away, I do it again, loving the feeling, and wondering if he's just always hard when he wakes up or if my ass firmly planted in his crotch has something to do with it. I know I shouldn't, but my body is on fire, his body surrounds me, all firm and practically naked except his boxer briefs. Only the thin fabric of our underwear separates us now.

It's been so long since I've been touched, and everything Liam and I have been doing, with him watching me, has only stoked the fire. I need more. I need to be consumed by someone other than my own hand. And whether I want to admit it or not, I want Liam. I've never felt this way before and it's so confusing. But the way I feel when he's with me, that's real. Whether I'm desperate for the attention and affection or not, I've never felt so wanted physically, and it gives an added layer of bewilderment. I want him, but I know I shouldn't.

Liam's arms tighten around me, and I close my eyes, completely content, and let myself wonder what it would be like to wake up like this every day, with Liam holding me close. Everything in me screams *yes,* to lean into this bizarre arrangement, but the smart, realist part, is giving me a hard bitch slap to wake up and not jeopardize this relationship for all of our sakes.

But I've always trusted Liam, and he wouldn't lie to me or do anything to hurt Charlie. If he says something, he means it.

So maybe I need to just go with the flow, knowing he'll protect all of us from burning to the ground. My brain just won't fully commit yet, the fear of hurting our loved ones and Charlotte, or even us, too great to be one hundred percent in.

I sigh louder than I realize, Liam stirring behind me again.

"Mmm. It's Sunday, do you have to leave?"

"Yes, dummy. I run the only coffee shop in Aspen Ridge, I think people would riot if it was closed again. Owen threatened to arrest me if it happened again.

"I'll kill him."

I smack his arm. "Don't joke about killing people. I love being there and you know it. What do you have going on today?"

"I'm going to wait for Charlie to wake up, take her ice skating this morning at the high school, and then come help you the rest of the day."

I sit upright, his arm falling from my stomach to my thighs, his hand not missing a beat and flexing around one of them.

"You don't want me to take her with me?"

"And have her be grumpy later? No, thank you. We'll have fun, and we'll see you before lunch."

"I don't deserve you, Liam Hayes."

"You've got it all wrong, beauty. You deserve everything."

Chapter Seventeen

Liam

Today I'm marrying my best friend of the last twenty-three years, who I've secretly been in love with for a long-ass time. Today I make her mine in every way that matters. I just wish she was doing this for love and not convenience. I want Hannah's love. Period.

With Bean Haven closed at its normal business hours—per Hannah's demand—Charlie with Hannah's sister Hailey, and us lying out the ass about where we are headed, I drive us into Clallam County for our appointment to get married. I hold her hand tightly in mine, resting on her thigh, as I keep my other hand on the wheel of my truck. I keep checking on her out of the corner of my eye, her dejected demeanor filling me with nerves, overshadowing how excited I am to make Hannah my wife.

A long, cream-colored, bohemian style dress that's covered in a gorgeous, patterned lace, with a tie at her waist drapes perfectly over her body. I'm still speechless when I look at her. She wore her hair half up and loosely curled in large waves. She's always gorgeous, but today she really stands out. I want to convince her to allow me to take a photo because I want to remember her like this forever. I want us to have one piece of today to look back on, I just hope she doesn't regret it. Needing to hear it again, I ask for reassurance.

"Are you sure about this?"

"Yes." I don't sense any hesitation or worry in her tone, which surprises me.

"And you're sure you don't want a wedding? Or Charlie there?"

"I don't want to hurt anyone more than they already will be, bear. They don't deserve it."

When is she going to learn? I press on the brakes harder than I should, jerking us forward, and pull over to the side of the road.

"What are you doing?"

Unbuckling my seatbelt, I lean over and place my hand around the back of her neck, pulling her toward the center.

"No one is getting hurt, because this isn't going to end badly, Hannah. I'll keep saying it until you understand. I will never let anything come between us or hurt Charlie. You two are my priority. Nothing else. Get out of your head and start taking control. What do you want?"

"I don—"

"What do you want, Hannah? Don't think."

"Love."

A soft, small chuckle puffs from my lips as I smile at her. Easiest fucking thing she could ever ask for.

"What else?"

"A family."

"Done, beauty. We are a family. Whether you marry me or not we're a family. Now, are we getting married today?"

Her gorgeous bright brown eyes turn glassy as they fill with unshed tears. She gives me a sad, hopeful smile but tells me exactly what I was hoping for.

"Yes."

"Good. Now get out of your head, and let's do this."

By the time we pull into the courthouse parking lot, the air in the truck is thick with nervous energy, but Hannah's mood isn't as sour, my little pep talk having given her the kick in the ass she needs. Now, it's me who's freaking out.

I'm about to make Hannah Haven *my wife*.

She reaches for my hand on her own, squeezing it lightly, and together we walk into the building. My heart pounds in my chest like a jackhammer, a hard, quick rhythm slamming into my ribcage. This isn't how I imagined marrying Hannah would go, not even close.

Having already applied for our marriage license, we pick it up and wait our turn to meet with the officiant. The hallway reeks of wood polish and dirty mop water as we sit together and let our nerves consume us. The two together create a great fucking ambiance for a wedding. We're quiet, unable to get out of our own heads long enough to say anything. Our hands stay clasped around each other in a silent comfort that we both need.

The next thirty minutes happen in a blur. We're taken into a room where two clerks stand as our witnesses since we didn't have any to bring with us. The judge talks to us briefly before starting the ceremony, even cracking a joke that we both look like we're heading in for colonoscopies instead of marriage. Hannah stands in front of me in her pretty dress, her little hands dwarfed in mine, our eyes focused on each other as the rest of the world melts away.

This is what you want. This is what she needs. I repeat the words in my head like a mantra, but the truth keeps slipping through the cracks, trying to choke me with its weight. I don't just want to be married to Hannah out of convenience. I want her to marry me because I'm end game for her. I'm already the one she turns to when everything falls apart, the one who always has her back no matter what, the one who loves her without expectations or judgment, the one who wants to wake up beside her every morning and go to sleep next to her every night. But she hasn't seen it yet. *I'm right here, baby.*

Hannah looks at me with calm, relaxed features, and my pulse spikes. She's always had this way of making everything around her seem lighter and brighter, even when the world is crashing down. But right now, I see the weight of the decision we're making in the slight slump of her shoulders, in her tired eyes, and in how she's working hard to stay centered and calm. I can't even do anything to help while I spiral out of control myself.

This marriage isn't about love for her, I know she's here and why she's doing this, fuck, I pushed her into thinking it was the best thing for her right now. But, now that we're here, now that we're about to commit ourselves to each other, I wish the reasons were different. Just as I'm about to tell her we'll find another way, Hannah squeezes my hands, forcing my attention back on her.

"You and me," she mouths, giving me the smile that I love so much.

"You and me."

Back at Hannah's apartment, she tucks Charlie into bed as I glance down at the signed paper in my hand, the legal document that binds me to her in the way I've always wanted but could never pursue. A document that I'd never imagined I'd have because I couldn't imagine a married life with anyone but her.

Hannah's my wife.

My mind is heavy, processing how this is going to work, how I'm going to make her see me as more than her best friend. Really see me, not as her savior, because fuck, Hannah doesn't need saving. But see me as the man she's been searching for all along. The one she can lean on, the one she can finally let herself love. The man who's been in front of her all along. I want to give her all of my love and get that in return.

After pouring a glass of whiskey and walking into the bedroom, I loosen my tie so that it hangs open around my neck, unbuttoning the first few buttons on my dress shirt as I take a seat in the chair that sits in the corner of her room.

Relaxing back into the chair, I sip my drink, replaying the events of the afternoon. The reality of what's happened crashing down on me.

Hannah's my *wife.*

"I, Hannah, take you, Liam, to be my husband, to have and to hold from this day forward, for better, for worse, for richer, for poorer, in sickness and in health, to love and to cherish, till death us do part."

"I, Liam, take you, Hannah, to be my wife, to have and to hold from this day forward, for better, for worse, for richer, for poorer, in sickness and in health, to love and to cherish, till death us do part."

"Do you, Hannah, take Liam to be your lawfully wedded husband?"

"I do."

"Do you, Liam, take Hannah to be your lawfully wedded wife?"

"I do."

"By the power vested in me by the state of Washington, I now pronounce you husband and wife. You may kiss the bride."

Hannah walks into the bedroom and slowly shuts the door until it clicks closed, pulling me from the visions of earlier as she took her vows to tether herself to me. I look at her over the rim of my glass, the amber liquid nearly drained. I stare at the woman I've looked at millions of times, and feel desperate to give everything to her. Desperate for her to see me and make this real.

"I want you, beauty, all of you," I say the words out loud, my voice unrecognizable as my desire for her takes over.

She sits down on the edge of the bed, the large *Hellraiser* T-shirt she's wearing riding up her thigh. She bites the tip of her thumb while she thinks things through, but I know she wants me. I feel the way her body melts into mine when I hold her close, the way she shivers in my arms when I kiss her, and she comes out of it lust-drunk and in a haze, the way she comes just from me talking to her. Maybe this is how we connect.

"Tell me how you like to be touched, *wife*. Tell me how to make you feel good."

Her breath picks up as her eyes shutter closed for a brief moment. I expect her to say no. I expect her to give me a million reasons why this is a bad idea and why we can't cross this line. But she doesn't do any of that.

"I don't even know. I'm not really experienced. It's been so long since I've actually been with someone, and no one's ever taken their time with me before, so I just don't know . . ." Her words are barely above a whisper as she confesses what I already knew.

"Baby. *I* want to take my time with you. Don't make me beg, because I will. I want to learn how to give you what you like, what you want, what you need."

Her breath hitches, eyes lighting up quickly before her face transforms right before me. Oh, fuck. I can work with this. She wants touch but doesn't want to ask for it? Well, I will.

"You like that idea."

"I don't—"

"You do. You're flushed, your breathing is unsteady. I know everything about you, beauty. Let me learn your body, too."

"Liam . . ."

Moving from the chair, I bend slowly to my knees, keeping my focus on her, watching as her eyes get heavy and she struggles to get air into her lungs. Fuck, yes. I'll take this. Anything for this woman.

"Let me touch my wife." I lean down on all fours, taking a hesitant step forward. "*Please.*"

That does it. Her shoulders sag, her thighs rubbing together slightly, and I know I've got her.

"Liam . . . yes."

I've been prepared to beg for this woman for years, and I'll happily do it now. I slowly crawl across the floor, our eyes never leaving each other's, giving me a front-row view as she spirals with lust. I reach her legs, Hannah's eyes heavy with desire and arousal, until I'm sitting in front of her, waiting.

She holds my eyes hostage as she lifts her leg and presses her bare foot against my pec. Turning my head, I brush my nose across the inside of her ankle, her silky skin so damn soft at the delicate little spot. Goosebumps scatter across her body and I hum my approval. I wonder how responsive she'll be to other touches.

"Please, baby. Tell me what you want. Tell me what I can give you. I *need* to touch you."

"Kiss me, Liam. I want you to kiss me."

Grabbing her foot in my hand, I lift it off of my chest, placing a chaste kiss to the arch before moving my way up, peppering slow kisses, my lips brushing across her silky skin. I kiss the inside of her knee before inching forward and hooking her leg over my shoulder. I've never wanted anything more in my life than her. Just as my hands stroke the outside of her thighs, inching under the large T-shirt she has on, she stops me, putting her hands over mine and holding them back.

"Baby, *please*. Put me out of my misery already. Let me have you."

"What do you want, Liam? Tell me." Her words are breathy, a plea on a desperate moan that makes my dick throb hard in my pants.

"You. *All of you*. I want to taste you. I want to lick your pussy until you're a mess, I want you to flood my mouth with your cum, I want to make your legs shake and hear you moan my name. Let me make you feel good. *Please*."

"Mother above, so help me. Liam, when you talk like this . . ."

My heart is racing so fast behind my ribcage, you'd think I was going a few rounds in the ring with Sawyer. But I'm just fucking desperate to touch her, even more so hearing how no one has ever taken their time to learn what makes her body feel good. I want to be the one to change that for her.

"Let me touch you the way a husband touches his wife."

"Holy shit." Her eyes close and my heart stops, but then she begins nodding her head. "Yes. Yes."

Before the last syllable is released from her mouth I'm moving. My hands finally roam up the length of her thighs, pushing her T-shirt up as I go, and exposing her panty-clad pussy to me. The black lacy material barely covers her and my mouth waters at the sight. Leaning forward, I run my nose up the length of her seam, breathing in deeply as I go. She smells so fucking good—so sweet, so *her*.

I nuzzle my nose deeper, loving that her arousal is leaking through the thin fabric of her panties just from the anticipation alone. Sitting up straight, I hook my fingers through the scrap of material at her hips and begin dragging them down her legs. She lifts up, allowing me to peel them completely from her body with trembling hands. After freeing her, her legs fall open for me and I don't hesitate to run two of my fingers through her center, finding out just how wet she truly is.

"Is this all for me? You're already making such a mess, and I haven't even kissed you yet."

"Liam, please. Don't make me wait anymore."

"Now who's begging?"

"I don't care. I need you."

"Anything for you. I'll always give you everything you need."

My eyes flash quickly to hers, taking in the desperate, needy look on her face. Leaning back in, I inhale deeply again, taking all of her into my lungs, never wanting to breathe anything else in for as long as I live.

When I finally give in to our needs, I use my thumbs to spread her lips wide open for me and take a moment to admire her glistening pussy as she squirms. With her spread open, I get a perfect view and my dick throbs violently, leaking precum from the tip into my pants.

"Fuck." My voice is a breathy whisper. "You're so soft, so fucking pretty. I bet you taste as good as you smell."

Dipping my head down, I run my tongue along the entrance of her pussy, pushing inside the tight channel. I moan into her, loving her sweet, musky taste as it explodes on my tongue, and I nearly fucking lose it right there. Licking her cum from the vibrator has nothing on getting it straight from the source.

"Mmm. So fucking good, beauty. I've been thinking about doing this since I licked your vibrator clean." *And much, much longer.*

Her hips buck and she lets out a breathy moan that goes straight to my cock. Flattening my tongue, I lick up her center, easily finding her clit and flicking it several times with the tip before moving back down and repeating the process. She tastes so fucking good. I can't believe I'm here after wanting this for so long.

Grabbing her hips, I jerk her closer to me, lifting her ass slightly to hold her to my face while I devour her sweet pussy. Her hips start to move of their own accord, her moans getting louder, her legs straining on my shoulders as they tremble. Goddamn, I love making her lose control like this, but we need to keep it down if this is going to continue. And I have plans to continue all fucking night.

"Baby, your noises are wrecking me, but you need to stay quiet, grab a pillow."

Her hands reach down, sliding through my hair instead and pulling my mouth harder onto her. My nose presses against the short strip of pubic hair she keeps, my tongue lashing against that swollen nub that's making her go wild.

"Holy shit, Liam, ohmygod! Make me come. Make me come! I can't take it anymore, please. Nothing has ever felt so good."

Because you hadn't been with me until now. I suck her clit into my mouth and pulse with little sucks as I plunge two fingers into her tight little pussy, feeling her walls around me for the first time ever. She's so damn warm, and my cock leaks at the thought of pressing into her tight heat.

"Fuck, you're tight, beauty. Your pussy is gripping me." My

fingers pump a few times before pushing in deep and motioning in a come-hither motion toward her navel. Based on the way her body spasms, I'd say she likes it. Her breath hitches, her moans getting louder and louder, even as she tries to muffle them.

"Come for me, *wife*. Let me finally feel you let go."

As if her body was waiting, she falls apart, her clit swelling, throbbing against my tongue, her pussy walls clenching around my fingers, sucking them in like it needs to be filled. Fuck do I want to pump my cock inside her, feel those walls stretch around my cock while I fill her with my cum. The image and the feel of her like this makes me groan into her pussy, jerking her body impossibly close by her hips, nearly suffocating myself as I bury my face into her, wanting to consume her.

I continue to rut against the edge of the bed, her orgasm flooding my mouth with her essence. I drink up all of it, swallowing her down and loving the sweet taste of her cum. My hips move, rubbing my stiff cock against the mattress until I'm coming, filling my briefs with a load that just won't end. I moan unfiltered and unrestrained into her pussy, licking her sweet, silky flesh through both of our orgasms.

"God damn baby, I'm addicted to your pussy."

"Good thing you married me."

A deep, primal growl leaves me. I stand and Hannah's eyes go wide when she takes in the outline of my still-hard cock through the thin material of my dress pants, a visible wet spot from where I came leaking through the khaki fabric.

"Did you . . . ?" she nearly pants as she points to the spot.

"Come from eating you out? Yeah. I did. Don't think that that means I'm done with you. That just gave me a little relief. Now, do I need to beg my wife to let me fuck her?"

Chapter Eighteen
Hannah

Liam undresses slowly, inch by inch, giving me pieces of his perfect, athletically built body. His wide shoulders are rounded at the top, leading to thick muscled biceps that forever look like he's flexing, his chest is chiseled, a light dusting of chest hair leading to washboard abs that I want to trace with my tongue. His shirt floats to the floor along with his tie as I lean back on my elbows and let myself take all of him in for the first time.

Liam hooks his thumbs into his pants, pulling the stretchy fabric over his massive cock, and letting them drop to the floor before stepping free of them—briefs in tow. My eyes are focused on his dick—long and thick, with a throbbing vein running up the length of the underside leading to an engorged, deep-red mushroom head. I figured he was packing, but seeing it face-to-face makes him seem otherworldly. He's massive. At least, he is to me, based on the limited experience that I've had with dicks in the past.

I've never had the desire to give a blow job before, but right now? That's all I want to do as I stare at him. I want to pull him to the back of my throat and make him feel as good as he just made me. His muscles ripple and flex as he grasps his big dick with his hand, his fist wrapping around the thick length and sliding upward to the bead of precum leaking from the tip. Holy shit, he is so hot.

All reservations about this have gone out the fucking window. I want him. Badly. Seeing him crawl on his hands and knees, hearing him beg, I could have orgasmed without him touching me at all. But his mouth? I've never experienced something so life-altering. Liam feasted on me like he would die without it, as if giving me pleasure was as much for him as it was about me. Which was proven by the fact that he came from going down on me alone.

This man, who's been by my side since I was three, has just obliterated everything I thought I wanted and needed. And he's been in front of me this entire time. My heart falls hard, and instantly, like blinders being removed, all I see is him.

"I know you want this, Hannah. Let me take care of you and make you feel good. Let me show you how good it can be when a man wants to take care of what's his." I hear his words through the rushing of my blood in my ears as I still work to come down from a life-altering orgasm and my brain attempts to catch up with my heart. But is he just lonely, too? Is this all because I'm readily available? I shake my head of the self-sabotaging thoughts and decide to just be in the now. Fuck it. If Liam wants to make me feel good, he can. His touch is *everything*.

Chapter Nineteen

Liam

"So, do I have to beg?"

She shakes her head as I stroke my cock in my hand, her legs still spread out in front of me, the sheets below her visibly wet. Stepping between her legs, I press two fingers in as deep as they can go, watching them slowly disappear inside her wet heat, while using my thumb to stroke her clit. Her hips nearly buck off the bed when an idea hits me.

"Have you ever squirted before?"

"No . . ." Her words are breathless as she arches into my hand.

"Good. Let's see what this pretty pussy can do."

I push two fingers in deep, curving upward toward her belly, circling her clit meticulously with my thumb. Releasing my straining dick, I press down on her lower abdomen, holding her down on the bed as I work her over.

"Oh, fuck, Liam!"

"That's it. Let me have it, Hannah. Pinch your nipples for me and just relax."

She listens, sitting up enough to pull her shirt over her

head, hands squeezing and kneading her perky breasts—that I've yet to give attention to, an issue I'll be remedying soon—tweaking and twisting her small rosebud nipples, pulling on those sexy as hell barbells as moans flow freely and softly from her lips. She sounds so fucking good, and I can't wait for her to feel this.

Hannah looks unbelievably sexy laid out in front of me, completely naked, legs spread open, my fingers pressing into her dripping pussy, her gorgeous lavender-colored hair splayed out on the bed. I use my fingers to fuck her, pulling out slowly before pushing in hard, curling and moving them against that spot deep inside her, all while rubbing that swollen little sensitive nub with firm pressure. Her legs begin to shake uncontrollably as she lets go of her breasts to grip the sheets on either side of her.

She's close.

"You're gonna be a good wife and squirt for me," I urge as her pussy walls start to flutter and clench around my fingers. I keep working her over, swirling my thumb over that sensitive little clit as her orgasm climbs, and I feel the moment she's about to combust.

"Bear down for me, baby."

Her back arches off the fucking bed as I press down on her lower abdomen, holding her in place as the orgasm pummels through her, her pussy squirting as she comes, liquid pulsing out of her as I pull my fingers back. It's the most erotic, thrilling thing I've ever fucking seen. The way her body did exactly what I wanted pleases me to no goddamn end.

I push my fingers in deep and replace my thumb with my mouth, sucking her clit with little pulses, prolonging her orgasm. She continues to squirt a few more times, flooding my mouth and face. It's the hottest thing I've ever experienced, and I'm already thinking about getting her to do it around my dick.

"Oh, fuck, Liam! That's—" Her next words are garbled as she covers her mouth with her hand to muffle her moans. I lick her languidly, pulling my fingers from her body and enjoying tasting her, lapping at her sweet, sensitive skin, and reveling in the feel of her on my tongue. I kiss her everywhere, licking at her lips, tracing every curve of her pussy with my tongue. When the sensitivity becomes too much, she wiggles free and I let her go, knowing that at any point she could freak out and put an end to this.

"So fucking good, Hannah. You just made a mess of me, baby. Fuck, I love it."

Crawling on top, I lift her by her lower back, scooting us onto the center of the bed and letting my body weight drape over her.

"Are you okay with this? We don't have to keep going."

"I've never been more okay. Please don't stop." Her body writhes underneath me, the head of my cock slipping through her folds and nudging her overly sensitive clit. Her hands roam my back, and feeling her soft skin on me, her touch, is everything.

"Fuck, Hannah baby, you feel incredible."

She rocks into me, my dick sliding smoothly as it gets covered in her arousal, working her back up slowly. My right hand cups her head, the other roaming down her side, grabbing her thigh and hiking it up to spread her wider.

"Kiss me, Liam."

"Anything you want, baby," I whisper against her lips.

My mouth descends on hers, our muffled moans filling the room as we consume each other, kissing like we need the other to breathe. We find a steady rhythm, not breaking contact as we rock together while kissing each other senseless. Her body arches into me as she rubs her hands everywhere she can reach, running them over my shoulders, grasping me, and pulling me closer.

"Liam . . ."

"Tell me what you want," I whisper into her ear, dropping open-mouthed kisses just below it. Her sweet little moans after each kiss fuel me, and I respond by pulling back slightly to look at her pretty face, nipping at her bottom lip and pulling it between my teeth. The sounds I'm pulling from her go straight to my dick, which is currently leaking like a motherfucker all over her wet pussy.

Hannah lifts her hips, grinding up and down across my hard length. I let her use me how she wants, releasing her mouth and peppering her neck with kisses, licks, and nips. I reach one hand up her side until I cup her perfect breast in my palm, rubbing and twisting her hard nipple between my fingers.

"Liam . . . I need . . ."

"I know, baby, me too. But you gotta tell me. Tell me exactly what you want. Take what's yours." *What's always been yours.*

She continues to writhe under me, releasing desperate little mewls as she claws at my back while I kiss down the length of her neck, sucking on the bit of skin where her shoulder starts.

"Fuck me, Liam. I want you inside me."

"Yes, baby."

I don't hesitate to give her what she needs, pulling my hips back and lining up my weeping fucking cock with her slick center. I push through her smooth, tight core for the first time and groan loudly as I take her mouth with mine again to muffle our noises as I slowly work to fill her. She feels like heaven, like everything in my life has led me to this very point right here with her. This woman had better get on board and fall in love with me because there's no way I'm ever letting her go. Not after this.

Chapter Twenty

Hannah

Every single part of my body is lit up like a live wire as Liam holds my head in one of his large, calloused palms, his other hand wrapped around my thigh, holding it up around his waist as he works himself inside me. Despite being drenched and my body primed, I can't help but wince as he wedges himself in.

"Baby, fuck, you're so tight, relax for me." His words are like a balm, coating me in so much affection that I instantly melt for him.

"That's it, my girl. Hell, you feel so damn perfect. You're taking me so well, Hannah." He talks me through it as he finally fills me to his hilt, my body stretched to its max to accommodate his size.

"Jesus Christ, beauty, you're so damn perfect. You did so good, baby. Look at you taking all of me."

"I don't want to inflate your ego, but you're fucking huge, I feel like you're ripping me open."

He laughs and I smile at him in return. I can't believe Liam's inside me. Everything about tonight has been surreal.

I've never been made to feel so good, never felt so wanted. His touch is everything, filling an emptiness deep inside me that I've been desperate for, that I've longed for.

My hands run aimlessly over his body, feeling every outline, every ridge, his large muscles taut and flexed as he starts to move within me, pulling out to his tip before slowly thrusting back in. Reaching for the back of his neck, I pull his lips down to meet mine in a searing kiss. Kissing Liam is all-consuming. I feel his want for me from the tip of my toes to the top of my head, and I never want it to end. He kisses me like he's been waiting for it his entire life.

Breaking the kiss before I'm ready to, he lifts up on his hands, hovering his upper body above mine while he thrusts into me. I drag my fingertips across his collarbone and down his chest when I notice something on him that has my heart beating in overdrive.

"Liam?" My voice cracks, emotion overflowing as I struggle to come to terms with what I'm looking at and wondering how I never noticed it before. But it's not like I've ever inspected his body or see him regularly without a shirt on.

"Beauty . . ."

His body stiffens as my fingers trail over the spot of skin at the very top of his ribs. Tattooed in very small script are the names Hannah & Charlotte. He doesn't give me time to think or process, but the knowledge is enough to make my heart beat wildly in my chest. He flips us over, staying seated deep inside me so that he's on his back and I'm straddling his waist. This position is so much deeper, my wince turning into a moan as he presses up from below me.

"Ride me, wife. I want you to take what you need."

For fuck's sake, there is something so delicious every time he calls me his wife that just makes me feel feral and wanton.

"I've never been on top before. I don't know what to do."

"Do whatever feels good, find it, chase your pleasure."

His hands on my hips guide me, rocking me back and forth and dragging my clit against his pelvis, rolling my hips and finding what lights me up on the inside.

"That's it, baby. Use my cock to make yourself feel good," he coaches, his voice deep and husky as his words coat me in burning heat and give me the confidence to do what he says. "Fuck, yes, Hannah, just like that."

I lean forward, pressing my hands flat on his muscular pecs, and begin lifting my hips, impaling myself on his rock-solid dick. Every nerve in my body is stimulated, the pressure rising and rising.

"Liam, I'm gonna come. Holy shit."

"Fuck, yes, Hannah, give it to me. Come all over my dick, baby."

The orgasm races through my nerves as Liam thrusts his hips up from under me, his hands holding my hips in a brutal grasp that I'll surely feel tomorrow.

"Oh, fuck, Han, yes, baby. You're squeezing me so tight. Shit. Shit."

His thrusts become jerky and then he's pulling me off of him, his cock sliding up between us and jerking. I watch as cum spurts from his engorged wet tip, covering both of us in his sticky, white release.

As soon as he finishes, he pulls me down on top of him, my body collapsing willingly, my head tucking under his chin as we both work to calm down and steady our breathing.

"Why did you pull out?" I ask after a few moments of quiet, only the sound of his steady heartbeat filling my ears.

"Because we haven't had a conversation about babies, and even though I know you have the implant, I'm not about to take any chances and force anything on you."

My body softens at his declaration. Liam is always putting my well-being above everything else, and even while deep in the throes of pleasure, he was still able to have enough control to not potentially cause me harm. I rest my head against his hard chest, listening to the steady rise and fall of his breathing and his strong heartbeat and I know without a doubt that I won't be able to walk away from this unscathed. I'm rapidly falling in love with my best friend.

Liam's hands rub up and down my back in comforting caresses, his body fully relaxed like he has no intention of moving from this spot any time soon, even as his release currently coats both of our abdomens.

"How are you feeling?"

How do I even answer that question? *Alive.*

"I've never experienced anything like that before," I whisper. "I'm perfect. I'm kind of at a loss for words. Is it weird for you?"

"Weird?" He chuckles. "No, beauty. That was the best sex of my life."

I squeeze my eyes closed, thankful that he can't see my face because he would read me like a book.

"Mine too. I didn't know it could be like that."

"When it's the right person, I think it's always like that."

When I don't say anything, he speaks again, his voice a whisper, "Even if I'm not it for you, beauty, at least I gave you something, so you know your worth. Don't you dare ever settle again. If your man doesn't make you feel wanted, then walk away until one does."

I nod my head, keeping my first thought to myself to hold on to. *But, what if you are the one?*

"Why are you so glowy?"

"I don't know what you're talking about. It's warm in here."

"Oh my fucking god. No you didn't. You fucked him, didn't you?"

I whip my head in the direction of my sister. She has the nose of a freaking bloodhound. She can sniff out bullshit quicker than anyone I've ever met. It's honestly annoying. Goddamn Scorpios.

"Piss off, Hailey. I've got work to do."

"Hannah, I thought this whole thing was bogus because Mom is a controlling dink hole?"

Needing to talk to someone—who wasn't Liam—about everything, I confided in my little sister, knowing she wouldn't hurt me by telling anyone else. Harlow is the one we have to worry about. She'd do anything to be in our mom's good graces. Including burying me alive or pushing me in front of an oncoming bullet train.

"It is bogus but we kinda did a thing yesterday . . ."

"He boned you. It's written all over your face."

"We got married."

"Well, holy shit, Hannah Jade. I didn't think you had it in you. I should have known better. Fake marriage, this is about to get interesting!"

"What do you mean fake marriage?" My hand jerks the buttermilk that I'm currently pouring into the mixer, splashing the rim and spilling everywhere. Setting it on the counter with shaky hands, I turn and face Harlow, standing at the entrance to the kitchen with her arms crossed. Fuck my life. "I fucking knew it, you filthy liar. All that shit about it being twenty years in the making, huh? Making me feel like shit for calling out your bullshit?"

"Lo, listen, you don't know what you're saying, and you don't know what conversation you just walked in on," Hailey says, trying to defuse the rapidly intensifying situation. I glance at my industrial-size mixer, and wonder if I chopped her up in small enough pieces, if I could mix her into batter and bake her into muffins to dispose of the evidence. Seems like my only option because her blabbing this information sure as fuck isn't.

"You gonna talk, Hannah? Or stand there mute?"

"Mother above, give me strength," I mutter under my breath. "Mom gave me an ultimatum that I need to settle down, preferably with Levi, and if I don't, she'd sell Bean Haven out from under me as soon as Grandma passes away."

Harlow just looks at me stunned for a minute before she starts laughing. I look at Hailey who winces, and my heart sinks.

"This is amazing. Levi didn't want you, so you managed to convince your best friend to marry you? How fucking pathetic and washed up do you have to be?"

"The fuck did you just say to her, Lo?" Liam's voice echoes through the kitchen as he rounds the corner from the front of the café. Harlow whips her head in his direction, not even flinching, the little wench. "I asked you a question."

"You really married her to deceive my parents?"

"They were trying to force her into a marriage she would have been miserable in or move her and Charlie to California with them. Do you not realize what your sister has been through the last few years? And you're gonna judge her?"

"This is a family issue, Liam, so why don't you leave and let me talk with my sister who has clearly lost her mind."

"I am her goddamn family, Lo. Or did you not hear the part

where she's my wife?" Harlow's eyes squint into slits at him. "Yeah, you heard me correctly. I don't care if you're her sister or not, don't disrespect my wife again. Now, are we going to have a problem with you running your mouth?"

"Our parents have a right to know."

"And it literally doesn't affect you, Harlow. Mind your own damn business. You couldn't give one single shit about what happens to Bean Haven, and it sounds like you just don't want your sister to be happy. So if you plan on being in our life, in your niece's life, you'll keep your mouth shut about this."

"Are you threatening me, Liam?"

"I wouldn't threaten you. I'm promising you. You fuck with Hannah, you're fucking with me, and I'm not going allow people in our lives who want to see us crash and burn."

Harlow storms out of the kitchen while I stand there frozen to the spot, staring at Liam like he's grown horns. Hailey winks at me and pats Liam on the shoulder like he did a job well done before following Harlow out the back.

Liam walks across the kitchen to get to me, his hands grabbing my face between his big palms and angling my head back to look up at him. His facial features are more relaxed than they were a moment ago, that part of him that he keeps locked up having receded.

"Are you okay?"

"I'm okay. I'm used to Harlow's bullshit. I hope she doesn't rat us out, I shouldn't have even told Hailey, but I just wanted to talk to her about everything going on in my head. Lo walked in and overheard us."

"Everything will be okay, don't stress over what she may or may not do. We'll deal with whatever happens together."

His confidence in every situation is reassuring but I know my sister, and I was just given one more thing to worry about.

"I trust you."

"Good." His lips press sweetly against my forehead. "Me and you?"

"Me and you."

Chapter Twenty-One

Liam

Arriving at Hannah's apartment, I let myself in, juggling the bag in my hand, so damn excited to surprise my girls. Hannah has been wanting to do this since their inaugural season, but we haven't been able to make it happen. Charlie's at the perfect age to enjoy it with us and I can't wait to see her face when we get there.

"Where are my girls at?" I yell through the kitchen. Charlie wastes no time barreling through the apartment to get to me. Hiding the bag behind my back, I drop down to my knees just in time to accept her hug, arms wrapping around my neck.

"I haven't seen you in two days, bear! Two! Where's Garbage? Aww, he's not here with you! Where is my puppy?"

"*Billy* is with Uncle Carter tonight, isn't he lucky?" She makes a face of disgust, and I can't help the laugh that bursts from me. She's not wrong.

"I promise, he loves Uncle Carter, and they have so much fun together, he loves to help out with him. Where's your momma?"

"She's folding laundry," she says, dramatically rolling her eyes into the back of her head.

"Where did you learn to do that?"

"Do what?"

"Roll your eyes. You're too young to be rolling your eyes at us, I'm not ready for it."

"Eliza does it after Ms. Katie tells us to stop chitchatting. It's funny!"

"Well, we're going to have to talk about that, okay? Let's go find your momma, I've got surprises!"

She gasps loudly, her hands flying to her mouth in excitement. "Surprises! I loooooove surprises!" Charlie turns and bolts from the kitchen yelling as she races. "Mumma! Bear's got surprises!"

I follow her into the living room, finding Hannah in nothing but an oversized *Carrie* T-shirt, her long legs on full display, covered only by the knee-high fluffy socks she has on. She meets my eyes, arching a brow as she watches me check her out. God, I'm obsessed with this woman.

"Surprises, huh?"

"Yep. But, I don't know, you seem like you're not really feeling surprises. Plus, you probably won't like this one. This one may just be for me and Charlie."

"Yeah, yeah. We'll see about that. Spill."

Setting the plain brown bag on the coffee table, I pull out both jerseys and quickly toss each one into their faces. Hannah gasps, grabbing it and holding it out in front of her, taking in the dark blue with the light blue S in the center. She turns it around, seeing the name of the Kraken goalie at the top and smiling so big.

Charlie looks at her matching one, and looks at me slightly confused, which is the cutest thing ever because what freshly turned four-year-old really wants a hockey jersey for a surprise?

"Thank you, bear! This is amazing. We'll wear them tonight while we watch them on TV. Want to stay up late tonight, munchkin?"

"Funny you should say that, beauty. We're not watching them on the TV tonight."

Her face lights up as she sucks in a quick breath of air, holding it in and waiting in anticipation.

"We're going to go watch them at Climate Pledge Arena!" I yell, throwing my hands in the air.

"Ohmygod!" Hannah screeches, jumping up and down, Charlie following suit.

"We're going to see them in person, bear?" Charlie asks.

"We are, and we need to hit the road, so go get changed, and wear a long-sleeved shirt under your jersey please because the arena is pretty cold, okay?"

Charlie jogs off to her bedroom and Hannah stands still, looking at me with an expression I can't read. Walking up to her, I trail the back of my fingers down the length of her bare arms, loving the scatter of goosebumps that follow my touch.

"Have you eaten?"

"Yes, I'm good, I promise."

"You excited, baby?"

"How did you manage this?"

"Crazy turn of events actually. The GM called me, looking for a specific rare year of our whiskey for a gift, and I hunted it down for him. To thank me, he offered me tickets. They arrived a few days ago, and it's been killing me to keep it from you. It was well worth it to see your reaction though."

"Don't you feel special, huh?"

"I do now. How about a kiss to show your husband thanks, huh?"

Her lips lift in a smile before she raises up on her tiptoes and kisses me. My hands find their home at her waist, holding her gently to me and letting her lead. She kisses me softly, just pressing her lips to mine, and I relish in the feel of her softness against me.

"Aww!"

Hannah pulls away from me, but I don't remove my hands from her waist. Waiting to see how Charlotte reacts.

"Aww? Don't most kids say eww?" I tease.

"Nope! I loooove it! You're sooooo cuuuuute! Now that you're kissing, can we move in with you, bear? Garbage wants me there, I know he misses me 'cause I can hear him crying, remember? And then we'd be able to sleep together every single night and then Mumma wouldn't be alone 'cause she's happy when you're here, bear, 'cause you're fun."

My face falls, knowing the weight those words will have on Hannah. She hasn't moved from my arms, her body relaxed, shoulders slumping forward slightly as she stares at her daughter. Instead of letting Hannah fumble, I release her and move toward Charlotte, bending down to my knees to talk on her level.

"I'm pretty cool, huh?"

"The best!"

"You know your momma is happy when she's alone, too, right?"

"Yep. But Evangeline said my mom must be sad 'cause she doesn't have a husband. Then she said I'm weird 'cause I don't have a dad. But I told her it's just me and my mom and we're besties and that sometimes we have bear and Garbage. But I want to live at your house and then we can have you and Garbage all the time and Evangeline won't call me names."

I sigh, my head falling forward for a moment, unsure how to proceed and explain things to her.

"Evangeline isn't being very kind and accepting of everyone, because every family looks different. Some kids only have one mommy, just like you." The words taste like ash on my tongue because, fuck, I've been an honorary dad to this girl since the day I pulled her from her mother. "Other kids have only a daddy, or two daddies, or two mommies, or they're raised by their grandparents and have no mom or dad at home. There are even families who have one parent at home, and the other parent is gone for a long time with the military, or with their job. Each one is okay and doesn't define you as long as you have love."

"Can I have two daddies?"

I look up at Hannah and raise my eyebrows at her in question, her hand flies up to cover the smile creeping up on her face and I have to stifle my laugh. I'd kill a fucker before I shared Hannah.

"Does what I'm saying make sense, munchkin?"

"Yep. It does. Evangeline should be nice 'cause it's okay that everyone is different."

"That's right. Are you happy?"

She bites her little lip and squints her face like she's deep in thought, my smile unrestrained as I watch her work through it. She's the cutest fucking thing ever created, and I'm obsessed with this kid.

"Yep. I'm happy. Buuuuuuut," she says, pointing her little finger at me, "I'd be happier if I could be with Garbage every day."

I laugh at her. "Noted. I'll take it up with the boss, sound good, munchkin?"

"Yep! Now, can we go to the hockey game? I want to see the goalie! Cause he's just like you!"

My heart swells with pride. I love these two so fucking much it hurts.

The arena hums with energy as Hannah, Charlotte, and I weave through the maze of people walking around. It's both of my girls' first big hockey game, and their contagious excitement buzzes through my body, even though I've been to more games than I can count. There's nothing in the world quite like your first NHL game, and now I get to experience it through their eyes, which is honestly better. The cold air bites, and I reach down to pull Charlotte's sweatshirt hood over her head. Her jersey is worn on the outside of it so she can rock our team proudly.

Getting in line for popcorn and sodas, I'm angsty, ready to find our seats and hear the familiar noise of the fans that will swallow you whole, the cracks of sticks, the skates cutting into the ice. It's an energy unlike anything else. Fuck, I miss playing but watching is such a good time.

After grabbing snacks, we head to find our seats, which is fairly easy when the GM gives you rinkside tickets—right next to the penalty box. Charlie takes in the enormous rink stretching out before us, her excitement written all over her sweet little face as she sees it all for the first time. Sure, I've been taking her to the high school rink since she could walk, determined for her to know how to skate, but this is different.

The Zamboni makes its slow passes around the ice, and she watches it with rapt attention while she munches on her popcorn. I take my seat between Hannah and Charlie, my hand moving to Hannah's thigh and squeezing to get her attention. The bright smile that I love so much fills her face, her cheeks pink, the gorgeous lavender of her hair reflecting the light and giving her a little halo. A knot forms in the center of my chest, aching, and I rub my fist against it. She's so goddamn beautiful, and I love this woman more than anything.

Leaning into her ear so she can hear me more easily, I whisper, "You miss watching me play?"

"You know I lived for those games, I think I only missed a few. Minus the ones you missed because of your suspension, those were pointless for me to go to."

"Worth it."

She gives me a little laugh, slapping my chest playfully. Grabbing her wrist, I bring her hand to my mouth, placing a kiss on the delicate skin on the inside of it. Threading my fingers through hers, I hold her hand with the back of mine resting on her thigh, my thumb rubbing back and forth slowly against her, giving her the touch I know she craves.

"This is seriously awesome. Thank you for bringing us, bear."

There's a sharp pinch in my chest when she uses that nickname, but it's slowly getting easier, especially after I know she'll moan out my name later when she's coming for me. I can be both for her. As long as we're together.

My phone buzzes in my pocket, and even though I don't want to, I take it out to check.

DALLAS:

How the fuck did you end up with Seattle tickets?

SAWYER:

Why are we looking at your ugly mug on the TV? RINKSIDE

CARTER:

Total bullshit

DALLAS:

You've got no room to complain. Weren't you the one invited to use the vacation home of some Washington elite asshole this coming summer?

SAWYER:

Yeah, fuck off, Casanova. Whose dick did you have to suck to get that shit?

CARTER:

Fuck off. Not my problem I'm personable and people actually like me over you growly fuckers

A laugh bursts from my lips, and I lean into Hannah to show her my phone.

"You didn't tell them? You're so bad."

"No way, they would have tried to make me take them. And then I'd have to choose between the three of them."

"Or they would have tied you down and gone just the three of them."

"Psh, not without one helluva fight. They'd be rolling in here with busted lips and shiners."

"So violent. Maybe that's what Lo and I need. A good brawl. I'd love to punch her in the nose one of these days."

"A little knockaround in a ring might do Harlow some good. And you," I tell her, bringing my attention back to my family chat.

ME:

Ya snooze ya lose, fuckers. GM called looking for a needle in a haystack and guess who found it for him?

SAWYER:

Those should have gone to the CEO

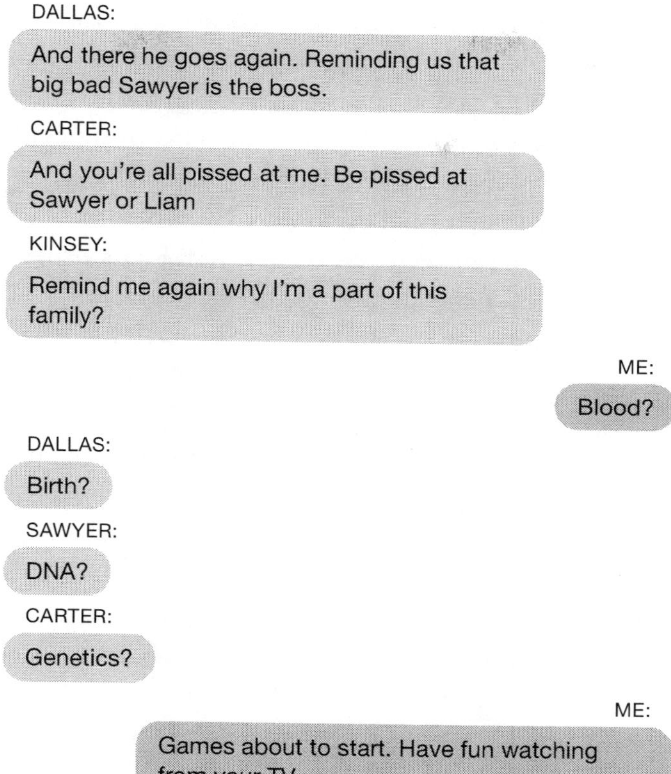

The massive scoreboard flashes above center ice, and the crowd goes wild as the players are introduced and enter the rink. Charlie sits up on her knees, cheering as the goalie takes his place in the crease. My heart swells some more knowing that she loves goalies because I used to play that position in high school and college.

The game starts and it's chaos from the moment the puck hits the ice, Seattle coming in hot, which pumps up the crowd, everyone cheering and yelling. Charlotte covers her ears when it gets overly loud, but after a little while, she opens up and screams at the players with the crowd right behind her. When a two-minute penalty for slashing is called on Boston, Charlotte screams, "Get in the box!" and I about die right in my seat. Hannah and I lose it, our laughter drowned out by the crowd's roars over receiving a power play so early on in the first period.

Any hockey game that I've watched prior to tonight has nothing on watching it with Charlotte. The game goes into double overtime, the three of us on the edge of our seats. This is where the goalies can really shine. We watch our player and hold our breath, Hannah and Charlotte repeating, "Don't blink, don't blink," over and over under their breath. One of the best Boston players takes the ice, and Hannah's hand squeezes mine tightly.

"He's got this," I reassure my girls. And thank fuck, the shot on goal is expertly deflected. The three rounds are quick, Boston getting one goal in, Seattle scoring two, delivering us the win on home ice. Charlotte bounds into my arms, squealing and screaming her excitement and joy, and I don't think I've ever been happier than right now.

I hold Charlotte, standing and cheering as our players line up to show thanks to the goalie, and catch Hannah watching me instead, a look of pure awe on her face. *C'mon, baby, see me. I'm it for you.*

Chapter Twenty-Two

Hannah

Liam carries Charlie into his house, laying her in the guest bedroom—a room that somehow has always been decorated for her—the dog jumping up and circling the middle of the bed where her still, small feet are currently under the blankets. She's out cold, all of the excitement of the night having drained her completely, passing out hard on the long drive back to Aspen Ridge. I gently kiss her forehead, following Liam out of the bedroom, pulling the door so it's only open a crack.

Liam grabs my hand, pulling me into his bedroom and shutting the door quietly behind us, flicking the lock. My heart starts thumping wildly in my chest, air getting harder and thicker to pull into my lungs, the tension in the room skyrocketing. He's on me a moment later, his hands grasping my face, the calloused skin of his palms feeling rough against my smooth skin. Liam angles my head exactly where he wants me, his eyes heavy as they roam my face. He looks at me like he's memorizing every single feature, committing them to memory, as if he hasn't looked at me nearly every day for the last twenty years.

"Tell me what you want, *wife*."

My heart gallops before nosediving into my stomach. Mother above, so help me, I want this man so badly.

"Kiss me, Liam."

I watch as his lips pull into a small smirk that is too damn sexy for his own good, chocolate brown eyes still dancing all over my face, desire thick between us. His thumbs caress back and forth against my jaw, making my chest rise and fall, my panties dampening—just from the anticipation.

Liam leans in, rubbing his lips over the shell of my ear, a ghost of a touch that travels down the length of my neck, igniting goosebumps in its wake. I start to shift on my feet, my hands reaching out and grabbing a fistful of his T-shirt at each side, gripping, pulling him closer.

He still doesn't give me what I want, his lips torturing me as they ghost over my sensitive skin. When his tongue traces the outline of my ear, his lips pulling the lobe into his mouth and gently sucking, I moan, my core clenching, wanting him so fucking bad.

"Take what you want, beauty. I'm yours." The words are spoken low, husky, his warm breath on my ear tickling and turning me on further.

I snap.

Pulling him closer to me, I lift on my toes, wrapping my arms around his neck and hauling his face to mine where I capture his lips. That's all he needed apparently, because Liam becomes just as feral as I am. In an instant, we're a mess of hands, mouths, and tongues as we claw at each other to rip clothes off, teeth clashing together as we race to get naked and not break the connection of our kiss for a moment.

Liam's body is a work of art, and I let my hands roam everywhere—his rounded shoulders, hard chest, toned abs. I work my way down, obsessed with his skin under my fingers, loving his reaction as he breaks out in goosebumps, his sharp intakes of air as I explore new parts of him. When his dick jumps between us, my hand tentatively grasps it, running over the silky smooth flesh that's desperate for me. Kneeling, I drag my hands over his hips and down his thighs, so ready to make him lose control like he's done to me.

"Baby," he breathes the word out roughly. "You don't have to . . ."

I look up at him from my knees, his strong body before me, and I know without a doubt, there is no "have to" anything with this man. This is a want and a need.

"You told me to take what I want. This is what I want," I tell him, sticking my tongue out and flicking his tip, licking across the slit and gathering the bead of precum there.

"Jesus Christ, anything for you," he gasps as his hands thread through my hair to hold the strands out of the way.

Grabbing his thick length with my hand, I jerk him from root to tip, loving the reaction I'm pulling from him. He moans, deep and low, and it sounds so damn hot. I never thought listening to a man's moans would be something that did it for me, but I had never been with Liam before.

I open as wide as I can, trying to relax my throat as I take him in as far back as possible, gagging slightly around the large intrusion.

"Oh, fuck, Hannah baby. That feels so good. Breathe through your nose, relax for me." His words fuel me, giving me the confidence I need to keep going, to make him feel as good as he makes me. I pull back up, using my fist to squeeze him while moving it up and down on his shaft to make up for all of him not fitting down my throat. My saliva works as lubrication, easing the way, my lips suctioning over his swollen head, tongue flicking around it.

"Fuck. Yeaaah. Just like that, Han."

His hips buck forward, his grip on my hair getting slightly

tighter. I love this. Love making him feel good, making him lose control. Popping off of his cock, I look up at him with swollen, wet lips, my voice slightly hoarse from him hitting the back of my throat. His thumb swipes at my tender lips, back and forth, smearing the moisture there around.

"I want you to come for me. I want to taste you."

A deep primal growl works its way up his chest and makes me even wetter.

"Jesus, Hannah. Yes, baby."

Liam guides my head back down, feeding his huge dick past my lips. I suck him down the best I can, continuing to use my hand to jerk him in time with my mouth. It's not long before his body tightens, thighs stiffening, his cock swelling on my tongue and in my hand.

"Hannah baby, I'm gonna come. Swallow me down, fuck. Fuck. Fuck."

He comes, and comes, and comes. And I love every single minute of it. I suck hard, trying to draw out every bit of pleasure for him, swallowing the mouthful of cum I'm rewarded with. I've never enjoyed giving a blowjob before, but this was incredible, and I can't wait to do it again.

Before I know what's happening, Liam has me lifted in his arms, gently settling me in the center of his king-size bed.

"Fuck, you were amazing. I can't even think straight. Shit, Hannah."

I melt under his praise, my heart pounding erratically in my chest, yearning for him, for more. Liam must understand because not a moment later, his large body is sprawled out on top of me, kissing the life out of me. I moan into his mouth, running my hands through the long hair at the top of his head, dragging my nails lightly over his scalp. He kisses my bruised lips until we're both panting, my hips grinding on him, dry humping him like a desperate teenager who doesn't know what she wants.

He releases my lips and I finally suck in a deep breath of air as Liam peppers open-mouthed kisses down my jaw, tracing the outline of my collarbone, grasping each of my breasts in his hands, his thumbs swiping over the cool metal of the barbells there.

"Your skin, beauty. You're so soft, so smooth, and perfect," he whispers as he continues to plant kisses and licks. "I'm addicted. Insatiable. I can't get enough. It's not enough, baby."

His mouth reaches my chest, lapping at my nipples gently before sucking each one into his mouth and gently tugging with his teeth. I look down at him and find his eyes on me, a smirk pulling at his lips as he repeats the motion.

"Mmm. Fuck, I like that my sweet little wife has these. I've never been able to play with them before, and now I'm fucking obsessed."

My eyes nearly roll to the back of my head. I've never been given so much attention, so much time. Everything he does makes me feel so good, so wanted. There's no way I'm going to come back from this.

Liam continues to kiss down my body, his tongue flicking and circling the barbell at the top of my navel, repeating what he did to my nipple piercings, my pussy a wet, dripping mess at this point. I'm desperate for him, wanting his talented mouth on me, my pussy clenching and empty. I squirm under his body as his tongue licks a line from hip to hip, his fingers threading through the short hairs of my pubic area.

"Say it, baby. Tell me what you want, how to make you feel good. Tell me what you need."

For fuck's sake, when this man talks to me like this, I'm putty.

"I want your mouth, Liam. Make me come."

Grabbing my hips, in a move that only Liam could do smoothly, he flips us, my legs forced to straddle his head. We're too far away from the headboard for me to brace myself, so I hover above him, my hands on my thighs as I look down at him, a devious smirk filling his face, mirth dancing behind those brown eyes.

"Be a good little wife and sit on my face."

Oh, fucking hell, he's going to kill me. How can he possibly get better than he already is?

"Anything for you," I reply with an equally devilish look on my face, throwing his words back at him and owning the pleasure he's teaching me to take. I drop myself slowly down onto his waiting mouth, his hips guiding me exactly where he wants me. The moment his warm tongue meets my wet center, I nearly combust. I'm so worked up from giving him head and all of the foreplay that I'm already so close. My clit throbs, swollen and ready for him to send me over that explosive ledge.

Liam manipulates my clit, flicking it and lapping like it's his last damn meal and all he wants to do is take his time with it. But I want to come. I start to rock my hips on him, giving myself more and more friction. He moans into my center, urging me on, the vibrations adding to the rise of my orgasm, pushing me closer and closer.

Fingers probe at my center from behind, sinking deep inside me. I lift slightly to adjust, but then he's curling them while sucking my clit into his mouth and pulsing until I'm falling.

"Liam! Oh, fuck! Yes, Liam!" I cry as the pleasure ricochets through my entire body, my muscles tightening, and the release is *so* fucking good. The warmth of the liquid from my body stuns me for a moment but it's followed by Liam's deep moans, the hand currently on my hip digging into my flesh, his head lifting and burying himself further into my center.

"Fuck, I love that my wife can do that," he stammers, picking me up by my hips and moving me down to his waist, not bothering to wipe the moisture covering his mouth and cheeks. My face flames, my body still shaking, coming down. I lift up on my knees as Liam lines up his cock with my drenched center, and then I'm sinking down onto him in one easy motion. My body fights the intrusion, my walls clamping, tightening and making him groan, but I don't care. I want this, the sting of pain as I adjust to him just makes me want him more.

I start to move, lifting my hips and then dropping back down and rocking before doing it again and again, finding a rhythm that feels good for both of us. His hands are everywhere, pulling at my nipples, gliding over my hips until he grips the globes of my ass tightly.

"That's it, beauty, ride my cock. You're gonna squirt again for me, do you understand? I want you to drench my cock."

"I don't know if I can."

"You can and you will. Lean forward."

I do as he says, laying down on top of him, his hands guiding me to lift just my hips, arching my lower back and then dropping back down. The position rubs my clit onto his pelvis but hits an entirely new place deep within me, that place that only his fingers have found.

"Oh, fuck, Liam, that feels . . ." My words are lost on a moan as I fuck him, his big dick hitting that sweet spot deep inside me while my clit is being stimulated just enough to edge me closer to release. I lift my head up enough to kiss him, his tongue spearing into my mouth, our tongues clashing. Liam's hands massage the meaty flesh of my ass until he's using a hand to spread me apart, and then I feel it. His fingers slip through all the moisture that's covering both of us, my pussy weeping for him and easing his way. His fingers rim the tight muscle there, and I don't hate it. The opposite actually.

When I press back slightly against him, he moans into my mouth, deep and feral. It would be scary if I didn't know this man would die before causing me pain. A finger breaches my hole, slowly pressing in and staying there. But I want him to move. I lift my hips quicker, falling back down onto his thick shaft,

"Does my wife need more?"

"Yes, Liam, please."

"So greedy. Anything for you, baby."

And then his hips are jerking up into me as I slam down onto him, his finger pulling out and thrusting back in sync with our thrusts. He pulls out completely before adding a second finger, and the stretch feels so wickedly good. My orgasm climbs until I'm floating away on a high so good tears spring to my eyes, my toes curl, and my stomach tightens until I'm coming so hard I nearly black out. I feel the release, the sudden gentle flow of me squirting, coating his dick and pelvis, his moans growing louder and louder.

"That's my girl. Fuck, so good, Hannah. Such a good wife."

His thrusts become erratic, my body draped over him, pliable and boneless as he holds me down by my lower back and thrusts up into me, chasing his release.

"Oh, baby, I'm gonna come. Fuck, I want to fill you up, Han."

God, I want that, too. But Liam won't take that chance. Just as he's about to come, I feel his already big dick thicken inside me, swelling, and then he's pulling free from me, white spurts of his milky cum shooting out between us as he moans out my name.

If I questioned it before, I know it now. There is no recovering from losing Liam after feeling this with him. He's mine.

. . .

"Do you think Charlie's going to be okay?" I ask Liam after he cleaned us both up and changed his sheets. We're currently wrapped up together under his blankets, my face resting on his strong chest, his steady heartbeat a near lullaby in my ear, so relaxing and comforting. His arms are wrapped tightly around me, my leg thrown over his hip, and my fingers tracing aimlessly over the tattoo he has of mine and Charlotte's names.

"Beauty, you've always done the best you can, she's a happy, healthy, smart little girl. She doesn't need a dad to be well-rounded. She is showered with love every day. She's got three honorary uncles, three aunts, and two sets of grandparents, even if two of them are assholes and the other two aren't actually related to her. She doesn't know any better, and she's so damn happy."

"I want to believe you. This is confusing for me, so I can't imagine how it is for her."

"If you really take a moment and think about it, our routine hasn't changed, and Charlotte is still so little. She was happy to see us kiss earlier. I know you panicked, but for all Charlie could understand, we've been together this entire time. I'm such a huge part of her everyday life. I don't think she's confused; I don't think she notices that anything has changed between us."

I give his words thought for a moment, and I know that he's right. Our routine hasn't changed, and the transition to married life was seamless because we're such a huge part of each other's lives already. Everyone who has found out we're dating hasn't batted an eye. Tomorrow is the first family dinner since things with Dallas and Blaire have calmed down, and we're announcing that we eloped. The thought of his parents' and siblings' happy reactions makes my heart flutter, but it also scares me that this could all crash and burn and I'll lose the people that mean the world to me.

"Promise me, no matter what happens between us with all of this, that you won't leave. I won't survive it, Liam."

"Hannah, never. I will never abandon you. It doesn't matter what title I carry, it's me and you. Till the fucking end. Do you understand?"

His thumbs brush away the rogue tears. God, I want to believe him more than anything, because I wouldn't survive it if we lost him.

Chapter Twenty-Three

Liam

Walking into my parents' house for Sunday dinner holding Hannah's hand feels like I'm living someone else's life. Everyone is sitting in the living room talking when we arrive, which couldn't have been a better setup. I pull Hannah behind me, her small hand clasped firmly in mine as we step into the room, and silence falls upon us.

"Liam?" my mom asks, hesitantly questioning.

"So, we've got a little announcement to make," I say, my mom slapping a hand over her mouth as she gasps. Hope fills her eyes, and I know that she has wanted this for Hannah and me for so long. It's going to kill me when she finds out the truth.

"Hannah and I have been keeping a secret, and we don't want to hide it anymore."

I lift up our hands, turning Hannah's to show off the thin, ornate, gold wedding band that adorns her left-hand ring finger.

"We got married!"

"Holy shit!"

"What the fuck?"

"What?"

"Oh my god!"

"Wait, are you serious?"

Everyone has something to say, and I watch as Hannah's eyes get big. I move my hand around her little waist, pulling her flush against me. My thumb rubs aimlessly over the bare skin there and I don't miss the way goosebumps scatter across her body or the way she shivers in my arms. I lean in to whisper in her ear.

"Smile, wife. We need to sell it, remember?"

She looks up at me, her eyes wide as she searches my face for something. God, I hope things have changed for her and she isn't faking it anymore. Lord knows I haven't been. I lean down, placing a chaste kiss on her forehead. Fuck if I don't want to kiss those lips again, spend all night worshiping her like I did last night. When she looks back at the room filled with my family, my mom is already in our space and pulling Hannah from my arms to wrap her in a hug, and a feeling of rightness flows through me. Hannah was always supposed to be my wife, I've never felt so sure about anything before.

My eyes connect with Dallas, who's looking at me, shaking his head. I toss my head to the side, signaling for him to meet me in the other room. I turn my focus back on Hannah as she smiles and talks with my family, who she has known her entire life. She wore her violet hair in a complicated side braid that hangs slightly off of her shoulder, a pair of jeans, and a cream sweater that ties up the back with thick ribbon. She could wear PJs every day and would still be the sexiest woman I've ever laid eyes on, but she's exceptionally beautiful today being reintroduced as my wife.

Knowing she's in good hands, I head to go deal with my brother. Turning the corner into the kitchen, a hard slap connects with the back of my head. I rub the spot with my hand, wincing.

"What the fuck did you do?" Dallas' voice pierces through the throbbing in my skull.

"What's it look like, dumbass? I took care of it."

"By *marrying* her? Did you think about how confusing this will be for Charlotte? How crushed Mom is going to be when this falls apart?" Dallas pauses his rant to laugh, his head thrown back like a dickface. "Wow. You one-upped me for sure, idiot. Now look who's the dumbass. Hold on, let me text the group. You need a new nickname."

Dallas pulls his phone from his pocket, and I slap it out of his hand. He slowly turns his head like a deranged sociopath, watching it scatter across the hardwood floor with a thud.

"If that's broken, I'm gonna rip off your arms and beat you with them."

"No one can know, you dumb fucker. You can't tell anyone, or I'll kick your ass."

"Look, I know I've had a lot going on with Blaire, but you could have come to me. You didn't have to do it this way. It's going to go up in flames."

"Dal, I've got it under control. I'm more worried about people finding out how it all started. Hannah and Charlie have always been mine. Now it's official."

"Charlie isn—"

Dallas doesn't register my movements as I quickly get into my brother's space, shoving my forearm into his throat and forcing him to fall back on the wall behind him.

"Finish that fucking sentence, dickhead, and I'll crush your fucking windpipe. You'll spend the rest of your life with Blaire feeding you through a goddamn tube." I press my arm a little harder into his throat. "Try me, I dare you," I fume.

He puts his hand up defensively and I ease off of him, taking a large step back. I rip off my hat and run my hands through my hair in an attempt to calm myself down before speaking.

"Those girls are mine," I seethe, pointing to the living room. "Hannah has always been mine."

"How long?"

"Ha. Long time. I planned to tell her I was in love with her the day she told me she was pregnant with Charlie. I've always loved her. Just didn't realize that's what it was until she left me at college and there was space between us. I fucking hate being away from her. The sun doesn't rise if I don't see her every day. She and Charlie are everything to me. I'm so in love with that girl I don't—"

"Liam?"

My body freezes. The sweet, feminine voice that I would recognize anywhere cut off the rest of my words, suspending the room in silence. The air leaves my lungs in a whoosh, my heart clenching painfully, my eyelashes closing involuntarily.

"I'm gonna let you two talk through that bomb. Definitely going to need a new nickname now. But I'll work on it. Don't worry, little brother, I got you. It'll be a good one."

Ignoring the idiot retreating from the room, I focus on my girl standing shocked in front of me. Her arms crossed over her chest, her eyes squinting into slits.

"Beauty. How much of that did you hear?"

"Enough. Was all of that you acting in front of him?" she whispers, looking behind her to make sure no one is there. "Or was that . . . do you feel that way?"

Fuck. My momentary pause to think for a second immediately backfires.

"Well, the look on your face just answered me before your words did. Was this just some elaborate way for you to get me to fall for you?" Her face contorts, eyebrows pinched, lips pursed as she looks at me.

"Fuck, no, Han. God, no. You needed help. I would do anything for you."

"But you're also in love with me. And sounds like you have been for some time."

Taking several steps in her direction, I grab her little wrist and pull her into the bathroom down the hallway, closing the door behind us and flicking the lock. I move quickly, my hand grabbing her hip, pressing her back against the wall, my other hand cupping her cheek. I rest my forehead against hers, sharing air as I speak my next words, our lips brushing against one another.

"Yeah, *wife*. I'm in love with you. What are you going to do about it?"

"You duped me, Liam!" She tries to push against my chest, but I don't budge. Her face flushes, eyes moving frantically across my face. "You tricked me into marrying you! All of this has been real for you while I've been faking it!"

Her words piss me off. There's nothing fake about anything between us. Instead of talking this through like we should, I remind her, connecting with her the way she likes to be shown. Holding her head in my palm, the other keeping her firmly pinned between my body and the wall, I kiss her, pressing my lips hard against hers, my thumb rubbing back and forth across her cheek. I kiss her like I always do, with every bit of love that I feel for her behind it. Her body softens, melting into mine just the way it always does, and my heart settles slightly in my chest. When I break away, I meet her eyes.

"Baby, does this feel fake to you?"

For the first time in over twenty years, I can't read her expression. Her blonde eyelashes flutter closed momentarily, and I hold my breath. She sighs, her silence so resolute, and I feel the moment my heart starts to fracture. Even if she can't love me the way I love her in return, I know I'm giving her everything she needs, and even if it kills me, I won't walk away because I would do anything for her.

She suddenly opens her eyes and there's a fucking inferno swirling in them. Her hands grip around my neck, yanking me to her mouth, my hat falling to the floor. I don't hesitate to respond, grabbing her ass in my palms and lifting her, shoving her back against the wall, her legs wrapping around my waist, not giving a single shit where we are right now.

She grinds her pussy against my stomach, tightening her legs around me as I devour her mouth, our tongues clashing and caressing. My fingers dig into the meaty flesh of her ass, guiding her to ride me any way that she needs to.

"That's it, baby, work that pussy on me. Make yourself come."

She pushes harder against me as I pull her mouth back to meet mine, sucking on her tongue, not able to get close enough, my dick rock hard against the zipper of my pants, wanting to feel her tight pussy around me. She pulls away from my mouth, burying her face into my shoulder as I rock her back and forth, her nails digging into my back as she hangs on.

Her legs start to shake, body tightening around me, and I know she's close.

"That's it. Come for me. Right now, Hannah, come for your husband."

She combusts, her orgasm rolling through her as she shakes involuntarily in my arms, her moans muffled as she keeps her face buried into my neck.

"Liam!"

"Fuck, my wife looks so pretty when she comes. I love you like this. I'll never get enough, baby."

She comes down from her high, and like a light switch going off, she pushes me back, scrambling out of my arms. I release her legs so that her feet touch the ground before allowing her to put space between us, which is the last damn thing I want. I run my hands through my hair and look at her, my heart sinking into the pit of my stomach.

She's flushed from her orgasm, her hair falling out of the pretty braid, but her eyes shine with unshed tears that pool at the bottom. I reach for her face with my hands, wanting to pull her back in close, to keep her with me, but she bats them away just as fast. My heart fractures, a weight I've never felt before settling on my chest.

"Holy shit. I am such a desperate idiot. What an absolute fool I've been," she mutters under her breath while I stand there frozen, at a loss for what to do or how to fix it, panic consuming me and pulling me under. The dam finally breaks, tears flowing down her gorgeous face. A face that I've looked at and loved for my entire life. The first time I saw Hannah, I made her cry over a fucking stuffed bear, and I never wanted to ever be the one to make her cry again. And here the fuck we are. I try to suck in air but it's no use. I don't register my own tears at the sight of hers.

"You're getting in my head! What are you doing to me? I can't think with you around, you're muddling my thoughts, and you use your touch to fucking blind me! Fuck! What have I done?"

Her words crush me, fear gripping me stronger than I've ever felt before, terrified that I've ruined everything and I'm going to lose her and Charlie.

"Baby."

"No. Fuck this. I need some space. I need space from you and to get you out of my head so that I can think clearly. I can't believe *you* would do this. Of all the people in the world, I can't believe . . . I need to go home. Please take me home. After, you should . . . I don't know what you should do but I need a beat to process everything. Away from you, bear."

Bear.

Not Liam.

Nausea hits me next, the stomach acid churning over, making me sweat. She's really fucking bolting. She's going to leave me, and I'll lose both of my girls. She had to have known I was in love with her. Was she really ignoring everything? There's no way she doesn't feel what's clearly between us. This is deeper than anything either of us expected. But I know my girl, and she can't be pushed in the heat of the moment, so I'll concede to her . . . for now.

"Yeah, beauty. Whatever you need, you know that," I reply, not able to mask the lump of emotion currently lodged in my throat. I can't help the tears that continue to spring to my eyes as she walks away, leaving me standing in my parents' bathroom wondering what the fuck just happened and if I just lost everything that I've ever wanted, when I've only just gotten it.

Lying in bed is fucking pointless when there's so much uncertainty going through my head. So, I do what I do best. Work. After Hannah and I left my parents' house, claiming that all the excitement made Hannah feel sick, I reluctantly dropped her off behind Bean Haven, where she got out of my truck and didn't say a word to me. Never have I been more grateful that we decided to let Charlie spend the evening with Graham and his daughter, Mila. She didn't have to witness how quickly the excitement turned to ash. The pain in my chest is insurmountable. I've always been the one person she wants close when things go to shit, and in my attempt to save her from more heartache and stress, I've added to it.

So, I drove to the distillery and threw myself into the familiarity of one of the rickhouses, walking up and down the aisles. It's cooler and darker here tonight, nature dictating how it feels, but I thrive in it no matter what. The warehouses give off a comforting smell of the charred oak barrels—deep wood, vanilla, and spices from the aging process. As I get farther toward the back where the older barrels are aging, I can just barely notice the smell of the whiskey itself evolving, with the older casks releasing notes of dried fruit, leather, tobacco, and caramelized sugar.

I used to do this as a kid, anytime I got overwhelmed or had an issue, pacing and running my hands through my hair at a near obsessive rate helped calm me down. The long aisles between the barrels are a familiar, quiet comfort that I need right now.

How Hannah could be blind to how I really feel about her, while it was obvious to everyone else in this town, isn't just disappointing—it's heartbreaking. I'm not willing to let her go without a fight. Consequences be damned. But it's hard not to wonder if she just got caught up in the acting of it all, and because she's been so touched starved, inadvertently used me to fulfill a need. A need I was more than eager to satisfy for her.

I lose track of time when my phone buzzes in my pocket. With shaky hands, I pull it out to see a text from Dallas.

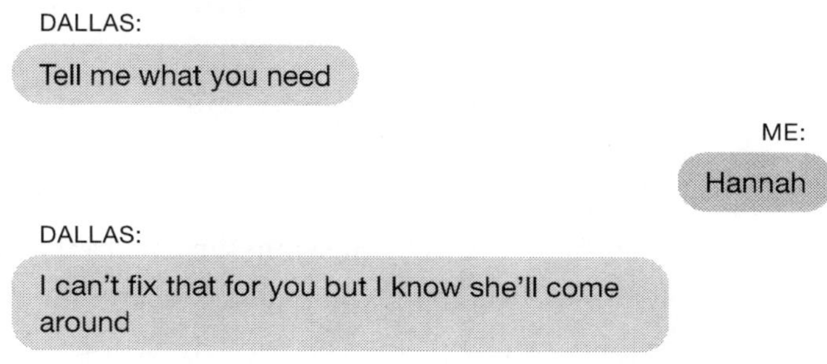

DALLAS:

Ring or drink?

I let his question hang in the air while I try to figure out what I need and if I want to be alone or have company when all I want is to go home and curl around Hannah to watch a horror flick.

DALLAS:

Walking around the rickhouse isn't gonna make you feel better, brother. Pick one or I'll pick for you.

I answer with the first thing that comes to mind.

ME:

Ring

DALLAS:

Meet you at Dom's. Leaving now.

Locking everything back up, I jump in my truck and take the drive back into town, feeling like shit the entire way. Spring is in full force, the remnants of our long winter gone, the tall Sitka spruce having shaken the heavy weight of snow off and returned to their former glory. As I get closer and closer to town, the urge to stop at Bean Haven and see Hannah is so strong my hands white-knuckle the steering wheel. I don't want to give her space, but I know after everything she's been through, she needs to process.

I walk into Knockout, the gym that my brothers and I have grown up in, adrenaline coursing through my veins and ready to knock Dallas on his ass to make myself feel a tiny bit better. The smell of sweat, rubber, and leather punches me in the nose and settles in my chest, making me immediately regret my decision to box over a beer or two at The Night Owl. But Dallas would just hunt me down and drag my ass right back here, knowing that this is what I need right now. Not alcohol. Damn, I really missed my brother, hate that he's had so much heavy shit going on in his life lately with Blaire that's kept him preoccupied, but fuck if I'm not grateful to get time with him right now.

I make my way to the locker rooms to change into workout clothes, stuffing my bag, keys, and phone into a locker before returning to the front. The receptionist, Emma, sits on the lap of one of her boyfriends, Cruz, his arms wrapped tightly around her waist in a possessive hold while her other boyfriends, Dom and Aidan, lean over the desk, doting on her. Emma was dating our friend Dom who owns Knockout, and then a few months ago, surprised the shit out of the entire town when Cruz and Aidan started openly dating her as well. Everyone except her parents have been supportive of them.

"Hey, guys, Dallas already here?"

Dom stands up straight, nearly my perfect match in height and weight. He typically works weights with me when I come in a few times a week to lift and not punch out my older brothers.

"Yeah, beatin' the shit out of a heavy bag in the back. It's good to have him back in here. Was worried for a minute."

"Yeah, we all were. Let's see how out of shape he's gotten, huh?"

"Put 'em on his ass, Liam!" Emma tosses over to me, and I give her a curt smile. Dom looks in her direction, his voice lowering, his tone sweeter, his affection for her clear.

"*Milaya devochka*, careful, after they're done, it's your turn in that ring."

Jesus fucking Christ. I don't even want to let my mind go there right now.

"I'm gonna let you get back to your weird-ass foreplay, Dom. I'll catch you guys later."

The rhythmic thump of gloved fists hitting a bag signals my brother's whereabouts as I walk toward the back of the open gym. It's empty here except for us, and I'm surprised that Dallas was willing to leave Blaire at all.

I work my way over to him, prepared to get stretched out before we hop in the ring to go a few rounds. Dallas turns to me, dropping his hands to his sides and giving me a goofy-ass grin that he wears when he's about to stir some shit.

"About damn time, spunk rag. Thought I was gonna have to beat this bag to death instead of your face." He jabs it with a firm punch, making it sway.

A laugh breaks through my shitty mood at my idiot brother. Dallas, Carter, and I aren't as trained as Sawyer—who wanted to fight professionally—but Dallas and I are a good match. I'm bigger than him, but he's quicker and carries a bit of a darker side that he unleashes in the ring. He and Sawyer have been battling it out this way since they were pre-teens and they both lean on it to work through their shit.

"You haven't been here in a long-ass time, you'll be lucky if you can get a hit in on me, dickhead," I shoot back at him. "And for fuck's sake, don't even try to get the spunk rag bullshit to stick, time to pick a new nickname."

"Not gonna happen. You gonna tell me how it went with Hannah?"

"She freaked and bolted. I'm gonna give her a day and then work toward fixing it. But she's lost her damn mind if she thinks she's going to push me away."

He laughs and I shoot him a glare while stretching out my shoulders. "Something funny?"

"Once a Hayes is all in, he's all fucking in and there's no turning back, consequences be damned. If you're in love with her, make sure she feels it. Hannah hasn't ever had that before."

"That's my plan. I think she's been so focused on proving to everyone that a man and woman can be platonic friends and just living her life, that she's missed all the signs. We didn't even have to change much for people to buy that we're together. Nothing about what we were doing was fake."

"She's had blinders on. Are you prepared for her to not feel the same though?"

Am I? It's one of a few fears weighing heavily on me, but then I think about how she looks at me when I walk into a room, how she melts into me when I tuck her in close, how easily we slipped into the sexual parts of a relationship. I'm her person. She's just fighting it because she's a stubborn ass sometimes.

"Short answer? No. I'm not prepared for that. But I know she could feel the same. She was heading in that direction before my big-ass mouth wrecked everything. Thanks for that, brother."

"Anytime. You know I've got you. You'll thank me later, I just know it. You ready?"

"Bring it, dickhead."

After wrapping up my hands and wrists, I pull on my boxing gloves and climb under the ropes to join Dallas. I roll my shoulders to loosen up a little more, the tension and weight of the afternoon creeping down my spine as I get my head to focus. Shaking my hands at my sides, I crack my neck, bouncing on the balls of my feet, bracing myself for what's to come. Dallas hasn't fought in a bit, he could either be a sloppy, lazy mess, or need a serious fucking outlet right now and pick it up like no time has passed. Hard to tell if I just got into the ring with Mickey Mouse or Mike Tyson.

Instinctively, we both step forward, touching our gloves in

the center and nodding to each other, the world shut out around us—just me, him, and our fists—and then it's go time.

We circle each other for a moment, feeling the other person out, but then like a dance we've done so many times before, we're in it. Dallas' first jab is aimed straight for my face, coming in hard and fast, his signature move that I'm always anticipating. My body reacts on autopilot, stepping out of the way to barely miss the contact. His movements are sharper than I expected, precise, letting me know it's definitely not fucking Mickey Mouse in here with me right now.

Knowing I need to get the upper hand, I duck his next swing, my left hook ready and connecting with the hard muscle of his side. He stumbles for a split second, but I've known him too long and know I just woke up the bear. Dallas falls into a trance, fully in control of each of his movements, blocking several of my punches like he knows exactly what I'm going to do before I do it.

"C'mon, baby brother. This all you got?"

"You're not as lazy as I thought you'd be. Or weak."

I throw another left hook, his right hand blocking the punch and pissing me off. Fuck this. We go at it, and I let him think he's got the upper hand, giving him a false sense of victory, and waiting for him to relax slightly. The pressure builds inside me, ready to unleash this pent-up bullshit festering inside me.

His next punch pulls back before it connects, but I see the move too late, my body reacting to dodge it and instead pushing me into a brutal hit to my ribs that momentarily stuns the piss out of me. My whole body shudders from the force of his blow, my breath whooshing from my lungs. I bite down hard on my mouthguard and hold back the wince that wants to break free.

"Ooo, that one must have hurt, spunk rag! Thought you were better than this. Looks like only one of us is out of practice and it sure as shit isn't me," Dallas continues to taunt, exactly where I wanted him to be.

I don't reply with words, instead, I push forward, crowding his space and holding him in a clinch before shoving him back hard enough that he staggers, throwing an immediate right uppercut to his chin. The noise reverberates through the small space, his head jerking back slightly before he recovers and cracks his neck side to side, a creepy-as-fuck grin spreading across his face. I don't waste any more time, my punches raining down on him fast and heavy. Sweat coats our skin as we exchange jabs, uppercuts, and calculated combinations—neither of us ready to stop, fighting longer than we should be.

Our chests are heaving as we finally break apart. I revel in the ache of my muscles and skin, the burn in my arms as calmness and clarity wash over me. My dad put his four stupid-ass sons into these lessons for the majority of our lives for an outlet, but these fights don't just release the pressure, they settle something within us and give us a way to speak to each other that only the four of us can understand.

Dallas swings his arm around my neck, and I rest my forehead against his. "You better?"

"Yeah, you?"

"Much. I got you. You're gonna figure this out. You and Han are perfect for each other."

"Yeah. I'll make it work. It has to. Love you, dickhead."

"Love you, spunk rag."

Once I'm back in my truck, I pull out my phone and bring up Hannah's chat, sending her a quick text before driving home to my empty house.

ME:

This changes nothing

BEAUTY:

It changes everything you jackass

ME:

You're my wife now, Hannah. And I'm seeing this through. You want out after Bean Haven is yours? We'll deal with it then. But I'm not bailing on you just because you don't want to face what you've always known

Three little dots appear and disappear several times before she leaves me on read. Fine, so be it. She can have a little space, but I meant what I said. This changes nothing. Hannah is going to get everything she wants in this life, and I'm not going to allow her to push me away because she refuses to see what's right in front of her.

Hannah is mine, and I'm going to prove it to her.

Chapter Twenty-Four
Hannah

"Did you seriously fuck up the best thing that's ever happened to you?"

I shoot my sister an evil glare from where I'm currently kneading dough. I had to come clean to someone about Liam and me. The one person I wanted to talk to was the other party in this fucked-up situation we've found ourselves in.

Yesterday was the most emotionally draining day I've had in a very long time. It made every tear shed over Levi look like child's play. It was difficult to mask my emotions in front of Charlie, but after she went to bed, I spent the night crying. Walking away from Liam was challenging when all I want to do when he's around is be close to his warm, strong body. But I need time to think away from him. Finding out that he's been in love with me this entire time rattled a foundation that I thought was unshakable.

"Charlie is the best thing that's ever happened to me, asshole. Don't you have a job now you need to get to?"

"Okay, she's obvious. But Liam is right up there with her. You really didn't know that boy was actually in love with you? We are absolutely not done talking about the fact that you eloped by the way. Sorry, Lo kinda soured you telling me."

When I think about Liam, my heart flutters in my chest, but there's also a gnawing sensation in the pit of my stomach. Liam is comfort, safety, fun, he's my peace. But he's also exhilarating and charming, and hell, he knows exactly how to touch me to light my body on fire. He's been the single constant thing in my life for as long as I can remember, never abandoning me, no matter how hard it gets. Was I naive to think it was all because of our deep friendship?

"Yeah, dummy, you were."

My head shoots to Hailey, suddenly realizing that I said the last part out loud. I drop my head back to moan at the ceiling.

"Ugh! What have I gotten myself into?"

"Sounds like Liam is what's gotten into you. How's the sex by the way? He's always looked like he knows his way around a woman's body."

My body heats thinking about how Liam touches me, the way he speaks to me as he does it, and the look of pure need on his gorgeous face.

"Oh my god! It's amazing, isn't it! You should totally see your face right now, Han. Damn, way to go. You're finally getting dicked down the way you deserve!" Hailey throws her head back as she laughs.

"Why the hell are you laughing right now, you little hussy? This isn't fucking funny! My life is literally crumbling around me."

"Because it's about damn time, Hannah! Wake up! The two of you have been acting like an old married couple since the very beginning. It's actually mildly exhausting to even witness."

"That is so not true. How can you even say that? We're best

friends, Hails. We've seen each other through everything, why does everyone assume that there's more there?"

"Look, I know that this must be strange for you because I'm the younger sister and I'm the one giving you advice, but you've got to seriously be blind, or stupid, which I haven't ruled out yet. That man has been in love with you for years. You can't tell me you don't see it, because everyone else does. It's so dang obvious to everyone who has ever seen the two of you together; when either of you are in the room, nobody else exists. I guess we've all just been waiting for the two of you to catch up. Or rather, for *you* to catch up. He lives and breathes for you and Charlie, Hannah. So, are you blind or just stupid?"

I let out an exasperated sigh, defeat weighing heavily on my shoulders. Unable to look her straight in the eye, I continue to work the dough with my hands, attempting to let my mind relax through the movements.

"That's the thing though. I feel it, Hails. Once he no longer held back, it was instantaneous. Like a light switch flicking on, and suddenly everything was so clear. I've never felt like I do when I'm with Liam, but that's also confusing as fuck. I'm struggling to separate my bear from my Liam.

"He's the same person, Han. Both sides of him have only ever operated because he loves you."

"But that's just it. Knowing that he's been in love with me all this time makes me rethink every interaction we've had prior to knowing. Even before all this madness between us, Hail, he's seen me in nothing but my underwear and bra, for fuck's sake, I've peed in front of him before, granted I was drunk, but still!"

"Which is no different than a swimsuit!" she interjects. "And as far as peeing goes, whatever. Maybe he's into that. But didn't your water break on him? Why are you worried about peeing in front of him if he's literally had birth juice all over him?"

"Whatever, stop focusing on me peeing. My point is, that while I was behaving as I would with my lifelong best friend, he was behaving that way because he's in love with me. I don't know how to let that go."

"That's fair. But, in Liam's defense—because you clearly haven't noticed—that man has only ever acted like he was in love with you. Like I said, it's been plain as day for all of us. And you're an even bigger idiot than I thought if you haven't realized your own feelings for him yet."

I wish I didn't feel so blindsided. But am I though? Because when it's laid out for me like this—the way everyone in town was so happy for us with their stupid "finally" comments, and how easy it was for both of us to fake this relationship, we've been operating as a married couple for years. Now that sex has been added to the mix, everything is just much more transparent. Was I really refusing to see what's right in front of me?

"He told me he hasn't been with anyone in a long time."

"I haven't been in Aspen Ridge full-time, and even I know that he hasn't come close to sharing himself with any woman other than you. He acts like a married man, Hannah. And he was doing so without getting his dick wet. What more could you ask for? So what if he has screwed some people before you? Hello, pot, meet kettle. You literally impregnated yourself with another man's baby. A man who he despises, by the way. So if those things don't make you wake up, then let Liam go."

I huff out a sigh and shake my head, starting the process of rolling out the dough for the cinnamon rolls, needing to be done with this topic. Hailey and I sit in silence until Charlotte starts to wake up over the monitor. I give Hailey a knowing look and she jumps up to jog upstairs to get my little one ready for school for me, leaving part of me wondering if Liam is going to show up or not, and what it'll be like when we see each other again. His text last night was exactly what I expected from him.

He's not going to bail on me now, and regardless of whatever is happening between us, he's going to make sure that Bean Haven is mine.

Hailey made a good point, not that I'll tell her that. Liam has been operating day in and day out as if he were a married man, without all the husband perks. He shows up for me constantly, helping with Charlie, holding me through my bad days, laughing with me through the good ones, pushing me to keep going. I was so stuck in this cycle with him as my best friend and trying to make things work with Levi, that I was too blind to see it. But now that I do, and now that I've connected with him that way, I can't go back from it.

I need to have a conversation with my parents and Grandma and let them know that Liam and I got married, and hope to mother above that it's enough for them to see me settled so they get off of my case and are happy to leave Bean Haven to me. They haven't even explained what that would look like, too busy making me feel less than for my life choices.

Lost in my thoughts, I successfully put in two large batches of cinnamon rolls and whip up the batter for my apple cinnamon muffins. The day I stop being able to get apples supplied to bake these things is the day the town will riot.

Hailey and Charlie clomp down the stairs together and round the corner into the bakery's kitchen. Charlie is wearing jean overalls paired with rubber rain boots and a yellow T-shirt. She looks so stinking cute.

"Morning, my munchkin!"

"Hi, Mumma. Where's bear and Garbage?"

My face falls. Was I seriously so busy thinking about my own feelings that it hadn't occurred to me how all of this could impact my daughter?

"Bear and the dog are at their house. Auntie Hailey is going to take you to school today before she goes to her big girl job!"

"Aww. I want to see Garbage. Can I see him after school today? He misses me, Mumma, I just know he does!" She clasps her hands together under her chin and bats her eyelashes rapidly at me. "Pu-pu-pu-puleeaase!"

"I will see if they are busy or not, how about that?"

"Okay! They won't be busy. Bear loves me. He'll come over, I just know it."

Hailey and I laugh, even though I'm dying on the inside, as I give her a massive hug, breathing her in and saying our see-you-laters.

"Have fun being a full-time nanny, Hails!" I tease as she walks out the back door of Bean Haven.

Pulling out my phone, I suck it up for the sake of my daughter and text Liam, but not feeling ready to face him yet myself. I chew on my lower lip while my fingers hover over the keypad.

ME:

Hi. Charlie is asking about you and Garbage

BEAR:

Billy.

Of fucking course it is. Because why wouldn't I just now be registering the fact that he named his damn dog after the killer in *Scream*, my favorite movie?

BEAR:

I can pick her up from school today, if that's okay? I'll take them to the park so she can play with Billy for a little while.

ME:

Thank you, she and I both appreciate it.

My phone starts buzzing in my hand with an incoming call

from Liam. I answer right away, holding my phone to my ear and not saying anything.

"Don't give me that professional bullshit, beauty. I pick her up all the time, this is not anything different from our normal routine. I love spending time with her. You think I don't know that you appreciate it?"

"I was just being polite. I'm not sure what to say."

"That's fine. I'll give you today, Hannah, but that's all you're getting. Please have a good day for me."

I sigh into the phone, "You too."

We hang up the phone, and for the first time in my life, I feel a distance between Liam and me that makes my heart ache painfully in my chest. My phone buzzes with an incoming text message, I open it, and a sharp pain is added to that heavy ache currently throbbing behind my ribs.

BEAR:

Me and you

It doesn't go unnoticed that this hurts more than anything Levi has ever done to me. If that doesn't say something, I don't know what does.

HARLOW:

Are we going to talk about this ticking time bomb?

Deciding to leave her on read for a moment, I bite the metaphorical bullet and call my mother before Harlow's big-ass mouth can, if she hasn't already.

"Hannah, what a nice surprise. How is Charlotte today? Liam?"

Because why the hell would she ask how I am? I drop the phone to my side and sigh before bringing it back to my ear.

"Hi, Mom. That's actually what I was calling you about, I have good news," I try to say with as much cheer as I can muster.

"Oh? I'm listening."

"Liam and I eloped."

The silence stretches long enough that I look at the screen of my phone to make sure the call hasn't disconnected.

"Mom? Did you hear me?"

"Yes, sorry. A bit stunned. Didn't you just start dating?"

"Not really, like I said the last time we spoke—we've been seeing each other, we were keeping it to ourselves while we made sure this is what worked for us. Trying to keep things as normal as possible for Charlotte since he's been such a constant in her life since she was born."

The words feel like ash on my tongue. I'm such a fucking idiot. That man is hurting so much right now because I was a blind asshole. An image of Liam's tear-stained face flashes across my eyes and I wince, my heart aching in my chest.

"Yes, he has. You both have been lucky to have him around. I don't know what you would have done without him."

Well, I would have fucking figured it out! Because that's what people do! But she couldn't relate to any of this.

"We're lucky to have him. I just wanted to let you know our good news."

"Well, it sounds like a celebration is in order. Your dad and I will push up our trip back to Aspen Ridge and plan something for all of us together. While I shouldn't be surprised you eloped since you can't seem to do anything the correct way, we still need to have a party."

Mother above, give me strength. I am going to lose my shit on this woman.

"Mom, there's a reason we eloped. We don't want a big celebration. It's just between Liam and I, and we want to keep it that way."

"Nonsense. I'm having your dad change our flights to return next weekend. I'll start working on everything now."

"Mom. Do you even hear me? Thank you, but no thank you."

"Hannah, you don't know what you want. You never have. I will take care of this for you, though. Give them my love. See you soon."

She disconnects the call with my mouth hanging open. She's un-fucking-believable. I toss my phone onto the counter and lean forward, dropping my head into my hands. Why does everything have to be such a mess? Why can't she just see what a hard worker I am? That I'm happy . . . most of the time anyway. There is nothing wrong with being tired. She equates it with being stressed, but being tired just means you put in the work, that you're hustling to reach your goals.

"Ugh! Why are you so judgmental, Mom? Why can't you just love me for me?"

"She's always been that way. Not sure what your father saw in that one." I nearly jump out of my skin as my grandma walks into the kitchen.

"Shit, Grandma. Make yourself known. I think my heart stopped."

"I talked, didn't I? That's making myself known. What else do you need? Want me to walk around with a bell around my neck?" I can't help but relax in her presence as I smile at her. To be her when I get old is ultimate life goals.

"What'd she do this time?"

Maybe now is as good of a time as any to bring up the plans for Bean Haven.

"Grandma, can I talk to you about something that makes me super uncomfortable to bring up?"

"No sense in letting anything make you uncomfortable, my darling girl, life's too short. I don't got much left so you had better get to talking before I join your grandpa."

On that note, I decide to just go for it.

"What happens to Bean Haven when you pass away?"

"Better question—what is that wretched daughter-in-law of mine telling you?"

I give her a puzzled look that clearly expresses my confusion. Shouldn't she already know? Then it hits me, and I feel even stupider than before. Control.

"She's been pushing me to settle down, with Levi, and told me that if I didn't get my shit together and marry him and prove that I could handle being a mother and businesswoman, she was going to sell Bean Haven."

My grandmother tosses her head back in a deep laugh that I haven't heard from her in ages. My eyes widen at the sheer boisterous level it reaches. But her reaction confirms what I suddenly suspected. What an evil freaking woman. My own mother.

"My darling girl, that woman doesn't have a lick of say over what happens to Bean Haven. It's in my will, and it will belong to you. And now that I know this, we're going to fix this before I die so she doesn't try to do anything fishy. You've been in this kitchen working your little tush off since you were six. You pour your heart and soul into it, just like I did. It's already yours. Bean Haven is just as much a part of you as it is me. It's in our bones."

I sigh with huge relief, weight lifting off my shoulders. Wiping away my tears, I walk over to my grandma—who has been more of a mother to me than my own—and wrap my arms around her shoulders, whispering to her that I love her.

The lengths my mother was willing to go to trap me in a relationship with a man who doesn't love me, just so that I can fit into the mold she wants to force me into, is astonishing. She's been trying to get me to conform by any means necessary for as long as I can remember, but now, she's really crossed a line she can't come back from.

My heart sinks as the realization that the entire reason Liam and I got married in the first place no longer exists—or didn't exist to begin with—hits me. I know now that Liam is in love with me, but that doesn't mean he would want to stay married. The thought hits me with force and I nearly stagger on my feet. For the first time in longer than I can remember, I'm happy. Liam marrying me wasn't for nothing, it opened my eyes to *everything*. I'm not ready to lose him. I won't ever be.

Chapter Twenty-Five

Liam

After a sleepless night in my empty house, just me and my dog, I'm up before the sun, ready to get things back on track. As hard as it was, I gave Hannah all day yesterday to think things through, but today, I'm moving forward. After spending the afternoon with Charlie and Billy, I'm even more determined to make her see the light. Those girls are moving in with me, and we're going to act like a married couple. I'm seeing this through, no matter what. Her head will catch up with her eventually.

As I step into the hot shower, my eyes flick to the clawfoot tub, memories of her spread out under the water while I watched her come over and over again on repeat. Even before she allowed me to touch her, she was giving me parts of herself that no one's had before.

My dick hardens, throbbing as I replay our first night together, claiming her, finally being able to taste her sweet little pussy. I could have eaten her out all night. Fuck, if she was here right now, I'd pin her up against the shower wall, hook her legs over my shoulders, bracing the weight of her with my arms, and devour her until she came at least twice. That's how we both should start our day from now on. Not with her waking up on the other side of town alone. Yeah, fuck this. Hannah is mine now. Sweet, laid-back, easygoing Liam just went out the fucking window.

I pull myself together as quickly as possible, throwing on a pair of denim jeans and a plain white T-shirt with a random plaid button-up thrown over it. Running my hands through my still-damp hair, I push it back the best I can and throw on my backwards hat. Filling up Billy's water bowl and breakfast, I pat his little head from where he sleeps at the foot of my bed before heading out.

The entire drive to Bean Haven, I'm focused on one thing and one thing only—showing her that I'm the man for her, that I've always been the man for her. I'm her person. That starts with me teaching her exactly how a wife should start her day. Everything else can wait.

The sun still hasn't risen over the mountains by the time I'm pulling my truck into a parking spot on an empty Main Street. The entire town is still fast asleep, except my girl inside the town's little bakery, working her ass off with no appreciation from her family. That'll be my next task to tackle with her. Enough is enough from those ass clowns.

Using my key, I let myself in through the front door, not bothering with attempting to keep the bell from announcing my arrival. By the time I pull the door shut and flick the lock, Hannah is popping out of the kitchen, barely illuminated by the lights behind her, everything still dark in the front of the shop.

"What are you doing here so early?"

"I wanted to see you before I started my day. You were on my mind."

She smiles hesitantly at me, the air between us thick with

tension and confusion. That won't do at all. This isn't us, and we've never had distance like it. She's standing there in a little navy T-shirt dress that comes down to her knees, an apron over her head and tied around her waist. She's so damn cute.

"Are you hungry? I can get you something to eat. Chocolate croissants just came out, so did the blueberry scones. I wish I had started your favorite sooner, or I'd have the lemon blueberry muffins done for you." She's nervous, fidgety, and trying to occupy herself so that she doesn't have to face the tension in the room. Face *me.* Such a drastic difference from Hannah's normal desire to take things head-on, not afraid of confrontation. Too bad for her, I'm not letting her hide from me.

"All of that sounds delicious, beauty, but not what I'm craving right now."

I prowl her farther into the kitchen, not bothering to rearrange my hard, aching cock. I know it's visible in my jeans as I watch her eyes take in the bulge. She walks backward until her ass bumps into the large butcher block island in the center of the kitchen, her chest starting to rise and fall deeper. I slowly stalk her until I've caged her in, placing my hands on either side of her hips, resting on the counter.

I lean down and take her bottom lip between my teeth before descending on her luscious lips completely in a heated kiss. Her body is stiff at first, but it's only a moment before her tongue meets mine eagerly, my hands moving on autopilot, picking her up by the waist and resting her ass on the edge of the table. Her legs part for me as I step between them, bunching her dress up around her waist to access what I came here for.

My hands move up her body, threading through her hair, pulling the strands to arch her neck, deepening the kiss. Using all of my restraint not to fuck her senseless right here, I kiss her until she's pushing herself against me, desperate for friction.

"Such a needy wife."

"Liam . . ." she whimpers, and that's my undoing. Hearing my name on those lips I love so much.

I take a step back, kneel before her, and rub my hands up her legs, spreading them farther apart for access to her sweet, pretty pussy.

I can't help but smile as I spot the small glass bowl next to us filled with melted chocolate. Reaching over, I lift the wooden spoon from the bowl, watching the smooth, glossy liquid drip from the end until it stops, bringing it between Hannah's legs. Her little gasp has me looking up and meeting her eyes as she watches me.

Focusing back on my meal, I glide the flat side of the spoon down the inside of her thigh, painting her with the rich, velvety texture, loving how she looks covered in it. Dropping the spoon back into the bowl, I slowly lick up the inside of her thigh, cleaning the sweet chocolate off of her luscious skin.

My moans vibrate against her flesh, loving the taste of her skin mixed with the chocolate, my own dessert for breakfast. I continue to lap at her, nipping her in places, sucking on her sensitive skin until she begins to push herself forward, chasing my mouth. Once I've thoroughly cleaned her up, my mouth salivating for what I really want, I pull back enough to meet her eyes from where she's looking down on me.

"You may be pissed at me right now, but you're still my wife, and I'm not going to stop showing you that I love you. Just as I always have. And right now? I want to start my day with my face between my wife's legs."

My hand presses lightly on her chest, pushing her to lean back and rest on her elbows. Grasping her hips to pull her completely to the edge, I hold her ass in my hands, putting her in a perfect position for me to devour. Pressing my face right to her perfect center, I take a deep inhale of my wife's delicious, sweet scent.

"I can't get enough of you, Hannah."

I lick up her center, right over the thin lacy fabric that separates her silky smooth skin from me.

"You're going to come on my tongue. Right here in this kitchen that you love so much. So every morning while you bake, you can remember how you came undone with your husband between your legs."

I push her panties to the side and take my first long, languid lick of her flesh from her core to clit with the flat of my tongue, soaking up her delicious taste, loving the little tremble in her body as the sensations travel through her. She's already so wet, my tongue slipping through her wet pussy lips as I kiss her deeply.

"Ohmygod, yes, Liam, shit, you're so good at that," she moans as I hold her in place, pushing my tongue into her tight little hole and probing her with it. Her walls flutter around me as I lick deep into her, swirling my tongue around.

Moving my thumb over her clit, I rub gentle teasing circles while I fuck her with my tongue, licking and pumping it into her. Hannah's little moans urge me on, using my hand around her waist to pull her forward, burying my face into her pussy, devouring her because I can't fucking get enough. I feel desperate, unhinged, not able to get close enough to her. My cock strains behind the fabric of my jeans, begging to be released and sheathed within her tight, warm walls. Goddamn, she feels like fucking heaven. *My wife.*

"Oh, shit, Liam, fuck. Oh, fuck, yes! That feels so good." A hand moves to my head, pushing my hat off and running her fingers through my hair. God, I love making this woman feel good. Her hips gyrate against my face as I consume her. Looking up her body, her chin is to her chest, her face pinched in pleasure, mouth slightly hanging open as she watches me consume her.

I lap up her seam to her little clit, replacing my thumb with my tongue and sucking it gently into my mouth before using my tip to swirl around it. Her moans grow until she shatters for me, coming so damn pretty, her body convulsing, my name a mantra on her perfect lips.

"Liam! Fuck. Fuck! Yes!" I could come just from the taste of her on my tongue and my name on her lips as she reaches her orgasm. I almost do, the fucker throbbing in time with her spasms. I lick her through each wave of pleasure until she starts to squirm away from me. I give her pussy one last gentle kiss before adjusting her panties back in place and standing up in front of her. Grabbing her shoulders, I lift her to sit upright and face me. Her eyelids are heavy, cheeks rosy and flushed. She's blissed-out, and knowing that it was all because of me makes me feel like the luckiest man in the world.

"That's the best way to start my day."

"Eating me out?"

"Making my wife come on my tongue."

Her eyes flutter closed as her chest rises and falls hard, a new wave of arousal hitting her. Hell, I love the effect I have on her. Cupping her cheek, she closes her heavy eyes and leans into my touch, making me smile down at her. She won't stay mad at me for long.

"You look beautiful like this, baby."

She opens her lids and looks up at me, her gorgeous eyes swirling with post-orgasmic bliss, a fire burning in the center that tells me everything is going to be okay. I'm breaking through to her. Dropping my forehead to hers, I whisper my next words, "Me and you, beauty."

She releases a rough exhale, her minty warm breath caressing my lips.

"Me and you."

"Good. Now, there's a plumbing issue in your only bathroom upstairs. So pack your shit. I'll be by this afternoon to pick you and Charlie up."

Her eyes widen and she pulls back slightly to study my face.

"But there's no—"

"Yes. There is. As far as Charlotte needs to know, there is. I want my wife in my bed; that's where she belongs, and that's where she'll be."

The smile that spreads across Hannah's face is both sexy as fuck and hopeful. She's not fighting me on this, which makes me nervous because Hannah typically doesn't do anything that she doesn't already want to. Rather than pushing for a direct answer, I accept her silence and decide I had better get to work and leave her to hers before Charlie wakes up.

Kissing her on the forehead, I tell her, "Have a good day, *wife*. I'll see you later."

Satisfied and feeling more ready to get my shit done at work, I return to the distillery, having turned Hannah down for a to-go coffee, not wanting to wash away the taste of her on my tongue.

"Hey, spunk rag, you ready for this meeting?" Carter says as he walks into the still room, looking around.

"What are you looking for, Casanova? I left Billy at home, got too many meetings with you jackasses today."

"You left him at home by himself? What are you, a fucking monster? Go get him."

"No. I've got too much shit going on today and plans this afternoon once Bean Haven closes."

"I hope he pisses all over your pillow and eats all your stupid hats."

"I've got one hat and it's on my head, idiot. Fuck off."

"Whatever. I would never leave him at home all day," he huffs.

"Dude, what is with you and my dog? Getting lonely? Need a companion? Maybe find someone to spend your life with instead of fucking half of Washington State. Or hell, I don't know, just a random idea here, get your own fucking dog."

Carter shrugs and rolls his eyes. "Nah. Never met anyone that made me feel anything other than arousal. But maybe the dog thing. Give me Billy. Which is a stupid fucking name by the way."

I look up from where I'm checking on the temperature of the stills and give my brother a look like he can't seriously be that stupid.

"You really don't know? Billy Loomis? The killer from *Scream*?"

His eyes get huge, the pupils blown causing me to stand to my full height.

"You named our dog after a fucking psycho teenage serial killer?"

Satisfied with the progress of the stills, I start to head for the door, Carter hot on my tail.

"He's not ours, he's mine. And Charlie's."

"I want joint custody!"

"Fuck off, Carter! No. You can see him when you babysit Charlie next." Idea struck, I spin on my heels, causing Carter to walk directly into me.

"How about this weekend?"

"I have plans. No more babysitting."

"Not even to see Billy?"

His eyes narrow as he glares at me.

"Nope. You're on your own. Ask Mom."

"Fine," I huff.

We leave the still room and jump in a golf cart, heading to the large main building on the distillery grounds where we keep our offices, tasting room, and event room. Walking in silence, Carter and I give each other a look as we get closer to Sawyer's office and the distinct noise of rustling around and insults hit our ears. I roll my eyes, knowing exactly what we're about to walk into. Carter pushes open Sawyer's door, and sure as shit, Sawyer is on his knees, Dallas bent over in a headlock, throwing hard punches into Sawyer's ribs and side.

"Jesus fucking Christ. Why? Did you two never grow up? Fuck." I move to pull my asshole brothers off of each other, but Carter puts his hand out over my chest, halting me. I give him a look, and he shrugs. Agreeing with him for a change and taking our seats in front of Sawyer's desk.

"You're such a shithead! Give her back to me!" Dallas barks as he wrestles out of Sawyer's hold. Good on him, that one is typically hard to get out of, Sawyer's arms are like fucking death traps. A place where you go to slowly suffocate. Unless you're Ivy.

"I told you, dumbass, I didn't fucking take her!"

"Don't mean to interrupt, but I've got to leave early today, think you two could pick this up after we're done here?" I ask.

Sawyer shoves Dallas off of him, the force knocking both of them back from each other.

"Who's her?" Carter asks.

"Gloria! She's missing! I know he fucking did something with her!"

I look at Sawyer as he's rolling his eyes. "Is he seriously talking about his fucking beloved office chair?" I ask.

"Unfortunately. I caught him in here trying to steal mine. I didn't fucking take her, I gifted him the godforsaken thing."

"Then who did?" Dallas yells, looking at me and Carter.

"Maybe ask Blaire? Isn't she back at work? She hid her the first time."

"How's it feel to be back, dumbass?" Sawyer asks Dallas as they both straighten out their shirts.

"Good. But payback is a bitch to whoever took her. And I'll find out sooner than later."

"And if it was Blaire?"

"I have my ways of punishing her," he says with a wicked gleam in his eyes that I could have gone the rest of my life without seeing.

"Alright, to business. Let's get this meeting started," Sawyer tells us, and we all get into it, taking turns going over plans for the rest of the year, progress updates, and a slew of other things on the agenda.

My phone buzzes in my pocket, and not wanting to ignore it in case Hannah or Charlie needs something, I pull it out and glance at it in my lap while Carter goes on and on about his irritation over this stupid fucking journal article that still hasn't happened, and the elusive writer who is dicking him around.

CYNTHIA HAVEN:

I hear congratulations are in order, son-in-law. Jay and I will be returning to Aspen Ridge much earlier than planned. Looking forward to the reception this weekend to celebrate your nuptials, however untimely they were.

What the fuck? Blowing out a heavy breath, I look back up to find all eyes on me.

"Problem?" Dallas asks, breaking the new silence suspended between us.

I hold up my phone and wave it in front of us with

Cynthia's text pulled open. "You guys hear that Hannah's parents are coming back to town early? Apparently there's a reception this weekend to celebrate my marriage."

All three of them bust out in laughter. They know I fucking hate this kind of shit. When Hannah said she wanted to get married at the courthouse, half of me died in happiness, the other half only wanted to give Hannah her dream wedding and would have done whatever she wanted. But I hate having all eyes on me, and ultimately, was so thankful for something just the two of us. That's not to say I don't want to give her a redo. Preferably a ceremony where it doesn't smell like dirty-ass mop water.

I'm much quieter and typically more reserved than my brothers and even sister. I'd take a night in watching movies with my woman by my side over going out any day of the year. I know that Hannah isn't going to want a reception either, but I'm not sure if I should speak for both of us without talking to her first.

"Sounds like Cunty-McHaven," Dallas says. "What's with these shitty-ass parents and how'd we get so damn lucky?"

"I don't know, but that shit isn't happening unless Hannah wants it to."

Over my dead fucking body.

Chapter Twenty-Six

Hannah

Surprisingly, when Liam arrives at my apartment, Charlie is walking into the kitchen with a duffel bag dragging behind her while I sit at my little table and deal with the bullshit texts I just received.

"Bear! We get to stay with you! Can Garbage sleep with me every single night?"

Liam drops to his knees, always talking to her on her level.

"His name isn't Garbage, it's Billy, remember?"

"Yeah, I guess so. I like Garbage better though. Soooo, can he?"

"He sure can. You have to promise to keep him nice and snuggly warm. He likes to cuddle."

"I promise. I can do it. Yippie! I'm gonna go get Mr. Pancake, and Spaghetti-o, they're coming with me to your house, too!"

Charlotte runs off toward her bedroom and then Liam's attention is firmly on me. I feel his eyes wash over me and I know there's no sense in hiding it when he can read it so clearly on my face and body language. He takes a seat across from me at the little table, just big enough for my daughter's and my needs to be met.

"What'd he do now?"

I sigh, my shoulders slouching even more.

"Mistakes were made. I reminded him that he still hasn't given me an answer on whether or not he's going to step up with Charlie. I had threatened him months ago, bear, and I didn't follow through. Now he's saying that she's his kid and he wants to have rights to her."

Liam's face transforms from that easygoing man I know to the one he keeps pulled back and hidden. His hands clench into fists on the table, his jaw ticking subtly, his head moving ever so slowly to crack his neck.

"That so? Can I see it?"

ME:

Levi, you haven't seen or spoken to Charlotte in months. Before that it was sporadic at best. Are you going to step up and be in her life or are you moving on with yours without her in it?

LEVI:

Always the bitch, Hannah. How dare you insinuate I wouldn't want to be in her life. I have the right to see her whenever I want and you've been keeping her from me.

ME:

I've never kept her from you, Levi. Ever. Up until recently, I've begged you to spend time with her, or even just call her.

LEVI:

Always with the lies and drama.

LEVI:

Fuck off, Hannah. I'll see her anytime I want and when I want, you can't stop me

"Beauty, this is all bullshit, don't get yourself worked up over this. All this is, is him saving face in front of his new baby mama. You and I both know that's not what Levi actually wants. I would bet money that he opened that text and she was next to him, and he needed to cover his ass so she didn't spook. He's not gonna want to look like a pussy in front of her. Let him say whatever he's gonna say, Levi is a big talker and doesn't have the balls to back it up. Trust me, he's been doing it his entire life."

My heart settles in my chest. Liam is right, if Levi wanted to be in Charlotte's life, he would be. I just worry that this new woman of his may have a brain and push him to be in her life, and I don't know if that's best for Charlotte anymore. I really need to meet with an attorney and see about a parenting plan, at least then he would be held accountable.

"Don't give him or your mother power over you. I'm not going to treat you like you're made of glass, Han, because you're the strongest woman I know. Fight for what you want, what you deserve."

"You're right. I don't need to deal with any of this anymore. We can't force people to be in our lives, and we can't force the ones who are there to accept us for who we are, but that doesn't mean we have to put up with any of their bullshit."

"That's my girl. Now what is this I'm hearing about a reception for us this weekend?"

"The mothership is apparently returning to Aspen Ridge, and she is just so overjoyed to marry her beloved eldest daughter off to the wealthy and successful Mr. Liam Maverick Hayes, heir to the Aspen Ridge Distillery empire."

Liam bursts out with a laugh before talking. "What a lucky woman you are, Miss Haven. I promise to keep you well looked after. I assume you can read and write? Play the pianoforte?

Your hips are a bit narrow, but I'm otherwise sure you'll have no problem producing me multiple male heirs."

"Oh my fucking word, for real, though! I wouldn't be surprised if she has a dowry stashed away for you."

Liam and I stand at the same time, laughing at the audacity and absolute ludicrous behavior of my mom, and take a load of Charlotte's things and bags to Liam's truck and my car. Even though Liam's confession is weighing heavily on me, he's still the only one I want by my side when shit hits the fan. He's my person, my best friend, and there's nothing that can change that. It feels good to see that he's still my bear, making me calm, relaxed, and centered, bringing a lightness and peace to my life. I'd be lost without this man.

There are few things that I know to be true. Running Bean Haven fulfills me and gives me a place to spend my days living out a passionate dream. Being Charlotte's mother is the most rewarding gift in the world. And I am irrevocably, unconditionally, and wholeheartedly, madly in love with Liam Hayes. I just don't know how to come clean and tell him about Bean Haven before I tell him that I love him.

The week goes by faster than I wanted it to, especially with my mother returning to Aspen Ridge today. I wish things weren't so strained, I would give a whole helluva lot to get my mom to see me for who I am, but she's never been able to, and my expectations are only leaving me disappointed.

I'm unloading the dishwasher when my phone rings from the bar, seeing my mom's flashing name from here, I take a deep breath and prepare myself for whatever vitriol she's got on reserve to spew my way.

"Hello parental unit, how was your trip?"

"Where are you? I'm at your apartment but you're not there. And Bean Haven is closed."

"Yes, well, I don't live there anymore. I live with my husband, and Bean Haven always closes at three."

"And where is that, might I ask?"

"Far into the deep, dark woods. Charlotte is looking forward to seeing you."

"Fine, keep it a secret. The party is tomorrow at four, at our family home. I've already spoken with the Hayes, and they will all be in attendance. Anyone else I should invite for you besides your father and I's friends?"

I blow out a deep breath of air in frustration. Didn't I tell her that I didn't want a party? Fuck's sake. Whatever, maybe this will be fine, it could bridge the divide, and at least Liam's family will be there with us.

"You know what, Mom? I really appreciate it. We're looking forward to it. I think just the two families would be great."

"Just the two? As in ours and the Hayes?"

"Yes, mom. Just those two. Intimate. Liam and I aren't crazy about big parties, we're pretty low-key."

She sighs loudly, gotta make sure I hear her frustration and disappointment, after all.

"Fine, Hannah. We will see you tomorrow at four. Please try to be on time for a change, I know that it's difficult for you."

"Thank you for understanding. See you tomorrow!"

Liam rounds the corner as I drop my head back and look up at the large skylight above me, his arms coming to wrap around my waist. He smells strongly of a rickhouse, the sweet char of the whiskey barrels bleeding off of him.

"Mmm. You smell so good."

"Damn, baby, so do you. Like vanilla and chocolate." His teeth nip at the sensitive skin at the base of my neck. "You handled her well. You don't mind going tomorrow? We don't have to."

"I'm okay, I promise. Your family will be there, and I'll have you with me. I can handle it. It's not like I'm going to get a new mom. I'm going to have to face her sooner or later."

"Everything will be fine. No one's opinion matters but your own. Where's Charlie?"

"I have to go pick her up from the park with Hailey and Mila in about an hour."

"Good. Tell me what you want, because I want to bend my wife over and eat her delicious pussy. I'm hungry."

I'm a goner.

Chapter Twenty-Seven
Hannah

Liam and I walk up the steps to my parents' house, the same one I grew up in, and I can't help but feel like this is my coming out party. The Washington weather is gorgeous today, the sun giving us its last gracious rays as it starts to dip behind the mountains and cloud cover. Liam squeezes my hand as he knocks on the door with the other. He leans in, whispering gently into my ear, "You've got this, beauty. Whatever happens, it's me and you."

"Me and you."

Jay and Cynthia Haven meet us at the front door, opening it wide as we walk through the entryway. We're twenty minutes late, which wasn't my fault—we had a shoe crisis with Charlotte before dropping her at a friend's house. Liam's parents, all of his siblings, plus Ivy and Blaire, my grandmother, and my sisters, stand in the formal dining room with drinks in their hands, except for Ivy, who is rapidly approaching her due date.

"Welcome back to Aspen Ridge. How was California?"

Liam asks my parents, starting the next twenty minutes of greetings and small talk. We all move to take our seats at their large dining room table, reserved for hosting dinners just like this one.

"So, Liam, what made you decide to run off and marry our daughter without speaking to us first?"

The fucking audacity. But Liam doesn't miss a beat, putting her in her rightful place.

"Well, I'm in love with her, and she's a perfectly sound-minded, twenty-seven-year-old, fully functioning adult who runs her own business, raises her daughter alone, and doesn't need the blessing or permission of anyone."

"I see."

"We had no idea, either," Liam's mom, Amy, adds, sensing the tension in the room climbing. "We're beyond happy for them. It's so romantic that they couldn't wait another moment to be husband and wife."

"My god, I can't sit here for a second longer and listen to this. You all realize they aren't even married for real right?" Harlow spews, slapping both hands on the table.

Dallas chokes on his drink and I cock my head at him, did he know, too? My mom gasps and looks at me with a level of shock and disappointment I've never seen before. Liam stiffens next to me, his hand moving to my thigh under the table and squeezing, a silent reminder that he's got me. There are so many reactions and too many people.

"Lo! What the hell is wrong with you? Do you even know what you've done?"

"She had a right to know the truth before she gave you Bean Haven! Maybe if you weren't shacking up with your best fucking friend like some desperate dog, I wouldn't have had to tell her."

"Wow. Newsflash, Lo! Bean Haven is already mine! It was never Mom's to hold over my head to begin with!" Harlow's eyes get big as she takes in that little piece of information she was missing. "Yeah, idiot."

"Excuse me?" my mom asks, truly confused. My dad is quiet, as always. It's then I realize what I announced and how no one knew but me and my grandmother.

"Will you all shut up already? Thought we were gonna have a nice dinner celebrating Hannah and Liam, but you all are ruinin' it with your bitchin'. Bad enough I couldn't bring my Winnie because the fishy one is here and she'd lose her mind, but now I've gotta listen to all of this," my grandmother admonishes, and I melt into my seat, so fearful of seeing Liam's face as he takes in my grandmother's confession. I've never been more thankful for my decision to let Charlie have a playdate tonight. "Cynthia, you're ruining your relationship with your daughter. I signed that deed over to Hannah already. It was mine to give and now it's hers. Worry about yourself. Your girls are fine. Except for you," she continues as she turns to Harlow, "you need to get your jealous head outta your ass before it gets stuck there."

"Liam, is there truth to this?" his mom asks.

Everyone goes completely quiet, all eyes on Liam and me, and I want to disappear. This was my biggest fear, crushing everyone we love with false hope and promises.

"I married Hannah because I'm in love with her, because I can't go a single day without seeing her before I lose my mind. She's been the center of my world since she cried for the Charlie bear I was playing with in preschool. There's no me without her. This isn't fake."

His words wash over me, and I can't stay here for another moment. My chair squeaks across the hardwood floor as I jerk back in it, standing, and walking briskly out of the dining room, out of the house, and then darting up the street to the only place that I can think of where I'll get a break and to someone who will make sure that I get it.

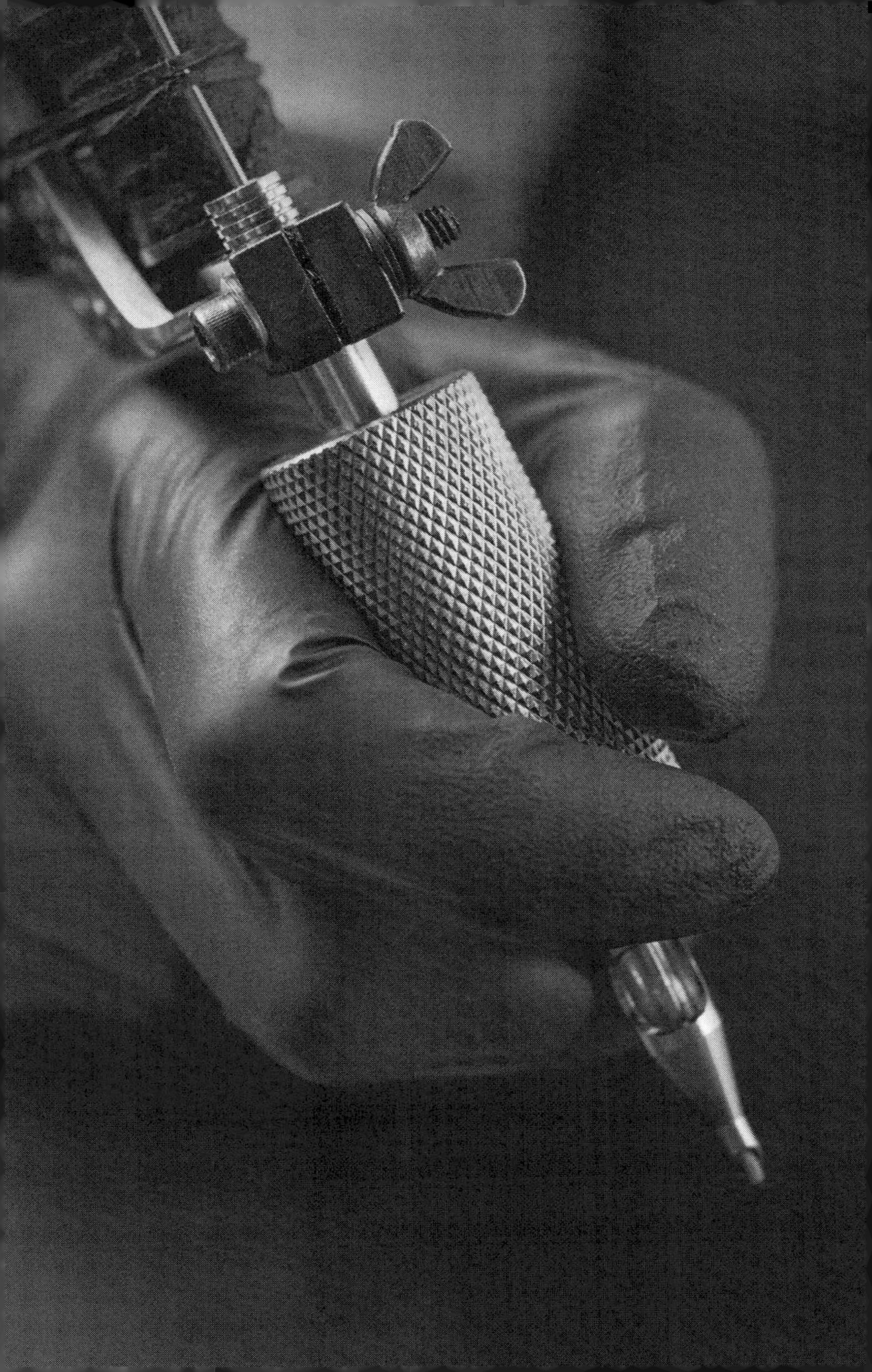

Chapter Twenty-Eight
Reid

The frantic tapping on the door of Rogue pulls me from the art tablet in front of me. Pulling off my glasses, I drop them onto my workstation and head toward the door. Sliding the blinds out of the way, I see a bleary-eyed Hannah and rush to get the door unlocked, letting her inside and relocking it.

"Are you alright?"

"I just need a moment to think, to breathe, it's so much pressure, Reid."

I pull her into a big hug, bounding my arms around her shoulders.

"Whatever it is, it's not the end. You'll see the other side, you're so strong, Hannah. How many people do you know who can sit through a nine-hour tattoo session with no breaks?"

She laughs a little at that and starts to pull away from me. I place my hand in the center of her upper back, guiding her to my office and handing her the box of tissues.

"Do you want an ear to listen, advice, or just someplace quiet for a little while? I got all three in spades."

"Mother above, Reid. I don't even know where to start.

Everything is a mess, and I think I just hurt both Liam's family and mine. Liam married me to help me get Bean Haven from my parents, but then they didn't even have the right to hold it over my head to begin with, so it was all pointless, Liam's in love with me and has been for years, my sister found out it was fake, and just told everyone at dinner. I love Liam but I haven't told him yet and it's just all so messy and complicated." She unloads everything on me, and I sit back and listen, giving her the space she so clearly needs to get everything off of her chest. Those goddamn Hayes men love their women fiercely but damn if they don't each share the possessive, obsessive gene.

Knocking at the front door echoes through my shop and Hannah's eyes go wide, knowing it could only be one person.

"What would you like me to tell him?" I ask, putting it all in her court, prepared to lie to him if I need to. She comes first.

"You can let him know I'm here, but that I'm not ready to talk. I need space."

I nod at her before rising and opening the front door, keeping my foot on the outside of it so that he can't push his way through, not that he could strong-arm me.

"Hey, man."

"Is she here?" Liam says, eyes frantically looking behind me.

"Yeah, but she said she just needs a little space."

"If you so much as touch her, Reid, I'll fucking kill you."

"Go find your dumbass brothers. I thought you were smarter than those two, but you're clearly not. I wouldn't touch something unless it's *wholly* mine. She'll be okay, just give her a beat to process what's going on."

Liam looks distraught and my heart hurts for him, but I've got no doubt he'll be able to figure it out. It's clear he loves her more than anything. We've all seen it.

Liam nods, running his hands through his hair. "Just tell her that I love her, please."

"I will. She'll be okay."

Returning to Hannah, I find her standing in the doorway of my office, facing where I just came from.

"You hear all that?"

"Yeah . . ."

"You love him, Hannah. Just tell him. Everything else be damned. You never know when you won't wake up tomorrow, so go love on your loved ones for me, yeah?"

"You're a good one, Reid Knight. You're gonna get your happily ever after someday, too."

Not knowing what to say to that, knowing that's not in the cards for me, I rub the back of my neck uncomfortably. She gives me one last hug before slipping out the back door of Rogue to figure her shit out. Glad I could give her a tiny reprieve, I fall back into my office chair and open my desk drawer, pulling out a small Polaroid photo and running my thumb over the young brunette smiling back at me, wishing like hell I could hug her one last time.

Chapter Twenty-Nine
Liam

The next day goes by in a blur and not being able to spend yesterday evening with my girls at home and my night inside Hannah, has made me a huge asshole today. The bomb that was dropped last night at dinner didn't rattle me. I don't give a fuck if Hannah kept that news to herself, it means that she wanted to stay married to me when she could have bailed now that there wasn't a reason for us to stay married for Bean Haven. For however long she's known, she has been choosing me every day and not doing it because of the arrangement or her situation.

But not knowing how she feels about me for sure has slowly started to eat me alive, not knowing where we stand is killing me. I need to hear the words from her lips. The last twenty hours have ripped me open. When I couldn't find her at home, at Bean Haven, or the apartment, I knew there would be only one other place she could be. Reid Knight. He's been known to go above and beyond to help women—his redemption, he calls it.

He sent me a text letting me know that she was picking up

Charlie and heading back to her apartment above Bean Haven, which I appreciated. I didn't mean to offend him by insinuating that he would ever cross a line. The man just belongs on the cover of a fucking magazine and women seem to flock to him as their best buddy. Hard not to be slightly insecure. Even Sawyer was nervous he'd be able to steal Ivy away from him.

My phone vibrating in my pocket pulls my attention from the massive to-do list I'm staring at.

SAWYER:

You ready to finally talk?

The sibling group chat has been annoyingly incessant since I bolted after Hannah at dinner the night before. I've talked to my mom and explained, and thank fuck she's the most understanding, accepting human on Earth because all she did was call me an "idiot, just like the rest of the men in our family." But I've been ignoring everyone else, the only person I want to hear from is Hannah.

ME:

I'm fine

DALLAS:

We can smell the lies from here

SAWYER:

We don't hold it against you

DALLAS:

I mean, I told you this would backfire

CARTER:

Wait, dickhead knew?

SAWYER:

???

DALLAS:

But we don't hold it against you. Any of us would have done the same thing

ME:

That's what Mom said

SAWYER:

So this is what you've been working through all this time?

DALLAS:

Yep

ME:

I can answer for myself dickhead

Yeah. But, I'm in love with her and I'm going to fix it. Hannah is mine.

CARTER:

For fuck's sake you sound just like shithead and dickhead

KINS:

I agree with you, Li. You two were made for each other. Who cares how things started? Get your girl.

CARTER:

This will never be me. You all have fun

KINS:

Just because you haven't felt love yet doesn't mean it won't wreck you once it hits you in the face. Never say never.

ME:

🙄 I've got it handled

Pocketing my phone with a frustrated sigh, I stand and head for the door.

"You're grumpier than usual. Starting to confuse you with Sawyer," Graham quips from where he's currently walking next to me to check on our crew working with the mash for the straight bourbon whiskey.

"I'm not grumpy, just agitated."

"Isn't that the same thing?"

Changing the topic, not wanting to get into my issues at the moment, I turn the conversation onto him. "How's it going with Hailey?" Hannah's younger sister started working full-time for Graham as a live-in nanny.

"She's incredible. Mila's mood has changed so much since Hailey moved in. As much as I was trying to convince myself that only having a dad around was enough, she's getting to that age where she clearly needs a woman's touch. Hailey's been a huge help. I know you've got your issues with Jay and Cynthia, and I would agree with you about Cynthia, but Jay is a good man, and he did good by those girls. Hailey is well-rounded and a good role model for Mila."

"They're good girls. I'm glad you've finally accepted some help. You needed it, man."

"Don't I know it. It worked out. And Jay feels good knowing that his baby girl is being taken care of and making their move to California easier on him. Everyone's happy."

I nod, feeling like an ass for not communicating much today. We walk into the building to check on the progress and ensure the mash will be ready for fermenting when my phone goes off with a chime that's only for one person, alerting me to a text from Hannah.

BEAUTY:

We need to talk

My heart drops into my stomach, bile churning around and making me feel nauseous. No one on planet Earth wants to hear those four little words. When have they ever not caused immediate alarm in the person receiving them?

ME:

Are you and Charlie okay?

BEAUTY:

Yeah, can you meet me at the apartment?
Charlie's with Hailey and Mila.

ME:

Of course I will, anything for you. Be there in 10

"Hey, Graham, something's up with Han, do you have this covered? I need to take off."

"Yeah, man, you got it. Let me know if you need anything."

Pocketing my phone, I jog out of the mash house and get into my truck, ready to do whatever it takes to show her how much I love her. I just hope that she loves me in return, or she's in for one hell of a fight, because I'm not letting them go.

After a quick drive into town, taking those familiar roads faster than I should, I park behind Bean Haven and jog up the stairs, letting myself into the apartment just like I always have.

I find Hannah standing in the living room, pacing, waiting for me. Everything I was going to say goes out the fucking window as I see her red-rimmed, puffy eyes. Fuck, her tears bring me to my goddamn knees.

Walking right up to her, I clasp her face in my palms, holding her head as I bend my knees to look her over in concern.

"You were crying?"

She nods slightly, a tear slipping free and trailing down her face.

"Baby, please don't cry. It kills me when you're hurting."

I pull her into my chest, wrapping one hand tight around her waist, the other holding her head to me. She grips me back, her arms snaking around my thick waist, fisting the loose fabric of my T-shirt. I give her a few moments before pulling back slightly, my hands resuming their position framing her face, my thumbs gently sweeping away the lingering tears.

"You are so fucking beautiful. Tell me you feel this, Hannah."

"Bear . . ." she whispers as she pulls away from me, taking several large steps backward. There might as well be a fucking cavern between us with the way my heart is aching right now. Distance, arguing, these things have never existed between us.

"No. No, don't do that. Don't put me back in that zone. I want more than that. I've always wanted more than that. We have more than that, Hannah. You have to feel it, baby."

Her eyes glass over as tears pool, threatening to spill over the edge again. A crack forms in the center of my heart, a knife plunging in and dragging. She doesn't feel the same. Fuck. My hands begin to shake as my knees threaten to give out on me.

"Everything that my grandmother said is true, Bean Haven is mine. My parents never had the rights to Bean Haven, they—mostly my mother—assumed that my dad would inherit it and they'd be able to sell it if I didn't conform. But it was never going to be theirs. It was always mine. My grandmother signed it over to me. She didn't want to wait until she passed away and chance leaving me to be devoured by the sharks."

"How long have you known?"

"A little bit. I didn't want to chance you leaving me now that we didn't have a reason to be married."

"Han, I would never leave you. You're my fucking wife, the most important thing next to Charlie. You're all I've ever wanted," I remind her, pulling her into me, grateful that she allows it. I nip at her bottom lip before scraping it with my teeth. "I can't believe you kept this from me, though."

"Yeah, well, you manipulated me into getting married so

you could try to get me to fall in love with you, so consider us even. How long?"

I know exactly what she's asking. She finally wants to know the truth. How long have I known I was in love with her. Took her long enough to ask.

"How long? Han, I've always loved you. There hasn't been a day that you weren't my first thought when I woke up, you and Charlie my last thoughts before I fell asleep. I've only fallen more and more in love with you as the years pass."

"But, wh—"

"I'm not done yet. I realized it was more than just the way a best friend should love you when you left me at college. It was the first time we'd ever been apart, and it was fucking torture. It's why I drove back home almost every fuckin' weekend. Do you remember the day you told me you were pregnant?"

"Of course I remember."

"You remember I had something to tell you?"

"Oh my god."

"Yes, Han."

"You were going to tell me?"

"Was hopefully gonna make you mine. See if you were willing to give me a shot."

"So, what, bear? You've just been slinking around waiting for the perfect moment to swoop in?" Her voice raises as she steps out of my arms, her fists at her sides. "You used the worst time in my life to get closer to me, then you made me fall in love with you, instead of just being open with me and giving me a choice? Just been biding your time? I'm not some damsel that needs rescuing and I've been trying to just keep going, but I know we need to face this in order to move forward!"

"What did you just say?"

"I'm not a fucking damsel in distress!"

I'm on her before I realize my feet have moved, grabbing

her face between my large palms and tilting her head up to look at me.

"You're in love with me?"

"Of course I'm in love with you, you idiot!"

She barely has time to finish the last word before my lips are on hers, crashing down on her like a tidal wave. Her arms wrap around my neck, pulling me closer as I angle her face to take the kiss deeper, my tongue plunging into her mouth. It's a frantic race to strip each other of our clothes, my hands only leaving her body to grab at fabric and bare the perfect body underneath.

Once she's completely naked, her arms return to my neck, my hands grabbing her ass and lifting, legs wrapping tightly around my waist. I walk us toward the bedroom, and she reaches between us to grab my cock, lining it up with her core. Bracing her in my arms, I drive home, filling her completely in one smooth thrust.

"Ohh, fuuck!"

My hips piston into her, driving her back harder into the wall. It feels like nothing we've ever experienced before, it's frantic, primal, consuming. Her soft, silky walls grip around my cock so tightly, her wetness coating every inch of my thick shaft, already dripping down onto my balls. Soft hands grab my face, pulling me back into a kiss, tongues tangling, teeth clashing as we fight to devour each other.

Holding her in my arms and not withdrawing, I let us fall back onto the bed, my body collapsing on top of hers. Her legs stay wrapped around me, heels driving into the top of my ass, holding me close to her.

"Baby, you feel so good."

"So damn good. I've never . . . it's never felt like this. Only with you, Liam."

"Fuck, I love you, Hannah."

"I love you, too. I'm sorry I didn't see it."

"I wouldn't change a goddamn thing, baby."

Pulling from her body, she relaxes her legs from my waist, letting them fall open. I kiss across her jaw and down her neck as her hands run across my back and shoulders, her thighs rubbing against my hips and thighs. Her skin is so soft and smooth against mine, warm, and absolutely perfect.

I shower her body with a mix of delicate pecks and deep French kisses as I reach her breasts, sucking and lapping at each pierced nipple, taking my time to worship each one, grasping them in my hand, and feeding them into my mouth. I suck on each peak, flicking the barbell with my tongue, her breasts heavy and aching in my palms. I move downward, her heavy breathing increasing the lower I get. My tongue circles her belly button, taking a moment to flick the barbell that's pierced through the skin there.

Dragging my tongue over the curve of her hip and across her pelvis to repeat the same motion on the other side, she wiggles under me, trying to force me where she needs me the most. Face-to-face with her sweet pussy, I slide my palm down across her pelvis and over the light tuft of hair there, and I slowly drag my middle finger through her slick folds until I get to her center, wetness dripping out of her and onto the bed. I circle her entrance lightly before dipping in and out, torturously slow.

"Liiiiiaaaaaam," she moans, eliciting a grin from me, I'll never get used to how responsive her body is. I want to give it attention every moment of every day, always wanting to make her feel good. And now that I know Hannah loves me, I plan to do just that.

I plunge my fingers deep, finding that spot that makes her wild, and use my mouth to suck on her throbbing clit until her orgasm makes her body shake, and my name echo off the walls.

After her body has come down, she lays there languidly, blissed-out, legs open wide for my big body to settle between them. Sitting up on my knees, I grab her hips and hoist her ass into my lap, her back still lying flat on the bed, and run my cock through her overly sensitive lips.

"Fuck, you feel so goddamn good. But I need to get a condom, baby, 'cause I'm not pulling out."

She grabs my wrist, using my body to lift herself up on top of me, straddling my thighs. Reaching between us, she grabs my hard dick in her fist, lining it up with her center. Her eyes are hazy and heavily lidded, but she's coherent, so I hope she knows what she's doing.

"No condom. I want to feel you."

I hold her hips firmly, only letting her hover over me, just the tip of my dick rubbing against her entrance.

"Don't want anything between us, wife? You want to feel your husband's bare cock fill up your pussy?"

"God, Liam, when you talk like that . . ."

"Say it, my pretty wife. Tell me you want your husband's bare cock."

"Yes! I need it. I want my husband's bare cock inside me. Nothing between us."

I slam her down onto me, impaling her on my hard dick. She doesn't miss a beat, grabbing onto my shoulders and riding me hard.

"Jesus, fuck. You feel so goddamn good," I praise her, running my hands all over her soft skin, pulling her body close as she grinds her pussy against me. She stays seated, rocking back and forth hard, popping her hips out and changing up the motions, moving however it feels natural. I love that she's using me to figure out what she likes, I want her to explore, to let go and be wanton and lost to the feeling we're giving each other.

"God, it's building again, I'm going to come, Liam. Fuck!"

"Who's making love to you right now, Hannah? Say it. Let me hear it."

"My husband."

"That's right, wife. Your husband. The only man that'll ever get to make you feel this good, who will ever know what it's like to fill you and have all of you." I thrust hard into her. "Your mind." Thrust. "Your heart." Thrust. "Your body." Thrust. "All of you belongs to me."

"Yes! I love you, Liam. I love you so much it feels like my heart could claw its way out of my chest to get to yours."

"We're a part of each other, baby. I'm right here. I'm not going anywhere."

"You and me?"

"You and me."

After sucking my fingers into my mouth, I slip my hand between us, finding her clit and circling, it's only another minute before her pussy is clamping down around my cock, choking the shit out of it as she comes again.

"Shit, baby, you're gonna make *me* come. You're so damn tight."

"Ahh!" Her moan is louder than it can be for such a small apartment, so I grab her around the neck, jerking her mouth to meet mine and capturing her lips in a searing kiss. She continues to ride out her climax as I swallow each of her moans, my orgasm rapidly approaching. Just as she relaxes against my chest, I thrust up into her once. Twice. Three more times, before I'm filling her pussy with my cum for the first time. My balls draw up, my cock throbbing violently inside her, her walls fluttering from aftershocks around me and prolonging my orgasm. Coming inside her feels fucking incredible. My forehead rests on hers, sharing air as I unload.

"Hannah. Fuuuuuuck."

Her hands reach up, holding my face between them,

forcing me to look at her. Our breaths are coming in hard pants, our bodies slick with sweat and cum, but she's never looked more beautiful than she does right now.

"I love you, husband."

"I love you, wife."

Flipping her onto her back, I drive back inside her and spend the rest of the time we have reminding her who she belongs to and how good it feels to be truly wanted.

Chapter Thirty

Hannah

Knowing that I need to set my mother and Harlow straight, I set up a meeting with them at Bean Haven after the store has closed for the afternoon. Surprisingly, neither of them gave me a hard time about it. Hailey has checked on me a million times and I'm forever grateful to have one sister who has my back. Even if we weren't close while growing up, I'm thankful for the adult relationship we have now.

The two of them walk in together, looking so much alike in both appearance and personality. I take a deep breath to settle my nerves, giving myself a silent pep talk that it doesn't matter how this conversation goes, at least I said my piece.

"Hannah, you wanted to talk?"

"You don't?"

"I don't know if there's much to say."

Sweet mother of Earth, maybe I will make that arrest record two.

"Yes, Mom, there is! You pushed me to do something insanely drastic like marrying my best friend just so I could be seen as something other than a massive fuckup in your eyes. Imagine if I had married Levi! You were pushing me toward a life of misery and unhappiness! Why can't you see how hard I work? Why can't you see that I'm okay? Why can't you just see me and love me no matter what? I'm over here alone day in and day out, and I'm happy! HAPPY! I know you can't possibly see that it's okay to be both tired and happy, but I am."

"Hannah . . ."

"No, mom. No. You've only ever made me feel like a disappointment. Ever. For dying my hair. For wearing the clothes that you didn't like. For getting my belly button pierced, well guess what? I've got both my nipples done, too! For dropping out of college, and getting pregnant with Charlotte. I've only ever been a fuckup. It's exhausting and I can't do it anymore." The words that I've been holding in for so many years finally release, and the world around me lightens—my raw, honest words setting me free.

"Hannah, I've never been truly disappointed in you. I just want better for you. I want to see you succeed and not ever have to worry."

"First of all, there's nothing wrong with worry, that's life. And did it ever cross your mind that maybe your version of success and happiness isn't mine? I have never asked you for help—physical, emotional, financial, or otherwise. I've been raising my daughter by myself and running Bean Haven successfully and happily for years, and it will never be good enough for you. You need to think long and hard about the type of relationship you want to have with me and your granddaughter moving forward because I won't listen to you spew hurtful things at me any longer."

"And you"—I turn to the Wicked Witch of the West—"you need to dislodge your head from Mom's ass. Be your own person and stop being such a hateful bitch."

Her head bops back like I slapped her, and she's lucky that I don't reach across the table and do just that after what she did to me in front of everyone.

"I do love you, Hannah. I'm sorry I've made you feel that way. I am proud of you. I just saw you on a path that I wouldn't have chosen for my girls, and I've done what I could to help steer you back to what I thought was best," my mom admits.

"But you see how that's wrong, right? You're supposed to love your children no matter what and support their choices as long as they aren't harming themselves or others."

"It's going to take me some time to change my behavior, but I'll work toward it. I can't imagine not seeing you or Charlotte."

"Then let's work toward it. But I mean it, I won't take any abuse."

"Understood."

"Anything to say, Satan?"

"I'm sorry for being such a jealous, hateful bitch."

"Glad we can both agree to that."

"Truce?"

"Fine. Truce."

Feeling hopeful that things will change but knowing that if they don't, I'll still be okay, is freeing. I lock up Bean Haven after they leave and head straight for the distillery, wanting to see my husband and not able to wait until he gets home tonight.

Pulling into the lot, I put my Jeep in park and climb out, hoping like hell it doesn't take me a year to find him. I decide to just text Carter to see if anyone knows.

ME:

Any idea where I can find Liam on campus?

CARTER:

Just left him in rickhouse B. Don't knock the fucking place down.

Easily finding the correct rickhouse, I sneak into the building, using the darkness to my advantage. I silently walk down the rows until I find him about to insert a whiskey thief into a barrel for tasting. His back is to me, so I sneak down the row as quickly and quietly as I can, at the very last minute, jumping up and yelling, grabbing his shoulders.

His scream echoes loudly through the large warehouse, bouncing off the walls at an alarming pitch. I bend over in laughter, my stomach cramping from the force. His arms bound around me, hauling me to his large chest.

"You think you're funny?"

"Payback is a bitch, remember!"

"Yeah, you're gonna pay right now."

He spins me around so quickly, putting me down on my feet and making quick work of my pants, pulling them over my hips and down my thighs.

"Liam . . ."

His hand slides between my legs, cupping my pussy, feeling how turned on I am already by him. I let him play, his fingers toying with my seam, gently stroking up and down, never dipping between my lips. When I've had enough, I grab his shoulders, bracing myself to grind on his hand, wanting, needing more.

In one quick motion, his hand is gone, and I'm bent over the barrel he was about to taste from, his hands running over the back of my thighs, my ass, my lower back.

"Fuck, beauty. Do you know how often I've thought about taking you here, seeing your perfect ass bent over one of *my* whiskey barrels?"

All I can do is moan as I feel his fingers finally breach my center, fucking me quickly with hard thrusts. He withdraws them just as fast, and then I hear the rustling of his jeans as he tugs them down to free his cock. And then his fat head is nudging at my pussy, slipping right through and filling me deep.

"Aah. Fuck, yes, Liam!"

"That's a good little wife, scream my name. I want to hear it echoing off these old walls."

Liam fucks me hard, staying brutally deep, never withdrawing more than halfway and driving back home hard and quick. It only takes me moments before I'm spiraling out of control, my orgasm slamming into me like a freight train.

"Shit, baby, I'm going to come, where do you want it?"

"My mouth, Liam. Come in my mouth," I gasp.

"Fuck, baby, yes, get ready."

I brace my hands on the whiskey barrel, and just as Liam pulls out of me, I turn around and drop to my knees in front of him, opening my mouth just in time to suck his head as he comes. I swirl my tongue around him, letting him fill my mouth with his cum, loving his flavor mixed with my arousal, loving making him feel so crazed.

He's made me the happiest woman in the world, and I hope I can make him just as happy. Liam is everything I ever wanted and then some, I don't know how it took me so long to see it, but I'm so thankful that he never gave up on me.

Chapter Thirty-One

Liam

The vibration of my phone pulls me from looking over my communication with a farmer in Walla Walla on the anticipated wheat crops for the season. Pulling it out, my sweet sister's face lights up the screen.

"Hey, baby sis. You on lunch break from the snot-nosed monsters?"

"Hey, so we gotta little, teensy problem here at the school."

I stand up quickly, pulling my keys from my pocket, ready to head there if she needs me.

"What is it?"

"No need to go all Hulk smash, but Levi is here trying to excuse Charlotte from school. Hannah didn't answer her phone when I tried her."

"Say that again?" My body is already moving, jogging out of the building and heading to my truck.

"I was in the office making copies and I overheard him getting a little heated with Ms. Newbury. He's not on the emergency contact list, so technically they won't let her go with him, but it's Aspen Ridge, Li, everyone knows he's her dad."

"That asshole is not her fucking father, Kinsey. Where is Charlie?"

"She's in my classroom, I'm standing outside the door. I went and grabbed her just in case. He hasn't seen her in so long, Li, I wasn't about to just let her go, she doesn't know who he is."

"You're so smart, Kins. I can't thank you enough. Don't let my girl out of your sight, okay? I'm on my way."

Peeling my truck out of the distillery parking lot, I wait the few seconds for my phone to connect to Bluetooth before I call Hannah. I'm at least ten minutes away, nervous energy flowing through me. What the fuck is he thinking showing up here unannounced? He hasn't made any attempt to see her or even fucking call her. The bare goddamn minimum. Hannah picks up on the third attempt.

"Hey, is everything okay?"

"Hey, baby, stay calm for me because everything is fine. But Levi is at the elementary school trying to pick up Charlie. Kinsey has her, she's safe. I'm on my way there."

"What? That motherfucker! I'll meet you there."

I hear the rustling of Hannah moving throughout the store, probably making sure her ovens are off and everyone leaves so she can lock up the doors, and then the line goes dead. Fuck, I hate that this is her life.

Hannah is pulling in at the same time I am, her little Jeep whipping into the parking lot behind me. I'm already out of my truck and moving in her direction before she gets hers in park. Pulling open her door, I grab her hand and haul her out, the two of us jogging together to the front of the school from the side parking lot.

My eyes are on him just as he's seeing me, the asshole stiffening and ready to run his vile mouth.

"Hey, asshole. What are you doing here? Heard you've been fucking my sloppy seconds. Still pissed I got to her first?"

I see fucking red. I move in his direction, but Hannah gets to him first. It catches him off guard because he expected me to lunge for him and not her. Her arm pulls back and flies hard right into his fucking nose. She doesn't stop there, grabbing his shoulders and driving her knee right between his legs so hard that I can't help but wince.

"You stupid fucking bitch!" Levi cries out. Hannah moves for him again but I grab her around the waist, lift her off the ground, and haul her back. This time I'm the one to get in his face, leaning over him from where he's dropped to his knees on the gravel with his hands cupping his shriveled balls. I grab his shirt and force him to look up at me.

"Speak to my wife like that again and I'll fucking end you," I grind the words out, my tone menacing, pinning him with a look that dares him to fucking try me.

"Your wife?" he sputters the words, and if I wasn't so fucking pissed right now, I'd laugh in his face.

"You heard me. Mine. Your days of fucking with her are over. Now you get to deal with me."

"Fuck you both. Hannah, you're fucking done for. This is assault!" Like the pathetic piece of shit that he has always been, Levi jogs over to his car, pulls out his phone, and connects a call. Ignoring him, I turn back to Hannah where she stands, fuming. Moving slowly in front of her, I reach down and gently lift her right hand, checking her knuckles and fingers for any damage before bringing them up to my mouth, where I drop a tender kiss on them.

"Are you alright, beauty?"

"I've been wanting to do that for so long. But fuck if that didn't hurt. How do you do that so regularly?"

I chuckle at her through my simmering rage. "Practice, and we never bare knuckle it like you just did. I knew my wife was a badass, but you just blew me away. I'll see if they have some ice inside. Do you want to take Charlotte home?"

"No, she's safe. I don't want to cause an interruption to her day. She isn't any the wiser of what happened, and it will only alarm her if I rush in there to bring her home. But I owe Kinsey a drink. God, Liam, what if they had let her go? What if he had taken her? Can he even do that?"

Cue Hannah spiraling as her adrenaline starts to come down.

"He didn't though. We're going to figure this out."

Just as Hannah opens her mouth to no doubt fight me on it, we hear the siren. My head whips back around to find Levi sitting smugly on the hood of his car, a wad of tissues held to his nose to stop the bleeding. I stomp over in his direction, watching him flinch back but trying to hold his ground and not cower.

"Bitch rebroke my nose! She's not going to get away with that!"

"You want some fucking broken ribs to match? Get the fuck out of here, Levi. You want to start being in Charlotte's life? You show up every fucking day. Not when it's just convenient for you to show face for your new woman. Charlie is the only priority. That's it. HER! You haven't been able to do that for four fucking years. So, if you're not going to find a way to treat her mom with the respect she deserves and be a positive, active role model in Charlotte's life, then get back in your fucking car and drive back to your shithole in Seattle. There's no fucking in and out when you feel like it," I yell the words into his face, my body heated and ready to drop this asshole six feet under. Over my dead body will he set Charlie up for a lifetime of fucking disappointment because he never wanted to grow up.

The police car pulls into the parking lot as Levi scrambles

to get away from me. I laugh as Owen steps out of the car and gives me a nod. This should be interesting.

"Levi, what the hell did you get yourself into?"

"Hannah assaulted me. She broke my fucking nose and kneed me in the balls like a crazy bitch."

I'm on him before anyone can react, wrenching him backward by his shirt, pulling my arm back, and letting it go with every bit of power I reserve for the ring with my brothers. It lands hard into his abdomen, and before his knees hit the ground again, I've pulled my second, landing it right to his cheek, shoving him hard and letting him fall to the ground.

"Well, fucking shit, Liam, now I've gotta arrest both of you. Get your ass in the back of the car. Where's Bonnie, Clyde?"

I put my hands up in the air, showing that I'm done.

"You make sure he doesn't go anywhere near that school, Owen. Promise me. He came here to get Charlie without talking to Hannah first. He's a damn stranger to her at this point." Owen nods and walks over to the shitbag moaning on the ground. "Han! C'mon, baby, we're getting a ride in the back of a cruiser and there's something I've always wanted to try in one of these!" I yell over to Hannah. Before getting into the waiting police cruiser, I lean down into Levi's space where he's moaning like a little bitch.

"I mean it, Levi. You try to fuck with either of those girls ever again, I'll fucking end you," I promise.

Hannah walks over and throws her hands in the air, stomping the rest of the way over to Owen, who's holding the back door open to his cruiser.

"For fuck's sake, Owen, are you for real? He deserved it!"

"I don't doubt that, but the law is the law, you can't go around assaulting people. Get in. And don't you dare try whatever you're planning back there, fucker, or I'll make you pay the cleaning fee," he says in my direction.

"It'll be well worth the fee, plus, payback for getting a BJ from Savannah Matthews while I was driving senior year."

"Jesus, don't remind me. Girl was a stage ten clinger after I let her do that. Get in the damn car, let's get this over with. Levi, get the hell up, you look pathetic man. Get your shit together and get the fuck out of here. You want to see your kid? This isn't how you do it. You show up without a plan and notifying Hannah first, you'll be the one in the back of my cruiser, make fuckin' sense? Do shit the right way."

We watch as Levi scrambles into his car and throws it in reverse, peeling out of the parking lot. He had better stay the fuck away unless he gets a goddamn plan together first, or I'll fucking ruin him.

Hannah climbs into the back of the cruiser and I follow behind her, Owen slamming the door shut and walking to the front of the car. I'm on her in an instant, grabbing her face between my hands and slamming my mouth onto hers. She meets me in the middle, grabbing my shirt and hauling me closer as Owen climbs into the front seat and starts to drive us away.

"Fuck, I'm so proud of you," I breathe through wet, sloppy kisses. "That was so hot. He's not going to fuck with you anymore."

One of my hands moves to her waist, yanking her so that she's forced to straddle my lap, her pussy meeting the length of my already-hard cock, pressing herself down to grind against it.

I kiss the shit out of her, our tongues clashing in the middle, nipping and sucking at her bottom lip, pulling her as close as I can with our clothes on. Fuck, I want her so bad. I briefly wonder how pissed Owen would be if I fucked her right in the back of his police car, but then toss the idea because like hell will I let anyone see Hannah like that.

"Hey! Hey! Bonnie and Clyde!" Owen yells, smacking the window that separates the front and back seats. "Cut the shit!"

Hannah and I break apart, her forehead falling to my own as we simultaneously break out in laughter.

"Yeah, real fucking funny. Who we calling to bail your asses out? Hannah's parents were pissed the last time she got arrested. Pick someone else this time, will ya?"

"Mother above, give me strength. Owen!" Hannah snaps, slipping off my lap. "It was a bullshit arrest, and you know it! Am I ever going to live that down? It was a street sign, it's not like I was out corrupting America's youth!"

"Laws the law, Han."

"Kiss my ass, Owen, no more free coffee for you. You pay double now."

Owen laughs as Hannah turns to face me, igniting me all over again. I grab her face between my hands, unable to stop myself, and haul her lips back to mine, claiming them in a bruising kiss. I can feel how wet her pussy is through her clothes, and I know it wouldn't take much to make her come. The adrenaline still coursing through me, I grab her hips, urging her to dry hump me as she moans into my mouth, hands knocking off my hat and threading through my hair.

"Jesus fucking hell on Earth. I'm gonna kill you for real this time, Li. For fuck's sake."

"Owen, will you shut the fuck up so I can make my wife come?"

"For fuck's sake. Liam, I'm gonna beat your ass."

The cruiser slows quickly as Owen breaks, the tires crunching on gravel as he pulls off to the side of the road. His door slams a moment later. I don't waste any more time, unbuckling Hannah's pants and dipping my hand into them, easily sliding through her slick center.

"Baby. So wet for me. Now let me make you come in the back of a police car, my little criminal."

It doesn't take long before Hannah's coming for me, so fucking pretty as she goes over the edge, her little pussy gushing just enough for me to have something to lick off my fingers. She lays her head down on my chest, getting her breathing under control while I bang on my window to let Owen know he's good to come back. I know he's not going to let me live this one down, but it was worth it.

"So, husband? Who are we calling to bail our asses out of jail?"

An hour later, Hannah and I are sitting together against a cement wall, her legs pulled up to her chest as she casually sips on a water bottle that was so kindly given to her at booking.

"You really had to put them in the holding cell?" Reid's voice rings out through the room, and I laugh under my breath. This is about to get interesting. His heavy footsteps echo through the large, barren, cement jail.

"Had to get a few photos to really mark the occasion, which pissed Hannah off, so I decided to leave 'em there," Owen tells him, the dick. "Not to mention, they did lord knows what in the back of my fucking cruiser. I'm gonna have to get it detailed. Should charge them with indecent exposure."

"Our pants stayed on you big fuckin' baby," I add, raising my voice so that they can hear me.

"Look at you, sitting behind bars. Never thought you'd be the one to get arrested," Reid says as he comes into view.

"Agreed.. Definitely thought that'd be Sawyer or Dallas."

"And, Hannah," he tsks, shaking his head in mock disappointment. "A respected member of our community, her second offense I hear," he playfully chastises.

"Wow, Reid Knight, I didn't know you had a joking side. Good to know, Drogo. Now, kindly get Owen to let us out."

"I don't know, you two seem pretty lawless. Maybe we should leave you overnight."

"I swear I will poison your food and drink if you two don't let me out of here right now," Hannah scolds, her face twisted into a scowl.

"You really shouldn't be threatening a police officer, Han," Reid continues to taunt.

"Yeah? And you guys really shouldn't be playing with the girl who handles your precious coffee and sweet treats. I've got shit to do, let me out."

Owen shrugs and opens the door for us to leave, and I take Hannah's hand in mine and follow Reid outside.

"Heard you got a good punch in, Hannah. Proud of you. Don't know Levi well, but he's a worthless piece of shit for what he's done to you and Charlie."

"Thanks. He can go to hell. I'm so done with that asshole."

Reid drops us off in front of Bean Haven where she unlocks the front door. The lights are all turned off, and I flick the lock behind us as Hannah walks through the main area and into the back kitchen. She fiddles with some items, trying to keep herself busy. I'm sure her brain is going a mile a minute right now with a colorful assortment of what-ifs.

"Baby."

She continues to flit around the kitchen, reaching for a mixing bowl and pulling ingredients out. Her pretty face would appear stoney and focused to an onlooker, but I know her better than anyone else. She's working on autopilot, but her thoughts are somewhere else, spiraling into different scenarios and outcomes.

"Baby. Talk to me."

After a fleeting moment, she meets my eyes from across the kitchen, her pretty brown irises wild and stormy. Fuck, I wish I could fix this for her. I can't face the terror that would come if Charlotte had been taken from school by Levi. Not that I think he would ever hurt her, but she's a barely four-year-old little girl, and being taken away by someone who has only seen her a handful of times would be terrifying, and Hannah would feel it on a completely different level.

Her face sinks slightly as she speaks and my heart pounds in my chest, a heady mix of anger over the situation and sympathy.

"What if he had taken her, bear? What if he took her and refused to give her back? If he was just a part of her life, this would be a different story, but he's a goddamn stranger to her! I tried so hard for so long! She was never on his radar, never a priority. What kind of parent misses their child's birthday party? Today had nothing to do with seeing Charlotte and everything to do with me."

I let her vent her frustrations but my mood simmers as she does. Levi isn't going to do shit. Right now, he's running with his tiny tail between his legs back to Seattle. I'm sure it won't be long before his current fuckbuddy realizes what a piece of shit he is, and Hannah and Charlie's situation will rinse and repeat. He came all the way down here to piss Hannah off because he said he was going to. Think it's a fair assumption he won't repeat that mistake.

I let her calm down before talking some sense into her, knowing that she won't see reason until she's ready to.

"I really hate him. But damn it felt so good to punch his stupid, smug face."

I laugh. "Right?"

"Sooo fucking good."

"I know it scared you, but he isn't coming back. And if he does, we'll get a lawyer and do things the right way. Today was just Levi flexing, and I think he learned real quick we're not fucking around. I'm not going to let him hurt my girls. We'll go down to the school and make sure they're aware of the situation and just wait it out for now. Trust me. He's not coming back."

Her shoulders finally relax as she nods and vocalizes her agreement with me. Feeling confident everything is going to be okay, I want to do what I can to help her decompress—in a way that only I can.

Coming up behind her, my hands find their home at her trim waist, gently pulling her ass flush against the top of my thighs, my rapidly hardening dick pressing against her lower back. Brushing her hair to the side off one shoulder, I lean my head into her neck, taking a deep inhale of her sweet, vanilla scent, filling my lungs with her. Hannah's hands stay firmly rooted in front of her, bracing on the counter as she arches her back and presses her ass into me.

I run my hand slowly from the base of her spine up to the center of her shoulder blades, guiding her to lay flat on the counter.

"Tell me what you want," I ask as I slowly work her pants down over her ass and thighs. My hands glide up her soft skin, lifting the perky cheeks of her ass and gripping them tightly in my hands.

"Mmm. Fuck me, Liam. I want you inside me."

"Anything for you, beauty."

Dropping to my haunches, I grab onto her ass and spread her wide, sinking my face right between her legs. My tongue laps at her slit, finding her already primed and ready for me. Using two fingers, I rim her tight little pussy before sliding them in, the lewd sounds from her arousal and the intrusion filling the quiet space of the kitchen making my cock leak with precum. She's so goddamn sexy. Removing my fingers, I slide up to her little ass, loving that she's let me play here, wondering if I'll ever be able to fuck that tight hole. She moans and pushes back against me, and it's my breaking point.

I unbutton my jeans quickly, pushing them down just enough to free my aching cock. I give it a few firm strokes, base to tip, before sliding the latex over it and lining up with her pussy. I sink in slow, watching my dick disappear into her tight body. Pleasure scatters through me, intense desire and feral need overtaking me.

"Damn, Hannah, you're drenching me, baby."

"You feel so good. Always so, so good."

"That's right. My pretty wife looks so good bent over, taking my cock. Fuck, Hannah, do you have any idea what you do to me?"

I look at the wedding band she has on her finger and lean over her, threading my fingers over the top of hers and clasping her hand as I rut into her over and over again, the tight walls of her pussy gripping me, spasming around my dick, making my balls draw up.

Pushing up her shirt, I drop kisses up and down her spine, taking one last long thrust into her pussy and staying deep, grinding my pelvis into her ass, hitting a new place deep inside her.

"Oh, aah! Yes!" Her moans fuel me, moving my hand around to her front, sliding through her pussy lips and finding her swollen little clit. "Oh, yes, please, Liam. Make me come!"

She shatters the moment I pinch her clit between two fingers, her pussy clamping down on my cock like a goddamn torture device. My balls draw up, my impending orgasm coming from out of nowhere, her pussy milking the life out of my fucking cock. I pull my hips back and slam back into her repeatedly, the vulgar slap of our wet skin filling the room, Hannah's body vibrating underneath me.

"That's it, Hannah. Fuck, I love making my wife feel good."

"Come for me, Liam, I want to feel you."

"Yeah, baby. Fuck, yes, Hannah!"

I erupt into her, my hips stuttering as I find my release, filling the condom with my cum, reveling in the feeling of coming inside her. I collapse on top of her back, doing my best to hold my weight up with my forearms so I don't crush her.

"God, baby, you're so perfect. I love getting to have this side of you. I love you so goddamn much, Hannah."

"I love you, my husband."

Chapter Thirty-Two

Liam

A month later, the sun slowly dips behind the mountains, erasing the last of the daylight as the three of us walk down the dirt road that leads to the house. The evening is cool, Charlie skips ahead of us, and I tug Hannah closer to me by the hand I'm holding. Her shoulder bumps mine forcefully, nearly knocking me off my feet from the unexpectedness of it.

"You're such a little shit."

"Yeah, but apparently you love it. Who knew?"

"Not you."

"Ooo! Ouch, Liam Hayes! Too soon!"

I can't help but laugh, throwing my arm around her shoulders and pulling her in tight, just as Charlie's voice fills the air.

"Shh! Did you hear that?"

"Oh, mother above, please no."

"You hear it right?" I ask Hannah in a whisper as Charlie releases my hand and walks up ahead, following the little cries. "Do strays just flock to her?" I say, slightly shocked that this is the second animal that has found its way to Charlotte.

"It's a kitty! I know it! Bear, save it! It's crying! Ms. Katie said kitties should never cry!"

Releasing Hannah's hand, I join Charlie where she's peeking into a sewer, looking for the crying animal. Not knowing what to expect, even though I'm fairly certain I know what it is, I ask her to take a step back and let me look just in case.

Bending down on my hands and knees, I peer into the open slit of the sidewalk and my eyes immediately connect with glowing slivers staring back at me, followed by the unmistakable cry of a kitten. Laying down so that my stomach is flat on the ground, I inch closer to the opening and stick my arm in as far as it will go until I reach the fur of the animal, grabbing it behind the neck and lifting, pulling it out of the small crevice it was hiding and into the open.

"Ahh!! It is a kitten! Sewer!"

"Charlie, we've been through this, we can't name things after where we found them or where they were born. I'll start calling you Kitchen, and I mean it."

"Fine," she huffs. "What do we name her then?"

"He's actually a boy kitten and his name should be Penny, obviously."

Hannah starts laughing hysterically from behind us and I slowly turn my head in her direction, arching a brow and giving her a devilish grin.

"Oh, it's actually perfect. Of course his name is Penny. It has to be."

"So we're keeping him? He'll be best friends with me and Garb-Billy."

Hannah dips down next to where we're crouched and looks at the tiny ball of fluff in the crook of my arm.

"Yeah, we can keep him. But no more animals after this one. The next one you find we have to place in a new home, we're not a rescue," Hannah tells her, but I give her a look that suggests that becoming a rescue isn't a half-bad idea. We've got the space for it. She picks right up on that and stands, walking in the direction of our house.

"Not a chance, Mr. Hayes," she singsongs.

"I don't know, Ms. Hayes, I'm kinda digging this idea."

She turns to face me, her expression a mix of surprise and satisfaction. I walk up to her, Charlie trailing right behind us, dropping my head so that my mouth is right next to her ear.

"Oh, baby. You like that, don't you, wife?" I whisper, causing a chill to spread through her body. "Do you want to change your name?"

"I never thought I did. I always wanted to stay a Haven because of the shop, but nothing has ever sounded so right before."

"On that note, there's something I've been wanting to talk to you about. Let's get inside."

Nerves suddenly plaguing me, we walk into the house, Billy meeting us at the door and wagging his tail, already smelling the little furball we just found. After getting him thoroughly washed and warm, which was not a good fucking time, Charlotte is fast asleep in her new bedroom with Billy, and the new furball is snuggled in a blanket next to the fireplace. Hannah and I sit down on our bed, her pretty hair now dyed a slightly darker shade of lavender floating around her face haphazardly.

"C'mon, let me hear it."

"I want to adopt Charlie." Deciding to just go for it.

Hannah's mouth falls open forming a little "O" as tears fill her eyes.

"Beauty, don't you dare cry. It kills me."

"You really mean that? You want to adopt her?"

"I've loved that little girl since the moment you told me she was inside you. I hope I've proved to you that I'm not going anywhere and that whether you say yes or no, nothing changes."

"Yes. Fuck, Liam, yes. How would that even work?"

"I wanted to talk to you first, but I have an attorney ready for me if I got the go-ahead from you. Levi is either going to agree, or I'm taking him to court. A judge will hopefully look at him as a parental abandonment case and grant the stepparent adoption, but I don't want to leave it up to chance. I'm confident he'll sign the papers."

Hanah looks at me with so much love and affection, something I had only allowed myself to dream about. All I've ever wanted was for her to love me back, and now that she does? My life's complete.

"I love you. I couldn't love you more."

"I love you, beauty."

"Now fuck me so we can go watch *Scream*."

"How about I fuck you with the mask on while you watch *Scream*?"

She pulls away from me, moving her head back far enough so she can read my face and see I'm dead serious. Her eyes are heavily lidded, her red, puffy lips pulled up in a shocked smile. I know she can tell how serious I am, I've been thinking about it since that morning at the bakery.

"Tell your husband what you want. Let me make my wife feel good."

"Yesss, Liam."

"Me and you."

"Me and you."

The next few weeks pass in a blur, the three of us falling into our normal routine, except my nights of sleeping on Hannah's couch are long gone, and I've got the two of them in the home that I hope they'd occupy someday. As soon as Hannah gave me her blessing to adopt Charlie, I contacted the attorney and made a plan to move forward. We plan to tell Charlie after we know that it will be possible, and that starts with the paperwork currently sitting in the manilla folder next to me in the passenger seat.

After three hours of major highway, I pull up in front of the stupid-ass Seattle apartment, not feeling a damn thing except annoyance. Last time I was here, the anger overrode logic and all I wanted to do was smash his stupid fucking face in. But now? I've got everything and he's going to go away, with or without a fight. I'll win in the end.

I jog up the steps, rapping my knuckles on the door and waiting. Levi opens it just wide enough for me to be able to stick my boot in as he tries to immediately close it once recognition sets in.

"Nope, we're gonna have a little chat."

"Get the fuck off my property, Hayes, or I'll call the cops."

"Yeah, see, that's not gonna happen. You're gonna hear me out or I'll break your fucking face. How many times do you think a nose can shatter before it leaves permanent damage to your breathing?"

"What do you want?"

"Like I said, to have a little chat." I push my way through his door, knowing the dickface won't actually call the cops. Levi leaves the door open and spins on me but I'm already taking a seat on his couch, dropping the manilla folder on the coffee table.

"This is more than you deserve, but because I'm a man, I'm coming to you like one first. I'm gonna give it to you straight, Jenkins. You don't want Charlotte. You never have. You've never made an effort and she's just a little girl who deserves more than that. So, here's your out."

I slide the paperwork I had my attorney draw up across the table, his stupid fucking face looking at it without touching it.

"What is this? You serving me now, Hayes?"

"Nah. That'll come next, Jenkins. This is a relinquishment of rights. You see, I've been helping raise Charlotte since the moment she was put into her mom's tummy by your sleazy, ungrateful ass. I'm her dad. I've been there every single day. Diaper changes, late night feedings, her first cold, holding her in a steamy bathroom while she had croup, every birthday, her first day of school, her first scrape, her first time on the ice. I've. Been. There. Not you." I pause before I launch myself at this sonofabitch. "I'm adopting her. We're going to do an easy and quick stepparent adoption and it'll be like you never existed at all. You sign the paperwork, and you disappear. If you don't, I'm going take you to court and make sure it is long and painful, and in the end, I'll still adopt her. It's your choice how expensive and miserable you want to make this. But I'm her father, and I'm going to see this through."

Levi fucking smirks at me, and it takes everything I have, the strength of a fucking monk, not to rip his throat out and shove it up his ass.

"You can have her. But you'll raise her and spend the rest of your life knowing she'll never truly be yours, she's got my blood running through her veins, and knowing you have to live with that makes me feel like I fucking won."

A toothy smile fills my face, and based off the slight tick in his jaw, I'd wager I look slightly unhinged and demonic.

"That's the thing, I love that little girl so much, I've never given thought to what blood she has in her. She's mine in every way that matters. I wouldn't change a goddamn thing because I would never change who she is, and if that means she doesn't share blood with me? Then so fucking be it. You'll cease to exist in her life, and I'll get to spend mine knowing I chose to be in hers every day because she's the most important thing in the world. I'm the fucking winner here, Jenkins. You're nothing."

Levi signs the paperwork, his stupid ass initialing all the places I've marked. Once I've checked that it's legit, I stand and walk away without saying another word.

Chapter Thirty-Three
Liam

I walk through the door with brick oven pizza from Barrel House, my excitement over talking with Charlotte tonight through the roof. Hannah is extra emotional, on the verge of happy tears and barely containing them, which is keeping a thick knot in my throat as I get ready to explain this to Charlie.

After dinner, the three of us grab our blankets and move to the couch to talk, Billy and Penny crawling up into Charlotte's lap just like they always do. For the first time in a long-ass time, I'm nervous. Hannah rubs my back as I lean forward, bracing my elbows on my knees.

"Charlie, can we talk?"

"Yep!"

"Remember the hockey game we went to and the conversation we had before we left?"

"About different kinds of families and how Evangeline should be nicer."

"That's right. Well, I left another type of family out by accident."

"What kind?"

"Adoption."

"What's adoption?"

"You know how you have just your momma?"

"Yep. And now you and Garb-Billy and Penny now."

"Right. Well, adoption is when a parent who didn't birth you gets to raise you and be your parent."

"Kinda like you, bear."

"That's right. I'd like to adopt you, Charlie, so that I can be your dad."

She stops petting Billy and looks up at me, those chocolate brown eyes lighting up so big.

"You want to be my dad, bear?"

"Yeah, munchkin, I want to be your dad more than anything in the world."

"Can I call you Dad?"

"I'd really love that."

I can't help the tears that flow from my eyes, but I smile through it so that she doesn't think I'm sad.

"Don't cry, Dad."

And the tears flow more freely now, a slight laugh releasing as I hear those words for the first time.

"I just love you so much, munchkin."

"I love you, my dad! And Mumma, and Billy and Penny!"

Grabbing Charlotte and tucking her in under my arm, Hannah takes up my other side, wiping away her tears that have drenched her pretty face. We smile at each other before I lean down and kiss her sweet lips. All I ever wanted was to give Hannah my love and get hers in return, but I got so much more instead. I got a family.

Epilogue
Liam

Five Years Later

"Are you ready to taste it, little brother?"

"Been waiting five long years. I'm more than ready."

I'm surrounded by my entire family and friends, my wife next to me, our second daughter in her arms, Charlie tucked into my side, looking up at me with all the pride in the world. Carter fills a Glencairn glass for everyone straight from the barrel, passing them out to everyone except Ivy, who is expecting another member of their hockey team.

"A few words, Liam?" my dad urges, tears in his eyes. I feel the lump forming in my throat, and I have to clear my voice before I begin talking.

"My goals in life were simple—marry my best friend, raise a family together in the woods, and continue to work and produce a product at our distillery that our family is proud of. I'm a happy, lucky man to be in my early thirties and already accomplished all of them. Thank you for trusting me and supporting me. Please raise your glasses, let me introduce the newest product for Aspen Ridge Distillery, the Charlotte Signature Straight Bourbon Whiskey."

Everyone sips and applauds, and I dab my eyes free of the few rogue tears that escaped my eyes. Hannah looks up at me with Asher in her arms, with all the love a wife could have for her man, and it fills my heart with everything. I drop a kiss to her lips, pressing firmly, loving the feel of her sweetness against me, before breaking away and kissing Asher on the forehead. Then I turn to my not-so-little anymore, and getting entirely too tall, Charlie.

"I'm proud of you, Dad, you worked so hard." She swats at her cheeks, batting away her tears. I wrap my arms around her and kiss the top of her head firmly.

"I love you four, more than anything."

"Thank you for loving us."

Books by Jenn Plummer

Not ready to leave Aspen Ridge? Check out other Books by Jenn Plummer

Contemporary

Aspen Ridge Series

Unravel Me

Crave Me

Love Me

Wreck Me

Complete Me

Aspen Ridge Holiday Novellas

Ready or Not (Halloween)

Sweet Girl (Valentine's Day)

Daddy Issues (Father's Day)

Acknowledgments

Thank you all for coming along on this journey with me. I hope you enjoyed reading Liam and Hannah's story. Writing best friends to lovers was so much fun but also emotional. The pair already knew everything about each other, and their connection was so deep. It was fun to let them explore each other in new, exciting ways while also continuing to show up for the person you love through thick and thin. Stepparent adoption is such a beautiful thing and I'm so glad to have been able to give them all their happy ending.

My readers,

You are making my dreams come true! Thank you for picking up my books and reading! I am so grateful that I get to create stories to share with you and I hope you continue to enjoy my words.

Michael,

Real life friends to lovers. Falling in love with you was the easiest thing I've ever done. Thank you for spending your life with me, thank you for making us a family, thank you for fighting for us in more ways than one. You know the rest but that's just for us and our family. I love you.

Momma,

Thank you for supporting me, and checking on me every day, for pushing me to keep going and chase these dreams. I finished this book the same month you were diagnosed with cancer, that was some of the hardest news I've ever received. You have consumed my thoughts but I know how important it is to you that I finally live this dream so I've continued to push onward. You're my hero, in every way. Your strength, resilience, your fight. Life hasn't always been easy on you but you have never let it hold you down. I strive to be like you every day. You've got this, just like everything before it. I love you.

My friend and editor, Katie,

Is this really book five? Last book of 2024. To think we wrapped up five books this year. We're a well-oiled, badass machine at this point. Thank you for keeping me sane, and for always knowing what to say. For taking my manuscripts and turning them into gold. I wouldn't do this without you. I love you!

Meighan,

Thank you for taking care of everything under the sun for me so that I can focus on writing and creating stories to share with the world. I'm grateful to have you in my corner, for creating an image for me that I'm proud of and being the best PA and friend I could ask for.

Harlots,

You're part of the best reader group out there and I am so thankful for your support! You all keep me going and fill me with so much love and encouragement. Having you along on this journey with me has been such an amazing, surreal experience. Thank you for being with me!

My personal ARC team,

Thank you for believing in me enough to support me

through my permanent ARC team. I am so grateful to every single one of you. You're all my favorite humans and I'll be forever thankful for each of you. Thank you for being such a huge part of making my dreams come true.

To every bookstagrammer, reviewer, and blogger,

Thank you for reading. Every post, review, and tag mean the world to me. Thank you for your support!

About the Author

Jenn Plummer resides on the beautiful island of Oahu with her husband and four kids. As a military spouse, she has had the privilege of living all over the world. Originally from Maine, she is looking forward to her husband's retirement from the Air Force and returning to cold weather. She has always been a lover of books and is constantly dreaming up stories that will make you blush.

When Jenn's not writing, she can be found reading a spicy romance novel, spending time with her husband and four kids, baking, and watching hockey.

Follow along for updates on new releases and book news by following below or join her Facebook Reader Group here https://www.facebook.com/groups/jennsharlots

Instagram @authorjennplummer

Goodreads @jennplummer

Amazon @jennplummer

Threads @authorjennplummer

Made in the USA
Monee, IL
10 February 2025